# SOMETHING IN
# MADNESS

# SOMETHING IN MADNESS

## THE DARKHORSE TRILOGY BOOK 3

### ED PROTZEL

INTEGRATED MEDIA
NEW YORK

ISBN: 978-1-5040-7797-2

This edition published in 2022 by Open Road Integrated Media, Inc.
180 Maiden Lane
New York, NY 10038
www.openroadmedia.com

# Praise for *Something in Madness*

"A gripping work of historical fiction! . . . I was captivated from beginning to end."
—*Readers' Favorite*

"Something in Madness has a wonderfully unique voice and chromatic characterization for all of its characters which really brings the story off the page."
—*Literary Titan*

"Stands out as a powerful saga of ongoing strife." —*Midwest Book Review*

"Despite the dark forces at work in Something in Madness, it is ultimately a tale of hope and determination against seemingly insurmountable odds."
—Terry Baker Mulligan,
author of *Sugar Hill* and *Afterlife in Harlem*

"The life of the freedmen smacks you in the face with racism from the first page to the last . . . the reader can feel the pain and share the grief of the characters. Tension builds until the final page." —Jeff Westerhoff,
Historical Novel Society

"Gets to the central problem of early Reconstruction: how to remake a society that rested on slavery into a society that would become more fair to whites and Blacks alike." —*St. Louis Post-Dispatch*

"A remarkable job of highlighting the prejudice and violence faced by newly freed slaves suddenly thrust into a tumultuous world."
—Heidi Slowinski
(Amazon reviewer, 5 stars)

"Illuminates the harsh ugliness that accompanied Reconstruction through the Negro Codes, and the constant dehumanization of black men and women. . . . Protzel's work will linger with readers long after the story ends!"
—*InD'tale Magazine*

To those courageous souls who suffered the horrors of slavery and the brutality of Civil War and its aftermath, as well as those brave enough to aid them along their perilous road to freedom and dignity—a hard road which, sadly, must still be traversed today.

# SOMETHING IN MADNESS

". . . not madman, no: since surely there is something in madness, even the demoniac, which Satan flees, aghast at his own handiwork, and which God looks on in pity—some spark . . . which we call human man."

—William Faulkner, *Absalom, Absalom!*

# PROLOGUE

On a quiet evening, when a pebble is tossed into a placid pool, scientists say ocean tides on *the* opposite side of the world are affected. Likewise, the courage and vision of a few obscure people can reverberate through time, moving us in profound ways of which we are unaware.

Such is the tale of Durksen Hurst, Antoinette DuVallier, and Big Josh Tyler. Their story is strange, complicated, as agents of change tend to be. In 1859, Durk, a lonely and ambitious drifter, a man we would call a hustler, rode into the hamlet of Turkle, Mississippi, needing to prove something to the town that years before had killed his father, leaving him orphaned. Fortunately for Durk, he was taken in by the Chickasaw and raised to manhood. But with no roots in the outside world or formal education, he became an itinerate promoter of schemes he claimed would help blacks and whites throughout the South.

And this time Durk was lucky. He encountered a dozen slaves hiding in the Chickasaw swamp. Wary, but having little recourse, the men agreed to Durk's proposal to build their own plantation—secretly as partners. But Durk would need land. So he swindled fifty square miles from a Chickasaw chief, and the clearing of forest and the raising of their mansion soon began. They named their venture *DarkHorse* after Durk's Chickasaw name.

But Turkle's power structure could not stomach the new rival. Looming over the town was the shrewd widow, Marie Brussard French, owner of *FrenchAcres*, one of the largest plantations in Mississippi. Ironically, the widow was hiding secrets of her own: she'd been a notorious quadroon in a New Orleans bordello who'd abandoned her small daughter, Antoinette, to marry a wealthy Mississippi landowner named French.

Once married and settled in Turkle, the young Mrs. French gave birth to another daughter, Devereau. Upon her husband's sudden death, with the town's notables poised to steal the plantation from the vulnerable widow, the wily Mrs. French seized on a ruse to ensure her control. She concealed the infant's gender, thus forcing Devereau to masquerade as a male throughout her life, becoming, in effect, the late-owner's *male* heir. Consequently, the pair's grip on power was as tenuous as *Dark-Horse*'s façade of legitimacy.

Sadly for Devereau, her male subterfuge allowed no room for friendships or love, which played havoc with her mind and emotions. By adulthood, she'd become increasingly erratic and uncontrollable, to her mother's mortification.

Meanwhile, Antoinette, now grown, prospered in New Orleans, marrying and having a son, Louis Edward. Learning this, Mrs. French, desperate to assuage Devereau's wrenching loneliness, resorted to clandestine means to "adopt" the boy for her.

Frantic to recover her son, Antoinette, now widowed, journeyed to Turkle, unaware that the child was already dead and buried. There, she encountered Durk and his partners, and they soon aided each other's efforts. As fate would have it, Antoinette and Durk fell in love—galling a jealous Devereau, who was consumed with the notion of getting Durk for herself. One night, gripped by utter hopelessness, Devereau confronted her mother, shot her, and fled.

With the war raging, Durk pleaded with the townsmen not to throw their lives away on a fool's crusade. But he failed miserably. Consequently, the town turned on Durk and his partners, forcing them to run for their lives north to Missouri.

Both the venerable *FrenchAcres* and the upstart *DarkHorse* plantations were no more.

By 1863, after working as contraband labor for the Union army, Durk and his partners established a colored regiment to help fight guerrillas, naming it *DarkHorse* after their lost plantation. Peculiarly, although blacks were encouraged to serve, according to the rules of the day, black units were required to be led by a white officer. Naturally, Durk agreed to serve in that capacity.

It is now 1865, and the fighting has ended. Durk and Antoinette, along with the two surviving partners, Big Josh and Long Lou, have returned to Turkle, with a young boy they'd rescued, Caleb, in tow. The opportunistic Durk hopes to recover the *DarkHorse* land. And with slavery abolished, Josh is determined to dedicate his new life to helping his people. Their aspirations seem within reach, so logical . . .

But what will they find waiting for them?

# SECTION I

# CHAPTER ONE

# POISONED HARVEST

## 1865. TURKLE, MISSISSIPPI

The slaughter on the battlefield had come to an end, but a scourge more insidious and enduring now descended upon the shattered land.

Under the glaring sun, the rusted-out train dragged a load of bales past dust-blown fields, like a one-legged soldier taking to the plow again. Inside the train's lone passenger car, a weary Durk Hurst wiped his face and neck with his damp handkerchief, then loosened his clinging shirt. Closing his eyes, he settled his head against the hard seatback, bare of its original leather and stuffing, struggling to conjure visions of his beloved plantation, *DarkHorse*, which he hadn't seen for four years. But instead of its vast, lush green forests, and swamps rich in tangled cypress and tupelo, his thoughts were overwhelmed by the grotesque images of his ten dead partners he'd left rotting under the plains of Kansas.

*He rode into their camp outside Lawrence to discover his unarmed men scattered upon the surrounding field, their black limbs and bodies twisted in the gruesome poses of failed flight, their uniforms rent by pistol balls, heads crushed in by rifle butts and caked with dried blood. As he drew nearer, his nostrils were assaulted by the stench of desiccation, his face assaulted by frenzied swarms of flies. There's Samuel, poor Samuel. And Little Turby! Turby, they broke your glasses! Oh, hell, your damn glasses . . .*

He swallowed hard, forcing his attention back into the train. With many of the windows boarded up, having been broken out during the war, there was little movement of air to relieve the early summer humidity, nor to dissipate the pungent odor pervading the cabin. Durk couldn't help stealing glances at an elderly farmer seated on a coffin at the front of the car, his face etched in sorrow. "Your son, sir?" Durk inquired.

"Our one child," the farmer replied, voice quivering. "Fetchin' him home to bury him right."

"How long you been traveling?"

"Three weeks, mostly hired wagon and riverboat. Yankees done tore up the tracks pretty good." The man's head sunk into his hands, and Durk looked away.

He turned to admire Antoinette sitting beside him. Now in her late-thirties, with her lovely chiseled face and dark, almond-shaped eyes, she was everything he'd ever dreamed of, a wonder to behold, wise and loving. To avoid standing out, she'd felt it expedient to dress in simple calico, her long hair pinned modestly in a bun; yet she remained every inch a lady, bearing a dignity beyond disguise.

"Are you sure you don't want to just stay on this train, Durk? To keep going? No telling how you'll be received," she whispered. "The last time you were in Turkle . . ." She didn't have to remind him: *the torches in the night reflecting a sea of angry faces, the long guns, the shouts, his frantic escape . . .*

He patted his pocket, absently reassuring himself that a crude, handwritten agreement giving him the rights to his deserted plantation was still there. He swallowed hard. Regaining the rights to that land could make him a man of substance, he hoped. Or was this notion just another in his long, sad history of foolhardy quests?

"Do you?" he asked. "Being here with me could be dangerous for you, too."

She took time to consider her reply. "I'm with you, whatever you decide," she assured him, placing her hand on his arm.

Durk swept his fingers through his long black hair, trying to ignore a passenger across the aisle glaring suspiciously in his direction. He was accustomed to that look. With his Seminole mother's high cheekbones and dark features, Durk was always a stranger—and that can spell real trouble in a land where hatred and resentment always rumbled under the surface, at the point of erupting into violence and sudden death.

Durk glanced at his two black cohorts, Big Josh Tyler and Long Lou Jones, seated in the rear of the car. They were determined to reunite with old acquaintances at the French plantation, assuming everyone hadn't deserted the place, and Durk had promised to help them get established in the changed South.

His gaze settled on Josh, an older man of substantial girth. Josh was a warm-hearted soul whose true merit was often obscured by his black skin and stutter, yet he could intimidate with a mere stare. In fact, it was Josh's wisdom that had made him the group's true leader, whether building their plantation or fighting rebels. And Durk loved him. Reading and writing had been proscribed for slaves throughout the South, and Josh, having been educated in army schools set up for black soldiers, was determined to educate his newly freed people.

Catching Josh's eye, Durk nodded toward the grip beneath his seat, knowing it contained Josh's blue uniform.

*You sure you want to be carrying that around?* his glance asked. He'd tried to convince him to abandon the telling attire before his return South, as he and Lou had done. But Josh had insisted that he'd worked too hard and lost too many brothers-in-arms to ever give it up, regardless of the danger.

Josh returned Durk's hint with a dour look, which stated unequivocally: *I am a free man; I ain't giving up my uniform.* Durk knew the subject was closed.

Durk studied Long Lou who, after stopping in Turkle, planned to make his way to the Carolinas to search for his wife and children, whom he hadn't seen in seven years. He had no idea where his family was or how he'd find them, or even if they were still alive, but he ached to be with them again. This was a solitary trek many newly emancipated freedmen were making to unite with lost loved ones—slaves having been sold, on average, five times in their lives. Durk's eyes met Lou's, and the two men nodded, acknowledging that their years together would soon be at an end.

Through the cracked window, Durk watched the countryside pass, marked by scorched chimneys lording above burnt-out homes, grim memorials to four years of random destruction and mass murder. In the distance sat clumps of dilapidated shack colonies inhabited by black people in rags and threadbare clothing, the flotsam of four million people who'd suddenly found themselves liberated from bondage, but without the means or direction to create new lives.

The group's journey from Missouri over the past weeks had been perilous, a hodge-podge of potentially deadly traps. Grant's soldiers had destroyed many of the South's trestles and railroads, firing the iron rails and wrapping them while hot around trees. As a result, their group had been forced to make its way by boat, wagon, ferry, and train. En route, they had no way of knowing which strangers might prove treacherous among the roving criminal bands preying upon travelers and emaciated Confederate soldiers returning home.

Jerked from his reverie by the squeal of brakes and a blast of steam, a surge of fear shot through Durk's veins. They'd arrived in Turkle. Durk picked up his suit jacket and donned his hat. With a reassuring glance to Antoinette, he lifted his grip and shuffled into the aisle alone, while the others remained in their seats. No need for signals; they knew the drill. He made a final check on young Caleb, sleeping peacefully on the seat. Caleb had been orphaned after Union troops murdered his rebel-sympathizing father, but Big Josh and Lou had rescued him, and he'd been attached to them ever since.

Making his way forward, Durk descended to the platform, then paused to study the situation. The destruction immediately struck his eye: one corner of the station roof had collapsed and two nearby sheds were stripped of their sideboards. *What have we stepped into?*

Durk spotted the sheriff, Bake Stubbs, a few yards away, his mass of flesh perched on an empty barrel. Beside the sheriff squatted a lanky deputy resting on his heels like a country man in a field. Durk lowered his hat to obscure his face and made for the steps, but the sheriff slid off the barrel, pulled the deputy to his feet, and waddled over to confront him.

"Now you see why we watch this train crawl through ever' week, Aaron?" the sheriff told the deputy, then spit tobacco juice. "Never know what come steppin' off. Pull your pistol, boy, and keep it trained on that man in the hat. Don't you pay no attention to nothin' else, hear? He put us in the grave 'fore we know we dead." Then he whistled with astonishment. "Well, well," he said, "Mr. Durksen Hurst himself. I didn't expect to see you back here—after the friendly send-off we give you."

"I see you're still keeping the town safe, Bake," Durk replied, putting on his best folksy manner. "It's a free country now, ain't it?"

"We see about that. What's your business in Turkle?"

Durk thought this over, searching for a plausible response. "I'm here to open a school," he offered, Josh's idea popping into his head.

"A school?" The sheriff puzzled over this notion over, then gave up. "I think you' better talk to Colonel Rutherford 'fore you get any notion of taking up residence. Aaron," he ordered the deputy, "search his person and his belongings for any firearms."

His pistol-hand trembling, the deputy approached Durk as he would a cottonmouth displaying its fangs. "Sorry, mister, but I gots my orders." Durk slowly set down his grip and nodded benignly, then raised his arms. The deputy patted him down, then searched his effects. "Clean, Sheriff."

A wry grin spread on Durk's face. It seemed the gossip-driven tales of his prowess as a marksman still clung in folks' minds. In truth, he was a bad shot who'd sworn off firearms after his army discharge. But a tinge of threat couldn't hurt, should less-than-friendly encounters ensue.

At that moment, Antoinette and Caleb descended from the car and paused to see what was transpiring. Seeing her, the sheriff was taken aback. "Shoot," he said, "looks like I ain't going fishing anytime soon." Without a word, Antoinette took the boy's shoulder and led him to the edge of the platform where she waited for their two compatriots.

"Who's this Colonel Rutherford?" Durk asked the sheriff.

"Well, it ain't my place to say, rightly. He's ..." the sheriff began, slightly befuddled, "... why, he's, he's Colonel Rutherford. He can explain hisself better'n I can. He be in town this afternoon for you to meet."

"Why do I have to see this colonel? Is that some kind of law?" Durk asked.

"Ever'body that settles in Turkle meets the colonel. Especially you. You ain't under arrest or nothing, if that's what you mean." Feeling intimidated by a man he could only vaguely recall by reputation, Durk grimaced, his immediate plans temporarily sidetracked.

Big Josh and Long Lou, the last to depart the train, stepped onto the platform, assuming a wary but nonchalant stance. The sheriff seemed startled by the sudden appearance from the public conveyance of two black men wearing store-bought suits and carrying worn valises.

"You two hold it right where you are." The sheriff turned to Durk. "And don't you move neither, Hurst. Aaron, keep your pistol on him."

The sheriff confronted the pair. "What you two want in this town?"

"Just coming to w-work, Sheriff," Big Josh said impassively. "Just here to work."

"Well, let me inform you that we have laws here. Do you have travel papers? Negros can't wander loose in Turkle without them papers."

Durk watched Big Josh grow tense but merely shrug, indicating he didn't.

"Aaron," Stubbs ordered the deputy, "we got ourselves two vagrants. Place them under arrest. And search their bags." Josh gripped the valise containing his blue uniform, not about to relinquish it.

Durk struggled to think of something to say. If the sheriff found a Union uniform in Josh's bag, it was certain he and Lou would suffer. He examined Josh's face to gauge his reaction. As regimental sergeant, Josh had spent two years giving men life or death orders; now he was being treated no better than a slave. Durk feared Josh would be unable to control himself—and the lawmen were armed.

Twelve-year-old Caleb quickly stepped forward. "Them crows is mine!" he shouted. "You keep your hands off'n them." The sheriff smiled at this.

Antoinette pulled the boy back and walked toward the sheriff. Her sure manner left no doubt about who was in charge of the situation. "Vagrants? What do you mean, Sheriff? What do you intend to do with these men?"

"See, mam, the town passed Black Codes, like they is doing all over the South. All freedmen, free Negros, and mulattoes over eighteen got to be under a' annual labor contract; otherwise, they is considered vagrants. They is jailed, the judge fines them, and if they can't pay, their services is auctioned to the highest bidder. This way, they get put to work to pay back their fine. See? So both sides win."

"I do see," Antoinette said, not surprised after what they'd seen since Missouri. "Now that the planters can't buy slaves at auction, this vagrancy law is a way for them to keep a fresh supply of cheap labor working their fields. You scoop up every poor freedman wandering the roads and chain them to a worthless contract. Isn't that it?"

The sheriff winked conspiratorially. "Them fields need workin', mam, and there ain't the white folks to do it."

"I do have these men under contract, Sheriff," Antoinette stated firmly. "Furthermore, the bags they're carrying are mine, and you have no right to search my possessions. Is that a problem for you?"

The sheriff took a long, angry measure of Antoinette. "I remember you, Mrs. DuVallier." He gave Durk a foul look, then turned back to Antoinette. "And just where are you taking them people?"

"Wherever I please, sir. Thank you for asking," she quipped.

The sheriff thought this over. "There ain't no more *FrenchAcres*, you know, Mrs. DuVallier," he said. "You may want to get back on that train and take these people someplace more hospitable."

Antoinette looked to Josh for his decision, which he communicated to her by a subtle wince, before returning his expression to stone. "Thank you for informing me, Sheriff. I'll make that decision in due time. Right now, we're here."

"All right," the sheriff said reluctantly. "But if I see one of these men in town unescorted, with no traveling papers, I'm gonna throw him in jail. That's the law. You understand?"

"I do. It looks to me like we only thought slavery was dead."

"Oh, they ain't no more slaves; no, mam. The Yankees done seen to that. But we got to keep order somehow. All right, Mrs. DuVallier, you go on with your bidness. But remember what I tole you."

Antoinette turned to leave the station, followed silently by the boy and the two men. Watching them depart, Durk exhaled with a sigh.

The sheriff turned to Durk. "Well, I thought the pigs done ate the rotten apples, but here you is. Trouble don't just *follow* you. You *is* trouble."

They arrived at the town square and spread a blanket for their noonday meal, dismissing concerns that passersby might be offended by the five of them eating together. Despite the relief they felt at nearing the end of their arduous travels, the condition of the town weighed heavily on their hearts. The patchwork of ruins and vacant houses among the standing homes and intact businesses told the story of war's ebb and flow. On the streets, dispirited women in patched gingham and calico and men in work clothes wandered aimlessly as if in a dream. It wasn't a heartening sight.

Durk ate hurriedly and headed for the courthouse. A half-hour later, he returned with a bounce in his step. "I've arranged a wagon to take us to *FrenchAcres* after I meet this Rutherford person."

"It's past noon already," Antoinette cautioned. "The sheriff's probably waiting."

Josh placed his hands firmly on Durk's shoulders, facing him squarely, eye-to-eye. "You be careful, Durk. I know you. You hopin' to figure a way to get *DarkHorse* back, ain't you? How you gonna do that? Don't you know it's gone?"

Durk shrugged, brushing Josh's hands aside. "Maybe, Josh. We'll see."

"*DarkHorse* almost get us all k-killed, my friend. Look, if'n you and Antoinette want to get on the n-next train outta here, n-nobody hold it against you," Josh said, his stutter creeping into his speech. "Anyplace in the whole country be safer for y'all than Turkle."

"Whether you help or not, Josh, I still consider us partners. I'm doing this for all of us. You sure you won't. . . ?"

Josh just grunted. "I'm back here to build a school," he stated flatly. "That's all, Durk. I ain't getting mix' up in none of your flimflam. Done had enough of that to put us all six feet under."

"But, Josh, I'm the legal owner. There are records."

"Ha," Josh growled. "It'll be like wolves settin' on a carcass. All that land there for the taking! The law ain't g-gonna matter one bit, and you knows it." He paused to think. "No, nothing gonna happen f-fast in these parts. I'm building a school, t-take it one step at a time. Listen, Durk, there gonna be a day—I see it!—where freedmen are full citizens, own they own land and businesses. That means we can vote, too."

"Getting the vote's gonna be hard," Durk said.

"They say we can't vote 'cause black folks can't read—least they think we can't," Josh harrumphed "Well, most whites here can't read, and they vote, don't they?"

Josh continued, "You better put a lock on that tongue of yours when you with that Rutherford. He seem to have the power 'round here these days."

"I'll do my best, Josh, but it's not my tongue that resents being pushed around. Who won the damn war anyway?"

Antoinette anxiously gripped Durk's arm. "What matters, Durk, is not who won, but who's still angry about the result."

# Chapter Two

# CITIZEN RUTHERFORD

While his companions waited near the wagon, Durk met Sheriff Stubbs at his office, and together they made their way down the street until they came upon Turkle Bank. Unlike the row of dilapidated and abandoned buildings, the bank was well-maintained, having a fresh coat of whitewash, clean windows, and intact plank sidewalks. Sheriff Stubbs entered the front door and led Durk through the lobby to a door leading to the back office. "Bringing this man to see the colonel," he told the teller.

The teller, a slight, balding man in wire-rimmed spectacles, slid from his stool and unlocked the door, letting the pair enter. "The colonel be back shortly, Bake," he called. "Go on in and take a seat." The sheriff waddled in and held the door for Durk.

Peering into the shadowy, shade-drawn room, Durk let his eyes adjust before venturing in. He made for the guest chair facing the large oak desk that dominated the room and sat, examining his surroundings. Immediately catching his eye was the stained, torn battle flag hanging on the wall behind the desk, bearing the words "Turkle Company One" stitched across its top. The flag was split by a wavy blue cross, representing the convergence of Turkle's major two bodies of water: the Mississippi River and its Chickasaw Branch. Fixed in brackets above the flag was an officer's sword and scabbard with a gold tassel. The surrounding walls were lined by neat rows of rifles and pistols, many sporting elaborately etched steel barrels. It was quite an impressive collection.

The door behind him opened, and Durk turned as Colonel J.B. Rutherford entered his office, wincing with every step of his left foot, likely from a war wound. An imposing figure in his late-fifties, with thick salt and pepper hair, Rutherford stood well over six feet. He wore a tailored gray wool business suit and leather cavalry boots, as if immune to the heat.

Durk recalled that Rutherford had owned a thousand acres before the war; plus, the man had been active in the regional slave trade. Yet Durk had often heard rumors about his problems with debt.

Easing himself carefully into his chair, Rutherford ordered the lawman to leave. "Got to go. Leeland's pig done broke into Ernie Dobbs' corn crib again," the sheriff muttered, jumped up, and scurried from the room, shutting the door behind him. Seeing Bake so intimidated put Durk on guard.

Durk rose and offered his hand. "Durksen Hurst, Colonel. Good to meet you."

Waving Durk's hand away, Rutherford lifted his left leg and placed his foot on a cushioned stool. "I know who you are, Mr. Hurst," he snarled. "I remember you future-selling cotton at the county seat before the war. Your wager on the collapse of the South's fortunes, likely a product of luck rather than foresight, was subsequently confirmed. Shame your sudden departure from the region precluded your cashing in on your accidental prescience."

Chastised, Durk lowered his hand and sat down. "What is your role in Turkle, Colonel Rutherford? Why was I brought here?"

"This is merely a friendly get-acquainted, Hurst. Why? Do you have a troubled conscience? Frankly, I am surprised you would show your face here again."

*So the man knows about me.* "No, sir, nothing on my conscience. I'm just a peaceful citizen returning home."

Rutherford's eyes narrowed. "Not that it is your business, but my friends own this bank, and I am an officer, Mr. Hurst. Plus, I have a few other interests here and there. You may remember I had a substantial plantation before the war. I am attempting to get what little is left operating again while I negotiate with our Yankee occupiers about my property rights." He paused, the creases in his brow deepening. Durk understood what that meant: Rutherford had refused to sign a loyalty oath to the Union, likely from sheer stubbornness, leaving his legal status and that of his land uncertain for the moment. Undoubtedly, the man believed his political influence in Turkle would be enough to regain his rights once the current situation settled.

"When the Union invaders blew through in '63, they took all my livestock and feed. Indeed, my own slaves—my own chattel!—sabotaged my plantation and ran off, many to fight for the Yankees."

"The ingrates," Durk remarked, trying to restrain his sarcasm: the brutal methods Rutherford employed to run his plantation had been the talk of the county. That these methods were ineffective, indeed counterproductive, did not seem to matter to the embittered landowner, who, for years, had only managed to keep his family estate solvent by selling off pieces of his property.

"What's important, Hurst," Rutherford stressed, "is folks these days look to me for guidance through these difficult times."

"As I understood it, Colonel, when I left Turkle, Mrs. French was the majority stockholder in the bank. With her gone, wouldn't ownership fall to her heir?"

Rutherford sneered. "If that sissy-boy Devereau French ever shows up to claim his mother's legacy, I'll see that the sheriff has a discussion with him about her sudden and tragic passing. More than one witness has claimed Devereau shot the old woman. Yes, I almost hope he does show up," he added. "That conversation will be *lively*."

"I suspect it would," Durk said. "Now, what are these Black Codes everybody's talking about?" Durk had heard about Black Codes being instituted widely; yet actually encountering them had been a shock. "I can't understand why you'd need such a thing."

Rutherford slapped the desk with both palms and stood, leaning forward. "Understand, Mr. Hurst, people here are suffering. By freeing the slaves, the North has violated our constitutional right to own private property. In so doing, they have overturned the South's entire system of labor."

*If you want to call slavery a system,* Durk thought.

"When I returned home from the battlefield," Rutherford said, his face growing red, "I found nothing but hunger and chaos. Negros were slithering everywhere, believing emancipation gave them all the rights of white men."

"Most are simply trying to find their families after being sold apart," Durk said, thinking of Long Lou's imminent quest.

"They're a hazard to public safety," Rutherford snapped. "They're even attempting to establish their own settlements. My job here, Mr. Hurst, is to restore order so that our society can function. To that end, I'm proud to say Turkle became one of the first towns in the state to pass the Codes, and I have been assured the Mississippi legislature will adopt them statewide in November, as will states throughout the South in time. In our ongoing conflict with the Federal government, we have no other choice."

Stunned, Durk sank into his chair. It took a moment before he could speak. "Your ongoing. . . ? But the war is over, Colonel."

"General Lee may have surrendered; I did not," Rutherford huffed, indicating the flag on the wall. "No, sir. The war is *not* over. It will never be over. Too many of Turkle's finest died valiantly to preserve that flag to merely go on with my business as if nothing happened." He paused to make certain his words had sunk in.

Durk vividly remembered trying to convince the farmers working their patches of *DarkHorse* to resist running off to fight for the Confederacy. It wasn't merely that their refusal to heed him was humiliating, though they'd knocked him into the dirt and spat upon him. It was that, when Turkle Company One marched off in a cloud of dust, the hopes of Durk, his partners, and the men's own families disappeared down the road with them. He wondered how many had returned to Turkle, and how many were dead, wounded, damaged for life. *No, Colonel,* Durk thought angrily, *do not attribute your actions to civic duty. As a slave owner, you led those poor men to their deaths for your own gain.*

Rutherford continued, his voice elevating in pitch. "By emancipating the slaves, the Union stole over two-hundred-million dollars' worth of private property in this state alone. How are we to recover from that without a reliable source of labor?"

"I'm not so sure the freedmen see things the same way."

Rutherford's eyes narrowed, as if Durk had cursed in church. Then, shifting his demeanor, he sat back down. "Incidentally, Mr. Hurst, we haven't seen you in four years. What in Heaven's name did you do during the war?"

Durk paused. "I was a captain in the cavalry, Colonel."

"Yes? What unit, Captain?"

There was no way to evade the topic. "The Ninth, sir."

"Yes, which organization, sir?"

Durk hesitated. "Missouri State Militia."

"So, Hurst, you wore blue, is that what you're telling me? You are a traitor, sir—a traitor to your country!"

Durk's face reddened. "No, sir. I am a Southerner, but also a citizen of these United States. I simply did not believe in secession."

"Nor slavery either, it seems. You are, in fact, the same son of the drunken abolitionist, correct?" Durk nodded reluctantly, his heart sinking. "Yes, and because of his misguided beliefs he came to a very bad end, did he not?

"Captain Hurst," Rutherford continued, "it would be a tragic state of affairs if you were to follow in your father's footsteps." It was clear what he was intimating. There had been many Southern abolitionist preachers in the twenties who'd convinced some planters to manumit their slaves. But preachers of this stripe were often "persuaded" to ply their religion up North. Some were even murdered. By the thirties, such clergy no longer existed in the South.

"I'm just a simple citizen, Colonel, neither a preacher nor a politician. I merely believe it is good when folks get along."

"Let me tell you, Hurst, I am a practical businessman. But there is far more at stake here than one's livelihood. God Himself has ordained the sovereignty on earth of the Caucasian race. That is the natural order of things; it's in your Bible. Our land is oppressed now by Northern tyranny, by evil forces intent on seeing a subject race ruling the master. But never in history has this been done. Never."

Rutherford paused to study his effect, then continued. "Our land is in turmoil, Captain. But out of this disorder we will restore a white man's government and a white man's laws. Do I express myself clearly? Do you see the whole picture now?"

Durk's heart quickened. Clearly, there was no reasoning with this man.

"Now, Mr. Hurst, let's get to business," Rutherford said. "What are your intentions here in Turkle?"

"I intend to build a school," Durk replied, presenting the innocuous notion he used to disarm the sheriff.

"But we already have a school. A little run down, but folks will fix it up when the town's back on its feet."

"I want to build a school for the freed slaves, Colonel, especially for their children."

"A school? For Negros! Hurst, these people can't learn to read and write. The whole notion is ludicrous."

Hearing this, Durk burned, and it took every bit of his self-control to keep his face from showing his fury. Durk's young partner, Little Turby, had loved books; indeed, Durk thought Turby could have had a great future in law or education. Durk bit his lip, knowing he needed to keep his plans quiet.

"That is a major problem the South will face if not confronted directly—and soon," Rutherford said. "Negro schools have sprung up like mushrooms after a storm; hell, they're starting them themselves. These so-called schools are a plague descending upon our civilization."

"Colonel," Durk said, "I can't see the harm in teaching these people to read and write. Shouldn't they be able to understand the labor contracts you're forcing them to sign? It only makes sense."

"Sense for whom, to what end, Hurst?" Rutherford replied, fingers tapping the desk. "Listen, I want you to keep me informed of their schoolin' activity. Hear? And if you participate, you will bear the consequences."

Glaring at Durk, Rutherford lit a cigar and took deep, thoughtful draws, studying him, before continuing. "Knowing your reputation, Mr. Hurst, you must have some other objective in mind."

*So the man figures I'm up to something. I may as well lay my cards on the desk.* "Well, to be honest, Colonel Rutherford, I still hold the rights to property south of town. I called it *DarkHorse* you might recall."

"Ah," Rutherford exclaimed, leaning forward. "Now we're getting to the heart of the matter. What evidence do you have of this claim, that it's even valid?"

"I still hold the deed, Colonel. I filed the record at the Honor Store myself."

"The Honor Store burned down in '61, Mr. Hurst. So you can forget that."

Durk was stunned. "How'd that happen, Colonel? Was it the Yankees?"

"No. The enterprise's demise was a town project, you could say. The deacon's granddaughter attempted to manumit the *FrenchAcres* slaves—illegally—and folks didn't appreciate her efforts."

The Honor Store had been run by the Purelys, an elderly senior deacon and his mousey young granddaughter, Ellen, Turkle's only admitted abolitionists. Folks tolerated the pair's unforgivable heresy because, poor as they were, they devoted their threadbare enterprise to aiding others as destitute as themselves.

The modest store never made money. However, Ellen did manage to earn a few dollars organizing the town's records: property deeds, notably Turkle's land and slaves; births, marriages, and deaths; and slave manumission papers, of which only a dozen had been filed by Durk for the partners he never actually owned.

"What happened to Ellen?" Durk asked.

"Oh, I see her now and then in church. They didn't lynch her, if that's what you mean."

"Yes? That's good. And what about her grandfather, Colonel?"

"Unlike some people, the Deacon died quite bravely defending his beloved South against the invaders."

Durk contemplated the irony of the elderly abolitionist sacrificing himself for the Confederacy. "And the town records?" Durk asked, calculating that there may still be records at the county courthouse in Lethe Creek. And the Indian Bureau probably had some record on the *DarkHorse* transfer that Rutherford couldn't get to.

"Oh, the town preserved those before they set fire to the place. But there is nothing in the records for you."

So, Durk surmised, Colonel Rutherford and his cohorts likely confiscated his deed, making his quest even more problematic. "And so, my property rights. . . ?"

"As you might well imagine, Hurst, there are a number of claimants for such extensive land, plus, there are taxes owed and a number of other complications. You'd be wise to think twice before getting involved." Rutherford paused to consider the situation. "And what do you propose to do with that land should you acquire it?"

"I intend to develop it into family farms which I will rent out, with eventual ownership going to the farmers, just like I started to do before the war."

"And who will you rent these plots to?"

"To any and all honest people who will work them."

"To *anyone*?"

"Anyone," Durk said firmly.

"Ah, that is your first mistake, Hurst. Under the Black Codes, it is illegal to rent or lease land to Negros. These people were brought here to work *plantations*, not to be independent farmers. Are you aware of that provision?"

"I see," Durk said, his heart sinking. The chains of slavery were to be replaced by chains of law. "So in effect you are forcing the freedmen back into plantation work."

Rutherford studied Durk closely, considering his options. "All right, now, Hurst. Assuming you prevail in your acquisition—or reacquisition—of the property, however unlikely, would you be willing to sell your rights?"

"Not for any price."

"Then what *will* you settle for? Would you be willing to accept a partner to achieve your aims?"

Durk considered the question. "Perhaps. Can you make me an offer, Colonel?"

"I will have to sleep on that." Rutherford rose and limped painfully to the bookcase, picked up a dog-eared volume, which he admired briefly, then handed Durk a clean copy from a stack of identical ones. "In the meantime, here is something for you to read. It was composed by a cultured gentleman respected throughout the South; copies even sold up North. Mine has been at my bedside throughout this entire conflagration, right alongside my Bible."

Durk examined the cover's gold lettering: *A Defense of the Divine Right of Slavery and Secession* by J.B. Rutherford. "Is this you, Colonel?"

"It is. You can keep that copy, Hurst; I have others."

Durk opened it and scanned the first paragraph, then shut the cover. "Thank you, Colonel. I will make a point to read this at my first opportunity. Perhaps the local freedmen can use your excess supply in their schools," he added as straight-faced as he could muster.

Hearing this, Rutherford pulled a knife from his desk drawer and began cleaning his polished nails with the blade, before leaning in to address Durk. "Let me tell you, sir, it is common knowledge that the Negro is doomed to extinction. Were his labor not needed to tend our crops, the South would be far into this process already." He paused to let that sink in. "Now, I know from your planter days you are a man willing to make substantial, even foolhardy wagers, so I have a piece of advice for you: aiding and abetting the Negro is a doomed proposition."

"Well, Colonel Rutherford, I am no prophet. I merely try to do what I think is right. I cannot understand how the Negro will somehow be erased from the face of our country. I would wager that the Negro has every intention of surviving, even if the odds are heavily weighed against him."

In an instant, Rutherford's hand whipped a backhand throw with his knife, which spun end-over-end and stuck deep into the wall. "Hurst, you are subject to the law here just like everyone else and to its enforcement, however draconian. Do you understand me?"

"Is that a threat?" Durk asked.

Rutherford's eyes blazed. "I do not issue threats, Mr. Hurst. The war taught me that. One is either alive or dead, and any remarks made in between those two states of existence are a waste of breath."

"I see. So you intend to rule by fear," Durk said, his voice low, tense.

Rutherford rose and limped to the wall, where he retrieved his knife. "An ounce of fear is worth a pound of persuasion, Hurst. You, too, will obey the law in full. Period."

"The law is our fortress, Colonel," Durk said through clinched teeth.

"No, our guns are our fortress. Our guns, sir." Rutherford scowled, then returned to his desk. "We are done here."

# CHAPTER THREE

# AN ENIGMATIC COUPLING

## FRENCHACRES, TURKLE, MISSISSIPPI

The shadows grew long as the sun slipped into its nocturnal burrow just beyond the western hills. Antoinette sat on the seat beside the skinner as the hired wagon plodded down the dirt road deeply rutted by decades of wheels laden with cotton bales. Behind her, Durk and Big Josh shifted uncomfortably in the wagon bed, while Caleb and Lou walked beside them stretching their legs. Pulled by a single horse, their trip from town had been slow, tedious, seemingly interminable.

The wagon passed the skeleton of an abandoned farmhouse, its sideboards and porch scavenged for cook pits by black families on the run, farmers fleeing to safety, riders on the prowl, and troops seeking fuel. The sight reminded the former cavalrymen of their near-fatal encounters against guerrillas in Missouri, of family abodes laid waste by rampaging armies and bushwhackers, of massacres and murders. *No matter where you turn, there's a reminder,* Durk thought.

Further on, the group was lulled into a dream state by the regular clip-clop of hooves and an overwhelming fatigue. Except for the cacophony of insects, frogs, and the scurrying of creatures, the air was silent, heavy. Passing the last scrub brush bordering the road, they came upon the once-imposing gateway to *FrenchAcres*, the county's most prosperous plantation, now a pitiful pile of fallen bricks and fencing slats.

They rode on. At the top of the hill, they passed the ruins of what had been the legendary mansion, a two-story, columned edifice. Somewhere in that pile of rubble rested Mrs. French's scorched bones. Looking upon the blackened timbers laying to rot, Durk could almost feel the reclusive widow's suffocating spirit hanging over the place, like a covetous ghost unwilling to release her grip on the town she manipulated and controlled for so long.

Durk tried to gauge Antoinette's feelings, imagining the bitter memories the place provoked within her. Although her face was impassive, he could sense a profound turbulence beneath the surface.

Fifty yards down the road they came to the family graveyard, now overgrown with tall weeds and vines clawing for sunlight. Its wrought-iron gate hung askew, barely attached to its wooden fence missing many of its pickets, like a gaping skull of rotted teeth. Amid the broken, over-turned monuments lying in the weeds stood one solid black headstone, a monolith rising above the ravages of time. As the wagon drew closer, Durk could make out the words chiseled in gold into its surface: SUFFER THE LITTLE CHILDREN. Nothing more: not name, dates, nor gentle remembrance of the interred child beneath.

Quietly, Antoinette told the skinner to stop. "Don't wait for me," she mumbled offhandedly. Then she climbed down and began walking slowly toward the grave.

Durk called after her, "Do you want me to come with you?"

Without looking back, Antoinette merely shook her head, preferring to be alone. As the skinner snapped the reins and the wagon creaked into motion again, Durk turned to see Antoinette lift her skirt and carefully enter the weed-covered yard.

*How can she bear this?* Durk wondered, wishing he could comfort her.

Roaring flames of yearning clutched at her heart as waves of sorrow and loss overwhelmed her. Antoinette knelt on the twig-strewn ground and, with one hand laid against the cold surface, touched her handkerchief to her eyes. "Sweet Louis Edward, a victim of your own grandmother's neglect. I pray you didn't suffer long. I miss you every day, my beloved . . ."

Rage welled up within her. "You cold, heartless witch. You nearly destroyed us all to serve your own selfish ends: my life, my child's, Devereau's."

Antoinette rose unsteadily to her feet, her fury unrelieved. She wiped her eyes and bent to gently kiss the stone, then made her way half-blindly to the road. "Damn you to Hell, Mother! Damn you to Hell . . ."

She began drifting slowly toward what had been the old slave quarters where the others had gone. Feeling lightheaded, she halted and sat down upon the damp ground beside the road. She had thinking to do.

Her mind wandered to her half-sister, Devereau, forced by their mother to live her life as a man to ensure the family dynasty.

*What a sad, solitary existence you must have had, poor thing. Had mother not given me up, had I known you, would things have been different for you? For both of us?*ntoinette had no doubt that Devereau, desperate for human warmth and contact, had loved Louis Edward. But the boy died in her mother's care while Devereau was away on business. Louis Edward's death drove a bleeding gash into her heart, a wound she knew would never heal.

Over these last several years, Antoinette's feelings of abandonment and despair, of loss and resentment, were ever present, poised to pitch her without warning into depths of anguish. She had hoped to find some relief by returning to this place, the last place her beautiful little boy had drawn breath.

The tears, held at bay for so long, began to flow.

*Sometimes I think it would be better if I could not feel anything at all.*

The sky revealed a vast profusion of stars singing their heavenly chorus as Big Josh, Lou, Caleb, and Durk finally reached the former slave quarters, a large cluster of run-down shacks, little better than tool sheds. Seeing the wagon approach, a group of six children stopped their play and scattered, shouting to alert their families. Relieved to have arrived, Durk and the others climbed down from the wagon bed, planted their legs firmly, and stretched their backs as blood flowed back into their limbs. The men fervently hoped that this was the moment they'd feel the war was truly behind them and their lives could begin anew.s word spread across the quarters, a few of the residents appeared, making their way cautiously to investigate the interlopers. Then a shout broke the air as one of the men recognized Big Josh. Soon an excited crowd surrounded their guests, welcoming them. Jumping and shouting children were quickly dispatched as messengers, calling everyone together.

The quarters had several empty cabins, so there would be no problem putting a roof over their heads. During the war, when the Union army passed through Turkle, most of the French slaves had run off in a great mass to follow the troops, deserting the property that had haunted their nightmares. With no French family left to interfere, many who stayed set to farming the land, as others who had scattered began returning.

The best available cabins were selected: one for Durk, Antoinette, and the boy; another for Big Josh and Long Lou. Once the greetings concluded, the community settled back to its routine, becoming a hive of activity. The women returned to their homes to prepare meals for the hungry travelers, find blankets and utensils for their cabins, and gather brooms, jugs of water, and lye soap to aid the cleanup. Taking charge as he always did, Big Josh sent one of the boys to watch for Antoinette.

Finally, the weary travelers headed to their temporary homes. Entering the dimly lit cabin with Caleb, Durk found five women cleaning and setting up the place. The one-room shack was sparsely furnished: a wobbly table, one of its legs held together with twine; a few chairs; a corncob bed; and a palette on the floor near the stove. It was the best that could be thrown together in so short a time. Two of the women were scrubbing out a rusty stove, while the others swept away cobwebs and carried in firewood.

Their cleaning done, other new neighbors brought them an assortment of stews, breads, and root vegetables, which Durk and Caleb hungrily wolfed down. When Caleb finished, and Durk released him to play outside, it was like the boy had been let out of jail.

Thanking the women, Durk went to the porch to wait for Antoinette. She'd separated from them some time ago, and, concerned about her state of mind, he had to force himself not to go in search of her. At last, she emerged from the darkness, eyes bleary from crying. In seconds, they were in each other's arms.

"You need to eat. Then we can talk," he whispered, walking her to their cabin.

When she'd finished picking at her food, Durk poured two cups of water and joined her at the table.

"What have we fallen into, Durk?" Antoinette asked wearily. "Do you think there's the slightest chance of you getting back *DarkHorse*?" She paused, a shadow creeping across her features.

Durk sighed. "It's not going to be easy. I asked around in town while I was trying to hire the wagon. There are apparently a number of competing interests eying the property. And they want control of *FrenchAcres*, too.

"Another thing I learned," Durk continued. "Someone burned down the Honor Store, where they'd kept the property records. I'll have to visit the county seat to verify my rights."

"What will we do?" Antoinette asked, bewildered.

What, indeed? Durk gazed at Antoinette. Had she only agreed to return with him to placate his harebrained ambitions? He knew she could leave him—go west, north, or east—and be far safer than here.

"I've been thinking. We should get married," he said. "Otherwise, how will we explain being together? I think we have to. If not, that could be an excuse for folks to . . ."

"You know we can't," Antoinette replied, shattering his hopes. "That could put us both at risk." Durk began to object, but she continued. "Durk, those birth records in New Orleans; there are laws."

Durk lowered his eyes, angry and frustrated. He had far more Indian blood than she had black. Both their skins had a tinge of color, but didn't most folks down here to one degree or another? They loved each other; shouldn't that be enough?

"Look," Antoinette said, "I was thinking. Whoever gets the deed to *FrenchAcres* will likely take away the farms these freedmen have started, forcing them back into peonage. You know that."

"Yes, I'm sure that's true."

"Well, then . . ." Antoinette said tentatively, studying her hands. Durk could see she was deeply unsure about something and waited for her to reveal her quandary. Finally, she spoke. "Durk, I have to try to take ownership of *FrenchAcres*. I want to deed the plots to the freedmen; it's the only way these people can be independent."

Durk was stunned. "Take over *FrenchAcres*! How could you. . . ? You know Devereau will be named as your mother's heir, and she's locked up in a Union prison for a long time. Besides, she'd never sign the plantation over to you. She hates you.

"Moreover, you and I and Devereau are the only ones who know that Mrs. French was your mother," he said. "Heck, folks still believe Devereau's a man."

"I've been thinking about Mother," Antoinette said, her voice trailing off. "You know what she was like, Durk, secretive and devious. And she knew Devereau's weaknesses. I'm sure she wondered: what would become of *FrenchAcres* if something happened to dear fragile Devereau? How can I arrange to cede the plantation to Antoinette?"

"That's likely," Durk agreed. "But what could she have done?"

"She could have had a phony marriage contract drawn up between Devereau and me and had it filed. Think about the ramifications."

"I see," Durk said. "If Devereau—*Mister* French—were to die, or she's out of the picture for some reason, then you could claim the plantation through marriage, no questions asked."

"Yes, and that's another reason we can't get married. Our marriage would nullify any claim I might have to *FrenchAcres*."

"Do you think there really is such a document filed away somewhere?"

"Perhaps. What if Rutherford or someone produces it? You know he's likely to dig into every possible angle. Or what if Devereau suddenly shows up? They're letting wartime prisoners go home under various amnesty programs."

"They'd throw you in prison for bigamy and take *FrenchAcres* anyway. Pretty ironic, married to your own half-sister."

"Exactly," she said.

They sat silently, holding hands, contemplating the situation. Durk studied Antoinette. The gloom he sensed in her now had often presaged a far deeper hopelessness that crept upon her. Of course, she was weary from the travel and heat; moreover, she had visited Louis Edward's grave, which must have been heart-wrenching. Now, added to that, she might have to play a hazardous role to resolve the turmoil surrounding *FrenchAcres*.

Feeling exhausted and defeated, Durk could not imagine how he could go on if something happened to her.s Antoinette and Caleb settled in, Durk threaded his way between the rows of closely packed cabins toward the quarters' common area. There he spotted Big Josh sitting on a crate, deep in thought and clearly troubled.s Durk came into view, a smile appeared on Josh's face, and he rose to greet him. Wanting to talk privately, the pair made themselves comfortable under a sycamore.

"So what did you learn, Josh? How does it look for your school?"

"Oh, black folks here already start a school. They hold it in the old French stable. Fifty children during the day, and they folks come in from the fields at night to study them books, too. Everybody want to learn to read and write." Josh lowered his voice, becoming grave. "The Freedmen Bureau sent a teacher over, white college man from up North. Then one day he just g-gone. Nobody know if he shuck Mississippi and go home, or somebody kill him. Ain't never found no body."

"I bet Bake went right after the culprits," Durk snickered.

"So's we got a black teacher now," Josh continued, "doin' the best she can. A free woman from Jackson. Well, we all free now, ain't we? She understand our situation, help folks around Turkle with they contracts and such, too."

"How do they pay her?"

"Oh, folks done tax theyself. Do her laundry, cook, give her a place. It's fine for now. But I wants to raise money to build a real school— maybe someday a college. See?"

"You know I'll help you if I can," Durk vowed. Josh's demeanor grew dark. "What is it?" Durk asked. "What aren't you telling me?"

"There a lot to tell. Let's move over by the fire." Josh rose, and the two trudged toward the large bonfire built to celebrate their return. Durk could sense the palpable new spirit in the long-downtrodden community. These gatherings in the quarters—once merely a momentary break from unrelieved toil and grinding fear—had now burst forth into unrestrained joy, imbued with a real sense of hope.

Near the fire, several groups of men sat passing a jug, ruminating over serious matters, joking and laughing. Women gathered in their own groups near cookfires, sharing their truths, gossiping and exchanging stories. Around the periphery, children ran wildly about, shouting and playing games. Nearby, young men timidly approached shy young women, who laughed disdainfully at the men's exuberant displays of masculinity. Naturally, these perfunctory rebuffs were followed by coy smiles that refuted the finality of any rejection of their suitors. These people had been given nothing. Yet they were living without fear of the whip, without neck collars, coffles, and humiliating slave auctions, without being torn from their loved ones, without the loss of life or limb for simple infractions or disagreements.

Nearby, the rhythms of pulsating drums echoed through the darkness, accompanied by a catch-can of strings, horns, and homemade instruments.

With myriad African tribes thrown together on this continent, their diverse cadences were constantly evolving into a distinctively new American sound, more complex than the simpler European metrics of the day. Reflected in relief against the blazing bonfire, the silhouettes of men, women, and children danced in celebration, their bodies swaying in unison to the rhythmic percussion, like tall river grass, their feet stamping in double- and triple-time.

Durk turned to Josh. "What did folks tell you about this Colonel Rutherford? Anything?"

"He a bad one, Durk. *Bad.* The colonel heads up gun clubs to terrorize black folks. From what folks say, he's leading a faction of rich planters and such. He's hired some killers, too."

"Sounds like they intend to reverse emancipation, even if the war did not. Are you worried about *FrenchAcres?*" Durk asked, examining the area.

Josh sighed deeply, clearly distraught. "Folks know the colonel ain't the only rich man trying to take this land. And they got lawyers and courts and such. People scared to lose everything.

"And these new laws they got," he continued, "arresting folks on the road, taking them to jail. Then it's 'sign a contract or go to prison'. They leaving these folks out here alone so far; the stores in town want the business. But that may not last. By the way, I hear Rutherford got his old plantation going again."

"That's what he told me."

"So where does he get his labor? Men go from jail to his place—and they never seen again! People think something terrible going on out there."

Durk angrily broke a stick and threw it into the fire. "What else?"

"Durk, black folks can't own firearms to protect theyselves. Heck, people was using they guns to put food on the t-table. You caught with one now . . ." Josh grew grave. "These gun clubs I told you about, they ride around, cause trouble, take what they want. Twenty of them ride to Joe Rivers' place last week, tell him to give up his musket. But he ain't got no musket. See? They beat him something terrible. 'Give us your gun,' they say. What could he do? Well, they kill Joe and his wife, and burn down the cabin they built."

"And the army allowed it?"

"The army left the old Confederates in charge, same jobs as they had during the w-war. The meanest ones, pro-slavery and all, Durk. It's this President Johnson . . ."

"Another dividend from President Lincoln's assassination," Durk said glumly. "President Johnson just wants the South to return to where it was before the war: whites on top, blacks on the bottom. Period. Congress is working against him. The amendment to outlaw slavery should be ratified soon. There's even word of amendments to give black folks citizenship and the vote. But he's the president after all: he's making change down here hard."

"It can't hardly get worse, Durk. If you kill a black man now, it ain't murder. You steal from a black man, it ain't robbery. Durk, ain't one white man been charged with murder since the war, and lots of black folks been beat, killed. Everybody scared."

"But the army, the Freedmen's Bureau?"

"Sixty mile away, near Jeron's Ferry. Sixty mile. The army can't cover the whole state. We ain't nothing here, I tell you. Nothing." Josh stretched wearily and rose to his feet. "I need some sleep," he said. "Lou and me over in that cabin yonder."

Durk realized how exhausted he was himself. "We're over there," he said, pointing to his cabin.

"They ain't our old mansion," Josh chided.

"They are not, my friend."

"What you planning to do?" Josh asked.

"Tomorrow I'm going to town to see if the stable rents horses, maybe sniff around the public records. Sometime this week I'll ride out to *DarkHorse*; see what's left. Maybe visit the Chickasaw village. You want to come?"

"My business is here, Durk."

Durk rose to his feet, and the two grasped hands.

"Can't keep away from *DarkHorse*, can you?" Josh teased. "Listen, Durk, don't get that Colonel Rutherford mad, understand? You standing on the edge of a cliff already. I like you better alive." He wrapped an arm around Durk's shoulders and hugged him before trundling off.

# CHAPTER FOUR

# THE BITTER TASTE OF DECEPTION

## CHESTNUT STREET PRISON FOR WOMEN, ST. LOUIS, MISSOURI

Fearful, Devereau French sat in her room staring in the mirror, studying with horror the telling brown speckles across her face. She knew what they meant. In the fading dusk, her delicate, frail hands trembled as she struggled to draw a comb through her matted auburn hair, which had grown to shoulder length during her two years of Union army incarceration. At thirty-nine, her eyes had begun to show wrinkles, more from the nightmares of war than from age. Tonight was her chance to free herself, but she had no confidence she could pull it off. Listening to stories from other inmates, she knew that better-looking women, experienced in the ways of men, had tried and failed. What chance would she have?

Two days earlier, she had been transferred from the Alton Women's Prison in Illinois to St. Louis, to be held for transfer to a Federal prison in Ohio where she would serve the final ten years of her sentence. She would be an old woman by the time she was released, nearly the same age her mother was at her death. The Chestnut Street facility was originally a mansion confiscated by the army from Margaret Parkinson McClure, a Confederate sympathizer, and converted to a prison to hold female Confederates until they could either be deported South or relocated to more secure facilities.

Devereau knew that if by some miracle she did manage to wheedle her way to freedom, she'd have nowhere to go. She'd be just another helpless female in a city flooded with refugees and widows, with no money or prospects.

—*Return to Turkle, fool! Have you forgotten my legacy? Have you forgotten* FrenchAcres?

—You are insane, Mother! Have *you* forgotten that there's probably a warrant out on me for murdering you?

—*Nonsense. Just get yourself out of the hands of these people. You'll figure it out; they're only men. Do you think I spent my life preserving my empire just to turn it over to white trash and Negros? Do you?* FrenchAcres *is your only recourse. Just get yourself free.*

—But I'm not you, Mother. Look at me.

—*You're my daughter, my blood. Prison has been good for you. You've blossomed. Unbutton your blouse, idiot. More! Another button. See? This would be a simple endgame for me.*

—For you perhaps. But this is no game, Mother. It's my life.

The Union guard opened the door abruptly, bringing Devereau to the present with a start. A scrawny, bearded man in his late-thirties, his uniform rumpled and weathered cap worn at a jaunty angle, the guard was all business. "The provost's office is ready for you, Miss French."

Devereau took a final glance into the mirror, nodded, then rose. "Well, sir, let's learn my fate."

The guard led her downstairs and through the former dining room to a parlor that had been converted into an office with a U.S. flag perched in the corner. Behind the mahogany desk that dominated the room sat a tall blond officer in his mid-forties, bareheaded, his uniform neatly pressed. At his back was a large bay window that looked out on the mansion gardens.

"Please sit down," the officer stated, glancing up. He picked out a document, then dipped his quill in the ink pot. "Now, Miss French. My orders indicate you are to be shipped to Ohio tomorrow with three other women. Do you have any questions?"

Devereau felt her face flush, a headache starting to pulsate up her neck. She was nervous about the challenge before her, never having seduced a man before. But she had to try. Knees shaking, Devereau rose slowly to lean over the desk, pretending to examine the document, hoping the man would become distracted by her exposed bodice. Awkwardly, she pointed at the paper with her forefinger and asked in a tremulous drawl, "Why, are those my transfer orders, Lieutenant?"

"Yes," he said gruffly, clearing his throat, visibly uncomfortable. "Please sit down, Miss French."

She hesitated, unsure of what to do next, then sat down. "Lieutenant," she said demurely, her Southern accent thick as syrup, "I believe we should discuss this transfer thoroughly before we do anything rash. I'm certain you and I can come to a—to a highly satisfactory conclusion." There, she'd said it!

—See, Mother, I did it.

—*Well-played. You are your mother's daughter after all.*

—Shut up now. I need to concentrate.

Taken aback by her overture, the officer studied her closely, then laughed, which made Devereau's ears burn red. His laughter grew to a roar before he was able to regain his composure.

"Miss French, I am a married man with four children," the officer stated firmly, showing no trace of interest. "Others in your position have tried the same tactic. I assure you, there is no satisfaction of that sort that you and I can come to."

Humiliated, Devereau's chin sank to her chest, and with trembling fingers she buttoned her dress up to the neck, her mind spinning frantically. *What's my next play?* Finally, she lit on an idea.

"Sir," she continued, straightening her back, "I'll have you know I own a large plantation in Mississippi that was worked by hundreds of slaves before the war. Hundreds. Of course, these chattel are slaves no longer, but the land still belongs to me. Nevertheless, as you can surmise, ten years from now it will no doubt be gone. If you allow me to return home to claim my property, I will make it quite worth your while. Quite worth your while." She studied his face. "Many prisoners are receiving amnesty. Why not me? You know I'm no danger to public safety."

The officer rubbed his face wearily. "You should have considered all that before you became an accessory to that murdering Indian. Now, Miss French, I must warn you that attempted bribery of an officer will only lengthen your sentence. Is that what you intended?" Devereau shook her head, unable to reply.

"Good," the officer stated. "Gather your things. You and the other prisoners will be setting out promptly at ten o'clock tomorrow morning. Understand?" Devereau nodded humbly.

"Sergeant!" the lieutenant called out. "Return this prisoner to her quarters."

The sergeant, an unkempt man in his fifties, entered, appearing a bit sleepy, and saluted. Without a word, Devereau rose and the two left the room. Failed, she'd failed!

—*That's it, fool? You're going to give up your life and your birthright that easily? You should have shot yourself when you had a pistol.*

Devereau had one move left to play, dangerous, but possible.

"What . . . What's your name, Sergeant?" Devereau asked demurely, unbuttoning her collar at the neck.

"Why, Bill, mam," he said nervously. "Name's B-Billy Cooper."

Devereau stopped ten feet before they reached the stairs, continuing to unbutton her dress. The guard faced her, unsure of how to proceed.

"Listen, Billy Cooper, this is my last night here; I'm going to be locked up for ten years. Ten years. How about you and me have a little fun before they send me off?" she proposed nervously. "It'll be a night you won't soon forget. I promise you."

"Well, I don't know, Miss French," he said, transfixed by her fingers working the next button.

"That spot back of the garden behind the house, where the hedges meet. No one will see us. I've got a jug of excellent aged whiskey hidden there behind the bushes. You can have it—have it all."

"Well," he said uncertainly, stroking his beard, his breath accelerating. He thought for a moment, watching intently as she undid two more buttons. "We'll have to go out through the kitchen and circle around," he said quietly.

Without a word she took the guard's hand and led him on tiptoe to the kitchen. There, the pair eased through the back door, shutting it carefully behind them. Night was falling, but there was still enough light for someone to spot them. Hand-in-hand, the two scurried silently through the lush garden, which had been well-tended during the war by women prisoners with nothing better to do. Across a footbridge spanning a miniature stream, they stealthily dashed into a grotto and fell giggling beside a flowerbed bordered by large, flat stones and surrounded by hedges. Coming to rest in the secluded area, they took a moment to catch their breath. Then Devereau finished unbuttoning the last two buttons and pulled her dress over her head, dropping it to the ground beside her. The sergeant couldn't take his eyes off her, which, having little experience in these matters, made her uncomfortable.

"I'll get the jug," she whispered. She scrambled on all fours and reached into the bushes. Going through the motions, she began tugging on the thicket. Failing to retrieve the promised jug, she pretended to tug harder, to no avail. "Help me, Billy," she asked urgently. "It's stuck on something."

The sergeant crawled beside her as she pointed to a section of hedge. "There, Bill, it's in there," she whispered. "See it?"

Crouching on all fours, the sergeant moved in closer, lowering his cheek to the ground to peer into the hedge, but it was too dark to see through the tangle. Devereau slid away to give him room. The guard looked around, then stuck his hand deeper into the bushes to feel around. "I don't feel it," he whispered. "Where. . . ?"

Without warning, Devereau slammed one of the large border stones down on the back of the sergeant's head. He uttered a muted moan and touched his hand to his skull. Devereau struck him again harder and watched the man fall silent, motionless. She tossed the stone aside and knelt beside him. He was out cold, but still breathing.

—Again, fool! Finish him! He'll wake and sound the alarm.

—Shut up, Mother, I'm doing this.

Devereau removed the sergeant's cap and wiped off the bloody spots in the dirt, covering them passably with soil. Then she hurriedly began to undress the guard, pulling off his boots and belt. She paused once to check his state, but he was far into unconsciousness, so she struggled to remove his tunic and trousers. When he was down to his skivvies, she finished undressing, then slipped on the uniform. Once she had the uniform on and all the buckles fastened, she tore a ribbon off her dress and tied her hair into a bun, securing it under the blue cap.

—Well, dear, a bit awkward way of doing it, but you certainly did your mother proud. Men are born fools for women and drink. Best you remember that.

—You would know.

—Don't forget the dress.

—I don't want it. I'm done with that rag.

—*Fool, you can't leave it. Besides, you might need it. Never discard a potential gambit for yourself, never abandon an asset. You don't know what lies ahead, what you'll need to do.*

Reluctantly, Devereau gathered up the dress and slipped it under her arm. She crept to the edge of the grotto and peeked over the hedge. Under the moonlight, at the front gate she could see a slim young guard sitting propped up against a tree, his rifle beside him leaning against the fence. Her eyes searched the gardens and grounds, but she could see no other way out. She checked the lieutenant's office window, but, thankfully, the room was dark. Her heart beating madly, Devereau stood up, straightened her back, and fixed the cap firmly on her head. Then she marched confidently toward the gate.

—Welcome back to the world, Mr. French.

—Shut up, Mother; it's Sergeant French.

When she reached the front gate, the young guard pushed to his feet and saluted. In as deep a voice as she could manage, Devereau ordered firmly, "At ease, private, at ease. Sergeant McCoy to go out for a bit."

"I don't know, sir," the young guard said uncertainly. "Nobody said nothing."

Devereau held up the dress. "I've got a gift for my lady in town. Be back in two hours, maybe three. This is on my say-so, you understand?"

"All right, sure, on your say-so." He opened the gate, and Devereau was soon on the street. Free!

—*Was that so difficult? Now do you still think you won't be able to deceive a bunch of Confederates back home?*

The night was growing cooler, less humid, and tomorrow would likely bring an early summer rain. From Chestnut Street, Devereau made her way steadily toward Sixth, but not too hurriedly, remembering that if she saw an officer, she would have to make a complete stop and salute. Reaching Olive Street, she paused to stare eastward. No military figures could be seen for blocks. After all, it was nighttime. She turned, continuing down Olive until she reached Broadway and stopped. Looking around, she found a clear spot high enough to view the river, the central artery for Union supplies.

She paused to look over the wharfs. Below were docked a mass of riverboats, barges, and steamboats. Two steamboats were being loaded with large bales, and Devereau could hear music emanating from another upon which well-dressed couples danced. How she longed to be part of the frivolity on that boat or to bathe leisurely in a tub in a private cabin. What a relief that would be from the cramped cells she'd shared as a prisoner the last two years.

But here she was, dressed as an army sergeant, broke, and unable to do the heavy lifting and stevedore work she'd need to get hired-on. Out of ideas, she sat on a mound, arms draped around her knees, and cried softly. What now? Her eyes searched the docks, but most of the other vessels tied up looked like army transports.

—*Down there, half-wit. Get yourself on any one of them—any one!— and you're on your way to Mississippi, to comfort and wealth.*

Wiping her eyes, Devereau rose to her feet. She dusted off her uniform pants, stuck the dress under her arm, and began walking briskly, careful not to stumble on the irregular lay of the cobblestone streets. Reaching the river's edge, she continued along the bank to where the boats lifted and fell gently in the black running waters. She passed boats being loaded by black stevedores, but decided not to try them and continued a hundred yards further to where soldiers were loading military barges. Spotting one with a line of soldiers passing supply boxes, she approached a captain supervising the operation and saluted awkwardly.

"Are you going as far as Mississippi, sir?" she asked formally, deepening her voice.

"Yes, we are, Sergeant. Supplying our occupation units."

"Can I catch on with you that far?"

"That would be highly irregular," the man replied, examining this frail soldier.

"Look, sir. My mother's dying back home." She showed him the dress. "I must get this to her, to bury her in. It's not much, but it's better than what she has."

"Let me see your papers, Sergeant."

Devereau searched her pockets. "I must have left them in my coat.

Won't need a coat in Mississippi. With mamma dying, I just wasn't thinking."

"I could get in real trouble, Sergeant. I'm sorry."

"Look, Captain, I left my family in '61 to come up here and fight with y'all to save our country. Killed three Rebs at Pea Ridge before they caught me with a ball," she winced, holding her side. "They thought I was gonna die. I was laid up—oh, it was terrible. You're my one chance to give my mamma her goodbye kiss before meeting her Maker. Won't you help me? Her goodbye kiss, Captain," Devereau pleaded. "She's been through a lot while I've been up here fighting the cesh."

—*Goodbye kiss, ha! Your goodbye kiss was a bullet in my chest.*

The captain thought long and hard. "All right, Sergeant. But you'll have to sleep and eat with the privates."

"That's all I ask. Bless your heart. I thank you kindly."

"Then get aboard; I'm busy here."

Devereau saluted briskly and made her way up the gangplank, relieved to be one step closer to home. She had to squeeze through the loading line, but soon she was on deck. She found her way to the stern, holding onto the railing, and seated herself on a stack of boxes. Taking a deep breath of the evening air, she gazed out at the hundreds of bonfires along both banks flickering and dancing upon the calmly rippling waters of the broad Mississippi. Her eyes turned upward toward the stars twinkling in the black sky, remembering so many nights on the trail lying beside pit fires, shivering cold, wrapped in her blankets. Who knew open sky could be so precious? Next, she glanced back to St. Louis for the last time, its warehouses and wharves casting jagged shadows against the horizon. Then she turned her eyes south.

Her heart beat with a wild exhilaration she'd never before experienced. She could barely believe she'd been able to escape a decade in prison, and the euphoria quickly overwhelmed her. She was gripped by images of *FrenchAcres* in its prime: of its endless stretches of cotton fields; of its stable where she'd kept her prize horses; of its extensive woods and riding trails.

Her thoughts snagged on the family mansion, her prison for thirty-five years, causing a chill to run down her spine. Then she began to wonder what was actually awaiting her back home, knowing nothing would be the same as before.

Trying to shake off her doubts, Devereau re-focused her thinking along practical lines. Returning to Turkle meant resuming her male identity. But as much as she hated being trapped in that charade, it was her only chance of gaining back what was rightfully hers. Of course, she'd have to acquire a man's clothing somewhere along the way to shuck this Union disguise. She didn't have any money, so she'd have to use her wits, maybe even steal.

*What, oh what, would mother do?*

# CHAPTER FIVE

# THE JEW STORE

## TURKLE, MISSISSIPPI

Under the glaring noonday sun, Durk strode past the neglected and ransacked storefronts lining Main Street toward the stable, where he intended to rent a horse for his ride out to *DarkHorse*. He'd already been fortunate that morning, catching a wagon heading to town for supplies, and hoped his luck would continue. He passed the city hall on the town square, its defaced columns being repaired and painted and broken windows replaced.

Sweat pouring down his face, Durk removed his hat and wiped his brow with his sleeve, to little effect. Soon he approached a storefront he recognized. In contrast to the street's otherwise quiet activity, there was a flurry of comings and goings at the enterprise folks called the "Jew Store," owned by an older couple named Ahronson. Every Southern town had a "Jew Store," a place to buy sundries like cutlery, pots and pans, Sunday suits, dresses, and Easter bonnets. Durk hesitated, then edged closer, his curiosity aroused. When they were building *Dark-Horse*, Durk and his partners had purchased most of their supplies from the Ahronsons and knew the couple well. Durk was shocked to see shattered glass covering the sidewalk and quickly made out that the oak barrel, kept in front of the store, had been thrown through the window. Customers scurried in and out of the front door, propped open with a brick. Then he spotted the bloodstained dirt in the street. Whose was it? He hoped the Ahronsons were all right.

Stepping inside, Durk was horrified at what he saw. Broken glassware and dishes were everywhere underfoot. The store's shelves were empty of clothing and linens, which had been tossed into chaotic heaps onto the floor.

He looked around. While one woman was sweeping up broken items, two others were taking care to fold dresses and suits, neighbors helping a neighbor in her time of need. Sheriff Stubbs was there, too, and Durk saw him slip a plug of tobacco into his pocket. Other townsfolk were eagerly picking through piles of clothing and other merchandise. Then he spotted Mrs. Ahronson, a small, gray-haired woman in her late-sixties. Always lively and friendly when he'd known her, he could see she now was in great distress, mechanically cleaning up. A middle-aged woman approached her carrying a pair of salt and pepper shakers in the image of hound dogs, one white, one brown.

"How much, Mrs. Ahronson?" the old woman asked.

"A nickel," Mrs. Ahronson replied.

"I only got three cent," the woman offered sadly.

"Just take them, Mrs. Lowell," Mrs. Ahronson said kindly. "You've always been a good customer." The old woman hugged her, then shuffled out the door, clutching her booty to her breast.

"Mrs. Ahronson," Durk said stepping over dresses and broken children's toys to reach the proprietress. "What happened here?"

Seeing him, tears rolled down Mrs. Ahronson's cheeks. "Durk? Oh, they shot Morris, Durk," she cried. "They dragged him from the store and shot him to death in the street." She fell into Durk's arms and rested her head on his chest for several seconds before pulling away.

"But why?" Durk pleaded. "Why would they do that?"

"Because Morris treated the Negros like whites, everyone the same. Is that any reason to kill a man and do this to his business? We've lived here all these years, paid our taxes, and this is what they do to us."

"They been warning him for weeks," the sheriff interjected, drifting over beside him. "But you know Mr. Ahronson. No damn sense."

Ignoring the sheriff, Durk asked, "Who did this, Mrs. Ahronson?"

"Who?" she replied bitterly. "Who! About twenty men from those gun clubs, that's who." She cried again, dabbing her eyes with her handkerchief.

Durk looked the sheriff in the eye. "Do you know these men, Bake?"

The sheriff shrugged. "I don't know nothing 'bout what them boys be up to. Could have been any number of folks; maybe not even Turkle boys."

Directing a look of disgust at Stubbs, Durk turned to Mrs. Ahronson. "What are you going to do, Mrs. Ahronson? Can I help?"

"No, Durk, thank you. I'm going to move to Atlanta to live with my brother. He'll send a wagon for me. I'll take what I can, leave the rest to the wolves." She considered the situation. "Do you need a horse by any chance, Durk?"

"Yes, mam, I do."

"I'll sell you Morris' horse and saddle. It's at the old stable, now that they burned the blacksmith's place. How much can you afford to pay?"

Durk chuckled. "Only got thirty dollars. Yes, mam, only thirty dollars. The army don't pay captains so well."

"The horse is no yearling; the saddle's in good shape, but it is ten years old. I'll sell them both to you for the thirty dollars."

Durk readily reached into his pocket for his money, but the sheriff interrupted, "I'll give you forty, Mrs. Ahronson."

"I sold them to Mr. Hurst already, Sheriff," Mrs. Ahronson replied.

"Fifty," the sheriff countered. When he received no answer, he proposed, "Sixty."

"Talk to Mr. Hurst, Bake," Mrs. Ahronson stated flatly. "He owns the animal now."

Bake spit a wad of tobacco onto the floor. "For thirty dollars! You people just don't understand business," he exclaimed.

Just then the young owner of the general store across town entered, wearing an apron over a starched white shirt, suspenders, and a tie, and drew near to the proprietress. "I'm so sorry, Mrs. Ahronson, so sorry," he said sympathetically. "Your husband was a good man. A decent man."

"Thank you, Orville." She dabbed her eye. "Looks like you're the only store left."

"That's not what I ever wanted," the storeowner said, as the two embraced. "Colonel Rutherford's damn ruffians." Hearing Rutherford's name, Durk grew grim.

"What are you going to do, Mrs. Ahronson?" the storeowner asked.

"I'm leaving Turkle, Orville. I'll sell you whatever inventory I don't take with me. What can you offer?"

"Well, like everybody else, what with the war and all, I don't have much right now. Times been pretty tight, and then there's the wife and boys to consider."

The storeowner put his fingers to his chin, thinking. "But, mam, I know you must have hundreds, maybe thousands, of dollars on your books. Mr. Ahronson was always quick to take a chit when folks was broke, and with this war, folks been broker than usual for quite a spell. If you'll sell me your ledger, I could probably dig out enough of my savings to cover a nice burial for the mister, plus I could send you along a cut of what I retrieve from folks as time goes by."

"Thank you, Orville. That's most generous. But our customers will find some way to bury him nice for me. As for the ledger, I think I'll just burn it. This way, folks can start their lives fresh, from scratch."

"Are you sure, Mrs. Ahronson? I maybe could come up with a hundred dollars or so from my uncle in Vicksburg."

"My mind's made up, Orville."

Disappointed, Orville merely shook his head and gave her a last hurried hug. "I left Dooley in charge, so I better get back quick before I go broke. Meantime, I'll send over Spark and Tye to board up the window and help you out any way they can. Good luck to you, Mrs. Ahronson. Again, I'm sorry." He was quickly out the door.

Finishing up, Mrs. Ahronson took Durk's money and wrote a bill of sale for horse and saddle. Then, struck by an idea, she paused a moment to appraise him. Her wise eyes came to life, as if seeing into his soul. "Tell me, Durk, what are you planning now that you're back?" she asked.

"I'm not sure yet, Mrs. Ahronson," he replied.

"I'll tell you what, Durk, I'll sell you the store and everything in it for a thousand dollars: seven hundred for the building and three hundred for the inventory."

Dumbfounded, Durk didn't know what to think of this unexpected, disproportionately generous offer. The enterprise would be a lot of responsibility though, and he already had plenty of that. "I'm sorry, Mrs. Ahronson, but that thirty dollars was all I had."

"I know you, Durk," Mrs. Ahronson assured him. "You'll figure out the best use for the store, or at least for the building. Pay me when you can."

"Why me, Mrs. Ahronson?" he asked.

"Because your dealings with folks, white and black, have always been honorable, Durk, like my Morris," she said. "And unlike most of our town's upstanding leaders, you keep your word."

"Oh, I would get your money to you, mam," Durk said. "I can't say for sure when, though."

"I trust you, Durk," she said, growing calm for the first time since the deadly clash the previous night.

"But I don't know a thing about managing a store," Durk cautioned.

"You'll figure it out. Say, Durk, do you remember Ellen Purely from the Honor Store? I'd like it if you'd bring her into the operation—she'd show you how I do things. She's been helping me a bit here and there. I pay her a few dollars to keep her body and soul together as best I can. Of course, she has no head for business. Still, she's meticulous and honest."

Durk thought over the request. "Course, I'll keep her on, Mrs. Ahronson."

"Good," Mrs. Ahronson said with a relieved sigh. "When she stops by after church later, I'll tell her to help you with the store, that she'll be working for you."

Durk nodded agreement, wondering what he'd gotten himself into. Still, he now owned a horse and a storefront in town. And he'd hired an employee experienced at failing in business, so the store wouldn't depend on his expertise to produce fiascos quite as much. Durk snickered to himself. What unlikely kindred spirits they were! Ellen, now a grown young woman, always held the firm belief that God lived beside her; while Durk, well, Durk, having seen the cruel and seamy sides of the world, wasn't so sure.

Durk's mind was suddenly a swirl of visions and notions of what to do with his new-found circumstances. After warm hugs and wishes of good luck, Mrs. Ahronson placed a hand-lettered sign on the counter reading "TAKE WHAT YOU WANT & PAY WHAT YOU CAN," bearing her shaky signature at the bottom. Beside the sign she set a collection box. That done, Durk watched her trudge off to her living quarters in the back of the store, resigned to her new life as a widow.

Sighing deeply, Durk led the sheriff back to the street. "What exactly are these gun clubs, Bake?" he asked innocently. "And what's Rutherford's connection to them?"

"Now, you know me, Hurst. I don't know nothing 'bout them gun clubs."

"You spend all your time chewin' the fat with everyone in town; you must know something. What do you know about last night?" Durk asked accusingly.

"Last night? I was in bed sound asleep. Didn't hear or see nothin'."

"Figures," Durk spit. "You ain't changed a bit, Bake. Matter of fact, looks like nothing much has changed in Turkle. Nothing at all."

# CHAPTER SIX

# A POIGNANT FAREW

## FRENCHACRES, TURKLE, MISSISSIPPI

Durk awoke gradually in the arms of a sleeping Antoinette, sore from the corncob mattress. The cabin was still pitch, and he sensed sun-up was at least an hour away. Since they'd fled Mississippi four years earlier, he'd longed to see *DarkHorse*, and this was his last chance to get away for a couple days before Mrs. Ahronson left for Atlanta.

Carefully, he turned onto his back trying not to disturb Antoinette, pausing a moment to admire her peaceful face wrapped in a storm of wild black hair. Stretching, his nostrils were struck by the smell of lye soap, mold, dust, deteriorating boards, and fried meat from the night before. He had to get outdoors.

What he needed was to be in the saddle. Of course, there were things he had to do in town that morning, and tomorrow afternoon he would visit government offices at Lethe Creek seeking documents that could validate their claims to both *DarkHorse* and *FrenchAcres*, claims upon which the fate of so many rested.

But his real objectives lie in between the two. Like a pilgrim to sacred ground, Durk would forsake the direct route from Turkle to Lethe Creek this afternoon and take the long-abandoned road that ran past the old *DarkHorse* plantation—a heart-twisting, bittersweet journey through time and memory.

When he'd last seen *DarkHorse*, most of its vast reaches remained untamed except for the few hundred acres Durk and his partners had cleared for planting. What he'd been dreaming of seeing, however, was the mansion site.

After paying his respects, Durk intended to spend the night with the Indian woman who'd raised him. To reach her village, he'd pass through the Chickasaw forest, where he'd played as a youth. Perhaps, he imagined, this pristine setting would cleanse his mind of the horrors he'd witnessed in Missouri and Kansas. Perhaps being submerged in the living green would end his nightmares, would wash away the images of bloody, mutilated bodies; of the faces of starving, ragged refugees dragging their possessions and children down dusty roads; of miles of burned-out family farms.

How he had loved this arboreal territory. Certainly, over the years he'd often considered shucking everything to once again dwell with the tribe; but he knew in his heart that would never satisfy him. And, of course, there was Antoinette . . .

Dressing in the dark, he sat in a chair to pull on his boots. "Where are you going?" Antoinette, half-asleep, mumbled quietly, not wanting to wake Caleb.

"I'm taking Lou to the station this morning," he whispered. "The train doesn't normally stop here on Wednesdays, but they might for me." He knew a train wouldn't even slow for a black man trying to flag it down.

"Then I'm riding out to *DarkHorse*; I'll spend the night with the Chickasaw. Tomorrow I'll go through the county records at Lethe Creek, like we planned."

Antoinette said something he couldn't hear, then said, "I hope Rutherford offers a deal."

"We'll see."

"Be careful," she said, kissed the air, and rolled over.

Durk rose and walked into the pre-dawn, careful to shut the door softly. The air was humid, but not as oppressive as it would be later in the day. He quickly saddled his horse, mounted, and made his way through the dilapidated quarters to his friends' cabin. When he rode up, Long Lou was already dressed and waiting on the porch, bursting to be on his way to find his family. As Durk drew rein, Lou hoisted up a sack containing his belongings and tossed them over his shoulder.

"Got your papers?" Durk asked. Lou patted his pockets. Hoping to evade the restrictive patchwork of vagrancy laws, Durk had signed two documents for Lou. One was a formal contract indicating that Lou worked for Durk. The other was a travel document directing Lou, his "employee," to go to Carolina to work for the man who had once owned him body and soul. Of course, Lou didn't know where his family was, nor whether that planter or plantation had survived the war, but Durk hoped these papers would at least get him there safely.

Durk pulled Lou up behind him onto the mare and set out. After riding two hours, it was well into morning by the time they reached the train station. Durk tied up the horse, and the two men climbed the stairs to the platform. Not being a scheduled day for the train to stop, Durk had to bang on the window to get the stationmaster's attention. After buying a ticket for Lou, the men sat on the edge of the platform, hanging their feet above the tracks, and waited.

"You sure you won't take the horse?" Durk asked.

Lou spit in the dust. "Thanks, Durk, but one of the soldiers making his way home on foot might take a shine to riding, and I ain't looking to get shot. No, sir, I'll work my way down to New Orleans any way I can: work on a boat, hitch on wagons, walk—a lot of walking, I expect. Sign on there as a seaman going to the East Coast if they take me."

"And money?"

"Everybody throw in somethin' last night. Got a pocketful. They just happy I'm gonna see my kin again . . ." he stared at his feet, ". . . maybe."

"I'm going to miss you, Lou. All of us will. We've been through a lot together. So many are gone."

"I know," Lou said. "I' miss y'all, too. But I gots to find my wife. Made it through the war, so this won't be so bad. Least they ain't no slave catchers no more," he half-joked.

It was late-morning by the time the train huffed and smoked out of the east toward Turkle Station. Durk stood and frantically hailed it with his handkerchief. Luck was with them as the train came to a squealing halt.

Lou slid off the platform, sidled up to the passenger car, and peered inside. Then, waving his ticket overhead so the engineer could see it, Lou climbed clumsily onto a freight car.

"You're riding freight?" Durk asked. "You have a ticket, Lou."

"Too many white folks in there. Don't want to chance it."

Durk helped his friend climb up, knowing he would never see him again. They grasped hands briefly until the whistle let out a blast. Then letting go, Durk waved after Lou as the train chugged off. The *Dark-Horse* partnership was now down to two.

Durk mounted the brown mare and headed toward the store that he, inexplicably, now owned. Before the war, sleepy Turkle had been familiar to him, like an old alligator sunning by the river. But in the light of morning it seemed more like a lifeless log snagged on trash. Dead? Perhaps not. The hamlet had already begun to show its teeth.

Ellen Purely, with white-blond hair, brows, and lashes and ghost-white skin, made her way along the shelves, making precise notations in the ledger. Diligently counting out the pieces of dinnerware, she was irritated because all the damaged merchandise was playing havoc with her neat columns.

Blue-bordered dishware. *PLATES: 7 unaffected, 4 missing, 2 broken, 5 cracked. BOWLS: 5 unaffected, 6 missing, 4 broken, 2 cracked. SAUCERS: 11 unaffected, 3 missing, 3 broken, 4 cracked . . .*

And the torrent of customers! Having heard about the attack on Mr. Ahronson and anxious to get their bite of the plunder, they wouldn't stop bothering her. Didn't they see Mrs. Ahronson's sign on the counter? Ellen knew many of them either couldn't read or felt guilty setting their own price, so they insisted on bargaining with her to assuage their conscience. *I have work to do!*

Small and frail on her best days, today Ellen was exhausted and appeared to have shrunk further into herself. The morning had been terribly difficult.

She'd worked half the night cleaning up from the catastrophe and putting the shelves in some semblance of order, aided by well-meaning, but feeble, townswomen who wouldn't know how to organize merchandise if God Himself was directing them. It had been easier just to step in and finish up herself than to talk any sense into their thick heads.

Then there was the matter of consoling Mrs. Ahronson. Thank goodness the woman wasn't averse to a little wine, which enabled Ellen to get her to sleep last night. Ellen also needed sleep, yet there was much to do before the store was in proper order. *God give me strength.*

On top of all that, Ellen was tortured to distraction by the visions of Mr. Ahronson's murder. She couldn't understand why her God would allow a beast in human form to kill such a good man. You'd think that after the suffering she'd seen, she would have come to understand His reasoning. But she didn't. She'd overheard old Mrs. Petty telling people that the murder was God's will because the Ahronsons weren't Christians. But that didn't stop Mrs. Petty from making quite a haul from the St. Louis cutlery shelf that morning, leaving in exchange only a wrinkled dollar and a few coins in the box. The spinster had invariably treated the Ahronsons with scorn when transacting her modest business there, ignoring her nearly half-page of debts on the store's books. No, there were plenty of Christians in Ellen's own church whom God would gaze upon with sadness and disappointment before turning His wrath on the Ahronsons, that was for certain. Moreover, Ellen wondered why providence let these killers roam at will, seemingly immune from divine retribution. It didn't make sense. The whole thing was a nightmare!

The sound of boot steps coming through the door shook her from her reverie. *Another customer!* Paying no mind, she continued counting dishes, hopeful that whoever it was would transact his business quickly and not ask after Mrs. Ahronson or pose any inane questions. But she expected there was little chance of that.

"Ellen?" a familiar voice inquired softly. She ignored it, hoping he'd take the hint and leave. "Ellen?" the man repeated a little louder. The interloper would not go away. Ellen sighed, turned, and immediately recognized the face of Durksen Hurst.

Forever etched into her heart was the day Durk entered the Honor Store to have her draw up manumission papers for his slaves. That was the moment, she knew God was calling upon her for a higher purpose.

She studied Durk. Still ruggedly handsome of face, she could see the war had been hard on him. She wondered, after how the town had treated him, why he'd returned.

"It's Durk, Ellen. Don't you remember me?"

She emitted a single involuntary, incredulous gasp, paying no heed to the question, and returned to her ledger.

Seeing she wasn't going to reply, Durk continued. "Did Mrs. Ahronson mention she sold the store to me?" Ellen merely stared at him, dazed, as if watching him from under water. "Well, she did," he said, "and I hope you will stay on; I could use your help. Would you like to do that?"

She tilted her head, his voice a distant echo. Finally, she stated flatly, "I'm busy scoring inventory," and returned to her work.

Durk looked the store over and could see that, unlike the night before, it was now in some semblance of order, though many shelves remained empty or disheveled by the frenzy of bargain-seekers looking to benefit from the tragedy. "Well, good," he said.

Just then a local farmer in patched overalls entered, carrying a sack, which he laid on the counter. "Here's taters on my account, Miss Ellen," the man said. But Ellen stood mute, unsure how to answer him.

Durk placed his hand on the man's shoulder. "Not necessary, Mister. Mrs. Ahronson rescinded everyone's debts." The farmer looked puzzled. "I mean, nobody owes the store any money from before last night. Understand?"

"I don't owe nothing?" the man asked, bewildered.

"Nothing. The slate is wiped clean for everyone. Spread the word to folks that their debts here are cancelled, will you?"

"Well, I'll try," the man said. "We don't get much company out our way."

"Ridley, just take what you want and go home," Ellen said impatiently. "We're talking business here. You can take the taters with you."

"No, I'll leave them. Thank you kindly," the farmer said, tipping his hat and going about gathering what he needed, nothing more.

Durk turned to Ellen. "You're looking pretty worn out. Why don't you shuck that ledger and go in the back to get some sleep? The store will look after itself." He reached in the moneybox, pulled out a few bills and shoved them in his pocket. Then he changed Mrs. Ahronson's sign. Where it read PAY WHAT YOU CAN, he scratched out the last three words, wrote AS MARKED, and signed his name above Mrs. Ahronson's. He felt safe leaving the box out while Ellen slept, since folks wouldn't steal from a store they frequented, and the amount was too petty for rich folks to bother with.

"Well, I don't know . . ." Ellen said, uncertainly.

Durk studied Ellen's homely, misshapen dress, then gave her an order.

"And go pick out the nicest dress in the store for yourself. The prettiest one. Shoes, too. I'm buying. Go on. I need you looking your best in my store."

"You sure?"

Durk nodded. "Listen, Antoinette, me, and a boy we've taken in, Caleb, are moving in here. But you'll stay back of the store, too; no more board for you. Would you like that?"

"I would."

"That's good, because you'll have lots to do. I'm going to open a legal practice here in town, and your time keeping records at the Honor Store would be a big help. We're going to offer our services to poor people, Ellen, white and black."

"I'd like that."

"That's fine. When you get a chance, will you make up a sign for the window to that effect? Your calligraphy was always so lovely as I recall. Make it read: LEGAL REPRESENTATION, FREEDMEN AND WHITES. Put my name on the bottom." Ellen nodded, then suddenly grew troubled. "What? What's the matter?" Durk asked.

"The sheriff was by, asking if you're gonna charge freedmen the same as white folks like Mr. Ahronson did. That's what got him shot, you know."

Durk considered his options. "Put a second box on the counter reading FREEDMEN PREMIUM, Ellen. That ought to satisfy the colonel and his friends."

"Freedman premium? What does that mean, Durk?"

"It means freedmen will pay an extra dime, or anything they can contribute, when they make purchases here. The money will go toward a school Josh wants to build." The two of them laughed, delighted with the subterfuge. "By the way, Ellen, I was sorry to hear about your grandfather. He was a righteous man."

"Didn't do him much good against Yankee rifles," she said bitterly, her bottom lip trembling. "A body can't always understand God's Ways."

Then she was struck by a spiritual revelation. *God has brought Durksen Hurst back into my life. If that ain't a sign, I don't know what no sign is!*

Leaving the store, Durk strolled down the street. Reaching Turkle Bank, he went inside and asked to speak to Colonel Rutherford. One of the clerks went into the back office and returned to let him in. Thanking him, Durk entered the shade-drawn office to find Rutherford seated at his desk perusing bank ledgers, a foul expression on his gnarled face.

"What is it, Hurst?" Colonel Rutherford snapped, not looking up.

"I wanted to discuss the *DarkHorse* land, Colonel," Durk said, trying to sound confident.

"All right. Have a seat." Rutherford pushed the ledger aside, clearly not pleased. "What is it you have to say?"

"You told me you might consider making me an offer . . . about a . . ." The next words stuck in his throat. He gulped, ". . . about a partnership between us." Durk found it profoundly disturbing that the word "partnership," which meant so much to him and his friends, was so distasteful at the thought of teaming with Rutherford.

A steely stare came into Rutherford's eyes. "Yes, I thought about it, Hurst, and I've concluded that my odds would be better without you involved. So I think that closes the matter between us. Now if you want to take your claim to court, that's your business. But I will save you the trouble: you haven't a chance, sir, not in Turkle. Now, do you have any other business with me?"

"Yes, Colonel. It's these Black Codes. It's obvious to me they are intended solely to keep blacks as a permanent underclass."

"Nonsense. Those regulations have codified the Negro's rights, protected them you could say, much to their advantage. I don't know why some folks can't see that. Under the Codes, they can now marry legally, establish contracts, file legal suits, even testify in court cases involving other Negros. Going any further, however, would lead to the collapse of Southern civilization."

"I'm sure the Freedmen's Bureau will have something to say about that."

"Hurst, the Bureau has no say in this matter. The Codes were passed unanimously by the elected officials of Turkle's town council . . ."

"Yes," Durk interrupted, raising his voice. "The same people who ran Turkle during the war, the most ardent Confederates."

"Look here, sir," Rutherford interrupted, silencing Durk. "We have an election coming up. If you want to change the Codes, that would be the way to go about it. Understand?"

"*If* you allow Negros to vote." Durk figured blacks made up nearly half the citizens in Turkle and perhaps slightly more than that statewide.

"Oh, I see," Rutherford said, smiling wryly. "So you are in favor of granting the franchise to the Negro, is that right?"

"Yes, certainly," Durk replied growing angrier by the second. "They're free now, aren't they?"

"Hurst, understand, these people are children, ignorant. They lack all the Anglo-Saxon virtues that enable men to govern themselves. Why, when I came back home from the war, they were out of control . . ."

"Searching for their families! Colonel, these people have been kept as slaves for generations, it will take some time . . ."

"The present situation is intolerable, Hurst," Rutherford bellowed. "Intolerable."

"All right, Colonel," Durk said, seeing no way forward, trying to calm the situation. "On another matter, I want to know what you and your cronies plan to do about the freedmen on *FrenchAcres*. These people merely want to earn an honest living. Why can't you just leave them be?"

"Why, indeed, Hurst?" Rutherford asked with unconcealed sarcasm. "Why, indeed?"

Durk saw that Colonel Rutherford had no intention of leaving them in peace. Antoinette's idea of claiming the land and deeding it over to them seemed the only chance they would have to be fully free. He took a deep breath and continued.

"One final matter, Colonel, about schooling for these black children. The Freedmen's Bureau wants them to be educated in public schools together with the white students. The regular schools have better teachers and books; you know that. Can we arrange that between us, between you and me?"

Rutherford merely stared at Durk without a word. Durk could see this was going nowhere and rose to leave. "Colonel Rutherford, times have changed. Can't we simply accept things as they are and learn to work together?"

Rutherford retrieved his ledger and resumed studying the columns of numbers, ignoring Durk's presence. Clearly, there would be no sharing of ideas today.

# Chapter Seven

# A STALLION NAMED CONTRITION

## FOREST ROAD NEAR DARKHORSE

There are days that dwell outside of time, where chronology is meaningless, immaterial. In these dream-like moments, during these epiphanies, one's life becomes illuminated, crystalline, eternal. So proved this diurnal passage for Durksen Hurst.

By mid-afternoon the sun was behind Durk, casting the horse's shadow ahead down the rarely traveled dirt road. The former Chickasaw territory was a pleasant ride, shaded by a dappled canopy of bald cypress, spruce pine, and Southern magnolia, and bordered by thickets and forest scrub. Durk relaxed in the saddle, breathing in the fragrant vegetation. As he drew within a quarter of a mile of the once-formidable mansion site where he and his partners had lived, the land grew increasingly familiar, sparking profound memories and emotions.

The horse, reliable like its former owner, had done passably well. Durk knew it would never be fast enough to escape trouble like his old roan; but if he could reach woodland on foot, pursuers would have a devil of a time catching him.

He drew rein at the property's entrance: two unevenly stacked towers of rough stone connected by a thick cedar sapling arch, which, surprisingly, no one had torn down and nature hadn't budged. *Well,* he mused, *it withstood war better than Turkle had.*

With a pain in his heart, he remembered the day Isaac had climbed up these rugged stones to hang their carved wooden horse, symbolizing their *DarkHorse* plantation. *Our horse is long gone,* Durk thought bitterly, *as are you, Isaac.* Durk owed his life to Isaac, who'd died in his arms on a St. Louis street trying to protect him, guts knife-slashed by the murderous Chickasaw, Wounded Wolf. Durk flicked the reins, and the brown made its way up the long drive.

At the site of their mansion, he paused to stare, arms resting on the saddle pommel. They'd been desperate—just a drifter and fugitive slaves—but, miraculously, they'd built their home despite formidable obstacles. How proud they had been the day they'd painted the final brushstrokes on the structure, a two-year labor of love. In his mind, he saw his friends' faces beaming, heard their laughter, felt their euphoria. But now most were merely ghosts.

The visions receded, bringing the chimney into focus, a scorched monument to another of his Big Dreams vanished into smoke. And their home, hewn from nearby stands of cedar and oak? A pile of burnt timbers rotting amid encroaching forest.

He wasn't sure how long he'd spent clinging to these memories before he noticed the sun dipping lower in the west. Throughout the war he'd longed to see his *ishiki,* the woman who raised him as his mother—if she was still living. He knew he'd best head for the Chickasaw village without delay or he'd have to navigate the swamp by night, never easy even for tribal members familiar with the territory.

As he rode his mind flashed back to his boyhood, to his terror fleeing through the predator-infested swamp, drenched and starving. Then ahead, through his delirium like a mirage, a Chickasaw village. He dragged himself to the closest fire, as near to death as he'd ever been. A kindly widow took him in, fed him, and raised him, becoming his *ishiki.*

*These people saved my life. And how did I repay them? I stole their land and named it after myself!* His conscience, seldom gentle with him, stung his heart at the thought. *If there was some way I could repay them,* he wished. *But no man can ever repay all the debts he owes to the people he hurt. And what I owe these people is far beyond my meager prospects.*

Durk knew the swampland well; yet nature had done its cruelest on the ever-metamorphosing landscape, and much had changed. As night fell, the swamp grew black, and terror seized him. Clouds covered the moon; slough and backwash lay like black ink across broad stretches, deadly sinkholes from which neither horse nor rider would return. The forest itself became a living nightmare of threatening branches and twisted shapes. Panther, moccasin, and gator lurked alongside every path and riverbank, hidden within brush, bramble, and thicket. There were no drums to guide him as he steered the mare through a dense stand of pine where he'd once played as a boy. Finally, he caught the welcome glimpse of light ahead: the village fires.

He rode past the village's ball field beside its empty log fort, which the tribe had built to retreat to when attacked. This was one of the tribe's smaller villages, holding fewer than one hundred families, each with its own summerhouse, a sturdier winter house, a grain storage structure, and a menstrual hut.

Like removing his hat in church out of respect, Durk dismounted and led the brown slowly through the village on foot, pausing only briefly to greet and embrace an old acquaintance. A night breeze from the west cleared smoke from the dying cook pits. Children played their last games of the day, as the women cleaned the clay and wooden bowls at riverside. He passed a group of men seated around a bonfire, smoking and laughing, who paused in their storytelling to examine the curious intruder in their midst; but Durk did not break stride.

Then he stopped in his tracks as the muscular figure of his enemy, the vicious Wounded Wolf, headed directly toward him, strolling hand in hand with another Indian in his late-thirties. Both were bare-chested, black hair to their shoulders, wearing buckskin breech-cloths and thigh-high deerskin boots. Spotting Durk, Wounded Wolf halted abruptly. As if frozen in place, Durk and Wounded Wolf stared at each other for several long moments. But Durk sensed something different about the man.

Durk spoke first. "You look naked without your knife," Durk growled between his teeth.

"I buried it," Wounded Wolf said flatly. "I will kill no more."

"We'll see how long you keep that vow," Durk said mockingly.

"Forever, Dark Horse. Forever." He placed his arm around his companion's waist, who had grown tense amid the obvious bitterness between the two old adversaries. "I am at peace," Wounded Wolf stated, gazing warmly into his companion's eyes, which calmed the man. The

Chickasaw stuck out his hand in friendship toward Durk; but, suspicious, Durk refused the gesture.

"I am sorry about stealing the life of your friend, Isaac," Wounded Wolf said with deep remorse, lowering his hand. He spread his arms wide, baring his chest. "You are free to kill me, Dark Horse, if it will lighten your spirit. I will not resist."

Wounded Wolf's companion, hand to a hatchet hanging at his side, edged him aside and interposed himself between the two, facing Durk threateningly. But Wounded Wolf eased his friend back. "My offer stands, Dark Horse. You need only bargain with your conscience to have your revenge."

Durk spit on the ground. "You know I won't do that, Wounded Wolf. Your offer is an empty vessel."

Wounded Wolf forced a smile. "I was a different man when I cut Isaac. But I am like you now, peaceful." Wounded Wolf got a puzzled expression. "If you do not want to kill me, Dark Horse, why have you come here?"

"I've come to see my *ishiki*. It's been many years."

Wounded Wolf sulked before speaking gravely. "I am sorry to tell you this, Dark Horse, but your *ishiki* is preparing for death."

Durk's eyes misted over and he had difficulty swallowing. He stood mute with shoulders drooped as Wounded Wolf wrapped his arms around his neck, pulling him closer and hugging him tightly before releasing him. Durk was dumbfounded by this loving gesture.

Wounded Wolf looked Durk over fondly. "I am happy to see the white man's war did not eat you, my old friend. Death is ever famished."

"I only hope I can survive the peace," Durk muttered.

"If you need anything, Dark Horse, I am here." Then Wounded Wolf and his companion headed for their dwelling, clinging affectionately to each other.

Continuing through the village, Durk neared a cluster of huts where he saw a young girl emerge from his *ishiki*'s summerhouse. The girl noticed him and gestured for him to go to the old woman's side, then disappeared into the night. That the girl knew which house he was visiting and wasn't the least bit curious about what this stranger was doing there, didn't strike him as odd: *Indians know things.* He dismissed the encounter and entered the old woman's dwelling, the sight and smell of which brought a herd of boyhood memories stampeding into his mind. *Funny how alien the Chickasaw life felt when I arrived and how familiar when I departed.* The structure was a standard Chickasaw summerhouse, with walls made of woven mats to let in the cooling air. Twelve by twenty feet in size, the hut, containing several pieces of handcrafted wooden furniture, was divided into two rooms. He entered her sleeping quarters.

There lay his *ishiki*, eyes closed, propped up in her bed, elevated off the floor with poles and animal skins in the Chickasaw manner. Despite the summer heat, she was covered to the neck by ceremonial bearskin, her hands crossed on her chest. He went to her bedside and knelt to study her face. He realized that, although her face may have faded in his memory, her cherished warmth and caring were always with him. Once the village beauty, a woman widowed young who'd never remarried, now she was much-shrunken and frail. As a boy, she seemed towering to him, a figure who, when she embraced him or nursed him through illness, encompassed the entire universe. Now she was thin with sallow skin, probably from her illness, with arms darkened and shriveled like sticks, fingers like twigs. It broke his heart to see this giantess of wisdom and courage so diminished.

Her eyes fluttered open. "Dark Horse," she sang sweetly, recognizing him. Her face lit up, and she smiled warmly with her broad, even rows of teeth.

"*Ishiki*," he replied, taking her small brittle hand. "I am here for you. What do you need?"

She coughed dryly and pointed to a clay pitcher. He poured water into a shell and held it to her lips while she drank. Then he patted her mouth with a cloth and set the shell aside.

"My son," she said lovingly. "Oh, how I've longed to see you these many years. You don't know how many nights I cried. I dreamed you would return before I departed. My heart is overflowing."

It hurt Durk hearing that she'd suffered on his account, and he recalled with regret the times he'd spoken sharply to her. At seventeen he'd felt compelled to leave the tribe, to seek what he believed was his special destiny, breaking their seemingly indivisible bond. "I thought of you every day, *Ishiki*." He kissed her forehead, which was surprisingly dry and cool.

"You saved my life," he said quietly.

"No, you saved *my* life," she replied cryptically. Their eyes met, and they stared into each other's souls for a long moment, silently revealing everything in their hearts, exchanging a love that needn't be spoken.

He lifted the bowl of *pishofa* the girl had left at her bedside, a stew of hominy and pork mixed with beans and squash. He scooped up a spoonful and held it to her lips, but she refused it, telling him to eat instead. The aroma of the dish he'd lived on during his childhood made him realize how famished he was. He tore off a piece of fry bread and ate hungrily, the rich taste bringing back the meals they had shared all those years ago.

The two shared stories far into the night. They even smoked together, although his mother only managed a few puffs. He told her about his *DarkHorse* plantation and his friends, about his time spent in the war. He even showed her the deep scar on his shoulder—never mentioning that the slash had been a gift from Wounded Wolf. When she could stay awake no longer, she told him his bed was still there for him.

Kissing her forehead, he said goodnight, then lay down to sleep in the adjoining room on a musty blanket rich with the aroma of smoke, cooking, and earth. As he closed his eyes, he saw her as it was that first night so long ago when she'd tucked him into bed, her face magically seeming to glow in the dark. He realized that his time living with her, within the tribe, was the only time he'd felt secure.

While asleep, Durk dreamed of his *ishiki*, of his youth among the tribe, even of his pa in their dirt-floor 'cropper cabin. He dreamed of hunting, of the exciting games of childhood, of trivial things that perhaps never really happened.

He awoke at first light and went to her, only to discover that her spirit had flown in the night. Sitting beside her, admiring her peaceful face, he vowed to keep alive memories of the happy moments and words they'd shared. Then he crossed her arms and kissed her cheek a final time before dressing and walking out into the sunshine.

In front of the summerhouse, the young girl from the night before approached. Durk nodded, letting the girl know his mother was gone. The girl reached up to place a hand on his shoulder, "They sometimes refuse to fly away until they can see a family member one last time. Know that she died in peace." Struck by such wisdom beyond her years, Durk watched her enter the old woman's place.

Still lost in the past, Durk strolled absently to where he'd left his horse. When he reached the spot, he was startled to see his saddle lying on the ground and, in place of the brown, a magnificent black stallion. Puzzled, Durk approached the muscular animal, angry that his horse had been taken while he slept, trying to understand what had transpired. Then he saw a leather patch tied to the horse's mane with a rawhide strip. He examined the patch: written in blood was Wounded Wolf's mark.

Durk saddled the stallion, realizing that he now owned horseflesh that no man in Turkle could ever catch. Perhaps this was Wounded Wolf's attempt to atone for murdering Isaac. Durk decided to name the stallion Contrition.

"This doesn't mean I forgive you," he muttered as he led his new horse away. "But at least I don't want to see you dead quite as much."

## LETHE CREEK, MISSISSIPPI

Astride his new black stallion, Durk rode proudly down the center of town in Lethe Creek. It was early afternoon, the ride from the Chicka-saw village having taken longer than anticipated; but he'd needed the time to shake off the gloom at having lost his *ishiki*.

It was clear that, like Turkle, Lethe Creek hadn't fared well during the war. Yet unlike Turkle, the town appeared to have escaped the burn-ings and carnage. Being an agricultural trading center with a regular rail stop, the town's surviving merchant class had managed to preserve enough residual wealth throughout the war to see to its gradual recov-ery. Passing the town's stately homes, Durk noticed workmen, black and white, busily hammering boards and giving fresh coats of paint. The stores were doing a brisk business, too. *Lethe Creek probably hasn't en-acted any Black Codes*, he surmised, examining the activity. Durk kept riding straight ahead, but he could sense people staring at him. Were they admiring his horse, or had they recognized him? He hoped it was the former.

At the courthouse, Durk dismounted, tied the horse, and, smiling and tipping his cap, made his way through the throng of citizens congregating on the steps. Then he followed the hallway to the county records office and bellied up to the counter. A pinch-faced clerk finished scribbling and shoved his papers aside.

"I'm here to check on two documents: a marriage certificate and a property deed," Durk stated.

"Yes?" the man said impatiently. "It'll cost you."

"I'm prepared to pay. I'm looking for the records of a marriage in Turkle to Devereau French. Possibly from 1859 or '60, but no later than April of '61."

"Two dollars," the man said. "Three, if you want a notarized record."

Durk laid out three bills, and the man scooped them up and disappeared into the back. Durk waited nervously, tapping his fingers on the counter and shifting from foot to foot. Minutes later, the clerk returned and laid a paper on the counter. There it was: a marriage license between *Mister* Devereau French and Antoinette DuVallier. The irregular, shaky signature at the bottom was, indeed, Mrs. French's, plain as day. The irony galled Durk, knowing that the future of the folks out at *FrenchAcres* hinged upon such a perverse subterfuge. The clerk filled out a form confirming the union, notarized it, and slid it across the counter. With a deep frown, Durk folded the paper and slipped it into his jacket.

"And the other document?" the clerk asked.

"I want to see the transfer deed to the *DarkHorse* property in Turkle from the Chickasaw to me, Durksen Hurst. April 1859."

"Sorry, Mr. Hurst. Property records were shipped to Jackson for safekeeping in '63. Folks were afraid the Union would burn us down. I don't know whether they survived or not. However, if it's an Indian sale, the Federal Indian Bureau there will have a record. You could wire them."

"I will," Durk said, tipping his hat, and headed back to the street, pleased to at least have the marriage document safely in his coat pocket.

Gathering his courage, Durk traversed two blocks and entered the wire office, where he was the only customer.

"I have three wires to send," he told the young man behind the counter, a purple scar on his left cheek, likely from a bullet. "How much will it cost me?" The man stated the price, and Durk paid him. Then he dictated a wire to the Indian Bureau at Jackson requesting a copy of the deed to *DarkHorse*. He knew the post office wouldn't deliver mail to *FrenchAcres*, so his wire instructed the bureau to mail the document to him care of the Turkle Post Office, where he planned to pick it up. Of course, he suspected the political appointee who operated the branch was probably tied to Colonel Rutherford, meaning any correspondence sent to him could be intercepted. But what choice did he have? Jackson was too far away to chase a piece of paper before he knew what the situation required.

"And the other two?" the man asked.

"Just send the first one," Durk replied, knowing, like in chess, you can't make moves in the wrong order. The clerk sent the wire to the Indian Bureau, then returned. "Now the others?" the clerk asked.

"This is to the Freedmen's Bureau at Jaron's Ferry," Durk informed him. The man gave him a nasty look. "Just write what I tell you," Durk said. "To the Freedmen's Bureau, Jaron's Ferry, Mississippi. *Rampant violence and murder against Negros in Turkle, Mississippi. Send army.*"

The clerk slammed down his pencil. "I'm not sending that!"

Seemingly blocked, Durk searched for an approach to get his wires sent. "Sign it from *Captain Durksen Hurst, 9MSMCC*." The man stared at Durk, fear and disgust flooding his face.

"MSM? What was that *Yankee* regiment again?" he spat, reluctantly picking up his pencil.

"*9MSMCC*," Durk related.

"All right," the man said between clinched teeth, poison in every syllable. "What's the last one?"

"To the U.S. Army commander, Jaron's Ferry. Same message: *Rampant violence and murder against Negros in Turkle, Mississippi. Send army.* Also, add: *Property rights need settling.* Sign it the same. I'll wait here until they're sent." Durk hoped that the army would settle the rights to either *DarkHorse* or *FrenchAcres* before Rutherford could steal them. That would simplify matters.

The clerk swept up the pair of messages and wired them under Durk's watchful eye. Then he barked, "Anything else, scalawag?" *Well,* Durk mused, *at least here I'm a scalawag, not a carpetbagger.*

"No, that's all, thanks," Durk replied, tipping his hat. He turned and walked out to the sidewalk, then doubled back to peer inside. Just as he'd suspected, the man was dashing off another wire. *Rutherford will know every word I sent.*

Durk made his way back to the courthouse where he'd tied the stallion. He was anxious to tell Antoinette about her "marriage" to "Mr. French." Even though he planned to take the new road directly to Turkle, he knew he wouldn't make it to *FrenchAcres* until after nightfall.

*How will she react to this news?*

By dusk, Durk was only a few miles from Turkle proper, riding along a stretch where the road passed through dense woods. Something in the forest didn't sound natural to his Chickasaw-trained ear. He drew rein and listened. A horse, two horses, were on top of the hill. He was being watched.

# Chapter Eight

# NIGHT OF HOOVES AND FIRE

## FRENCHACRES, TURKLE, MISSISSIPPI

It was dark when Durk arrived at *FrenchAcres*. As he approached the cabin where Antoinette waited, Caleb came running. "Durk," he shouted excitedly, "where'd you get this horse? Can I ride him, Durk, can I?"

Durk dismounted and the boy threw his arms around him, hugging him tightly. "It's late. Have you eaten?" Durk asked, tousling the boy's long hair.

"Sure, I did; long time ago," the boy replied. "He's a beauty. What's his name, Durk?"

"Contrition. His name is Contrition."

"That ain't no fittin' name for the likes of him! You should name him Black Lightnin' or somethin'. Can I ride him now, Durk, can I?"

"It's a fitting name, all right. You think you can handle him, son?"

"Why, Durk, you know'd I been around horses all my life. Riding this one won't be nothing."

Durk thought this over. "You can ride him half an hour to get acquainted," he said, "but not hard, no canter or nothing. That horse's been on the road since morning. And don't go farther than the big drainage ditch south of here. Then you groom him right. If you want to ride him again, you'll do what I say, understand? I'm trusting you."

"Thanks!" Completely enraptured, Caleb took hold of the bridle and began petting the stallion's nose. Talking softly, he blew into its nostrils. *Now that's love for a twelve-year-old boy*, Durk mused, and went into the cabin.

Stepping inside, Durk and Antoinette fell into each other's arms.

When they parted, Durk could sense her despondency. "How're you holding up?" he asked, his arms around her waist.

"Oh . . ." she sighed, unable to elaborate. "I'm merely . . ."

"Tomorrow we'll move into Ahronson's," Durk ventured, hoping to pick up her spirits. "What do you think? There's a kitchen, a little parlor, a few bedrooms downstairs, and room upstairs where Josh can stay when he's in town. With all the space, folks'll assume we have separate rooms. People will still talk, but we can avoid real problems."

"All right," she uttered, "if you think it's best."

"If you want to, we could leave Turkle entirely, go anywhere you want, start fresh," he ventured.

Ignoring the notion, Antoinette wandered to the table and filled their cups with water. "You must be hungry, Durk," she said. He sank into the rickety chair, making it creak in protest, while she fixed him a plate, then sat down to join him.

"By the way, you guessed right," Durk said, sliding the marriage certificate across to her. "Another unlikely fruit from your mother's tangled soul."

She glanced at the document, not seeing it. Then, snapping back to life, she read it again before looking up. "I'm not surprised," she said bitterly.

Durk laid down his spoon, unable to force any more of the fried vittles into his painfully convulsing guts. "Look now," Durk said, "if you don't want to bother with *FrenchAcres*, I'll understand; but who knows what will happen to the folks here."

"Let me think about it," she said, placing her hand on his. She sipped from her cup, and he attempted to force another bite into his mouth. Finally, after a long silence, she said, "You'd better tell Caleb to gather his things; we're moving into town in the morning."

Without warning, they heard a volley of shots coming from the quarter's common area. "Get down behind the stove," Durk yelled, directing Antoinette onto the floor. As the shooting ceased, he rose and dashed to the door. "Caleb!"

"Durk, wait, don't go out there!" Antoinette warned.

Ignoring her plea, Durk ran out to the porch, slamming the door behind him, scrambled around the corner of the cabin, and peered around the side. He could hear the hooves of riders headed his way. At that moment, Caleb rode up fast on the black stallion, slid off, and tied the rein.

"Durk," the boy panted, out of breath, "there's men a-coming on horseback. Must be fifty of 'em!"

"What's the shooting about?" Durk asked.

"Can't tell. They just shootin' in the air," the boy replied. "A whole mess of 'em!"

Durk tried to think of what to do. "Go inside with Antoinette," he ordered. "You hear me?"

"But, Durk . . ."

"She needs you; get in there. And do what she tells you. Hurry."

Durk watched as Caleb tramped reluctantly into the cabin. Then Durk heard footsteps running toward him. He tensed up, but was relieved to see it was Josh.

"R-riders, a whole m-mess of 'em, Durk." Josh said, his stutter pronounced. Watching and listening for more shots, the pair speculated on what was happening. Then the riders rode past, their torches shattering the night. Well-dressed men, mostly planters, rode in the vanguard. Durk recognized many from before the war. Then his eyes fixed on the lead rider: Colonel Rutherford, wearing his civilian suit and cavalry boots, a soiled Confederate officer's hat with plume and insignia, and his sword. As the mass passed the cabins, Durk saw there were, indeed, over fifty—a terrifying sight.

"They headin' to the stable," Josh said urgently.

"What should we do?" Durk asked.

"Le's g-go see 'bout this," Josh said. In agreement, they walked briskly, speculating among themselves. By the time they neared the main stable, the riders had already surrounded it. The planters sat their mounts twenty yards from the door, while six young men carrying torches dismounted, threw open the stable doors, and burst into the structure.

"Wait here," Durk said when they were forty yards from the stable. "Hide behind that shed. I'll talk to them." Gathering what little courage he had, he walked directly toward Rutherford.

"What's all this about, Colonel?" Durk demanded.

"Well, if it ain't the traitor," Rutherford remarked and spit in the dirt. "Traitor to his country and . . ." his eyes searching the area ". . . traitor to his race."

"I'm not a traitor to anything," Durk countered, holding his head high. "If you want me to respect your service in the war then you need to respect mine." Quickly surveying the leaders, he noted that seven pistols were aimed at him.

"This land doesn't belong to you," Durk told Rutherford. "You and these men have no right to be here. Show me your papers, sir."

"Here's all the papers I need, Mr. Hurst," Rutherford stated, indicating the pistols aimed at Durk.

Just then, the six men emerged from the stable waving aloft books with worn and missing covers. They rushed up to Rutherford. "Books! All kinds of 'em in there!" one cried.

Rutherford glared angrily at Durk. "Burn it. Burn it down," he ordered. A shout went out, and others carrying torches dismounted to join the six.

"Wait!" Durk shouted, backing toward the stable door. "This is illegal. Where's Bake?" The men with the torches paused, looking to Rutherford for guidance.

"This stable's been harboring Negro minors. That's in violation of the Codes," Rutherford said.

"What do you mean 'harboring minors'?" Durk demanded. "This is a school."

"It's in the apprenticeship clause; read it yourself. 'Any Negro under the age of eighteen shall be apprenticed to his former master'. We're going to roust out and round up the ones we can identify, get them where they belong." Rutherford faced the men with torches. "Go on, now. Set that building on fire."

Durk was frantic. They were about to raze the stable where the community held school and stored grain, and, more horrifying, tear the children from the arms of their parents. "Wait! You can't do this!"

"Go on, gut it," Rutherford ordered. "Hear me?" A group of twenty began putting the stable to the torch. Helpless, Durk could only watch as the barn caught. The men cheered, while more than a few of them, seeing the flames spreading, broke into a full-throated chorus of "Dixie," as if this growing conflagration were fanning an old flame that had never been extinguished.

At that moment, Antoinette came rushing up, holding her skirt, and stopped before Rutherford. "What are you fools doing?" she protested. "Put out that fire. This is my property."

"What do you mean, your property?" Rutherford asked, bewildered.

Antoinette waved the marriage certification. "I am the wife of Mr. Devereau French, and in his absence *FrenchAcres* is mine. Now, have these men put out this fire! Immediately."

"Let me see that," Rutherford said. Antoinette handed him the document.

Rutherford glanced at the paper, then handed it back. In thought, he gazed with satisfaction as the walls of smoke and flames poured from the door, lofts, and between the planks. Then he turned to the riders. "Anyone willing to volunteer to extinguish this fire?"

The riders laughed, hooted, and shouted. Furious, Antoinette said angrily, "I will have you arrested for destruction of private property, Colonel Rutherford. And I'm going to sue you and these people for the damage. That includes everything stored inside. Durk, remember their faces. I'm taking them to court."

"Yes, mam," Durk growled.

"Now get off my land, and take these half-wits with you," Antoinette demanded.

"We're not done here, *Mrs. French*," Rutherford said pointedly. "There's still the matter of harboring juvenile Negros."

"You get off this place," Antoinette said firmly. "Every person on *FrenchAcres*, young and old, is contracted to me. To *me*, Rutherford. If you want to make a claim on any of their children, I'll sue."

Rutherford leaned back in the saddle, considering his next move. Just then, Caleb ran from the darkness between the riders and torches to Antoinette's side. "You leave her alone or you'll have me to worry about," he said haughtily, waving his fists. "I'll take a shotgun to you."

Rutherford studied the boy, amused, as the flames consumed the stable. "Who are you, son?" he asked.

"None of your business," the boy answered. "That's a woman, you coward. You're shamin' your sword."

"Coward? I fought four years for Mississippi. Folks don't call me a coward lightly."

"I lost three brothers fightin' for the Confederacy," the boy challenged. "Don't tell me nothin' about fightin' no war."

"So we have a little rebel here," Rutherford said, chuckling. He turned to Durk. "Who is this boy? What's his name?"

"Name's Caleb," the boy answered.

"Look, Colonel," Durk replied, "this child doesn't know what he's saying. He saw his father gunned down by renegade Yankees."

Rutherford studied Caleb. "What are you doing living among these Negros with this damn charlatan, boy?"

"None of your business, Colonel," the boy repeated.

Rutherford faced Durk. "Does he belong to you?"

"He does."

"All right," Rutherford said. "I'll forgive your temper, son. You lost three fighting bravely for the Cause. You come to visit me, boy, hear? Ask for Colonel Rutherford at the bank. I've got something for you."

"Get off'n this land," the boy ordered. "If I come to that bank of your'n, I'll be bearing steel and powder. You hear me?"

Laughing, Rutherford turned to the riders. "All right, that's it for tonight. Y'all go on home."

"What about the younguns?" the planter beside him asked.

"Another day, Jeb." Shouting, he ordered, "Let's ride!" And more quickly than they'd come, the swarm of riders headed back toward the road to town.

Durk and Antoinette took a final, fatalistic glance at the lost stable, now little more than black smoke and orange flickers of flame. Durk gave Antoinette a quick hug, and she headed back to the cabin, leaving Durk and Caleb.

"Listen, son," Durk told him, "we're moving into town tomorrow: you, me, and Antoinette. You'll still be able to ride Contrition, but you'll have to live like a town boy. You'll go to their school with the white children. That means no getting into trouble and no fights, and being polite to folks. Think you can do that?"

"I can still ride him?"

"Yes, after school, if you're good."

"I'll be all right," Caleb said. "If'n none of them town boys don't start no fight with me. I ain't backin' down from nobody."

"That's all I ask. One last thing. Keep away from Colonel Rutherford. He's a bad man and only means to do us harm. Understand? Don't even talk to him if he speaks to you."

"I don't wanna talk to that buzzard nohow. He better stay away from me."

"Listen, Caleb, go on and groom Contrition," Durk said, placing an arm across the boy's shoulders. But the boy pushed Durk's arm away and stomped off toward the cabin, passing Josh.

"Well," Josh said, examining the catastrophe, "the stable gone. The books, all our seed and grain: gone." Durk could only nod.

"So tell me, Durk, what just happen' here? What did you say to get them to leave?"

"Oh, it isn't what I said at all, Josh. It's what the late-Mrs. French *did*."

"Mrs. French?" Josh replied.

"Yes, Josh, things may not be as dark as they seem," Durk said with a knowing grin.

# CHAPTER NINE

# DESTINY'S CONUNDRUM

## PARKER LANDING, FIFTY MILES EAST OF TURKLE

Carrying her dress in a sack, Devereau French made her way down the gangplank of the Union supply boat, striding nonchalantly along the wharf in her most masculine gait. She needed to find a secluded place to change out of her military uniform.

The morning was overcast; nevertheless, she felt exposed. She could see soldiers unloading boats up and down the busy docks. Outside a nearby warehouse, she noticed two men talking lazily while smoking pipes, so she avoided them. She approached a large shed, but when she saw a Yankee soldier posted nearby, she continued without stopping.

She drifted away from the river toward town, but little seemed promising. Soldiers, dockworkers, and civilians were everywhere. She knew she couldn't get too far from the army activity while wearing her Union uniform. She was small and unarmed, and news of Union occupying troops being beaten and murdered by vengeful civilians was common.

She turned down a brick-lined alley and found it deserted. Promising. She tiptoed forward carefully. Her foot struck a broken hammer lying on the ground, which clattered noisily as it skidded along the cobblestones. The sound stopped her in her tracks, but hearing no footsteps approaching, she continued. At last, she found a spot behind a stack of boxes and changed into her dress. Then she let down her hair. Next, she looked for a place to discard the uniform.

—*You'd better keep that.*

—This is the South, Mother. If I'm searched, just how do I explain that?

Disposing of the uniform, she left the alley, still adjusting the dress and smoothing her hair into place. When she reached the street, she noticed the clouds rapidly clearing, exposing a world suddenly not so solemn, not so dreary. She took a deep breath. For the first time since St. Louis, she had no need to hurry or to hide her female self. A great tension slipped away.

Reaching town, she strolled casually, innocently. No one gave her a second look. She couldn't help smiling.

It didn't take long to wend her way beyond the business district and through Parker Landing proper. Combat hadn't touched the Landing, so the neighborhoods were mostly intact. After being locked up for so long, she admired with wonder the grand homes with their iron gates, then the smaller houses, where women puttered in their gardens, men repaired wagons and porches, children played in the street. If she wanted to, she could just keep on walking. She could dissolve into another street, somewhere in another town and never have to fear capture, never have to make believe she was anything but the plain-faced woman she was. And maybe that would be a relief.

—*Don't be so smug. You still need a man's suit and a horse. The hard parts are yet to come.*

—*If* I decide to go to Turkle. *If* I choose to be Mr. French again, which I'm not sure I want to do.

—*Of course, you will. You have no choice.*

—Why, Mother? Everyone hated us there. Besides, I could end up in prison. Everyone knew I wanted to kill you.

—*You're no helpless female by any means. You've already gotten this far on your wits, haven't you?*

Devereau picked up her pace to clear the shanty shacks on the purlieus of town. Then came a stretch of small farms and homesteads. The birds were singing after the night's cooling rain, cows and goats huddled about the yards, chickens scratched and cackled, dogs curled up on porches. Fields of bright wildflowers stretched across broad meadows. It was proving a lovely day. Why not just keep going?

*Of course, there's still Durk to consider. What if he's returned to Turkle?*

Putting that troubling fixation from her mind, Devereau continued down the dirt road, her shoes kicking up dust. The world was an enormous, slow, empty place when one is on foot. Oh, for her horse.

## MCCORKLE PLANTATION, TWILLING, MISSISSIPPI

She heard someone at the door! Was it another hungry soldier straggling home? Sadly, she had nothing for him. Or was it a pack of Yankee devils coming to ransack the house? Thieves? Vandals? Murderers? A woman her age can't be too careful, especially in these times. Her handyman had left for supper an hour ago. Knowing she could ring the bell to summon him reassured her, but not completely.

She peeked through the parlor curtains. Why, it's a young woman fallen on hard times. Poor thing. Her eyes searched the broad front lawn and the circular drive. No one else was there. She went to the entrance hall, checked her gray-streaked hair in the mirror, and opened the door a crack. "Yes? Can I help you, Miss?"

"Yes, mam, I surely pray so," the young woman said sweetly. "My name is Diane Favreau, and I am trying to get home to my mother before she meets her maker. To give her my goodbye kiss so she can rest peacefully."

"I see. What do you want here?" the home's owner asked kindly.

"I was accosted on the road. You can see my dress is torn." The young woman fingered where a ribbon had been torn from her garment. "I managed to escape my tormentors, but you can see how vulnerable a woman traveling alone is in these times. If only you had some old men's clothing to lend me, I could cut my hair and make it to Mamma in time. Just any old suit will do. I would be happy to send you payment when I reach home."

"I'm not receiving any visitors. I am a widow alone here."

"Please," Devereau pleaded, "it's getting dark out, and I'm afraid someone will take advantage of me. I don't know if I can face another assault on my person."

The interloper sounded educated and well-mannered. But what could she do to aid her? The poor thing would want to be fed and to spend the night. Finally, after ruminating on her scant resources, the woman opened the door further. "Well, hurry in quick so I can lock the door." Devereau entered as timidly as she could manage. The owner closed the door, bolting it behind her, and studied Devereau's petite frame. "I'll give you one of my late-husband's suits, but you could never pass for a man," the older woman remarked.

"I'm going to try," Devereau replied, scrutinizing the interior of the mansion. But though the place held valuable appointments throughout its vast space, she immediately knew something wasn't right.

"All right, Miss Favreau, let's get you that suit. My name is Mrs. Daisy McCorkle. My husband was Darren McCorkle, brigadier with the Fifth Mississippi. But he died near Jackson."

Devereau took her hand. "Pleased to meet you."

"Follow me," Mrs. McCorkle directed, heading toward the stairs. Devereau trailed behind, examining the parlor and the dining room as she passed. The furniture was of fine quality, but showing considerable wear. The table tops and floors were covered with dust, and with papers, books, and dirty dishes strewn about, there wasn't the sense of order one would expect in such a residence. Mrs. McCorkle kept up a steady stream of commentary as they proceeded up the stairs, a lonely widow relieved at the chance to express herself to any visitor from outside her own walls.

"As you can tell, I'm by myself out here. When the Yankees bypassed the Landing in '64, the slaves ran off to follow them. Here I was, husband dead, and no one to work the plantation. What was I to do?"

"Yes, mam."

"House servants ran off, too. You aren't looking to hire out as a maid, are you, dear? Can't pay you much."

"No, mam. It's imperative I get home. My mamma, you see . . ."

"I've got a colored man helps me grow my vegetables, sharecrops some corn, and tends the bit of stock left to me; but most of my fields are fallow," Mrs. McCorkle fretted. "Can't afford to hire any white men, and the slaves aren't coming back. Mr. McCorkle was a hard man. A hard man. No, no love lost there. I don't know how I'm going to get by."

"I'm sorry to hear that, mam."

"I never trusted the Negros. Never trusted them. Oh, they'd smile when we'd come around, act like things were Jim Dandy. If a man with a whip held the power of life and death over you, you'd smile, too, I guess. Now that's all coming back to haunt us."

"Yes, mam."

They reached the second-floor landing and entered the master bedroom. The room was spacious, with green velvet curtains and gold and green carpets. The bed was unmade, and empty teacups cluttered the bedside table. Mrs. McCorkle led Devereau to a chifforobe and opened the door. "There they are, all his suits," she said. "Take your pick, Miss Favreau."

Devereau searched the chifforobe, lighting upon a dark suit that the late-Mr. McCorkle likely wore to weddings, funerals, and official functions, and which he probably would have been buried in had he not died on the battlefield. Devereau pulled the suit out, crossed to the room's full-length mirror, and held it against herself.

"He was a rather big man," Devereau observed.

"Yes," Mrs. McCorkle said, studying the situation. "You'll be swimming in this. We'll need to take up the legs and sleeves and take in the coat and trousers."

"And cut my hair."

"You have such pretty thick hair. Are you sure you want to do this?" Mrs. McCorkle asked.

"I do. I must, Mrs. McCorkle."

"Can you sew?"

"No, mam, I never learned how."

The two made busy tailoring Mr. McCorkle's suit, with the widow working the needle and thread, chatting like old friends. The hours passed, with Mrs. McCorkle spouting off whatever entered her mind and Devereau inventing background stories, as necessary. That done, they set to cutting Devereau's hair, an imperfect but passable job. Then they went downstairs to the kitchen and heated up whatever scraps they could find for supper. Devereau did her best, but Mrs. McCorkle could tell the young woman had never set foot in a kitchen. Never sewed, never cooked. This woman was not who she pretended to be. But Mrs. McCorkle was enjoying the company of another woman. Social activity had declined rapidly as the war had gone on, until the women of the region's great plantations had become nothing more than solitary ghosts haunting their own empty, cavernous mansions.

Clearing a space on the long dining room table, they sat down to eat together, lit by the stub of a lone candle perched on an ornate candelabra.

"You are welcome to spend the night, Miss Favreau, but tomorrow you must be gone. As much as I've enjoyed your company, I can't afford to feed a guest."

"Yes, mam, I'm most grateful. You've been very kind."

After they'd eaten, they chatted into the evening. Growing tired, Mrs. McCorkle took up the candle and led Devereau back upstairs, the wind hammering against the windows and the creaking of floorboards the only sounds. Mrs. McCorkle showed her to one of the spare bedrooms where Devereau laid Mr. McCorkle's suit neatly across the back of a chair. Then Devereau climbed into bed, and her hostess left, closing the door behind her. Devereau could hear Mrs. McCorkle's footsteps fade away into the master bedroom. Under the covers, Devereau stared at the ceiling, unable to shut her eyes.

—*When she falls asleep, kill her. She's bound to have kept her husband's horse in the stable. You can take it and be gone. If anyone saw you on the road today, they saw a woman. Right?*

—Kill . . . After her kindness? I couldn't. I just couldn't . . .

—You have no choice. She's going to die in this tomb eventually anyway.

—That's despicable, Mother.

—*Do what you must do. Don't be a fool. Tomorrow you could be miles from here. You'll be safe. They won't find her body for days.*

—Why don't you leave me alone! Please, Mother, leave me alone!

—*Oh, you'll be alone. If you don't do what I say, you'll be alone in a jail cell—or dead.*

# SECTION II

# CHAPTER TEN

# THE CONFRONTATION

## TURKLE, MISSISSIPPI

Sitting at the desk in the corner of the store, Ellen finished filling out the last of the documents, laid her quill aside, and slumped back. The stack of papers was ready for Durk to file with the court. No customers were about, so she had time to herself. If she wanted to, she could open her Bible to pass the hours as she was accustomed to doing, but she couldn't get the troubling sounds out of her head.

Lying on her cot night after night, she could hear them through the walls—and it wasn't innocent. She'd heard the creaking bedsprings, the kisses, the sighs, and although she couldn't make out the whispered phrases, she could tell they were declarations of endearment, of affection, of reassurance. Imagining them naked together turned her ears red.

They'd been kind to her, Durk and Antoinette, clearing out a crowded storage room and squeezing in a cot and an old chifforobe. They didn't charge her rent and promised they would pay her what they could. But as slow as business had been since the night of trouble, that wouldn't be much. All things being equal, she was glad to be helping the couple with government forms, and she liked running the store like Mrs. Ahronson taught her. But she was not content.

Durk had given Antoinette the larger bedroom at the back of the store and had taken for himself the smaller of the two children's rooms. And word was being passed among Negros in transit that a hot meal and sleeping palette were available under a tent behind the store. All well and good. Except Durk did not sleep in his room. Each night he'd tiptoe down the hall to lie beside Antoinette. And if Ellen strained her ears, she could hear the telling sounds and whispers.

Ellen had never even been kissed by a man, other than her grandfather, much less lain naked with one. Besides, she thought, such goings on was supposed to be the sole province of husbands and wives. Isn't that what the Bible says? It was troubling; still, she held her tongue.

She ruminated about her situation. The folks at Ahronson's were doing good, defending poor folks, and giving a helping hand to blacks and other travelers as the Good Book said they should. But having Durk so entangled with Antoinette was not what God had in mind. Not at all.

By the time Durk concluded his business and stepped outside the courthouse, the skies were overcast and growing darker. He paused at the top of the steps. Below, a large crowd had gathered around a group of wealthy planters, some of whom Durk had seen the night the *FrenchAcres* stable was burned down. In the center of the group stood Colonel Rutherford, flanked by four of his armed riffraff, making histrionic pronouncements to the rapt attention of his audience. Squatting on their heels nearby were the planters' overseers, gossiping in hushed tones, grim expressions donning their faces.

Around the edges of the main square, visiting farmers and locals paused to watch events unfold. Vendors hawked food and cigars to the crowd. Among them, a man in faded Confederate gray sold apples and peaches for ten cents a dozen; a woman in patched gingham was selling cornbread; and a black man offered a slice of bread, three fried eggs, and a portion of ham for a quarter. Behind a large maple on the purlieus of the square, a crippled black man sold cider from a jug, pouring the golden liquid into an old tinned salmon can for his customers.

Durk didn't know what to make of it. He descended the steps and, avoiding the preoccupied planters, circled to the street, where he settled fifty feet from the main gathering near a woman selling boiled ears of corn. Her lone customer, an old man Durk had seen loitering around the courthouse, nibbled on an ear, passing the time with the vendor.

Then Durk heard the sheriff down the street, barking orders to clear the way as if to a lame mule blocking the kitchen door at breakfast. Everyone grew silent and turned to see about the commotion. Marching down the street single file directly toward the courthouse were two dozen sullen black men, their wrists shackled in iron cuffs. Overseen by Bake, the prisoners were being shepherded by six men armed with rifles, three deputies and three of Rutherford's riffraff. One particularly ragged prisoner stumbled, nearly falling, as a deputy prodded him with his rifle butt. Regaining his balance and giving the deputy a fowl look, the man continued.

"What's happening here?" Durk asked an elderly white couple beside him.

"They gonna auction them off," the old man replied. "They does it ever' week."

"What do you mean auction?" Durk asked, horrified.

"They been arrested for vagrancy, see," the old woman explained. "They can't pay, so's them planters bid to pay they fines. If you ask me, they should just leave them rot in jail, is what I say. I wouldn't pay a plug penny to set loose a one of 'em."

"See, they needs to work out what they owes, is what she's sayin'," the old man added.

Durk saw immediately what was happening. He'd seen men patrolling Turkle's rural roads, apparently looking to arrest any blacks found without papers, just as Josh had described. Now they were being auctioned off. Clearly, de facto slavery had seamlessly replaced the old tried and true version.

"So," Durk asked, "if I paid a fine for one of these men, I could just march him off to do what I wanted with him?"

"That's right," the woman replied nonchalantly. "If'n you pay Bake."

"She mean, if'n you win the bid," the old man clarified.

*I thought Bake was looking especially well-fed these days.*

The motley caravan meandered to the courthouse steps, the deputies shouting and poking with their rifles, directing the prisoners to stand six to a step. Durk focused on the end of the line, unable to believe what he was seeing.

Bringing up the rear was Long Lou, who Durk assumed would be headed downriver by now. He examined Lou closely. The suit he'd bought when the war ended was torn and soiled, with rips around the pant cuffs. Lou was struggling painfully, with a pronounced limp on his left leg. Durk was furious.

A deputy shouted at Lou for falling behind and pushed him forward with his rifle butt, causing Lou to fall face-first into the street. The deputy continued shouting as Lou scrambled to his feet and continued, hobbling along as fast as he could manage.

Outraged, Durk ran to the deputy and grabbed the rifle by barrel and stock so they were face-to-face. "If you lay another hand on that man, you're going to answer to me," he shouted. Recognizing Durk, the deputy let go of the weapon and backed off. Durk threw the rifle aside.

Then he confronted the sheriff. "What's this man been arrested for, Bake? He works for me. He had a train ticket and a pass I authorized!"

"He ain't had no pass when we found him. He a vagrant like them others."

Durk turned to his friend. "Is that true?" Durk pleaded.

"That's a lie, Durk. When I showed them my papers, they laugh and say, 'This boy going to Carolina!' and tear them papers up."

"But why'd you get off the train? It would have taken you out of Turkle," Durk asked.

"See, that old engine break down," Lou replied. "I tried to go on foot to the next station, but they arrest me on the road."

"Why are you limping, Lou?" Durk queried. "You can barely walk."

"They beat me on the leg, Durk, just to be mean. It swell up fast. Then I had to walk into town. Ain't none of them riffraff would let me ride up behind."

Durk looked the crowd over, trying to think of a way to help his friend. His eyes fixed on Colonel Rutherford smugly watching the goings on.

"This man works for me, Colonel," Durk insisted, fuming. "He had a pass." He rushed to face the colonel, but two of the riffraff blocked him. "He doesn't belong here," Durk shouted over them.

"Oh, I see," Rutherford replied with feigned concern. "Do you have a work contract for this man?"

"Yes. Not on me," Durk replied.

The sheriff put a hand on Durk's chest. "We havin' a auction here today. Get outta the way."

"You can't auction off this man, Bake," Durk said, growing desperate. "He's no vagrant."

"According to the law, he is," Bake replied. "All right," he shouted to the crowd, "we're gonna begin."

"I'm a veteran of the war," Lou declared defiantly. "This ain't no way to treat a man done risked his life for his country."

Rutherford held up his hand and stepped forward, examining Lou. "You fought in the war?" he asked.

"Yes, sir," Lou replied.

"And who were you with?" Rutherford asked. "What regiment?"

"Ninth Missouri State Militia Colored Cavalry," Lou recited, straightening to attention.

"The Ninth . . . I think I've heard about that legendary regiment." Rutherford gave Durk a nasty look. "So you wore blue, did you?"

"Yes, sir. Served two years. And did hard camp labor 'fore that."

"Let's auction this one first," Rutherford told the sheriff pointedly. "I wasn't aware we had a brave Yankee soldier in the bunch."

"Whatever you say, Colonel," the sheriff laughed. "All right. This man, Lou Jones, owes a fifty dollar fine for vagrancy and resisting arrest. Do I hear any bids?"

Durk panicked. During the war, it was common knowledge that captured Negro troops were sometimes summarily executed, with the Union's response to the massacre of captured black troops at Fort Pillow becoming a turning point. Durk pulled out his wallet and hurriedly counted his money. "I've got twenty-four dollars," he shouted. "I bid twenty-four dollars."

"Two-hundred-fifty," Rutherford stated coldly.

"It's two-fifty to you, Hurst," the sheriff said. "I don't think nobody gonna offer more fo' this whelp."

Durk stared down Rutherford. The colonel was known to be tight on money, and Durk figured Rutherford's pent-up need for revenge over the South's defeat was his motivation for this extravagant bid. "I—I'll put up my store to guarantee one-sixty," Durk offered.

"Cash only," the sheriff said.

What else could he do? "I'll put up my stallion right now! That ought to be more than enough." The sheriff looked toward the colonel, an avaricious gleam in his eyes.

"I repeat, cash only," Rutherford said.

"Don't let this man take me, Durk," Lou begged. "He's crazy."

"He can't walk, Colonel," Durk attempted. "He's hurt. He needs a doctor!"

"I brought a wagon," Rutherford said. "He's well enough to ride."

"You can't do this!" Durk pleaded at Rutherford. "You can't."

"Sorry, it's the law, Hurst," Rutherford stated flatly. He turned to his men. "Well, looks like I've got me a Yankee prisoner, boys. Take him." The other planters sneered and laughed at this remark, as two of Rutherford's hired guns gripped Lou's shirt and led him to the wagon.

"Wait!" Durk shouted frantically. "That man's under contract to me. He had a pass . . ."

"Produce it," Rutherford said.

"Can't we make some kind of deal, Colonel?"

"Come see me at the bank, Hurst. Until then, I'll see this vagrant gets some honest work."

"I'll get you free, Lou!" Durk shouted after his friend, who was being forcibly shoved into a wagon bed. "Don't worry, I'll raise the money." Durk stared at his friend being taken away.

"Next," the sheriff ordered, nodding to bring another man forward.

Frustrated and enraged, Durk turned to Rutherford. "You're practicing slavery here," he screamed. "You'll pay for this, Rutherford, and pay dearly."

"No, you will pay: two-hundred-fifty dollars if—*if!*—a judge rules you have a valid reason to impound this man. Tell me," he mocked, "are you going to file suit under property rights or the rules of military engagement for prisoners of war? Neither seem too promising, with slave property not recognized by the state and the war presently a moot point."

Durk spit on Rutherford's boot, then turned and stormed off. Behind him, he could hear planters laughing.

# CHAPTER ELEVEN

# DAUNTING ARTIFICES

"Colonel Rutherford's got Lou!" Durk exclaimed, running like a man on fire through the front door of Ahronson's and into the kitchen. Startled, Antoinette and Big Josh, who'd shown up an hour earlier with legal business for Durk, ceased their lunch preparations, setting down their utensils. They'd never seen Durk's eyes so wild, and quickly closed in to settle him down.

"What?" Big Josh asked. "W-what you m-mean 'got Lou'?"

In the suddenly consuming quiet, they could hear the steady rain patter on the tin roof over the back porch. A crash of lightning broke the stillness, presaging a storm. Antoinette handed Durk a towel to dry himself, studying his face closely. "What are you saying?" she asked.

"They just auctioned Lou off on the courthouse steps! Rutherford bought his fine."

Josh just stared at his friend. "I thought you give him a pass."

"Stubbs' men simply tore it up. They arrested him for vagrancy." Durk looked frantically around the room. He grabbed a butcher knife, examined it a minute, and then stabbed it down on the counter, leaving it protruding in the air. Josh and Antoinette looked at each other, alarmed and perplexed.

"I've got to save Lou. No telling what Rutherford might do to him."

"Durk," Josh said, trying to calm him, "Rutherford's men just gun you down."

"Don't worry," Antoinette said, placing her arm around Durk, "we'll find a way."

Durk took a deep breath and exhaled, composing himself. "So what . . . what can we do?"

"You a lawyer now," Big Josh said. "Take papers to Judge Fairbanks. He a honest man."

Ellen, standing at the door, having followed Durk to the kitchen, spoke up. "Judge Fairbanks maybe ain't gonna be no help for y'all. You may have to see Mackey Devillin, and that ain't any good."

"What are you saying?" Josh asked.

"They have two courts," Ellen explained, "one for black folks, one for white. Judge Fairbanks sits for white folks. It's Mackey Devillin sits for black folks, and he ain't even no real judge; he's Rutherford's man. Lou ain't got no chance with Devillin hearing the case."

Stunned by this revelation, the room grew silent except for the rapid ping-ping on the tin roof as the three friends exchanged questioning glances. Durk collapsed into a chair and, his hand shaking, poured himself a cup of water. He drained the glass thirstily and set it down. "Those men they were auctioning off with Lou, some of them looked pretty bad, like they'd been beaten," he said. "One fellow could hardly walk; he had to be helped up the stairs."

"They kept the old penal code for Negros," Ellen explained, taking a seat at the table. "They just replaced the word 'slaves' with the word 'freedmen'. Whipping, pillory is still the law, just like before. Things white folks get fined for doin', black folks get beat—and worse. White folks can just take a oath of poverty; black folks get jail, fines, forced labor."

"The newspapers say they're doing that throughout the South," Antoinette advised. "They're not keeping it secret. What did we expect?"

"Rutherford inferred as much," Durk interjected. "I thought he was merely one bitter planter; but it's more than that."

"They don't recognize we free," Josh said, pulling up a chair. "To them, we just slaves who the Yankees done let loose, and now they needs to gather us up and ship us out to the cotton fields again. I heard one man they say was 'sassy' tried to escape—'to break his contract', they call it. The gun club catch and kill him. Yes, sir. Skin him and nail him on the barn as a warnin' to other field hands not to run off, like he was a weasel in the henhouse or something."

"Now that they don't own black folks no more, they don't have no reason to keep them alive, or even to treat them decent," Ellen stated. "Some do, some don't."

Clearly shaken, Antoinette wiped her hands and sat with the others.

Everyone was speechless, as a quiet despair descended upon the four like a ponderous dark cloud.

"After two years in the army, Lou isn't going to take kindly to being treated like a slave by that man," Durk surmised. "I'm worried something terrible . . ." There was a catch in his throat, and he fell silent.

Antoinette covered his hand with hers, but he could not be consoled. "We'll think of something," Antoinette assured him. Everyone remained quiet, thinking, until Durk spoke up.

"I can try Judge Fairbanks," Durk ventured. "I'll submit a claim for Lou as a property motion saying Lou is under contract to me. We'll make it a straight business issue: I'll say Rutherford illegally appropriated a man contracted to me. Ellen will help me draw up the paper."

"I think that's our best chance," Antoinette agreed, relieved to see Durk's mind beginning to catch like straw in a pit fire.

Josh and Ellen nodded their affirmation to Durk's approach. "I'll get started drawing up the papers," Ellen said.

"I can't get to Lou for his signature," Durk said. "Josh, will you sign for him? I'd do it, but they'd recognize my hand."

"Yeah, I'll sign Lou's name. Le's just get him free."

"This whole thing . . ." Durk bemoaned, spreading his arms, despairing that everything seemed stacked against them. He felt like he was trying to swim up the Mississippi against a ten-year flood. ". . . the Black Codes, the penal codes, we've got to do something. Something . . ." His voice faded as he fell back deep in thought.

Antoinette gathered her courage. Since that terrifying night Rutherford's riders had burned the *FrenchAcres* stable, she'd been contemplating a risky idea she'd come up with to provide security for the freedmen inhabiting the abandoned plantation. Now she was ready to expose herself to unknowable consequences to end the terrors hanging over them, while assuaging her own fury.

"The Black Codes say I can't *rent* land to freedmen," she stated firmly. "But they can *own* land."

Big Josh nodded, knowing that the going price was $5 an acre for whites, but $10 for freedmen. "So?" he ventured.

"So, you know my plan to claim *FrenchAcres* as Devereau's widow,"

Antoinette said. "Once it's settled that this land belongs to me, I plan to turn it over to the people there. They'll own their own farms, safe and clear. As for Devereau, I'm sure no one in Turkle knows she's alive, and I can't imagine she'd show her face here anyhow." Durk gazed at her, admiring her audacity, but fearful that Rutherford's friends would not be pleased when they discovered her ruse. People had been killed for less in Lethe Creek County.

Josh whistled. "If you do that, I don't know how we can protect you, Antoinette. I know you want to help, but getting killed won't do nobody no good."

"No, Josh, I'm determined to do it," she replied simply. "Draw up the papers, Durk."

"Are you sure?" Durk asked, studying her dark eyes for any sign of uncertainty. Antoinette's face grew stern, and Durk knew she would not be dissuaded.

"Just so I'm clear," Durk stated calmly, planning the paperwork, "you want to turn over *FrenchAcres* in its entirety to the people currently working it. Is that right? And keep nothing for yourself?"

"Exactly," Antoinette replied determinedly. "I want nothing to do with *FrenchAcres* ever again. The place has brought nothing but heartache to me and suffering to generations of black folks. If their descendants gain some autonomy by owning it, and maybe achieve some prosperity, perhaps justice will be served in some small way. For me, though, the place is eternally cursed."

"All right, we'll draw up the papers," Durk said, nodding toward Ellen.

"I hear they' going to hold the state constitutional convention in Jackson next month," Josh said, taking up the next subject. "Maybe that will lead to something good."

"Maybe we can we convince them to outlaw the Black Codes," Antoinette said wistfully.

"Outlaw?" Durk exclaimed. "It's just the opposite from talk I heard around the courthouse. Rutherford thinks they're going to pass Black Codes for the whole state. Not only in Mississippi either. He sounded very confident they'd get it."

"Rutherford will probably be selected to represent Turkle," Josh said, disgusted. "The planters and money folks are meeting tomorrow to pick someone."

"The whole thing will be a sham," Durk growled.

"That's frightening," Antoinette said. "What can we do?"

"Black folks already drawing up a petition; going to send a delegation," Josh explained. "We want to make peace with our white brothers. We know they scared of us being free, but ain't we both God-fearing folks? Well, ain't we?"

"Supposed to be," Durk mumbled sadly.

Josh got a faraway look in his eyes. "The scripture say, 'In the latter days all mankind, the small and the great, shall eat his bread in the sweat of his brow'. That's what the Lord say he want; that's what's going to happen."

A hard expression gathered on Durk's face as he rose from the table. He had to do something to change things. Without a word, he walked through the back door and out onto the porch. He didn't hear the hard rain on tin, didn't see the waterfalls streaming off the roof. He sat on a barrel to think.

He was not a brave man; he made no secret of that. Life had taught him to avoid angry confrontations, and he invariably looked to find some clever stratagem to get what he wanted. Why plow through a bear when you can divert his attention? But now he felt overwhelmed by forces capable of charging over him and knew he couldn't talk his way around them. Coward or no, he had to stand up to what was happening. He spent a long time ruminating over the situation, his mind searching for the one point where he could perhaps make a difference.

Finally, he snapped to his feet and took a deep breath, just now noticing the torrents of rain, the runoff below the porch cutting gullies in the mud. Then he strode purposefully into the kitchen, letting the door slam behind him.

"I'm going to that town meeting tonight," he stated. "And I'm going to speak my piece."

Astonished by this sudden pronouncement, Antoinette began to argue against it. She knew Durk could never convince the planters and merchants to send him to the convention, nor could he convince them to moderate their leaders' agenda for the new Mississippi government. But seeing the grim determination locked onto Durk's jaw, she remained silent; there'd be no stopping him from trying.

# CHAPTER TWELVE
# OPENING GAMBITS

Durk entered the courthouse shortly after noon carrying four motions for Judge Armstrong P. Fairbanks' attention. Shaking the rain from his hat and brushing off his coat, he squared his shoulders and followed the elderly secretary into the judge's chambers. Upon entering, Durk was immediately assaulted by the bitter aroma of cigar smoke and the sour mildew of old books lining the floor-to-ceiling shelves, rules, rules, and more rules created to impose fairness and justice upon the affairs of men. Then his attention fixed on the ornate chess table near the American flag and immediately saw an opportunity to become friendly with a man whose counsel and influence could help him navigate the torturous currents of post-war Turkle politics.

Judge Fairbanks, distinguished-looking with long gray hair and bushy sideburns down to his chin, sat behind his desk signing documents. Nearing eighty, wearing a white linen suit stained under the arms, his considerable bulk had shifted into a pear shape. He looked up from his paperwork and laid down his pen. "Thank you, Mrs. Howard," he said, and the secretary shuffled from the room, closing the door behind her.

Durk extended his hand. "Durksen Hurst, your honor. Pleased to meet you. Don't bother standing," he said warmly, deferring to the elderly man's age. Taking the judge's hand, Durk noted the soft, damp skin, the brown age spots, the weak handshake.

"Please sit down," Judge Fairbanks said perfunctorily.

"What a handsome chessboard," Durk remarked, his eyes drawing Fairbanks' attention to the set.

"Yes, an import from Italy; it's my most treasured possession."

"Are you willing to face experienced players, or are those pieces just for show?"

"I'm always seeking worthy challengers, Mr. Hurst," Fairbanks said, his face brightening.

"Well," Durk replied with a gleam in his eye, "I challenge you to a match at your earliest convenience. You can decide yourself whether I'm worthy or not."

"You don't need to slap me with a glove to accept that duel," the judge chuckled. "If you can play, as you seem to indicate, I'm your eternal enemy on the sixty-four squares. And your friend."

He reached into a walnut humidor on his desk and pulled out two Cuban cigars. He bit off the end of one, spat into the spittoon, struck a match, and lit his smoke, blowing a dense cloud into the air. The second cigar he offered across to Durk. After biting off the tip, Durk leaned forward for Fairbanks to light his cigar, and both men sat puffing, admiring the aroma of the indulgence.

"All right, Mr. Hurst," the judge harrumphed, growing businesslike. "Let's see what you have for me."

Durk removed the documents he'd secured beneath his coat to keep them dry, untied the thick brown package, and slid the first sheet across the desk. "I have several orders of business, Judge. First, I present the notarized document confirming the marriage between Devereau French, Mrs. Marie Brussard French's heir, and Antoinette DuVallier. Mrs. DuVallier-French is currently a resident of Turkle."

Durk paused while the judge examined the paper, before sliding a second document across. "And this is Mrs. DuVallier-French's claim to *FrenchAcres* as Devereau's widow."

The judge studied the paper, then looked up. "But, Hurst, a son cannot murder his mother and then inherit her estate. There is an outstanding warrant issued for Devereau French, charging him with shooting Mrs. French. We have sworn depositions that he did it."

"First of all, Judge," Durk responded, "Mrs. French's body was consumed by the fire that destroyed her mansion. Therefore, you have no *corpus* to prove she'd actually been shot. Being fairly immobile—a recluse confined to the second floor of the dried-out old place—she likely perished in the fire. Wouldn't you say?

"Secondly," Durk continued, "those testimonials are undoubtedly from her hired guards, who were the only known individuals in the house that night besides Devereau. The slaves would have been already confined to their quarters at that late hour. Am I right?" The judge nodded affirmation.

"It is almost certain that those ruffians started the fire, whether intentionally or accidently, which would make *them* responsible for Mrs. French's death. That gives them a compelling motive to blame Devereau. On the other hand, Devereau had no known motive to shoot his mother—no more than anyone else in Turkle, anyway—nor would he burn down his own house.

"Furthermore, Judge, that was four years ago. I suspect none of those itinerates who testified are around any longer. It's likely they're either dead or dead drunk somewhere far away. So the law has no real witnesses, only the depositions of unreliable gunmen who had a motive to swear falsely."

"Points well taken, Hurst."

"Regardless," Durk concluded, "even if Devereau had shot his mother, the next person in succession for the estate would be Mrs. French's daughter-in-law: Antoinette. Has Mrs. DuVallier-French any culpability in her mother-in-law's death? No one has claimed such. Therefore, Devereau's guilt or innocence is entirely a moot point; Mrs. DuVallier-French has clear, unimpeded rights to the plantation."

The judge put his fingers to his chin and rocked back and forth in his chair. Still thinking this over, he rose and crossed to the liquor table. "Would you join me in a drink, Hurst?"

"I thank you kindly," Durk accepted. Although he wasn't a drinking man, he figured he'd best go along to bond with the judge.

Judge Fairbanks opened the decanter sitting on the silver tray, poured shots of amber Bourbon into a pair of crystal glasses, and carried them back to his desk. The two men raised a toast and sipped.

"Do you have a death certificate for Devereau French?" the judge asked pointedly. "Without proof that Devereau is deceased, how can Mrs. DuVallier-French inherit the plantation?"

Death certificate! Durk hadn't thought of that. "Judge, if Devereau died in the war, there is no Confederate government now, and the Confederate army is disbanded. The records are piecemeal, missing, or destroyed. If Devereau hasn't returned to claim his land by now, he's likely one of the tens of thousands, military and civilians, residing in unmarked graves scattered throughout the country. Finding his body would be impossible.

"And even if he did survive, he'd hardly return to Turkle with a murder warrant waiting for him?"

The judge considered this argument. "That's true enough, Hurst. Regardless, I may have to allow time for Mr. French to show his face."

"If he is alive, he's deserted his wife, correct?" The judge nodded agreement. "Under the Mississippi Married Women's Property Act of '39, when a man deserts his wife, their joint property becomes hers. So legally, if Devereau is in hiding somewhere, *FrenchAcres* automatically belongs to Antoinette. Either way, you have to rule in her favor."

"Points well taken."

Judge Fairbanks sank back in his chair, clearly troubled; then leaned forward. "I must tell you, Mrs. DuVallier-French's claim falls into conflict with a claim for the property by Colonel Rutherford," the judge cautioned. "You are aware the colonel has been known to resort to extreme measures to get what he wants. It won't be pretty, Hurst. I hope you're prepared for that."

"I am. But the law is the law."

"Furthermore," Durk said, handing the judge another document, "I am requesting a court order restraining the colonel or anyone else from setting foot on *FrenchAcres* without Mrs. DuVallier-French's written consent. Can you imagine, dozens of armed men confronting the poor, distressed widow in the darkness of night and burning down her stable! In the name of Southern chivalry, Judge."

The judge's face grew deathly pale. He rose again and made his way unsteadily to the liquor table, where he refilled his glass, then returned to his seat.

"Hurst," he said, "there was a nasty case last month in Lethe Creek. Seems a freedman gave looks to a white woman or did not give up the sidewalk quickly enough for her to pass. Something like that. Not nearly as contentious as these conflicts you've burdened me with, not by a far piece. Nevertheless, the judge and two witnesses were shot down by friends of the defendants. Brought their pistols right inside the courthouse! Now, these things you're asking me to rule on could get us both killed. You understand?" The elderly judge paused to catch his breath, and took a deep swallow of the golden fluid before slamming down his glass.

Realizing the danger they could be facing, Durk felt dizzy. Recovering, he said, "Well, Judge Fairbanks, I'll work with you on my cases. I promise, it won't come to that."

The judge leaned forward, staring fiercely into Durk's eyes. "I have not ruled on Mrs. French's estate yet, Mr. Hurst. A death certificate for Devereau would help, but you don't have one.

"Regarding the restraining order," the judge continued, "the colonel has issued a claim on *FrenchAcres*, so I can't see myself denying him access to what may become his own property. So every one of your motions are on hold right now. Every single one. And I don't know when, or if, I will rule on them." The judge paused to collect himself, brushed back his hair with his fingers, and downed the last of his Bourbon.

Durk knew he had to get the restraining order, or Rutherford and his allies would burn out the freedmen. "You cannot allow Colonel Rutherford or the others free access to *FrenchAcres*, Judge," Durk pleaded. "It's clear from their actions they have destructive intent."

The judge took a moment to consider his logic. "You convinced me, Mr. Hurst. They burned down the stable; that gives me good cause to issue a restraining order. I shall see to it first thing in the morning. Your other motions are still suspended, however."

Durk downed his drink in one swallow and sighed deeply. At least the freedmen had temporary protection from Rutherford's depredations. It would have to do for now.

"Now, Mr. Chess Player, what other gambits have you for me? A man like you will reserve the cases closest to his heart for last."

Durk saw that none of this was going to be easy, nor particularly just, even with a reasonable old judge like Fairbanks. Of course, Durk had, indeed, saved two cases for last: his own claim for *DarkHorse* and, more importantly, his motion to save Long Lou from Rutherford's clutches.

Durk took the stub of his unlit cigar from the ashtray, gathering his courage. Contemplating what he would say next, he placed the bitter tobacco between his lips. Lou's life was on the line. He couldn't fail.

* * *

"This, sir, is my claim for *DarkHorse*," Durk said, reaching inside his jacket and retrieving a worn sheet of notepaper.

The flimsy document was fraying at the folds, with ink smeared from sweat and rain after being carried in his pocket for six years. He straightened the paper on the desk and handed it across. "This is the original signature document," he said, pointing to the scrawl at the bottom, "and that is the mark of the Chickasaw chief, Wounded Wolf, beside my own signature. Please excuse the condition the paper's in, but it fared better through the war than I did."

"Yes, your stealing that land from the Chickasaw is legendary, Mr. Hurst."

"I didn't steal it, sir. I won it fair and square."

"Regardless, this is a court of law, Mr. Hurst. Do you have anything to back up your claim besides this scrap of paper?"

"I've wired the Federal Indian Bureau in Jackson seeking documentation, but haven't heard back yet. Frankly, Judge, any missive from Jackson would have to pass through the local post office . . ."

". . . And Rutherford's appointee would be instructed to intercept it. Is that what you're saying?"

"That's right, Judge."

"You have a fairly strong case. But as with *FrenchAcres*, there are other interests vying for that land. I will refuse their claims for now to give you a chance to retrieve what you require. But I can only hold them off for so long."

"Thank you, Judge. That's all I ask."

The judge tossed the worn sheet with Wounded Wolf's mark back across the desk. "You'd best hold on to this, Hurst, at least until the matter is settled." Durk returned it to his pocket.

"All right now, it's getting late. Present your other petition to the court. Out with it."

Noting the darkness descending outside, Durk took a moment to examine his final motion. *I have to win this right now for Lou.* He took a deep breath and plunged into his well-rehearsed argument.

"Judge Fairbanks, this morning a freedman contracted to me, Lou Jones, was auctioned off on the courthouse steps, and I want him back immediately. He was on the road at my behest, carrying a traveling pass signed by me, and they had no right to arrest him. He was not in violation of the vagrancy laws in any respect."

"What was the fine, Hurst, and who paid it?" the judge asked, casting a jaundice eye at the petitioner.

"Two-hundred-fifty dollars; Colonel Rutherford paid it."

"That's quite a fine."

"Rutherford knew Lou was my man. He did this out of spite," Durk said, his face flushed, his anger unconcealed.

The judge relit his cigar and rubbed his chin. "Those vagrancy cases belong in Mackey Devillin's court. I don't handle Negro issues."

"You know I wouldn't have a chance in that court, Judge. Lou Jones had a legal pass."

"Still, it's not my jurisdiction."

"The vagrancy charge is not the issue. This is a simple property settlement between two white men. I need a ruling from you. Please."

"Why didn't the man show his pass?"

"Lou said they tore it up. You know these gunmen Rutherford has patrolling around here. Hunting black men is the only work they're capable of. They receive a bounty for each vagrant they arrest; that's why they kidnapped Lou, for the money, nothing more."

The judge peered into Durk's eyes. "I must be honest, Hurst. I'm not sure I want to get between you and the colonel on this matter. Can you tell me why this man means so much to you?"

Durk decided it was best to tell as much of the truth as possible.

"Lou was at my side throughout the war," Durk pleaded, his voice rising. "He risked his life to save me more than once, and you know very well how Rutherford treats Negros. I can't leave a man who served me so bravely exposed to Rutherford's arbitrary cruelties. Frankly, Judge Fairbanks, I can't stand to think of him being under the colonel's thumb for one night, not even for a minute. That would dishonor both you and me and all who served."

With a reluctant nod, the judge dipped his pen and made himself a note. "All right, Hurst, I'll draw up a writ. But this is highly irregular.

Come by any time after noon tomorrow to pick it up. Of course, you will have to reimburse Colonel Rutherford for the fine he paid."

Durk collapsed back into his chair, exhausted from his unrestrained outburst. At least he saw an end to his friend's dire jeopardy. "Thank you, Judge. You are a man of honor and respect."

The judge relit his cigar, allowing his guest time to compose himself. "I'm not sure how much weight honor and respect bear these days, Mr. Hurst."

His throat still tight from his emotional ordeal, Durk reclined into the cushioned leather chair. Taking a deep breath, he sipped from his Bourbon, feeling the warmth descending into his gut. Then, gazing out the window, he drew on the Cuban and blew smoke.

The judge sipped from his glass, drew on his cigar, and blew smoke toward the ceiling. Suddenly showing his eighty-plus years, he became simply a tired old man grateful for a younger ear willing to listen to his troubled thoughts.

"You know, Hurst, I was against secession. I lost more to these hotheads than I can ever recover: both of my sons lost their lives on the battlefield. Johnny and William were such promising boys, with fine futures ahead of them. Neither do I have any extended family; all dead. I had inserted a clause in my final testament to manumit my servants and farm hands upon my demise, but of course those provisions are moot," he chuckled at the now-anachronistic nature of a generosity he once thought magnanimous.

"There're only my two house servants left and an old couple tending my modest farm. I will leave my property to them; but the women will have to sell the house in town. Can't have a couple of old Negros living on my street, that's for certain. They'll probably get skinned in the transaction, poor things." Durk nodded in sympathy.

There was one last item still tugging hard, like a hook caught in Durk's gills. "I have one final request, Judge. I want to attend tonight's meeting, to be seated with the formal speakers," he said. He had no plan for what he would do at the meeting, no tricks up his sleeve, knew not what he'd say or if he'd remain silent. He'd simply have to make his way by instinct.

The judge set down his glass. "I don't think that's wise, Mr. Hurst.

The attendees are all established property owners, men of means. You cannot say the same."

"Yes, I can. I'm a business owner: I own Ahronson's."

"Not enough."

"I'm also owner of the *DarkHorse* property, remember. No one has yet won a judgment against my rights to the land. And further, I am the legal representative of Mrs. DuVallier-French, the heiress to *FrenchAcres*.

I would venture that I represent assets more substantial than many of the men who will be attending."

"And what do you intend to say at the meeting, Hurst?"

"I will speak against the Black Codes."

"You are mad, sir," the judge remarked. "If you speak on behalf of Negros in that company you'll be torn to shreds. Torn to shreds."

"Nevertheless, your honor, that is my right. I intend to be there."

The judge sighed deeply. "I don't know what you see in these people."

"People, Judge. I just see people."

The judge stared at Durk a long time. Then he wiped his hand across his face, like he was washing away a lifetime of mistaken beliefs. "All right, fool. I will write a letter of introduction entitling you to a prime seat, my own seat; I'm not going. Too bad. I'd hoped to have you as a regular chess partner. Now I see that this small boon late in my life will be denied me. Go get yourself killed if you want to, but don't say I didn't warn you."

"Thank you, your honor." Durk finished his drink, then grew philosophical. "So, do you think the South will accept the free black man in its midst?"

"Things have not changed the way I expected them to," the judge mused. "Frankly, in all except the results of the physical struggle, I consider the South to have been the real victors in the war. The masterly way in which the Southern powers have neutralized the verdict of Appomattox with regard to the Negro is the most remarkable thing ever witnessed in America politics."

Blood draining from his face, Durk ruminated over this stark observation of current developments. Momentarily, his strategies seemed of no consequence. He felt bitter, trapped, with prospects for the future seemingly hopeless. Would anyone, North or South, rich or poor, foolish or wise, ever escape the sordid past holding them in its iron grip? Would this division never end?

Outside, the rain had ceased as dusk settled over the town square. Durk noted the time on the judge's grandfather clock. "I must get home if I'm going to make that meeting," Durk said, rising to his feet. "As soon as you write that letter, I'll be on my way. We'll have to save our chess match for another day."

"I'll write you the note, Mr. Hurst—but I sincerely hope I'm not signing your death warrant."

# CHAPTER THIRTEEN

# HEADSTRONG

"Please don't go," Antoinette pleaded. "You know you'll say something you shouldn't."

"I have to," Durk said, hurriedly pulling on his jacket. The kitchen still retained the homey aroma of supper, the stove, though being allowed to die, still generating heat. It would be pleasant to stay, but that was impossible.

"You crazy to risk it, Durk," Big Josh said. "You be like a rabbit in a wolf den."

Durk looked his friend in the eye. "Aren't we all rabbits in the wolf den now? I need to see how hungry the wolves are, how sharp their teeth are, to hear what they're planning."

Through the kitchen window Durk could see the ominous, deep shadows of nightfall. He struggled to suppress his trepidations, to not acquiesce to his companions' entreaties. The tent set up for transients was empty. These days, few were evading the armed patrols along Turkle's roads; perhaps some were warned off against entering the hamlet's borders.

"Listen," Josh said, "they come to get you, I'll try to protect you. But I'm only one man."

"Nobody will come after me," Durk replied. "But if someone does, you get Antoinette, Caleb, and Ellen to *FrenchAcres* any way you can."

"Durk," Antoinette beseeched, placing her arm around him. "Do you really have to do this? Do you?"

Durk hugged her tightly. Then, standing at arms' length, he admired her face. "Believe me, love, I'll try my hardest not to get myself killed. But don't you see: I have no choice. It's for all of us."

Antoinette kissed him on the cheek, gave him a final imploring look, but saw he would not be swayed. Downhearted, she turned and disappeared into the living quarters.

Durk looked to his friend, but Josh merely shrugged. Then Josh gripped Durk's hand with both of his, drew Durk to him, and embraced him in a prolonged hug. Releasing Durk, Josh then straightened Durk's coat and collar.

Durk shoved his hat on firmly. Turning, he strode out through the store into the street, heading toward the stable, his heels clicking on the plank sidewalk boarding. The night had cooled, and storefronts were now shuttered and dark, the streets and yards empty. Halfway down the block, he noticed scruffy men in patched clothing wearing shapeless hats, pistols jammed into their belts, approaching from the opposite direction. Their gait was loose-jointed, unsteady, and he could tell they'd been drinking. As Durk neared them, they blocked the sidewalk, forcing him to halt. Durk's stomach knotted, his heart pounding rapidly. He made a fist without realizing it.

"You trespassin' this sidewalk," one said threateningly. "Your kind gots to walk in the street 'long with the cattle and nigras."

"Yeah," another chortled, "cattle and nigras."

"My mistake, gentlemen," Durk feigned politely. Tipping his hat, he stepped from the sidewalk into the muddy street. He walked another block and entered the stable, inhaling the familiar, comforting scent of hay and horse excrement. "Walker," he called out.

A fifty-year-old black man appeared from the back. When he saw who it was, a smile lit his face. "You want me to saddle up Contrition, Mr. Hurst?"

"Please, Walker," Durk replied.

"Well, you dressed for doin's," Walker complimented. "You ain't going to that big meeting, is you?"

"That's exactly what I'm doing, sir."

"Well, Mr. Hurst," Walker said haltingly, slightly embarrassed, "would you mind payin' me the two bits 'fore you go? Not that I don't trust you, but Mr. Hawkins make me pay if'n you don't come back. Um-hum. Learn my lesson on that long time ago."

Durk dug into his pocket and handed over a coin. "Can't let the two bits slip past us," Durk joked.

A half hour later, Contrition was trotting down the road to James Clifton's plantation. It was invigorating to be swaying in the saddle, feeling the breeze-blown drops from the tree leaves after the day's storms. As he spurred the horse to a gallop, forested brush and stands of pine passed on both sides. A whippoorwill sang out its satisfaction with the forest, calling to mate and continue life. Durk realized how constrained he felt staying in town. His vagabond life had taken him from one Southern hamlet to another, each little different from those scattered throughout Lethe Creek County. The myriad boarding-houses and widow's homes for transients all ran together in his memory, their smells intermingling, the warm meals proffered never quite right but welcome nonetheless. Out here he felt at home.

Finally, Durk rode up the left side of the circular drive leading to Clifton's enormous, white, two-story edifice. Four great pillars flanked the double doors, and a wide verandah filled with tables and chairs encircled the house.

Off to his right, dozens of townsmen, farmers, and other locals congregated on the lush, manicured lawn, eating and drinking at their host's expense. He tipped his hat, and a few returned the gesture. He preferred to renew old acquaintances with these men and learn the lay of the land, but knew he had to join the noteworthies gathering inside or his words, if he spoke at all, would have no weight. He rode on.

Nearby, among carriages and fine steeds lining the drive, black drivers huddled in clusters, gossiping and laughing, waiting for the men inside to conclude their business. One by one, they paused to watch the rider on the black stallion progress up the drive. One man gave Durk a subtle wave, having recognized him, then quickly crossed his arms. Durk made a point to tip his hat to each group as a respectful acknowledgement.

Reaching the trough that ran along the side of the house, Durk dismounted to water Contrition. Then he tied him to the railing and, taking a long, deep breath, headed for the door, only to be blocked by two deputies and two riflemen.

"Wait out there with the others," a deputy said, indicating the lawn. "We're only letting in folks what have a seat."

"I'm taking Judge Fairbanks' place," Durk commanded, displaying his letter.

Looking as if they'd been asked a complicated arithmetic problem, the deputies stared blankly at the sky and ground. Durk concluded none of them could read and pointed to the bottom of the page. "Do any of you recognize the judge's hand?" One of the deputies nodded affirmation. "Then I'm going in." With that, Durk folded the letter, slid it into his coat pocket, then strutted up the steps and into the foyer.

The entry hall was high-ceilinged, well-lit, and roomy, attended by two liveried servants taking hats. From his vantage point, Durk took in the breathtaking surroundings, the satin draperies, framed oil paintings, and expensive tapestries. The polished furnishings and floors, and ornate rugs were well-maintained, as if there'd never been a war. He believed he knew why. When the Union army passed through Turkle, Clifton likely had feted the officers in blue, offering them hospitality with a smile—and probably a bribe—before they moved on to play havoc elsewhere. During the war, he'd seen plantation owners perform this same farce, while the sons of their sod-breaking neighbors bled to death on distant fields.

Durk handed his hat to the servant, who directed him into a large ballroom. There, three rows of cushioned oak chairs faced a podium flanked by the Confederate and Turkle Company battle flags. The sight of the two flags replacing the U.S. flag burned Durk, but he understood: many in Turkle had lost family during the war and viewed the flags as a sign of respect for their departed. Nevertheless, they clearly represented what many of those in attendance wanted to resurrect.

Around the room, two dozen of the town's luminaries dressed in their Sunday best talked excitedly in groups. Durk had never been accepted by this circle when he had *DarkHorse*, even trading cotton beside them at Lethe Creek, and being among them here made him uncomfortable.

"Your name, sir?" one servant asked.

"Durksen Hurst in lieu of Judge Fairbanks."

"Mr. Durksen Hurst," the servant announced to the gathering, causing heads to turn. In the far corner, Colonel Rutherford was speaking privately with a tall, heavy-set man in his fifties whom Durk assumed to be James Clifton. Both turned warily to study him. Rutherford, visibly enraged, wagged a finger to summon the sheriff, who set down his heaping plate and pried his ungainly weight from the chair to join the pair. Rutherford whispered instructions to Bake, who then stormed angrily up to Durk, perturbed that his repast of ham steak had been interrupted.

"You don't belong here, Hurst," he growled under his breath. "Get out before I arrest you."

Durk produced the letter from the judge. "Judge Fairbanks signed this, Bake. I have every right to be here."

The sheriff stared red-eyed at Durk, then turned and waddled back to Rutherford and Clifton. The three discussed the situation, then Rutherford, followed by Clifton, confronted Durk. "What are you doing here, Hurst?" asked Rutherford, poking Durk in the chest.

Durk held up the judge's order.

"I object to this man being in this chamber, James," Rutherford complained to Clifton. "He has no place here."

The rich planter considered the situation. Finally, he rendered his decision. "If the honorable Judge Fairbanks says the man belongs, then he's welcome in my home." He then led Rutherford and the sheriff back to the corner. On the way, Rutherford pulled the sheriff aside and whispered to him. Bake got a pained expression across his face, then left the room. Durk did not like the looks of that interaction. Was Rutherford planning a surprise for him?

Alone, Durk scanned the room. From every corner, eyes were following him, the intruder invading the most sacred sanctum of Southern aristocracy. Even having dressed as best he could, Durk might as well have been a five-acre soil-breaker in torn overalls. His attention turned to a group of four men, two of whom he'd known around the Lethe Creek cotton auctions before the war. He approached them, a forced smile fixed upon his lips. "Gentlemen," he said pleasantly, and their conversation died as quickly as a squirrel blasted with buckshot.

Seeing he wasn't welcome, Durk turned away and sat against the wall apart from the crowd. After a while, the men returned their attention to their heated conversations. Feeling anxious, Durk examined his companions for the evening. A servant with a smile fixed on his face approached and offered him a drink from a silver tray. When Durk politely refused, the man departed, his smile fading to its blank, neutral state. Durk had seen this sphinxlike mask that slaves presented to their masters. Though these servants weren't slaves, what exactly had changed?

Hearing the clock chime, Clifton signaled to the head butler, who nodded acknowledgement and left the room. Then Clifton clinked his glass with a knife until he gained everyone's attention. "Please take your seats, gentlemen. The meeting will begin shortly."

Durk hung back to allow the others to find their seats. One man Durk recognized gave him a wink without breaking stride. Another, wearing a red velvet jacket and riding boots polished to a high gleam as if dressed for a British foxhunt, gave him a nod. When more than half had passed, Durk positioned himself at a seat near the middle of the center row, hoping to blend in. As others filled in around him, he nodded to many, but was mostly ignored. A bad sign.

James Clifton climbed the two steps to the platform and stood at the podium, followed by Colonel Rutherford, who limped up the stairs and sat to his right.

Shortly thereafter, the folks waiting on the lawn were ushered in, crowding into the roped-off space behind the seated guests. The room reverberated with a loud, penetrating buzz, as rumors and speculation flew about, until Clifton banged a gavel. As everyone quieted, Clifton ordered, "Shut the door!" whereupon the butler exited the room, closing the double doors firmly behind him. Durk chuckled to himself, picturing every servant outside the room with an ear to the door.

"The gentlemen of the Turkle Governing Council will now come to order," Clifton announced. The members halted their whispering, shuffling in their seats, then grew quiet. "For the first order of business, we will discuss a platform for the forthcoming constitutional convention in Jackson. After that, we will select our representative to the convention." He became jovial. "And after that, who knows!" There were chuckles and guffaws, but the mood in the room hadn't appreciably lightened. Too much was at stake.

"All right, motions for the platform. I believe Colonel Rutherford has something to say." Clifton turned to Rutherford, who rose to his feet, limped to the podium, and cleared his throat, as Clifton sat down.

"Gentlemen, thank you for being here," he announced with histrionic gravitas. "You are the rock of Turkle, the men upon whom the welfare of our society depends. I know we will make wise decisions tonight.

"Turkle Company One, which I was honored to lead into battle, was a heroic force for good from the war's very beginning. Though the evil forces set against us were monumental, our Cause was just and our efforts never flagged or faltered. Even facing tremendous odds, our brave citizens never backed down through the long weary years of conflict. I especially want to thank the gentlemen in the front rows whose generous support kept us armed and in the fight. Your contributions to the war effort were as powerful as any cannon, as swift as any cavalry brigade.

"I also want to acknowledge those of you who served or who had brave sons who served their country, especially those who lost their boys on distant battlefields for the most noble principles for which man has ever fought. As their commander, your sons made me proud."

Rutherford lowered his voice, growing deadly serious. "Men, we are now faced with bayonet rule by an invader who wants to turn upside-down not only our sacred institutions but our entire civilization. But we have not, will not, abandon our self-respect; we will not submit. This is a white man's country; yet the Yankees want to take it from us and give it to the nigra. We have sacrificed too much and lost too many of our best youth to bow to these scurrilous dictates. This constitutional convention is our chance, our best hope, to restore a white man's government to the great state of Mississippi as the Lord intended. In this, we must not fail.

"Therefore, I move that Black Codes be initiated statewide. Please consider the alternative." Rutherford bowed from the neck and took his seat.

The hair on the back of Durk's neck stood up. He'd promised Antoinette and Josh he'd hold his tongue, but being silent was not in his nature. Words were the tools of his trade and without them he felt naked, helpless. He dug his fingernails into his palm, trying to hold himself back.

*Surely there are reasonable men in this assembly who will speak out, who are seeking a new way to rebuild Southern society, a better way,* he conjectured. *I know them, I've heard them talking. Surely, reason can prevail.*

Meanwhile, Durk fumed, his palm bleeding. *Keep quiet,* he told himself. *Keep quiet!*

# Chapter Fourteen

# GLORIOUS DEFEAT

"It has been moved that the Black Codes become state law under the new constitution," Clifton called out. "Is there anyone who will second Colonel Rutherford's motion?" Several voices cried out in the affirmative, and Clifton brought down the gavel with a flourish. "Moved and seconded. The floor is open for discussion."

"Tell them to reinstate our property rights!" shouted a well-dressed gangly man with long, stringy red hair sitting in the front row. There was a grumbling undercurrent of amused agreement to this sentiment, mixed with nods and snickers, but no one took it seriously.

"We all want that, Evert," Clifton said benevolently to the redhead, "but our oppressors don't have to live here, and they set the rules. Now we've got a motion on the floor for discussion, and all other notions must wait. All right, your thoughts about the motion."

Durk studied Evert, who seemed awkward and a bit tipsy, marveling that a man of so little intelligence or sobriety could have held life-or-death dominance over anyone. The whole frightening and repulsive situation, the ugliness of what he was hearing and seeing, was starting to get under his collar.

"The vagrancy clause ain't being enforced like we want it to be," a man seated in the second row insisted. "We need more patrols. They is still freedmen running loose everywhere. Never know when one will come up on you. Caught one of 'em stealing my chickens. I know they got to eat, but . . ."

"Hire some of the returning troops; those boys'll know what to do," a man in the front row interjected. Calls of "Yes!" and "Right!" roared throughout the room to applause, hoots, and hollers. Clifton banged the gavel to quiet them.

"We'd have to supply their horses, Frank," Clifton replied. "While I agree with you, the town just hasn't got the money for purchase and upkeep for new mounts. Besides, our supply is awfully thin and of poor quality. This just isn't in the cards I'm afraid."

"What we need is more guns, horses or not," a man seated beside Frank shouted. "Look, everyone knows it: the Negros expect Washington to give 'em all forty acres and a mule on January first. When that don't happen, we'll have a revolt on our hands worse than Haiti. It's gonna be our heads and our families' heads." There was loud agreement on this point from every corner.

Clifton banged his gavel. "The supply of rifles is thinner than the horse market. Where can we get them? The Yankees aren't going to let anyone just ship in a supply. That item will have to be tabled for a later date. Tonight we're debating the platform and selecting a delegate to Jackson. Now let's hear what y'all have to say about the vagrancy situation."

"The vagrancy clause has helped some with the labor shortage," a man offered. "Though I'll tell you, a slave was worth two freedmen. Heck, three of them." Many in the front rows grunted their agreement.

"Yes, but now we have to pay them, just like they was white," a man in the back complained.

Durk seethed, knowing that black field hands were getting skinned by signing contracts they couldn't read. He squirmed in his seat.

"You can't find white men to do this work," added a man in the front row. "There ain't enough of them. So here we are, stuck with higher labor costs and whatever the patrols snare in their nets."

"My labor cost ain't gone up," a sunburned planter interjected, standing up. "I told my nigras after the war done ended, you can stay on my place. I'll provide the same clothing as before the war, and you'll get the same food, same roof over your head. But I ain't gonna to pay you. I ain't no charity."

"That, sir, is the old way of thinking," a white-haired gentleman in a black preacher coat said in a measured tone. "I always gave my field and house slaves a cash bonus when times were good. My place showed a profit until the war started."

Hearing this, a number of the attendees rose to their feet shouting. Everyone started arguing at once, until a loud din engulfed the room. "Order," Clifton shouted, slamming his gavel down repeatedly until everyone grew quiet. Durk studied his boots, trying to control his rage, but he could feel his pulse racing and a painful throbbing in his forehead and neck.

"Look," Clifton said, "this is getting out of control. If anyone wants to speak, you're going to have to raise your hand." He studied the group, who'd fallen silent.

Clifton pointed the gavel at Durk. Durk looked at surrounding men, then, shocked, realized he'd raised his right hand. "Mr. Hurst," he said, "you're new here and represent Judge Fairbanks. Let's hear what you have to say about our situation. From what I understand, you're practicing law; you're even willing to represent Negros in court. You might bring a different perspective to our gathering." Rutherford started to object, but Clifton overruled him. "No, Colonel, I want to hear him. Go on, Hurst."

Taking a deep breath, Durk rose to speak. "Thank you, Mr. Clifton. Gentlemen, we must adapt to the present, not by looking backward, but with our eyes set on new horizons. The South came to depend so much on unpaid labor, and became so corrupted by it, that we believe we cannot survive without it. But having seen slavery in all its enormity, the more I am satisfied that it was a curse to our country. In the South, outside of the towns, the people are a century behind the free states, which I implore you to join. Neighbors, the institution of slavery was as much a curse to the whites as to the blacks and killed improvements of every kind, deadening all enterprise and prosperity. After all, why should a smart fellow create a device to improve a farm implement, building a little family business, when a landowner could direct a slave to do the work for free?"

Hearing a few voices in the crowd uttering agreement, Durk was encouraged to press on. Perhaps there were enough reasonable people who would see the wisdom of peace between the races. He'd shoot the works, see where the cards fell.

"The Black Codes and laws like them evidence a desire to return to that state, if not in name, then in another form," Durk continued. "But those old ways will only lead to our downfall. Good sirs, I assure you, Mississippi will survive, even prosper, under a fairer system."

Durk could feel the resentment burrowing into him from every side. Angry grumbles filled the room, mixed with random cries of affirmation. But now that he was speaking his mind, Durk couldn't stop himself. In a seemingly friendly tone, Clifton encouraged him to continue. "Go on, Mr. Hurst. What specifically do you see as the problem the Black Codes present?"

"For one thing," Durk replied, "The Codes drive a wedge between us that will lead to untold unpleasantness. I know differences exist in Turkle between the two races, and I expect that will continue for a time. But with fair treatment, life can and will get easier for all, black and white. Laws like the Black Codes only make it harder to heal our country."

Shouts erupted from all around the room. The obese man at Durk's right, who hadn't yet said a word, laughed so hard his belly shook, his face beet red. A man sitting directly behind Durk spit in his direction. Clifton began slamming down the gavel.

"Mr. Hurst," Clifton barked, "just what are you saying? If you don't support the Black Codes, how do you propose we replace them?"

"Haven't black folks suffered enough, Mr. Clifton, gentlemen? Now that they are free by law, why shouldn't they have the same rights as any other man? This is our chance to enshrine the principles in the Declaration of Independence into our new state constitution."

The room quieted for several moments. Seemingly stunned, Clifton merely stared at Durk. Then he managed to sputter, "Are you suggesting the state of Mississippi grant equal rights to the Negro, Hurst? Is that what you're saying?"

"Yes, Mr. Clifton, that's exactly what I'm saying. I assure you, sir, everyone's life will be better for it."

"You'd let them vote, too?" a man shouted.

"Yes," Durk replied, "why not?

Suddenly, amid the hubbub, Rutherford snapped to his feet, his eyes spitting fire at Durk. The two men faced each other, combatants to the verbal death. "Vote!" Rutherford roared. "What would be the consequence of such an absurdity? I will tell you, Mr. Nigra-lover: you would have a superior race put under the rule of an inferior race. No free people, ever, have been subjected to domination by their own slaves. This is a white man's government, and we must denounce the tyranny to which the oppressed South is being subjected."

"I'm suggesting no such thing as black domination," Durk retorted.

Rutherford was furious, shaking his fists. "Be warned, Hurst. It has been the settled purpose of the leading white men to teach the nigra a lesson. Nothing but bloodshed, and a great deal of it, can answer the purpose of redeeming the state from nigra and carpetbag rule. Why, I'd think no more of shooting a damn nigra than I would of shooting a dog!"

Hearing this, Durk's pulse raced. His mind was flooded with visions of Rutherford taking out his vengeance on Lou, subjecting him to inhumane treatment. Durk lost control. "You know very well the Negro is not permitted to own firearms," he shouted. "What kind of courage does it take to shoot an unarmed man, Colonel?"

"Courage? You talk of courage?" Rutherford fumed. "My face is scarred, and I walk with a limp. I had three horses shot out from under me. I risked my life for four years for this land that our fathers and grandfathers built into a great civilization."

"What about the black men and women who built this country, too, who built your mansions and fortunes? Didn't their sweat plow your fields, pick your crops, and haul them to market? Didn't their women cook the bread you enjoyed, raise your children—in some cases, even bear your children?"

Rutherford's eyes narrowed. Lowering his voice, he snarled, "Before any of you gentlemen are swayed by this fool's sweet talk of junipers and butterflies, I'll have you know *Captain* Hurst fought for the Union! Yes. He killed your boys for our enemies. Isn't that true, Hurst? Do you see his boots? Those are Yankee cavalry boots! And he didn't scavenge them off no dead Yankee neither."

"I fought for this country, Colonel, the country into which I was born. I fought honorably for my beliefs, just as you did. You forget that no small number of people right here in this room were none too keen on entering a fight that was destined to bring misery down upon us all."

"Honor! Hurst, you don't fool me, and you don't fool any of these good folks," Rutherford continued, his vehemence unrestrained. "Oh, yes, word's done made its way to me. That nigra you came back with, the big buck. He fought for the Yankees. And Mr. Hurst here was their officer, directing them to kill your boys. You heard right: Durksen Hurst commanded a *colored* regiment."

Hurst's face flushed. *Of course! The telegraph operator in Lethe Creek!*

"You cannot deny that, Hurst. You, sir, are a *traitor* to the South. And what's more, you are traitor to your *own people*."

Shouts grew to a roar. Shocked, Durk realized with horror, *I've put a target on my friend's back and made things worse for Lou!*

Incensed and lightheaded from fatigue and the day's tensions, Durk barked back, "And you're a thief, Colonel! These vagrancy arrests —auctioning off unfortunate souls because they can't pay trumped-up fines issued by your sham court—are simply your method of stealing labor from the black man. Yes, stealing! You're using armed deputies to rob unarmed men, and that's the very definition of a cowardly high-way robber!"

By now, the hubbub was deafening. Durk examined the surrounding faces, bloated and distorted by rage. Fists shook at him. A man in the front row drew a pistol, but was restrained by his companions.

"And, Mr. Clifton," Durk continued heatedly, "you and your friends who are so proud of your fine establishments, y'all are no better than he is. You're thieves of the most despicable kind, lining your pockets with money stolen from the poorest of the poor. You should be ashamed of yourselves."

Clifton banged the gavel furiously. "Enough of your insults," he shouted until the room settled down. "Now, I was willing to hear your arguments, and we have heard your twisted proposals. Sir, I ask you politely to leave my house immediately; you are no longer welcome. Sheriff, please have two of your men escort my guest off this property. This is for your own protection, Hurst."

Realizing he'd gone too far, Durk regained his composure. Facing Clifton, he said contritely, "I beg the honorable Mr. Clifton's forgiveness for my foolhardy outburst. I also beg the forgiveness of Colonel

Rutherford and your other guests. My comments were ill-considered, inappropriate, and rude. I apologize deeply and hope we can put this episode behind us."

"Such a transgression in another man's home cannot be forgiven," Clifton stated. "You will please leave the premises."

"I don't forgive you either, Captain Hurst, and neither will anyone else in this chamber," Colonel Rutherford spit.

*What have I done?* Durk thought, his heart sinking. He'd failed to control his temper and his mouth. He'd failed his friends, and, worse, he'd placed Lou in greater jeopardy. Durk made his way down the aisle through a gauntlet of vengeful men spewing years of bitterness and loss at him. As he passed, a man kicked him in the shins, another elbowed him in the ribs, and another spit in his face. From around the room, he heard shouts of "Traitor," "Yankee."

When he reached the end of the row, two armed deputies were waiting. He walked between them to the rear of the room, vicious curses and blood-curdling threats pouring down upon him. Reaching the door, he was careful to open it slowly to give the servants time to scurry away before anyone inside could see they'd been listening.

Once outside the room, Durk slammed the door shut behind him. "May I have my hat back, please?" he asked the butler.

"Yes, sir, Mr. Hurst," the butler replied formally with a worried smile. "Follow me, sir."

As Durk continued toward the front door, the other servants silently parted to let him pass, a strange look on their faces. Never had they heard one of Master Clifton's guests speak on their behalf.

Then it struck him. *What am I going to tell Antoinette and Josh?*

## OUTSKIRTS OF TURKLE, MISSISSIPPI

—*I'm afraid, Mother.*
—*This is no time to turn cowardly, fool. You've come this far.*

Devereau drew rein, bringing the unfamiliar horse to a halt on the muddy road. She slumped in the saddle, exhausted from her ordeal, her shoulders and back screaming pain from her first ride since her incarceration. The chestnut mount was a fine one, easily identified by its markings: a white muzzle and matching stockings on both right foreleg and right hind-leg. It was already after sundown and, being exposed all day to the hard rain, she shivered inside her damp clothing. Still unable to shake the terror that had tortured her throughout her mad flight from the McCorkle plantation, she looked back over her shoulder, but as with the hundred other times, saw no one in pursuit. She didn't think she was lost but, having been gone from Turkle for four years, couldn't be certain.

Navigating the old road that ran east past the former *DarkHorse* grounds had been slow, wearying. Luckily, the rain clouds were passing, exposing enough dim moonlight to light her way. The side road to Jenkins' house couldn't be far off. She'd ridden out there on business errands at her mother's behest many times before the war, contracting for Jenkins' cotton crop and negotiating loans to him, merely one minor strand of her mother's web of suspect business alliances. The French name had meant something then. How folks would view her now, however, was anyone's guess.

—*Why Jenkins, way out here?*

—Mother, I'm on a stolen horse! When they find Mrs. McCorkle's body . . .

—*They'll search for a young woman in a ragged dress. You're a man in a suit. Stay calm.*

—We didn't have to kill her. She was a kindly old woman. She'd been good to me . . .

—*Yes, we did, fool. Do you think she would give you the horse? Just keep your mind on* FrenchAcres.

Desperate to find shelter and rest, Devereau spurred the chestnut, but the animal was near exhaustion and failed to quicken its pace. Jenkins had been practically a hermit when Devereau knew him before the war, so she felt safe making her first contact there. Besides, the man owed her mother more money than he was worth. Devereau had leverage over him, and she planned to use it.

Turning off the main road, Devereau followed the side trail to Jenkins', passing fields lying fallow, surrendering their boundaries and furrows to encroaching feral vegetation. A quarter mile further, she rode up his drive, flanked by rows of willows left unpruned for a decade, until she came upon his house. It was two stories, with walls peeling paint, its porch missing boards. She circled the structure and tied up the chestnut beside a water trough in the back where it couldn't be seen from the drive. Then she pulled the pistol she'd stolen from Mrs. McCorkle from the saddlebag and tucked it into her belt. With fine engraving on the barrel and handle, the dueling pistol had undoubtedly been a family heirloom. She sneered. *Typical of a man: willing to get himself killed for no reason other than pride.*

She circled the house and climbed the porch stairs, tripping on a loose board in the darkness. She cursed in pain, then limped carefully to the front door and knocked. No reply. She banged louder. Nothing. Frustrated, she pounded with both fists, shouting, "Jenkins, come to this door. Jenkins!" She continued until the door swung inward. Jenkins faced her rubbing his eyes, his dirty brown hair in a tangle, feet bare, wearing wrinkled, soiled clothing and feet bare. One suspender of his britches hung over his long johns. He carried a lighted candle in one hand, his rifle in the other pointing at Devereau's chest.

"I'll shoot you down," he threatened, voice shaking.

"Jenkins, it's Devereau French. Put that gun down."

Jenkins held the candle higher, squinting through sleepy eyes at his visitor. Then he lowered the rifle. "Mr. French? Is it you?" he asked.

"Yes, of course it's me. Let me in," she said impatiently. Jenkins stepped back, allowing Devereau to enter, before closing the door behind her.

"What in Heaven's name are you doing here, Mr. French? I figured the war done took you off't like it done so many."

"I've come to offer you my help—and to seek yours. Just like the old days." Devereau examined the place with a scornful expression. "Looks like you could use some help."

"Well, just don't stand there. Foller me," Jenkins instructed. He shuffled into the dining room where he leaned his rifle against the wall. Then he crossed to the table, which he wiped with his sleeve, making swirls in the dust. He pulled out a chair. "Sit down, Mr. French. Do you need eatin's? I ain't got much."

Devereau took the chair. "I ate along the trail. I would greatly appreciate some hot coffee and a blanket though. I'm soaked from riding in this deluge all day. And I need a bed. We can talk in the morning."

"I got one bed good enough for sleeping. The other rooms, the rain come in through holes in the roof. You'd have to share them beds with birds, squirrels, and field mice."

"Just get the coffee and blanket," Devereau snapped. Jenkins hurried to the kitchen and lit a fire to boil water, then went up the stairs. Soon he returned with a blanket smelling of dampness and dust, which he shook out and handed to Devereau, who, still shivering, wrapped it around herself.

"You look awful tired, Mr. French," the man said. "I'll get the coffee." Then he disappeared again.

When they were both seated, sipping from mismatched cups, Devereau gave Jenkins a penetrating stare. "You know, Jenkins, you owe me more than this place is worth, if you could even find a fool with a dollar in his pocket to take it off your hands. But that's not at issue."

"Well, what do you want? Listen, Mr. French, the war done cleaned me out just like ever'body. Ain't made a crop in over a year."

Devereau studied Jenkins' face in the candlelight. He wasn't telling the whole story; she knew him.

"I come to deal, Jenkins, not to be lied to. Now I can help get you back on your feet. I'm even willing to forgive your old debts. But you're going to have to help me out, too."

Jenkins sipped his coffee, thinking, then peered up. "I'd be willing. What's your needin's, Mr. French?"

"First, I don't want anyone to know I'm back yet. I want you to hide me and my horse for a time. I don't know how long."

"All right," Jenkins agreed, his voice trailing off, figuring there was more to come. He bit off a chew and spit into the corner. "Nobody never comes out this-a-way no more, not that they ever did much. Times are pretty slim; but I can sleep and feed two for a spell. What else you got in mind?"

"I want information . . . about *FrenchAcres*. That is the wellspring of our future prosperity."

"*FrenchAcres?* Far as I know, a bunch of nigras are workin' it. Probably some of them your slaves from the good times."

"I mean, someone must be trying to get his hands on it. What have you heard?"

Jenkins fiddled with his suspender, an old habit that Devereau knew meant he had a hard decision to make. "See, Mr. French," he finally said, "Colonel Rutherford and a couple of his friends are trying to take it. Got a lawyer and all."

"I remember him. Ran his plantation down to a nub. What's this 'colonel' business?"

"See, he done led Turkle Company in the war. Colonel's a big man in town now. You don't want to cross him." His voice faded off.

"And?" Devereau demanded, knowing the man was holding something back.

"He took over your mamma's bank."

"I may need your help with him. To find out what he's doing and such."

"Well, I'm not so sure I want to get on the colonel's wrong side."

"You've had dealings with him?"

"Plenty during the war. That's all I'll say." Jenkins spit again.

"I see." Devereau was thoughtful for a minute, the silence hanging between them. "What did you do during the war anyhow, Jenkins?"

"Me? Why, I kept to my business, is what I did, sir. I helped the Cause," he added defensively.

"Yes. And your business was. . . ?"

"Different things, different. War was pretty good to me for a time. Tell you the truth, I'm sorry it's over."

"Yes, and just how was it good to you? Come now, Jenkins, you know I'll find out. If you want my help, you'd better talk straight."

"Well, see . . . I helped supply the army."

"Which army?"

"Whichever one was around. No sense in being difficult toward nobody, now is there? Mostly our side, though."

"Yes, and what did you supply them with?"

"Oh, horses and such. All kind of things."

"And where did you get these horses?"

"Mostly borrowed them from the Yankees. Took a ball in the arm in one raid. Lucky, I didn't lose it."

"What else? Do you have anything we can turn into some cash?"

"Well, I haven't gathered much moss, as I tole you. Got enough Confederate script to light kindling, use in the outhouse. Ain't no shortage of that. Jeff Davis printed that stuff like mad to keep the war going."

"Come on, Jenkins. I know you have more."

"Let me think on that, Mr. French," he replied grudgingly. "Yep, been cogitatin' on that very question. Going to be hard to turn war material into peacetime gold, you see. No market for it no more." He spit in the corner again. "It's that Rutherford who troubles me."

Devereau slowly slipped her hand under the blanket until it rested on the pistol in her lap. "I must be able to trust you, Jenkins. Now, what is your connection to Rutherford?"

"Again, Mr. French, I don't have much truck with nobody these days. Dealt with him during the fighting, but now-a-days just see him in town time to time to say howdy." He thought his situation over, then decided to shoot the works. "He ain't no buyer of what I got, Mr. French. Nope. Nobody's no buyer of what I got."

"Yes, and why is that?" Devereau asked.

"'Cause I don't want nobody to know what I got, see? Especially the colonel. Don't trust him. The whole situation makes me nervous."

"And you have . . . what?"

"Oh, I got something of some value to somebody, left over from the war. But I've been needing a person with a business head like your'n to turn it into cash, somebody with connections like you used to have. Maybe outside the county. You think you might want to help me unload it some kind of way?"

"Depends. Let me see it."

Jenkins spit and stood up. Then he lifted the candle and tilted his head toward the back. "I'll show you, if you ain't too tired."

"I can manage a peek."

"All right, foller me. Careful in the long weeds; there' a mess of cottonmouths and varmints back there."

"Let's go," Devereau said, rising to her feet. She wrapped the blanket around her shoulders, concealing her hand on the pistol.

*This better be worth it.*

# Chapter Fifteen

# UNDER SIEGE

The forest road to town began to narrow. Durk drew rein, settling in the saddle while the stallion snorted its impatience. He listened closely, unable to see through the fading moonlight. The woods sounded unnaturally quiet; something wasn't right.

He'd been wary of an ambush ever since leaving the meeting at Clifton's, having seen Rutherford whispering something to Bake, who'd left the gathering and didn't return for some time. Durk had little doubt that Rutherford would order him killed.

Durk's keen ear pricked up: he could hear a horse whinnying and hooves snapping twig-laden earth from a hill bordering the road fifty yards ahead. As he'd done so often fighting bushwhackers in Missouri, he ducked over to interpose Contrition between himself and any shooter. But no shots came.

When he'd gone another hundred yards, the blast of a pistol sounded from behind him. Durk became tense, trying to collect his thoughts. He figured there was an ambush set up ahead. The shot from behind likely came from a sentry posted to signal he was on his way into their trap. They expected that, upon hearing the pistol, Durk would flush, as most men would, riding away from the sound straight into their waiting rifles. But Durk wasn't any man; he knew what to do.

Durk turned Contrition off the road, into the forest, and up a wooded hillside. He climbed steadily, listening, then drew rein. No one was following from the road. He spurred Contrition on.

Reaching the crest of the hill, he stopped and waited. Soon he heard a rider galloping from ahead toward where the warning shot had been fired, passing the spot where Durk had left the road. As he'd expected, the group had sent a rider to see if the warning had been a mistake. Soon they would come searching for him.

Through a flicker of clear moonlight, Durk detected a deer path running along the ridge of the hill parallel to the road. Turning the stallion to follow this narrow passage, he headed toward town.

Progress was slow in the darkness. Finally, believing he'd put enough distance between himself and the gunmen, he descended the hill and made his way back to the road. There, he spurred the stallion to a gallop. As he rode, he heard shouting and horses chasing him, but he knew they'd never catch this horse. Never.

Exhausted and disheveled, Durk collapsed into the kitchen chair, gulping deep breaths to calm himself. The harrowing chase had shattered his nerves and exhausted his last bit of energy. After a few minutes, Antoinette came into the room wearing a robe, her flowing black hair hanging loose upon her shoulders. She gave Durk a hug and put a coffee pot on the stove, then lit the kindling. "Do you want something?" she asked.

"Just coffee, thanks."

Shortly thereafter, Big Josh entered the room rubbing sleep from his eyes, joining Durk and Antoinette at the table.

Antoinette sighed deeply. "What happened tonight?"

"They tried to ambush me on my way home," Durk muttered, still shaken.

"Who tried to ambush you? Did they follow you here?" an alarmed Antoinette asked, trying to keep her pitch down. "Caleb's asleep in back. Should we get him out of the house?"

"I don't think they followed me into town," Durk assured the pair. "It's likely Rutherford wouldn't let them."

"And the m-meeting?" Josh asked. "You talkin' like . . . like it didn't go so good."

Durk rubbed his forehead, trying to clear his head enough to explain.

"Could have been worse; they didn't hang me or burn me alive. See, I got into an argument with Rutherford. It got nasty, and Clifton kicked me out of his house."

Durk paused to consider his next words. "Actually, I've been thinking. Because we argued before the whole town, Rutherford probably knows he can't get away with killing me. Everyone would know he'd be behind it."

"You're probably right, Durk," Antoinette remarked. "The argument may be good fortune in disguise."

"Not exactly," Durk replied. "Now, everyone knows I fought for the Union, Josh and Lou, too. If you weren't in jeopardy before, my friend," he told Josh, "you're in it now."

The three fell silent, contemplating their changed circumstances.

"So what's next?" Antoinette asked.

"Well . . ." Durk hesitated, so tired he had trouble focusing. "Course, I want to ride out to Rutherford's and get Lou as soon as I can. Tomorrow, if possible. We still need to find some money. How much do we have?"

"I have about twenty left, and the store has about the same," Antoinette said. "That's all. Ellen won't have anything to speak of."

Josh emptied his pocket. "I have about thirty. I can take up a collection from the black folks, but they ain't got much to spare. It'll take time."

"I'd be lucky to have ten," Durk added. He rubbed his chin, thinking. "We need to get some money in here quick. Maybe the store will get busy."

Antoinette took Durk's hand. "Folks are going to be wary about coming in after what went on at Clifton's tonight. You didn't make many new customers, I'm sure."

Durk perked up. "We'll have Ellen make a big sign to put in front of the store, 'Half Off of Everything'. Plenty of folks will overlook their political sensitivities at those prices."

Antoinette studied Durk's face as he cast his look away from her scrutiny. "What else happened?"

"Well, it wasn't all bad," he explained. "Some would like to get past . . . the past. Some were against the war to begin with. And now that it's over and the hotheads lost, they want to press on with their lives. They're asking themselves, what's next? Some planters, too. Unfortunately, Rutherford and his faction are busy keeping the uncertain ones riled up, throwing beehives into their bonnets."

"Exactly what did you say to the colonel?"

Durk sighed. "I called him a coward for shooting unarmed Negros."

"I'm sure that earned his good will," Antoinette chided. "What else?"

"It's the Black Codes. Whoever they send to Jackson will want them to become state law. I was just one voice against them." He grew quiet.

"So where do we go from here?" Antoinette asked.

"The courts. I'm going to pursue your claim to *FrenchAcres*," Durk said. "Our friends are counting on that. As for my *DarkHorse* claim, I suspect we'll never get the papers from Jackson. And this is no time to ride across state to get a copy; there's just so much hanging loose, so much . . ." His voice trailed off.

Antoinette gazed affectionately at Durk. "You'd better go to bed before you fall over," she told him and kissed him on the cheek.

He nodded obediently, pushing himself to his feet.

"This will work out, you'll see," Josh assured him, seeing how hard his friend was taking his failure.

Durk shrugged, then lumbered from the kitchen into back bedroom and fell face forward onto the bed. He was snoring within seconds.

Left alone in the kitchen, Antoinette and Josh talked over Durk's misadventure at the civic meeting and his deplorable condition upon returning. Finally, their conversation turned to themselves.

"You gonna be safe here?" Josh asked. "Maybe *FrenchAcres* be better for you right now. Durk got that judge's order to keep Rutherford and his people off'n that land."

"I'm not leaving," she replied firmly. "I've run enough in my life. This place isn't exciting like New Orleans or St. Louis. Turkle's just a small town, with people good and bad like any other. But Durk is here, and as long as he's here—as long as he's alive—that's where I'm going to be.

"How about you, Josh? I'm frightened for you and Lou. Maybe you should leave the county altogether. We can raise money some way to free Lou and get you both somewhere safe, at least safer than you'd be here."

"I can't leave, Antoinette, I just can't," Josh said determinedly. "I done promise' myself to do something for my people. 'Sides, Turkle is home to me now. Things going to change someday. I believe it; they got to."

"What have y'all been up to at *FrenchAcres*?"

"Us? Oh, we drawin' up a petition for the convention. Yes, mam. Black folks need to say our piece if things going to change. A whole bunch of us going, no matter what."

"I'd like to go with you, Josh. What do you think?"

"I think: welcome."

It was too hot to sleep; he was drenched in sweat. Laying on top of the covers with the window open to catch only the hope of a breeze, the boy could hear every word the three said. He could tell they were scared, and he couldn't stand to think of them that way. It was that Colonel Rutherford and them planters' fault. The truth was, they're afraid of Durk. And Caleb hated them.

He'd figure something out. They'd see.

The sun was already peering through the window when Durk awoke, sore from riding, a large boulder banging inside his skull. Seeing the sun's rays through the window, he chastised himself for sleeping so late. He worked his way to the edge of the bed and pulled on his pants and boots. Then he put on yesterday's shirt, buttoned it up, and tucked it in. Lou's captivity was the only thing on his mind.

He made his way into the kitchen where Antoinette and Josh were waiting for him, headed for the coffee pot, and poured himself a cup.

"There's breakfast warming in the oven; help yourself," Antoinette said.

"Mornin', Any business yet?"

Antoinette and Josh glanced at each other, reluctant to be the one to tell him. "Nobody come in yet," Josh replied. "But Ellen just put the sign out."

"That's what I was afraid of," Durk said, fixing himself a plate. "What're you gonna do today, Josh?"

"Headin' back to *FrenchAcres* on Earl's wagon," Josh replied. "A few of us working on a petition for the constitutional convention to take to Jackson. What you gonna do?"

"Getting that order from Judge Fairbanks, first thing, then over to the bank. Try to pry Lou from Rutherford's clutches. Wish me luck."

"Oh, friend, I do wish you that. That, and finding some kindness in that man's cold heart."

Durk halted across the desk from Colonel Rutherford and waited silently as the man continued to write, ignoring him. Finally, Rutherford looked up from his paperwork. "Yes, Hurst, what is it?" the colonel asked curtly.

"I want to apologize for my ill-considered insults last night. I lost my temper."

Scowling, Rutherford looked Durk over. "Words aren't bullets just yet, Captain Hurst. What do you want from me?"

Durk displayed a work contract with Lou's signature forged by Big Josh, returned it to his pocket, then dropped Judge Fairbanks' order to return Lou to Durk's employment on the desk. "I want my man back."

"There was a judgment issued by the court against this nigra."

"This is a property claim, Colonel; it overrules your sham vagrancy charge. Now, when do I get him?"

Rutherford examined the document, then looked up. "This says you have to repay me for the amount of his fine. Where's my money?"

"I'll get it to you," Durk replied.

"You mean you don't have it?" Rutherford smirked.

"Not at the moment, but I'm good for it."

"I want cash. I put up cash, and this document says you have to reimburse me in full before I hand him over to you."

"This is a bank. I'd like to borrow the money."

"Turkle Bank don't lend to you. That should come as no surprise."

"Everyone knows I'm good for it. I'll put up the store as collateral."

"Cash, Captain Hurst. Cash only," Rutherford repeated.

Stymied, Durk searched for another plan of attack. "I'll tell you what, Rutherford. I'll sell you part of my rights to the *DarkHorse* land. That property will be worth some real money, far more than the paltry sum we're discussing."

"Ha! Rights to land that's not legally yours and never will be. A bank that trades on pie-in-the-sky wouldn't stay in business very long, now would it?"

"I'll put up my horse, Contrition, Colonel. He's worth a lot more than two-fifty."

"Good day, sir."

Burning with anger, Durk examined Rutherford's smug face. "No harm better come to Lou, Colonel, or you will regret it. I promise you that."

"I'm a fair man, Captain Hurst," Rutherford stated. "I treat all nigras equal."

Crouched behind a barrel on the corner of the sidewalk, Caleb kept watch on the bank door. Seeing Durk emerge, he ducked down.

*Durk weren't in the bank very long. And he ain't lookin' very happy comin' out neither.*

Thoughts scattered through his mind like buckshot. *Poor Lou. We got to rescue him, we got to. He saved my life back in Missouri. Heck, I don't even think of him and Josh as crows no more; I'm sorry I ever did.*

*Maybe I could somehow rescue Lou. He done rescued me, didn't he? But how? I don't even have no horse . . .*

*What I got to do is get me a rifle. Why, back home I could shoot a squirrel at thirty yards. Wouldn't be nothing to plug that Colonel right through the heart. But Durk and Antoinette won't let no firearms in the house. But, heck, my birthday's a-coming. I got to ask for one. I'm almost thirteen dang years old. I'll tell them it's for huntin'. I'll say, 'the other boys go huntin' and I can't go along'. One way or t'other, though, I got to get me a rifle. Then I'll show that colonel.*

Watching Durk disappear, Caleb studied the street. Storefronts, fences, and alleys; barrels and crates; there were a lot of possibilities.

*Now where will I set up my huntin' blind for a good shot? Where I can skedaddle after I shoot? This ain't gonna be hard, not hard at all.*

# CHAPTER SIXTEEN
# STALEMATE

## JENKINS' PLACE

For perhaps the hundredth time that night, she peeked through the torn curtains, but no shadow of a rider was coming up the drive. It was long after midnight. She was bone tired and had dozed more than once leaning against the wall below the sill. When would Jenkins return? She checked her pistol again and secured her knife under her belt.

—I'm going to bed.

—*You'll do no such thing, weakling. There's too much at stake.*

Finally, she heard the slow thud of hoof beats approaching the house. She drew her pistol and peered out. A single rider. She listened closely, her eyes searching the area. The rider seemed to be alone. That, however, didn't preclude his being followed or others circling the house. She slipped behind the front door and waited in the dark, pistol raised.

The rider dismounted and tied his horse to the trough. Then he walked to the front steps and climbed to the porch. There he paused, eyes darting about, listening. Nothing but insects chirping, owls crying. He opened the door and paused again. Then he went in—and felt cold steel pressed behind his ear.

"Is anyone with you?"

"No."

"Were you followed."

"No. Now take that gun off'n me."

Devereau let Jenkins into the house, then went into the dining room and sat, laying her gun on the table. Jenkins followed and lit the candle, burned down to a scooped-out inch. "What took so long?"

"That road needs fixin'." Devereau gave him a dirty look. "I was talkin' to a couple fellahs, seeing what I could learn. Ain't that what you sent me to do?"

"Drinking with them, you mean. You stink of it."

"Drinkin's the best way to loosen folks' tongues. I'd be remiss in my duties if'n I didn't make certain folks was getting soaked, wouldn't I?"

"What did you learn about *FrenchAcres*?" Devereau demanded.

"*FrenchAcres*, now that's a far tale. Folks went out there one night, see?"

"Folks? Who?"

"Oh, a bunch. Led by Colonel Rutherford. I tole you, he the big man these days."

"And. . . ?"

"Well, see, they's a whole mess of nigras working the place. How it was, the boys was going to run them off, string up a few, arrest the others, the usual. They did burn down the stable. But then it got curious."

"Curious? How?"

"Well, they was all watching the stable catch good, when out of nowhere comes—you ain't gonna believe it—Mrs. DuVallier waving a paper, saying 'get off'n my land'. Yep."

"Antoinette? *Her* land? Listen, Jenkins, you're not making sense. What paper?"

"Marriage paper, 'tween you and her. Says she runnin' the place with you gone. That's all I know."

"Marriage to. . . ? Why, that's preposterous!"

"It's a fact. I stopped by the bank to say howdy to the colonel. He says it was your signature all right. Colonel was kinda busy to chat much, and I don't want to spend more time with him than I need to. I tole you why." Jenkins whistled, a silly grin crossing face. "I give you my respect on that one; she's a looker. You have to tell your partner what she's like . . . you know. Ever' detail."

Devereau's head swam. Then it came to her: the document was one her mother had her sign just as she was anxious to get away.

—This is one of your tricks! It figures.

—*I had to protect my interests, my darling, in case something happened to you. You'd better make your claim—and soon. Or else our land will be devoured by our former chattel.*

Devereau glared at Jenkins. "Where is Antoinette now?"

"She livin' in town, back of Ahronson's."

"The Jew store? Ahronson's?"

Devereau tried to make sense of the man's ramblings. Then she realized, where there's smoke, there's fire. And she meant *fire!* Her heart thumped hard. "Is Durk . . . Durk Hurst with her?"

"Course. He the one what owns it."

*So Durk's back in Turkle!* Her mood sank, hitting bottom faster than a boulder dropped into a shallow creek. Durk, the man she'd wanted from the first moment she'd seen him, who she'd pursued throughout Missouri, who'd cost her so much, even her freedom. Durk, who she must have but knew she never would—because of Antoinette.

"So the two are living at Ahronson's . . . together?"

"That's what folks tells me. Lots of talk about them two, you can imagine. Talk of the whole county by now."

"Are they married?"

"How could they be? She's married to you, ain't she?"

Devereau slammed her palms on the table in frustration. "All right, what else did you learn?"

"There's still Federal agents snoopin' around, hunting them missing Henry repeaters. Like we said during the war, 'Yankees load 'em on Sunday and shoot all week'. Mighta been a different war if'n we had 'em, 'stead of our old muzzle-loaders. But things is as they was. Yes, sir, they is as they was. We gonna have to go far afield to sell our stock, Mr. French. Yes, sir, maybe all the way to Jackson. Maybe Memphis or N'awlins. And getting them delivered gonna be another thing."

Jenkins took out his tobacco pouch and rolled a cigarette. Devereau grabbed the cigarette from his hand and lit if from the candle, drawing and blowing thick clouds of smoke, coughing till her lungs adjusted to the irritation. During her two years' incarceration, she hadn't been allowed a cigar, and the tobacco was making her dizzy, a weakness enhanced by her fatigue. Jenkins gave her a foul look and rolled himself another.

"Jenkins," Devereau asked, "did you corner the sheriff? Did he say anything about me?"

"No, he was with some folks I need to avoid. I waited a spell, but they had a jug, so it was going to be some time. I just went on about my bidness."

Devereau grimaced, disappointed. "Next time you go into town, don't come back till you fish him about me. Understand? But work your way around the subject. Don't let on you've seen me or you're asking for me."

"I'll do that, Mr. French."

Devereau stubbed out her cigarette on the table, licked her finger and touched it to the tip, shoving the remainder in her pocket. "I'm worn out. We'll talk tomorrow." Devereau rose and headed for the stairs, fear and frustration whirling like a hurricane inside her skull. She needed sleep, if she could silence her mind long enough to fall into its dark embrace. Yes, she certainly would visit that pair. Pay them a surprise visit, well-armed.

—*Forget that man! He means nothing to you. Your chasing him cost us everything, idiot! You have a chance to regain our legacy, and you're already planning to throw it away. For what?*

—You're wrong. I want what's mine, Mother. All of it . . . or there's going to be nothing left.

Having a weary late-supper with Antoinette at the kitchen table, Durk heard the front door open and close. He paused in mid-bite and laid down his fork. Without a word, he and Antoinette looked at each other: who would be shopping this late? The store had been devoid of customers all morning, but picked up gradually after the "Half Off" sign was posted, becoming quite busy. By the end of the day they had enough to free Lou. The bills and coins were neatly stacked on the table, having been counted while dinner cooked.

"Ellen's asleep, exhausted, poor thing. I'll go see who it is," Antoinette offered, starting to rise.

"Let's just see what happens," Durk said, picking up his fork again.

The pair resumed eating, but paused: light footsteps were making their way hesitantly toward them. Durk gave Antoinette a harried wave and tiptoed toward the sink, where he picked up the carving knife. Then he listened. No sound. The intruder must have halted temporarily.

Then the stranger was standing in the doorway, pointing a rifle at them. "Please discard that weapon and sit down," ordered a threatening voice. It was Devereau French wearing a broad-brimmed hat slouched over her eyes, brown suit hanging like oversized curtains—wielding a Union-manufacture repeater rifle. Where she obtained such a weapon Durk couldn't imagine. Shaken at the sight, Durk envisioned their hopes for *FrenchAcres* crumbling into dust.

"Well, isn't this a wholesome domestic tableau," Devereau oozed. "Sitting around the table in the evening counting your coins, discussing the sale of ribbons and penny candy. I thought you might go tame one day, Durk, but I never imagined this."

"What are you doing here, French?" Durk demanded.

"I came to gun you both down. That is my intention," Devereau retorted, ignoring Antoinette.

"I'm willing to work with you, Devereau," Durk said warmly, setting the knife on the counter. Glancing nervously at Antoinette, he returned to his chair. "You and me, we've got a history, haven't we? Sit down. Care for some coffee?"

Devereau felt her face flush. Clearly, Durk knew what she wanted. "Enough prittle-prattle," Devereau growled, turning the rifle toward Antoinette. "What's this about your claim on *FrenchAcres?* As my wife!"

Antoinette put down her fork and delicately dabbed her lips with a napkin. "Why, it's perfectly legal, Devereau. Mother arranged this sham marriage between us. You must have been aware of it; you signed the certificate."

"You know as well as I that . . . well, that woman had more tricks up her sleeve than a traveling Bible salesman," Devereau groused. She studied Antoinette, foul resolve in her eyes. "Well, I'm back to claim my legacy. Your management will no longer be required on *my* property, dear."

"Let's talk this through, Devereau," Durk interjected in a calming tone, searching for an approach to defuse the crisis. "Colonel Rutherford, some other planters, are lined up against us to take that property. It's going to take all three of us working together to stop them."

"As for you, Durksen Hurst, word is you've been sleeping with *my wife*," she said threateningly. "I could gun you down right now for adultery and no one would blame me. I've half a mind to do it, too."

"But that's the last thing you want to do, isn't it, Devereau? Shoot me?" He winked at her.

Devereau took a deep breath, trying to recover her equilibrium. "You shouldn't have said that." Frustrated, she raised the rifle to her shoulder. "Quiet! I came to shoot you both, and that's what I'm going to do. Any last words?"

Antoinette stared hard at Devereau. "If you kill us you're done in Turkle, Devereau. You must know that. Then where will you go? You're not looking very prosperous. Why don't you listen to Durk?"

"I'm not listening to anyone. Especially not that shifty weasel. Besides, I have assets you know nothing about."

"Listen, Devereau," Durk said, "you must know you're wanted for murder here."

"So?"

"So, Antoinette and I were in the house that night, too. We could testify to your innocence, *if* the three of us can come to some accommodation. You kill us, they'll hang you, just on general principles. Your mother, me, your *wife*: three murders. That's a lot of guilt in a trial. You recall, people weren't very partial to the family that kept Turkle under its thumb for so many years."

Devereau sat down, her rifle still pointed at them. "What are you offering, Hurst?"

"Well now, I'll have to think that one over," Durk drawled, maneuvering to force French to make the first move. "Your appearance has been quite a surprise, a revelation really. What do you suggest, Devereau?"

"You're so devious, Hurst. How do I know I can trust you?"

"Have you ever known me to break my word?" Durk eyed Antoinette looking for a suggestion, but Antoinette remained silent, having no idea of what to say. Durk turned back to Devereau. "Let us come up with something in the next day or two. I'll ride out to see you so you won't have to chance coming into town. Where are you perched?"

"None of your damned business. *FrenchAcres* is what I want. It's in my name; it's mine."

"All right," Durk replied. "What else?"

"Your testimony in my favor, of course, if I need it."

"What else, Devereau?"

"You know what else." Devereau gave Antoinette a snide look, which, surprisingly, Antoinette repaid with a sympathetic one.

"What are *you* willing to give, Devereau; what do you even have?" Durk asked. "So far, you've demanded much, but offered nothing."

Devereau paused to consider her limited options. "I'm giving you both your lives. And I'll give you a cut of *FrenchAcres*. The lower two hundred."

Durk laughed, then grinned broadly at her. "But your 'wife' already has the whole thing. You get hung; Antoinette keeps it. Why would we accept two hundred measly acres from you? I'll tell you what. You let us keep *FrenchAcres* and *DarkHorse* is yours."

"Wild swamp in exchange for an entire plantation that's been in my family for generations? You're crazy."

The three stared at each other in silence, but it was obvious they were at an impasse.

Suddenly, Caleb wearing a nightshirt drifted into the kitchen. When he saw the strange-looking man, he looked puzzled. Then his eyes fixed on the shiny new rifle.

"What's going on, Durk?" Caleb asked, rubbing sleep from his eyes.

"Get back to bed," Durk ordered.

"I needed a sup of water," Caleb replied yawning, his attention fixed on the intruder. The four paused as if frozen, not sure of what to do. Caleb broke the silence. "Who is this, Durk?"

Durk opened his mouth, but Devereau interrupted, saying, "It won't do any good for him to know that."

"Get a drink, dear, and go back to bed," Antoinette ordered sweetly. "There's no danger here."

"But the rifle?"

"The man's just showing it to us," Durk replied.

Caleb studied the weapon. "Why, that's a dang Henry repeater! Where'd you get that, Mister?"

Stunned, Devereau flushed red, not knowing what to do. The boy could tie her to Jenkins' stock of stolen Henrys—the very ones the Federals were seeking. In her panic, she considered shooting him, but knowing she couldn't pull the trigger. And if she shot Durk and Antoinette, the boy would be a witness. She was faced with a quandary.

"Do what Antoinette told you," Durk ordered.

Acquiescing, Caleb plunged the dipper into the bucket and drank, then gave Antoinette an affectionate squeeze. Drifting to the door, he turned back to look at Devereau a final time.

"Good night," Devereau said, forcing an awkward smile. Caleb nodded politely and disappeared into the hallway.

"Seems like a decent boy," Devereau remarked, eyes narrowing toward Antoinette. "I'd hate to leave him motherless." Keeping her eye on them, rifle raised, she backed toward the door.

"How can we get a message to you?" Antoinette asked.

"I'll contact you. And don't try to find me." Then she was gone.

Durk slumped in his chair. "This is sure a pretty mess," as they finished their dinners in silence.

The blackness of night frightened her. Terrified she'd be discovered, Devereau circled the corner building and slipped down the alley where she'd tied up Jenkins' horse. She'd left her own back at his place, fearing someone might recognize it as belonging to the McCorkles. Her eyes searched for the sheriff or anyone who might impede her escape; but, thankfully, she was alone.

Shaking uncontrollably, she leaned the rifle against the side of the building and sought a place to sit. Spotting a crate around the corner, she stumbled over to it and plopped down in the shadows. Then she let herself cry, body heaving with gut-wrenching sobs, oblivious to her surroundings. How could it all have come to this? Prison waiting up North, a murder warrant in an adjoining county, her mother's killing hanging over her head. And Durk here with Antoinette. It all seemed so hopeless.

Finally regaining some control, she breathed in the night air and rose. But the rifle wasn't where she'd left it. In panic, she searched around the area in the darkness, even crawling on her hands and knees. But it wasn't to be found. After a while, afraid of discovery, she gave up the hunt. The weapon had inexplicably disappeared.

Mystified, she untied the horse's reins and mounted. Then she turned and spurred the horse to take the circuitous route out of town, avoiding the main streets.

—*Why didn't you shoot him when you had the chance? He's what stands in your way. People would have understood killing the man sleeping with your woman.*

—I didn't want to; I won't . . .

—Killing him is your only choice.

Devereau reached the edge of town and made her way through a pine grove until she came to the old road east toward Lethe Creek. Once Turkle was behind her, she leaned back in the saddle and breathed normally, no longer quite so terrified.

Then she drew rein, the pull of *FrenchAcres* impossible to resist. She turned the horse around and spurred him, heading west. Yes, it was time to face her old home ground. She had to see it!

# SECTION III

# CHAPTER SEVENTEEN

# DAMAGED GOODS

The thick canopy of overhanging branches shaded the wooded road from the blasting mid-morning sun. Josh and Durk felt elated riding out to rescue Lou, having paid Rutherford the money they'd cobbled together dime by dollar. Old Walker at the stable had risked his job to lend Josh a good, strong roan whose owner was in Memphis. Durk had offered Josh Contrition, the bigger horse, saying he'd take the rented animal, but Josh had deferred.

After a half hour, they came upon furrowed fields and small farmhouses. Josh sighed. He had never seen Durk so haggard, with dark bags under his eyes and a grim expression etched across his face. Worrying about Lou had taken a lot out of him. "You and me, just like the old days," Josh commented, hoping to cheer his friend.

"And no secesh bushwhackers," Durk said, brightening a bit. "I can't wait to see Lou's face when we ride up."

"That'll be something," Josh agreed.

Nearing Rutherford's fields, they observed black men and women in rags being watched over by a large black man wielding a whip. Josh nodded toward the large man. "See him?" Josh said pointing. "Driver, just like in slave days. Beat the ones working too slow, or just having a bad day. Nothing much convicted prisoners can do."

"You had drivers back home?" Durk asked.

"When I run General's place, I put the driver in the field with ever'body else. Took away his whip and all. One night, some of the others beat him near to death. General had to sell him off'n the place just to keep him alive."

"About this so-called General. What was he the general of anyway, Josh?"

"Ha! He weren't general of nothing. Just made ever'body call him that. Fact is, he was generally drunk, and that's 'bout it."

The two laughed, but seeing the field hands around them, it was like laughing past the graveyard. Finally reaching the rutted drive to Rutherford's mansion, they grew quiet, stopping before a man lounging on the front porch, boots propped up on the rail, straw hat pulled down to shade his eyes.

"I'm Durksen Hurst. We're here for Lou Jones."

Pushing his hat back, the man spit a stream of tobacco juice over the rail and looked them over. "I know who you is," he said, working his way to his feet. "Tie up there and foller me."

"We won't be staying long," Durk replied. He and Josh dismounted.

"Suit yourself."

Leading their mounts, Josh and Durk followed the man around back to what was still called "the quarters, a collection of weathered shacks that had, indeed, once served as slave quarters and hadn't been repaired in decades. Finally, the man stopped at one of the hovels. "In there."

Handing the reins to Durk, Josh ducked inside the shack. "Lou, we're here to get you!" Durk heard him announce. Then things went quiet. Finally, Josh appeared in the door, waving Durk in. Durk dropped the reins and ran. There, lying on a blanket on the dirt floor was Lou, clearly in pain. "Durk," he said weakly. "Thank God you've come."

Josh knelt beside Lou and pulled up his right pants leg, exposing Lou's lower limb. The injury to Lou's leg had become infected. Lou's calf had already darkened and in places was turning black. Sickened, Durk closed his eyes, cursing to himself. He'd seen it often during the war: gangrene was taking hold.

"Come on," Durk said. "Let's get him to the doctor, quick.

Josh slipped Lou's arm around his neck, then carefully lifted him under his legs and carried him outside, where he set him on Contrition. Then he climbed up behind, wrapping his arms around Lou. Durk faced the man in the straw hat. "The colonel will hear about this."

"I' be sure to tell him," the man replied with a sneer.

Durk and Josh eyed each other, then made for town.

\* \* \*

Dr. Higgins returned to the parlor where Durk and Josh were waiting, his face grim. "It's gangrene, all right. Getting bad."

"Wh-what can you do? Can you save his leg?" Josh asked.

"Too late for that," the doctor replied. "If we saw it off, we might be able to save his life though."

"Do you mean. . . ?" Durk gulped.

"At the knee. Best I can do."

Durk and Josh groaned, shaking their heads. "Do you have any morphine?" Durk asked plaintively, having seen too many soldiers' limbs sawed off without painkiller; he could still hear the men's screams and cries.

"Sorry, medicine is in short supply. I'm hoping to get some kind of delivery from the army or the Freedmen's Bureau, but I don't know when, or if, that will be. I have some whiskey, that's about it. You two come with me to hold him down."

Josh placed his large hand gently on the doctor's shoulder. "I know you been treating the freedman, Doctor. I just wanted to thank you. There's a lot of misery going 'round."

The doctor wearily shook his head. "I'm seeing it all: malnutrition, lockjaw, whooping cough, diarrhea, hookworm. Epidemics, too: outbreaks of cholera, smallpox, yellow fever, typhoid, tuberculosis. I'm just one man, Josh. The planters have no stake in the health of these people any more. Sometimes they refuse to pay me for the visit or promise they'll pay me something after harvest. I'm at my wit's end."

"We'll pay you, Doctor," Durk said, "You'll be paid for this, I promise."

Sitting on the edge of the bed, Antoinette fed Lou the last of the soup, setting the bowl and spoon onto the tray. She wiped his mouth with a cloth before adjusting his pillow for him to lie back. She'd seen far too much of amputations, sickness, and death nursing the troops up North for any one person.

As Antoinette carried the tray away, Durk and Josh drew near Lou's beside. "How are you doing?" Josh asked.

"Still hurts bad," Lou managed to utter, wincing. "Bad."

"What do you need?" Durk asked.

"Just get me a good crutch. I got to find my family," Lou replied through clinched teeth. Josh and Durk looked at each other.

"Maybe we can raise money for boat tickets," Durk suggested. "Sure, a train to the river, a boat to New Orleans, a ship to Carolina. We'll get you there . . . somehow."

"Going to try to sleep now, if'n I can," Lou mumbled, closing his eyes.

Josh led Durk by the elbow into the hallway. "Damn Rutherford. It ain't right," Josh whispered.

Durk just shook his head. Then they noticed Caleb standing silently beside them, listening to their conversation. "What is it you want, Caleb?" Durk asked.

"I just want to say howdy to Lou," Caleb answered.

"All right. But make it short. He needs to sleep."

Caleb nodded agreement and tiptoed into the room. When he was gone, Durk fixed Josh in his gaze, his jaw set. "I'll make the colonel pay for this. I promise you, Josh. He'll pay like his slaves used to pay: with sweat and blood."

It was well past midnight when Devereau approached *FrenchAcres*, weary and sore. The new moon and stars lay hidden behind clouds, casting little light, but she'd taken this route home so often, she didn't need celestial guidance.

She headed for the mansion. But instead of a monolith looming before her with its broad verandah and tall white columns as she'd expected, she was shocked to find all that remained was an enormous pile of burnt rubble and the barren outlines of three tall chimneys reaching toward the darkness—in effect, her mother's funeral pyre, the fitting end of Turkle's infamous French family dynasty. This seemed just.

Profoundly shaken, she drew rein and dismounted, tying the horse to the sole standing hitching post. Stretching her back and legs, she clumsily rolled a cigarette in the dark, spilling much of the tobacco. She lit the cigarette, drew in smoke, and blew it out. As tired as she was, the smoke made her nauseous. Spitting away tobacco flecks, she sat down on the overturned horse trough to stare at the piles of burnt timber. And wept.

* * *

She must have cried herself to sleep, as she'd done most of the nights she'd lived in this house, her mother's house. Rising to her feet, it took some time before Devereau was able to take stock of the situation. The morning sun was peering above low clouds, providing ample light to make out details of the catastrophe around her. Then she had a thought.

The old miser had horded her many treasures in her bedroom suite: priceless paintings, statuary, and tapestries. Any one of the paintings would be worth more than Jenkins' stolen rifles she hoped to sell. Of course, she knew none of them could have survived the inferno that took the dry old structure.

Ah, but her mother also kept liquid assets locked in a large sealed chest beside her desk, neat stacks of paper money, stock certificates, and transferable bonds—which may have withstood the fire. If Devereau could retrieve the chest from under the rubble, she would have enough money to run away, to begin anew and forget Turkle. She'd take Jenkins' horse and leave him the McCorkle mount, a far finer animal, but evidence of a murder. That would be Jenkins' problem.

She climbed the rickety porch and entered where the front door had been, careful not to catch her boot on the missing planks, then began climbing over the piles of blackened rubble, slowly clawing her way, sometimes on all fours, to keep her balance. In the half-light she was stung by splinters and scratched her calf on jagged boards. It took some time to make her way to where the stairway began, with only the bottom steps not having collapsed. Then she turned left. The second floor had collapsed onto the first, but she estimated where the once-familiar hallway would have led to her mother's bedroom. She made out what she thought was the door frame and struggled forward, examining and discarding objects as she came across them: the burnt corner of a gilded frame, a scorched and shattered bust of a Greek god. Nothing of use or value. Then she worked her way to the infamous chest, lying open, its lid askew. Ashes.

Years of fire, rain, and even snow had done their worst. Reaching in, she a pulled out a few corner fragments of blackened paper, which fell apart in her hands. She tried to make out the print on a slightly legible, smudged, and waterlogged piece, holding the scrap up toward the sunlight, and moving the paper around until she could deduce what it was: the remains of a Confederate bond! That her mother, an astute investor, would have speculated on such dubious securities made little sense, except that she must have bought them at distressed prices, betting that, if Lincoln lost to the Northern peace candidate and the Confederacy survived, she'd harvest a windfall when the South paid off its war debts. Devereau crumbled the ashes in her palms and tossed them away.

—Wholly unlike you to lose money on such a wager, Mother. Confederate bonds! What could you have been thinking?

"That place been picked clean," she heard a voice shout from the drive. She turned to see a freedman guiding a mule toward the fields. "My daughter find a brass doorknob last year, but that's about all."

Devereau watched the man go on, laughing to himself. Of course, the French ruins would have been scavenged over the years. What did she expect?

She climbed back to the porch, brushed herself off, and mounted the horse. Then, instead of heading back to Jenkins', she decided to take a tour of the grounds. Spurring the horse, she continued for a hundred yards, passing the old quarters; but the aroma from a cookfire drifted into her nostrils, making her empty stomach churn and growl. She was famished.

She drew rein before a dilapidated cabin and breathed in the delicious smell, pondering what to do. It was possible whoever lived there, no doubt a freedman and his family, would recognize her. Word spreads quickly, and she didn't want it known she was back. But she was near starvation. She dismounted, tied the horse to a support beam, and went to the door.

How humiliating. She'd likely owned these people for much of their lives, and now she was about to beg them for a morsel of food. Unsure of what to say, she took a deep breath and tapped tentatively on the weathered wooden door.

"What you want?" a man said, cracking open the door.

"Just . . . just a bite of breakfast. I'm willing to pay. A dollar?"

"Sorry, we ain't got nothing to spare."

"Two dollars . . . Five?"

"Ain't got nothing but meal fried in bacon grease. This ain't the Grand Hotel in Lethe Creek."

"That's fine." Devereau reached in her pocket and counted out the money. She held it up to the crack.

The door swung open. "Come on in," the man said reluctantly.

Cautiously, Devereau entered the small, cramped space and handed the man the money, then removed her hat. Her host was in his early forties, skinny, and weary-looking. In the dimness, she saw two children sitting at the table, a boy of about twelve, a girl of ten. A round-faced woman in her late-thirties stood holding a pan, about to ladle a serving of watery gruel into the children's mismatched bowls. Two other settings were placed at the table.

The man pulled back one of the chairs and said, "Sit here." He looked toward the woman, who gave the man a scowl. But the man ignored her and took an empty chair for himself, cowering like a dog shying from a coming whipping. "Five dollar," he explained. "Fill his bowl first."

The woman callously plopped a portion of gruel into the bowl, then filled the children's before retreating to slam the pan down noisily onto the rusty stove. Devereau watched her closely, recognizing the deep scar running from her temple to her chin. This was one of the women she'd sold when the war began. The woman merely glared at Devereau, her arms crossed, her large brown eyes loaded with venom. Devereau remembered the poor woman pleading as the slave trader dragged her away, saw her reaching out in vain for her crying children—likely the very children sitting across from her.

Devereau ate the raw-tasting porridge, gulping nervously, hungrily, trying to ignore the woman and the children, their suspicious eyes fixed upon her. Her eyes scanned the spare cabin: a shredding mattress on the floor, with two palettes for the children; a cracked mirror atop a dilapidated dresser; a broken chifforobe set against the opposite wall.

She inhaled deeply, taking in the room, the thick smell of family intertwined with fried pork grease. A family nonetheless; she was envious.

The man sat across from her, staring as she ate, clearly recognizing her. "You back to stay, Mr. French?" he asked.

Startled, Devereau ceased shoveling the foul-tasting glob into her mouth. "No. I'm . . . I'm just stopping by to see the old homestead. I'll be on the road to Tennessee shortly."

"Um-hum," the man said, one eyebrow arched.

Devereau cleaned her bowl in silence, scraping the bottom with her spoon, avoiding their eyes. Finished, she looked up. "I thank you kindly," she said, rising. And without another word, she left, closing the door behind her. Her nerves were shot.

She'd hoped to tour the fields, but realized too many would see her. However, there was one final stop she was compelled to make. Yes, one tormented island in this tumultuous sea of despair.


Tripping over vines, Devereau made her way through the old French family graveyard, her pants gathering thistles and catching on thorns. She reached Louis Edward's grave and halted, then removed her hat and fell to her knees in the dirt.

Overwhelmed, tears poured down her cheeks. She was alone in the world, exactly as she'd spent every excruciating day of her miserable existence, just as she always would.

—I'm sorry I wasn't there for you. It was my fault . . . I'm so, so sorry . . .

Devereau clutched at her bursting heart, growing dizzy, sick to her stomach. She began shaking and threw up her breakfast onto the ground, vomiting until she was empty and continuing to heave when there was nothing left in her stomach. Finally, her body relented, and the spasms ceased. Weak and trembling, she tumbled onto her side in a ball, clutching her legs.

She wanted to die: right now, right here, beside Louis Edward. She breathed deeply, rolled over and attempted to stand, trying to stabilize herself, but she fell back, still lightheaded. She tried again, using her hands to push herself to her feet. Finally erect, she found herself able to walk. Still faint, she turned toward the horse: her pistol was in the saddle. She could end this agony with one bullet.

She stumbled through the graveyard, tripping over a headstone and nearly falling. When she got to the gate she came to a halt; a huge black man holding the reins of a bareback plow horse was standing between her and her horse—and her pistol.

"Too d-delicate to hold them s-slave v-vittles, ain't you, Mr. Fr-french?" the man said with a stutter. "Why you here?"

Shocked at the enormous apparition before her, Devereau's knees buckled momentarily. Did she know him?

Then a glimmer of recognition: this was Durk's man. But Durk couldn't have known she was headed to *FrenchAcres* and couldn't have gotten word here in time if he had. The family that fed her must have alerted the man. He was big enough to break her in half, and she feared he would do just that. But, studying him closely, she saw no malice in his face. Still, she couldn't be sure.

"What you doin' here, Mr. French?" Josh repeated.

"I . . . I just wanted to see the old place, what's left of it. I'm not stay-ing. I'd much appreciate you keeping our encounter to yourself," she cautioned, composing herself, "if you know what's good for you."

Josh examined the disheveled figure with a jaundiced eye, not be-lieving a word. "Don't worry, Mr. French. Ain't nobody gonna tell on you," he said.

She felt intimidated, afraid—and he was blocking the way. She couldn't simply order him aside; those days were gone. But if she could talk her way around him to get to her pistol, she could shoot him down or at least escape.

Josh glanced at her horse. "In town yesterday, ain't I seen that brown fleabag you riding? Why surely, it gots that scar on its flank. Who be-longs to that animal?"

"That horse is my concern. Listen, I just want to be on my way. Now let me pass."

Josh decided to take another tack. "You want to see the place? Come on, I'll show you around. Then you need to be gone." Devereau backed up, afraid Josh might lead her into a trap. "I'll make sure nobody harm you," Josh assured her. "You safe here with me." Without a word, he deftly mounted the plow horse and settled himself on its back.

When Devereau reached her horse, she hesitated, considering whether she needed to draw her pistol. Then, feeling less threatened, she mounted, and the two proceeded down the property's main road. Soon they passed fields once devoted exclusively to cotton to feed the looms of

Europe, now divided into small plots dedicated to corn, beans, and other subsistence crops. Where there were once overseers and drivers lording over slaves, whip in hand, now black men and women contentedly planted and plowed the rich soil. The world was turned upside-down.

As the two progressed down the dirt lane, people paused from their labors to gawk at them. Many appeared merely curious; some clenched their jaws in animosity. She placed her hand on her pistol.

"They look like they want to kill me."

"It's 'cause they remember you, Mr. French."

They passed a pasture. Sitting in the shade under a large oak were dozens of black children sharing books, a class of sorts, taught by a young black woman. This was, indeed, an odd sight.

—He's showing you this for a reason. Be on your guard.

—Thank you, Mother, I'm quite aware of that.

Further along, Josh broke the silence. "Listen, Mr. French, things ain't too safe for you 'round Turkle. You know you can't show your face. What you gonna do?"

"I'm not a bit afraid," she insisted. "I didn't do anything wrong, after all."

"Folks don't know you survived the war. You could keep on, and nobody the wiser."

"Don't be ridiculous."

"We could help you get to somewhere safe, maybe out of Miss'ippi. Start over fresh."

"I'm not going anywhere," she scoffed. "Mind how you talk to me."

The two drew rein. Josh turned his horse in order to face Devereau. "What would it cost for you to sign over *FrenchAcres* to Miss Antoinette? How much?"

"Don't waste my time. I have no intention of conceding my rights to my family estate."

Josh sighed. "Well, sir, I think you done seen enough. I'm willing to escort you off the property. After that, your safety is your own business. Understand?"

"Yes, I've certainly seen quite enough. Why don't you do that?"

\* \* \*

Devereau French, fugitive and former slave owner, dismounted onto the dirt trail, the layer of sticks and dry leaves crackling under the thud of her boots.

It was late-afternoon, with the sun still blazing, but she was spent and needed sleep. She led the horse to the secluded bank of a stream to let the animal drink. Then she collapsed onto her belly at the water's edge, drank thirstily, and washed her face. Struggling to her feet, she tied up the reins and nestled on her blanket under a large shade oak. Using her hat to block the sun's rays, she closed her eyes, expecting some much-need rest, when a voice intruded.

—*So you're going soft on the nigras.*

Devereau rolled onto her side and covered her ears.

—*Fool! They want your land. Half of them would wring your neck if they could get hold of you.*

—With good reason, Mother. With good reason.

—We treated them no worse than the other stock.

—Yes, actually we did treat them worse. Least you forget, Mother, it could have been us picking that cotton, us living in these shacks. Now would you let me sleep?

—*The big one recognized Jenkins' horse. Hurst will know where to find you.*

—I'll figure that out later.

—*You've got to keep Jenkins from going to town. Why don't you just get rid of him? Then the guns will be all yours.*

—I need someone who can move freely about for me. Now will you go away?

—*You're not giving up on your Hurst obsession, are you, fool? I can tell. You're still clinging to that romantic chimera.*

—Why should I give him up? He's mine, just like *FrenchAcres*.

—*The two of you nigra-lovers make a perfect match. You should have shot him when you had the chance.*

—I should have shot *her*, Mother. I should have shot the lovely Antoinette.

—*You will not touch her, do you hear? Now you've lost the Henry, clumsy fool. And Hurst can tie you to those rifles. You'd better start using your wooden head, child, if you want to survive this mess you've made.*

—Nobody can find where Jenkins hid those rifles, Mother. Nobody. They're way out in the swamp.

Devereau shut her eyes and rolled over. She'd show that witch. She'd get the guns sold and then have plenty of money in her pocket. As for Durk, knowing him, he'd talk himself right into her hands. Or else into a noose in the town square. And that would leave Antoinette at her mercy.

Comforted by these assumptions, she was able to fall into a deep sleep, troubled only by the usual nightmares.

# CHAPTER EIGHTEEN

# A TASTE OF VENGEANCE

His prey warn't no shifty squirrel or rabbit; he'd plugged more'n a hundred of them critters right through the heart back home using his old single-shot, smooth bore. No, this time his target was a limping man, his weapon a spanking new rifled Henry loaded for war. Why, at this distance, it'd be like spittin' in a well.

The boy peeked through the fence knothole, studied the bank door, then slipped back on his haunches. Looking about, he noted the sun over his shoulder—no problem—and the gap between the weathered boards just the right width. Over days, he'd meticulously prepared this hunting blind. From here, once he'd fired, he could melt away, quick and unobserved, through Turkle's back alleys and forested fringes. His hunting wiles would serve him well.

He made sure the safety was off and squatted on one knee. Then he froze, still as a stone, as if waiting for deer to show. He'd studied that door for two days and knew the time was near for Colonel Rutherford to make his midday stroll to his house for supper. The boy cradled the Henry under his arm and leaned in to watch.

Yep, there it was: the door swung out toward the street like always. Caleb lifted the Henry to his shoulder and took aim. The fat sheriff, Bake, stepped out first, a danger he hadn't counted on. But Stubbs stepped back to hold the door open. Then the colonel limped his way out onto the sidewalk, putting his full weight on his good leg. Caleb closed one eye, adjusted the rifle on his shoulder, steadied his aim, and squeezed the trigger. A loud blast rang out, echoing through the streets.

Perfect! The shot hit Rutherford square on the kneecap. The colonel shrieked in pain, grabbed his knee, and fell face-first onto the sidewalk.

Seeing the calamity he'd created, the boy experienced a moment of elation, celebrating his marksmanship and the Henry's accuracy; then he panicked. His eyes scanned the area for onlookers, but saw none. Relieved, he dropped the rifle and, crouching low, slithered away, his instinctive movements sure and fast. In no time, he was gone.

When he heard the shot, the sheriff hit the sidewalk with a thud, landing on his stomach, striking his elbow. He rubbed his arm and—when he saw no more shots were coming and was certain he hadn't been hit—crawled to the colonel, who was now writhing on the ground, howling in pain, pant leg blossoming dark at the knee. Bake removed his kerchief from his back pocket and hurriedly helped the colonel tie up the bloody wound.

Seeing the colonel fall, two bank clerks, plus a merchant and a passerby rushed to the fallen colonel and, together, propped him up into a sitting position. Then Bake rose to assess the area. "I think it come from that direction," he exclaimed, pointing toward Caleb's blind. "I'll gather my deputies, Colonel. We'll catch him!"

"Deputies? Fetch me the doctor, fool!" the colonel shouted. "Hurry! I'm shot."

"Yes, sir, right away, Colonel." Bake turned to a young bank employee. "Run get all my deputies. Run!" Then he took off at a rough approximation of a run, his body layers jiggling madly, leaving the colonel to grimace in agony. Breathing heavily, Bake ran to the building where the doctor lived, huffed and puffed his way up the flight of stairs, and burst into the office.

"At the bank, Doc . . ." he sputtered, bending over at the waist, and gasping for breath. "Somebody shot Colonel Rutherford! Come quick!"

Startled at being interrupted mid-meal, the doctor put down his fork, tossed his instruments into his bag, and rushed to Rutherford's side, Bake trailing as best he could. There, he worked furiously to staunch the bleeding while Rutherford howled in pain, screaming at him to hurry. Then the doctor paused to examine the damage. "It's bad, Colonel," the doctor said grimly, wiping his bloody hands on a towel. "Your kneecap's shattered. Just shattered."

"Can you save my leg, Doc?" Rutherford asked.

"I think so," the doctor replied.

"Will I be able to walk on it again?"

"I'll do what I can, Colonel."

Hearing this, Rutherford groaned. "I survive four dang years of war, and some fool cripples me coming out of my own bank. Find who did this, Bake. Reward, big reward. You hear me?"

"Yes, sir, Colonel."

Bake watched as the bank clerks, two deputies, and the passerby lifted the colonel and carried him to the doctor's office. Meanwhile, the other deputies spread out in all directions searching for the shooter. Shortly thereafter, one of them ran up carrying the Henry. "I found the gun, Bake. Back of that fence between them two stores."

Bake took the rifle and studied it closely, admiring the precise Northern manufactured machine of destruction, by far the best weapon he'd ever seen. Then it hit him: this was a Henry, probably from the stolen shipment the Union army had been searching for. They'd offered a substantial reward for the weapons' return, plus extra for the capture of the men responsible. He decided to keep this knowledge to himself—as well as the prized rifle.

"Show me where you found it, Dooley," he said, his thinking fixed upon that reward money bonanza—and the handsome rifle he now owned.

Durk looked up from the document he was filling out for Mrs. Reynolds, a townswoman whose husband had died the week before, as the sheriff stormed into Ahronson's carrying the Henry, venom pouring from his visage.

"Hurst," he growled, "where you been the last half hour?"

Taken aback, Durk replied, "Why right here, Bake, helping Mrs. Reynolds."

"I don't believe you."

"Ask Mrs. Reynolds." Mrs. Reynolds nodded affirmation. Durk

scanned the store. "Ask those two good women by the bonnets; they've been in the store for nearly an hour. Ask Ellen here."

Bake turned to the women in the store. All three nodded agreement. "You seen this rifle before, Hurst?" he demanded. "It's a Henry."

Durk studied the weapon. "Not since the war. Where'd you get it?"

"Somebody just shot Colonel Rutherford with this here gun. Busted his good knee all up. I'm gonna find the one who done it and arrest him."

"In the knee?" Durk mused, pausing to consider the irony—and the consequences. "Well, it wasn't me, Bake. I've been here all morning. You can search the place if you want."

Frustrated, the sheriff studied every face in the room, but seeing they were all women he knew and trusted, realized Hurst couldn't have been the one to fire the shot. "You coulda sent your nigra to shoot him."

"Bake," Durk tsk-tsked, "Josh hasn't been in town since yesterday. Besides, he couldn't hit the broad side of a barn at ten feet. No, you're barking up the wrong tree here."

"Shoot. Looks like I'm gonna be hunting some other nigra, most likely. That's a passel of snakes."

Durk saw a hurricane terrorizing blacks brewing in the sheriff's eyes and grew anxious. "Bake, Bake, Bake, you know very well you don't allow colored folks to bear no firearms, and none of them would have access to a rifle like that. Couldn't possibly afford it if they knew where to find such a fine weapon. No, sir, it was a white man fired that shot."

"Listen Hurst, you and your nigra hear things. I want to know where the man who fired that shot got that Henry, you hear me? Life in Turkle will be much easier for you if you can tip me off. Understand?"

"I'll keep my ear to the ground, Bake, and bring any news I find directly to you."

"Good."

"Listen, Bake, grab a plug of tobacco on your way out to relax you during your search. On the house, and God speed."

Bake merely harrumphed and made his way back to the street, pausing only to pocket the plug of chew on his way out.

Durk watched him go. *Blasted his good knee, eh? That was no coincidence.*

* * *

Caleb had to be called four times for supper that night, which wasn't like him, and when he showed he seemed preoccupied. Throughout the meal the boy spoke little and ate rapidly, not looking up. When he was finished, he placed his plate and cup in the sink and hurried off to his room, closing the door gently behind him. Antoinette and Durk eyed each other: he was hiding something.

After they'd eaten, Durk washed the dishes while Antoinette dried, then went to Caleb's room and tapped on his door. When Caleb grunted that he should enter, Durk went in and, closing the door behind him, sat on the edge of the bed. He had Caleb join him there so they could talk.

"How'd you spend the afternoon, Caleb?" Durk asked softly.

"Oh, nothing special, Durk. Playing. Mostly in the woods outside town."

"Did you know that Colonel Rutherford was shot this afternoon? In town?"

"He was?"

"Yes, on his way to dinner. You wouldn't know anything about that, would you?" Caleb's face reddened, and he lowered his eyes. "Now, Caleb, you and I never lied to each other, have we?"

"No, sir."

"Now tell me the truth, son. Did you shoot Colonel Rutherford?"

"It's his own fault; he got Lou's leg cut off! I had to do something, Durk. Lou saved my life."

Durk rose and paced, thinking, then turned to Caleb. "Caleb, when those soldiers killed your daddy, that was illegal, wasn't it?" Caleb nodded.

"Yes, sir."

"That was terrible, wasn't it?"

"Yes . . ."

"And when you shot the colonel, that was illegal, too, right? Caleb, do you want to be like those soldiers?"

"No, I don't, I don't. But Lou . . ."

"That was an ambush, right? That wasn't honorable, was it?"

"No, sir, but . . ."

"And how do you expect the colonel to respond? By forgiving his enemies? Do we want more dishonorable acts in the world, Caleb? Do we want the war to continue? Will that solve anything?"

"No, sir."

"We want to rid the world of those types of things, don't we?"

"Yeah, I guess. But I heard you tell Josh you were going to get even with Rutherford. And I know you still got it in your head. Tell me that ain't true. And these Black Codes y'all talkin' about all the time, ain't that dishonorable? Ain't the way some of these planters treat they coloreds working the fields dishonorable?"

Durk stopped pacing and sat beside the boy again. "Caleb, where'd you get the rifle?"

"I found it in the alley right around the corner," Caleb said haltingly.

"You stole it from that man that was here, didn't you?"

"Yeah, I did, Durk," Caleb said defiantly. "He was aiming that firearm at you and Antoinette. Darn right I took it from him."

"What was he doing when you took it?"

"Crying like a baby." Caleb looked up, but Durk was deep in thought with nothing to say.

"Now what can you do to make amends?" Durk asked rhetorically.

"Yeah, French was up here sniffin' around," Big Josh told Durk, relieved that the previous night's rain had cooled off *FrenchAcres*.

"That right?" Durk thought this over. "She must have ridden here straight from the store."

Durk and Josh paused to watch freedmen hammer, saw, and plane lumber, busily constructing their new community building, exuding a sense of pride and purpose.

"I'd sure like to know where French is holed up," Durk said.

"She was ridin' Jenkins' horse. I ask around; couple men know the animal."

"Jenkins? Lives off the old road to Lethe Creek? Not too far from *DarkHorse* land?"

"That's him, Durk. Dealer in arms and stolen stock during the war, folks says. Traded with the rebels and the Yankees both."

"She was in military custody. And I doubt she was freed on amnesty," Durk noted.

"Ha! Must have escaped. Ain't that something?"

"So, that would mean she's wanted by the army. That, plus the murder charge here, she's in a spot. I'd guess the freedmen are safe for now. So you talked with her?"

"I did; rode her all around the place so she could see what the war done. Dressed like a boy in his daddy's suit. I asked her if she'd be willing to sell the rights to *FrenchAcres*, but she won't. Why? You thinking of turning her in?"

"Not just yet, Josh. I've got bigger fish to fry."

"The colonel still? You ain't thinking 'bout doing nothing crazy, are you, Durk? I feel the same way 'bout Lou as you. But Rutherford's got killers working for him."

"I've got news for you, Josh: somebody shot Colonel Rutherford," Durk said, suppressing a grin. "Blew his good knee all apart."

"Durk, you didn't. . . ?"

"Of course not. Anyhow, that's not the way I settle things."

"You were pretty angry when the doc took Lou's leg," Josh noted. "I never seen you that mad. Mm-hmm. Looks like the sheriff and maybe the gun club, too, be paying us a visit. I better warn folks."

"I'm pretty sure I convinced the sheriff a white man did it, so there shouldn't be a lot of trouble blowing out this way. It'll be more like the random stings you get when somebody near you whacks a hornet's nest."

"You still thinking on taking the colonel to task for Lou, ain't you? Listen, he's gonna be angry enough to do anything. Anything."

Durk broke the branch he was fingering and tossed it aside. "That's what I'm hoping. The colonel ain't half as smart as he thinks he is, not by a long shot."

"It's not just him," Josh said, his face grim. "There's the fact that when most folks see a black man, they still see a slave. I can't stomach that."

Durk tried to cheer him up. "I received a letter from Illinois two days ago from our old friend Captain Turner. I wrote him a month ago, and his letter just came."

"Turner, the old abolitionist? What's he say?"

"Says folks in Washington ain't forgot us, even with President Lincoln gone. You don't read about these things in the *Turkle Tower*. The amendment to abolish slavery is being ratified. Yes, sir, putting it right in the Constitution. They're also working on an amendment that would make everyone born in this country, everyone, a citizen. They're even working on suffrage for your people."

"What about President Johnson? Can't he veto them?"

"Yes, but Turner thinks they have more than enough votes to override him, and there's nothing Johnson can do about it. We've just got be patient until the law takes hold."

"And until the powers that be down here begin to obey it. They already done seceded, so that ain't going to be quick. Or painless."

"No, Josh, it ain't going to be quick. But we've got to keep our boots moving ahead. Speaking of the election and the new state constitution, you ready for your trip to Jackson?"

"Ready to go. But while we're gone, don't do anything that will get you killed. Do that for me, friend."

"The way things are now could get any of us all killed, Josh. I've got to do something to change that or things will never get better for anyone."

The maidservant led Caleb into the colonel's bedroom. The dark chamber smelled of medicine and something foul, like desiccation, but out of politeness the boy resisted covering his nose. He stopped at the foot of the bed, facing the colonel, who was resting propped up on a stack of pillows wearing his bed robe, his knee wrapped in heavy bandages.

Colonel Rutherford waved the woman away, then studied the boy closely, his eyes narrowing. "Well, it's our little rebel: Hurst's boy, friend to his nigras. What do you want, boy?"

"I just come to see you, Colonel. To offer you any help you might be needing."

"You? Why would you want to help me?" Rutherford asked suspiciously.

"That was wrong what someone done to you."

"Yes, it was. But what does that have to do with you?"

"I just want to help. You fought in the war. Don't matter now which side you was on."

"You told me both your brothers died fighting for the Cause. And Yankees killed your daddy. Am I remembering right?"

"Yes, sir, that's true."

"So it damn well matters which side I fought on! It matters very much to me—and it should matter to you." The colonel paused. "What is Mr. Hurst up to, boy?"

"Durk? Why, he's busy with the store . . . and his lawyerin'."

"Yes," Rutherford said. "And busy with *FrenchAcres*? What is he doing with that?"

"Nothing. He don't go out there much."

"Yet he's out there today," Rutherford interjected, feeling smug about his intelligence on Hurst's movements. If the war had taught the colonel anything, it was the importance of intelligence. "So you want to work for me? I suppose whatever you overhear, you'll take right to Hurst. I'd be paying you to spy on me. Am I right, boy?"

"I ain't here for that, Colonel. Don't want no pay neither."

"But if I did pay you," Rutherford said suggestively, "you could let the old Colonel know what Hurst and his friends are up to?"

"I ain't here for that neither, Colonel. I'm just here to help you till you can get around good. I ain't lookin' to keep an eye on nobody for nobody."

Rutherford thought the situation over, then set a piece of paper and a writing board on his lap. He dipped a pen into the well on his bedside table and wrote. After he signed the note, he folded it to conceal what he'd written. "All right, boy, I'll try you out. Take this note to Captain Hurst."

"You're sending a message to Durk?"

"I am. But don't read it. Promise?"

"I ain't no spy."

"Good," Colonel Rutherford said. "Return tomorrow, mid-morning, boy. I may have other duties for you."

"My name's Caleb, Colonel."

"I understand. All right, Private Caleb."

"I ain't joining no army neither, Colonel. Just call me Caleb, not private or nothing. I ain't lookin' for no cause."

"Ha! The Cause isn't lost by a long shot, Caleb," the Colonel said, handing the boy the note.

As the evening shadows descended upon the street outside, Durk closed the store and joined Antoinette. He paused a moment to admire the quietness of dusk, the town's tranquility.

At that moment, a lone rider thundered up outside and drew rein. In an instant, the man hurled a large rock through the front window and galloped away, shouting wildly.

Durk ran to pick up the stone, and Antoinette followed. They read the note that was attached:

*Mrs. Antoinette French*

*We have been informed that you are 'lowing nigras to squat about your land. So, madam, your stable is burnt. If this is not sufficient warning, we will burn everything on your place. If that don't break it up, we will break your neck. If that don't break it up, we will shoot the nigras. Beware, madam, before it is too late, or you will be waited on by A COMMITTEE.*

Durk stuffed the paper into his pocket. "Look," he said, "I don't think you should travel to Jackson. It's not going to be safe for you."

"No, Durk, that note is just from a young tough blowing off steam, just one man. Whose imprint is on it? Nobody's. I'm going. Let's not even discuss Jackson."

Durk knew not to bring up the subject again.

# Chapter Nineteen

# CRUSADE

Despite the cool night outside, even with the windows flung open the jam-packed church was stifling. Tonight, however, there were to be no hymns sung, no sermons preached as everyone listened intently to Big Josh on the podium.

"Folks, don't come to town tomorrow to celebrate," Josh warned. "Stay away. This march to Jackson ain't no traveling circus. We don't want no crowd gatherin' to alarm the townsfolk. If you giving somebody a ride into town, just say your goodbye and go straight back home. If you don't have no reason to be in town, don't come. If you live in town, stay indoors or at work till we gone."

He looked at the row of dignitaries seated behind him on the dais: the preacher, a tall, thin man with iron-gray hair; a number of elders; and Antoinette. "Any of you got questions?" Josh queried.

One young firebrand leapt to his feet. "You taking a petition to the same folks who ran the slave government! You telling us any of them going to listen to y'all?"

"So, what you want us to do, Leon?" Josh retorted. "Give up? Not try nothing? Listen, friend, coming up from slavery is going to take a long time, a long time. Everybody know that. But we' planting seeds now. Many of them seeds going to die; the whole field going to lie barren some years. But everywhere ain't like Turkle; even here, there are good folks, white folks, don't like what's going on."

"But those folks is scared like we' scared," young Leon countered. "This new constitution ain't gonna be nothing. The white folks gonna have they election; we won't even get to vote. Then they gonna pass Black Codes for the whole state is what they gonna do."

"Maybe so," Josh conceded. "But should we let them go ahead, thinking we don't care? That they can do what they want to us without a peep? Or do we want to remind them that the country's founders said 'all men are created equal'? Remind them that we are men, just like they is men? You right, Leon, it's gonna be hard. Take a long time, too. But it's important they know what we expect from this country, our country."

A wizened old man rose, snow white hair crowning his wrinkled face, and spoke in an even voice. "People say I'm over seventy year. I been sold more times than I can recall, some men cruel to me and some treat me right. But nobody own me, not no more. I'll walk all the way, but I'm going to Jackson."

At that moment, the solemn crowd packing the pews stood and broke into loud shouts, amens, and hosannas. One woman with a rich contralto voice broke into "March Down to Jordon." A deep baritone joined her, and soon the room was filled with lilting voices. "You gotta march down / You gotta march down to Jordon / Hallelujah . . ." they chimed.

Pleased, Big Josh smiled and held up his hand. After a while, the people got his message and the church fell silent. But Leon had not finished his admonition. "They gonna shoot y'all down is what they gonna do."

The old man stood his ground. "They shoot us every day, young sport," he said. "Or hang us by the neck or beat us to death. They gonna kill us all if this keep up. It got to stop and ain't no other way. No, this sholy ain't no time to be scared. Why'n't you come with us, Leon? You afraid?" Hearing this, Leon got a sour look on his face, but had no reply. The young man sat down, followed by the old man.

Just then, a shot fired outside, and instinctively the crowd ducked. In moments, the sounds of hooves and pistol shots thundered up to the front door. People panicked, their eyes darting about, their bodies tensing to flee. More shots were fired. Then a half-dozen rowdies on horseback charged into the church firing pistols into the ceiling, hollering and catcalling. Pandemonium! People screamed and scrambled to dive through the windows; a confused crush of bodies collided at the back door. In the mayhem, men and women stumbled and fell over one another, rising or being helped to their feet by their neighbors.

Big Josh rushed to Antoinette's side and, shielding her with his body, guided her from the podium to the back door. There, he attempted to establish some sort of order out of the chaos, helping the elderly and those who were injured. After everyone had passed through safely, Antoinette and Josh made it through the door.

Outside, people scattered in all directions, and, in short order, the church grounds were as clear as a newly planted field. Josh and Antoinette took cover behind a large oak in the back and looked on as the rowdies left the church, laughing and cursing.

"That d-dirty Rutherford," Josh stammered bitterly. "Trying to scare folks from going."

"I wonder how many will show after this?" Antoinette mused.

The delegation gathered at the Turkle courthouse, euphoric and determined. Josh had spent the night worrying the raid on the church would frighten people away, but was pleased to discover it had had the opposite effect. As the last folks straggled in from the countryside, he noticed among them a number who'd previously refused to join the crusade, even scrappy young Leon. In fact, the crowd had swelled so much, Big Josh feared they might run short of passes needed to protect everyone against roadside stops.

The sky promised an overcast day, which would keep the heat down. Folks were dressed for the event in their Sunday best, with their everyday clothing stuffed in satchels or tied up in handkerchiefs. The elderly preacher was seated in the front wagon beside its owner, a farmer from *FrenchAcres*. Most of the pilgrims were black, but they were joined by two mounted white planters and a few townsfolk, men who were ready for a new society to be forged upon the ruins of the old. The hodgepodge included wagons, mules, plow horses, even a large group on foot willing to endure the long trek just to be part of the endeavor.

The smattering of well-wishers and family members in attendance were heeding Josh's caution to keep the send-off orderly. As the courthouse clock approached the appointed hour of eight-thirty, Durk strode across the town square leading a saddled Contrition and walked directly up to where Antoinette sat perched on a wagon seat beside the owner, a black man named Noble.

"We agreed you wouldn't be coming," a surprised Josh said to Durk.

"I'm not, Josh. I thought Antoinette should ride Contrition. If y'all run into any troublemakers, they'll respect a woman on that horse more than they would on a buckboard. Remember, the documents say these folks are contracted to her. Might help y'all out of a tight."

"No, I'm fine here beside Noble," Antoinette objected.

"Durk's right, Antoinette," Josh conceded. "It'd be safer for everyone. You, too."

"I know why you're doing this, Durk, and I appreciate it," Antoinette replied. "You think I'd be able to escape on your horse. But I have no intention of running out on these people, of abandoning their hopes and dreams. If they shoot me down, then I'll have done all that I can. There's no point arguing."

Then Durk stepped back and watched as the ungainly convoy departed. As agreed upon in advance, they sang no hymns, bearing only a dignified determination. They knew the odds against their ultimate aims; yet they ventured forth. As they disappeared down the street, Durk's eyes lingered on Antoinette and Josh, wondering if he would ever see them again.

The afternoon was proving long and lonely, with Durk's every thought swamped by torrents of worry. He grudgingly finished tallying the ledgers, then worked on a stack of legal documents he'd kept putting off. After a few minutes he pushed them aside, leaned back in his chair, and looked around the store. Ellen was waiting on one elderly townswoman; other than that, quiet.

His ears picked up faint hoof beats in the distance. He pushed his chair back and strode to the front door. The street was empty, with only a single wagon passing and a pair of women drifting under parasols raised against the midday sun. There was barely enough breeze to blow up the dust. Soon the pounding of a goodly number of hooves grew louder, fast approaching the town square. His first thought was the colonel's people were coming for him. The day before, Caleb had brought him a note from Colonel Rutherford bearing an unspecified but implied threat. Then a worse thought: were Rutherford's men chasing after the delegation to Jackson? He grew frantic.

Then relief: riding toward him was an orderly contingent of three dozen mounted soldiers in blue uniforms led by a brevet general. People filtered out of businesses, shops, and homes to watch.

As the soldiers passed, Durk ran inside, shouting to Ellen, "Close the store. We've got to finish these documents right now." He sat down and began filling out papers at a furious pace, while Ellen turned the sign to CLOSED and joined him.

Pausing, Durk instructed Ellen, "I want you to go out to Mr. Clifton's home. Tell him a general of the U.S. Army has arrived in Turkle. There will be Freedmen's Bureau hearings, and, as the head of the town council, he must be present to witness them. You're an important member of the church, Ellen; he'll listen to you. Tell him I'd like to chat with him after he's witnessed the proceedings."

Ellen was taken aback. "But . . . but how will I get out there, Durk?" she stuttered. "I don't have no horse and can't ride nohow."

"Take money from the box and rent a wagon. There's always someone for hire at the courthouse. Hurry, let's get these papers filled out."

This chore gave Durk time to think over his predicament. He knew the law: he'd won a big case in an army trial in St. Louis and, subsequently, studied law as his wartime duties permitted. If the local attorneys were his only obstacles, he believed he could figure out a way to win both the *DarkHorse* and *FrenchAcres* suits in court.

But casting a shadow over his efforts loomed Rutherford, who distained the law. Durk might win rulings from Judge Fairbanks, but still lose everything to foul play. This resort to violence pervaded the South. Only two days earlier in Lethe Creek a black man had been shot and wounded for refusing to tip his hat to a white man. No, if Durk were to succeed, he'd first have to eliminate the colonel from the equation, then take his final battle to court. A daunting prospect, but his only recourse.

When they'd finished the paperwork, Durk straightened the stack of papers and shoved them into a leather satchel, throwing its straps across his shoulder. Then he disappeared down the street, heading for the stable. A plan was beginning to form in his mind, and suddenly things didn't feel hopeless anymore.

\* \* \*

Durk found the troops bivouacked in a field beside a stream three miles outside town. The soldiers were leisurely finishing their midday meal, shoveling dirt on dying pit fires, and stretching their legs. Durk located the general seated at a table under a shade tree and rode directly toward him, but an aide intercepted. Durk drew rein.

"Durksen Hurst, former captain of the Ninth MSM Colored Cavalry, to see the general."

"Wait here, Captain," the aide said. "I'll ask."

"Who is the general, soldier?"

"Army Brevet General Stevens, commander of this military district," the aide replied. Then he went back to confer with his superior. Shortly thereafter, he returned with instructions to show Durk to the general's table.

Durk dismounted and tied Contrition to a sapling, grabbing his satchel. General Stevens rose to offer his hand. "Well, Captain Hurst, I received your telegram. I've been looking forward to meeting you. Sorry I took so long, but since the war ended, everything's been quite hectic." The two clasped hands firmly, then the general gestured to the spare chair, which Durk took. "It's good to see a friendly face."

"Welcome to Turkle, General. I can't tell you how much I appreciate your coming. Your duties cannot be easy these days."

"Hardly. I am forced to conclude that my command is the most turbulent and disloyal of any in Mississippi," the general noted. "The treatment of our uniform since I came here has been abominable: five of my men killed, a number wounded, and many fired upon. Without exception, no effort has been made by the citizens to bring the offenders to justice or to assist the military authorities. On the other hand, local ruffians and outlaws receive the kindest attention from the residents."

"Just like in Missouri," Durk noted.

"President Johnson has not made our task any easier. After Appomattox," the general continued, "they reinstated the state's civil officers without distinction. The men who'd held these offices during the rebellion were generally the most radical. By a stroke of the pen, the political structure was put into the hands of the most objectionable persons to our government. Consequently, the moderate and well-wishing became powerless."

The general paused, rubbing his chin in thought. "In your telegram, you referenced violence and murder against Negros. That is no surprise to me."

"I know you have yet to establish yourself, sir," Durk said, removing documents from his satchel, "so I have taken the liberty of preparing what you'll need."

"At great personal risk, no doubt," the general commented, perusing the paper.

Durk handed him the top two papers. "This is a list of the freedmen who've issued complaints and those who have injured them. Of course, many of the plaintiffs will be unable to attend a hearing without the army's protection—for obvious reasons." He handed the general other papers. "These are the freedmen who will need an escort to plead their case and the location of their transgressors. The relevant writs signed by Judge Fairbanks are attached to each. You'll have to send troopers to round the defendants up."

"Naturally. These proceedings will take some time, Captain. I'll have to send several men out on each."

"I understand. Thank you, General. I'm at your disposal to advise and assist you throughout your stay."

"I am grateful, sir." The General sighed. "All right, Captain, any other business for me?"

"Yes, sir," Durk said. "One more thing. Those stolen Union Henry rifles: you're aware of them?"

"Yes, of course. The weapons pose quite a danger to this command and to the stability of this region. Their possession by the wrong interests could spark an insurrection that would become most bloody. Most bloody. Go on."

"I believe I know who has them."

"Well, tell me," the general said, growing animated. "I will have those responsible arrested immediately."

"That's the problem, General. I know who has them, but I don't know *where* they're hidden. There's a lot of swamp around here. I do have a thought, though."

"Yes, let me hear it."

"Perhaps I can arrange to have the weapons surface of their own volition. At the same time, maybe we can kill two birds with one stone . . ."

Caleb ran into the bank, stopped to brush back his shock of hair, then continued to the colonel's office in the back. He knocked at the door and waited until given permission to enter. Once his eyes adjusted to the dark room, he saw Colonel Rutherford propped up in his chair, wearing his usual three-piece business suit, both legs resting on a cushioned bench under the desk.

The colonel took his watch from his vest pocket and noted the time.

"Well, Caleb, that was a fast delivery. Listen, son, I forgot: did I write in that note what time my friend should come to dinner?"

"Don't know, Colonel. You tole me not to read your messages."

The colonel leaned back in his chair, rubbing his legs. Standing there, Caleb surveyed the room's wall-to-wall gun collection and its bullet- and shell-riddled Confederate and Turkle battle flags. His eyes rested on an antique pistol with an intricately sculpted stock and chiseled barrel. He lost himself, longingly admiring the precious firearm.

The colonel's voice broke his reverie. "That gun belonged to an English nobleman over fifty years ago. It's a beauty, isn't it, boy?"

"Yes," Caleb answered, slightly embarrassed. "It sure is, Colonel."

"Can you shoot a rifle, boy? Did your daddy show you how?"

Caleb stared at the floor, uncertain how to respond. Then he announced proudly, "Pa gave me a musket for my sixth birthday, Colonel. He taught me to hunt."

Colonel Rutherford intently studied Caleb's face. "You a marksman?" he asked.

Caleb paused. "I shot squirrels and rabbits. That's all."

"Squirrels and rabbits . . ." the colonel mused. "Do you have a rifle of your own?"

"No, sir. Durk won't let me. He don't allow no guns at home."

"Is that so? Listen, son, I want to pay you a dollar a week for the work you're doing for me."

"No, sir. Durk ordered me not to take no pay from you."

"I'll tell you what, Caleb. Keep up what you're doing, and I'll give you a reward. I'll give you a good rifle for your service. Now that's not a payment, you see, that's simply a mark of my gratitude for the dependable contribution you're making to my efforts. How's that sound?"

"That's very kind, Colonel," Caleb answered. "But Durk won't let me have no gun."

Rutherford thought this over. "Well, I must accept that. Now look, son, I'm giving you a promotion. Can you ride a horse?"

"Dang right I can ride."

The Colonel handed him a message and a note. "I have a letter for Mr. Clifton that needs to get out to his plantation right away. Give this note to Walker in the stable. He'll saddle up Nancy for you. Old Nancy got me through some tights during the war, but these days I ride Rebel. See? Anyway, ride Old Nancy out to Clifton's fast as you can. Let's see how good a horseman you are. Can you do that for me?"

"Yes, sir, Colonel!" Caleb blurted and hurried for the door. "I'll be back before the ink dries on the paper."

"Oh, Caleb," Rutherford called after him. Caleb stopped and turned around. "In the future, you won't need a note from me. Just tell Walker, and he'll saddle Nancy for you. Understand?"

"Yes, sir!" And Caleb was gone, slamming the door behind him.

# CHAPTER TWENTY
# INTO A HEAVY STORM

## ROAD TO JACKSON, MISSISSIPPI

The sun blazed directly overhead, slowing the marchers' long slog to Jackson. When the large contingent of wagons, mules, and those on foot came upon a field of purple wildflowers bordered by shade trees, all agreed to stop for the midday meal. Those who wanted to could also change from their good Sunday clothing to something more appropriate. At Josh's signal, the ragged line broke, with folks dismounting and tying up their animals where they could water and graze. Big Josh gave Antoinette a hand down from the wagon, and the pair paused in the road to plan their next steps.

Suddenly, shots rang out from where they'd just passed. Then, within moments, shots came from directly ahead, as if responding to a signal. Everyone froze as riders galloped directly toward the crowd from both directions, firing pistols in the air.

Just when it looked like the riders were about to crash headlong into the crowd, they began to circle them. But the marchers stood their ground, instinctively drawing together. As the interlopers continued their noisy circular jaunt, they soon realized that the group would not be cowed, that their hollering and shooting were simply a vain exercise. Finally, the rowdies' leader drew rein and lowered his pistol. The others did likewise and gathered at his side, stuffing their guns into their belts, looking for guidance at this unexpected turn-of-events.

The leader rode directly up to confront Antoinette, ignoring Josh. "What do you think you're doing here with all these nigras, woman?" he asked.

"As you see," Antoinette replied calmly, holding his gaze.

Sitting his horse, the leader removed his hat and wiped his brow. "Just who are these people? They don't belong out here. Where you headed?"

"These people are contracted to me, each and every one of them. What I'm doing and where I'm going is my business."

"You better turn back," the man ordered.

"Listen, Mister, if you don't disburse this minute, I'll have you all arrested for disturbing the peace and interfering with legitimate commerce. Now go on, skedaddle."

Frustrated, the leader exchanged glances with the others, then abruptly turned his horse around.

"You ain't heard the last of us," he warned and spurred his horse. The other horsemen followed. Watching them ride off, the marchers broke into nervous laughter, which was replaced by a quiet apprehension.

## TURKLE, MISSISSIPPI

The afternoon session was set to begin. The steamy, crowded courtroom buzzed like a violated beehive, having been commandeered by General Stevens for the hearings. The seats were packed with white faces, including the defendants, many of them prosperous landowners who were furious at having been summoned by Federal subpoenas delivered to their homes by the occupying U.S. Army. These were complaints from their own black workers whom the landowners were accustomed to intimidating into servility over decades of enslavement. They were stunned that these people failed to be content with their lot and feared the old, orderly life of the town would never return. Around them sat their lawyers, families, curious onlookers, and the editor of the *Turkle Tower*.

Standing jammed together at the back of the room were the black plaintiffs waiting to be called forth. Three deputies bearing loaded rifles, not pleased with this duty, watched their black charges closely, as if they were criminals and the defendant's innocent victims needing protection. A rifle butt wasn't a whip or buggy trace, but it would have to do.

James Clifton, president of the town council, accompanied by his servant, sat in the center of the otherwise unoccupied jury box. General Stevens was to be judge and jury, so Clifton had appropriated this area for himself to observe the proceedings. The sheriff, fussing with his going-to-funeral suit, which he had outgrown twenty pounds ago, took his seat at the foot of the judge's bench, relaying orders through deputies.

Sitting at the plaintiff's table, Durk kept turning his head to snatch a glimpse of the courtroom entrance. He couldn't help it. Long Lou was on the docket with a complaint against Colonel Rutherford and Sheriff Stubbs. Durk hoped this lawsuit—and the criminal acts it would reveal—would bring down the corrupt artifice Rutherford and Stubbs had erected on the backs of black laborers. Or at least enrage the irascible Rutherford enough to bait him into a trap Durk was planning for him.

Durk had been anxiously awaiting this confrontation since the hearings were announced; but now his chances of attaining justice—and revenge—seemed to be draining away. That morning Lou had awakened with a high fever and chills, as on so many mornings since his leg was amputated, and couldn't get out of bed. Ellen had stayed behind to nurse him in hopes of getting him to the hearings, but it hadn't looked promising when Durk left the store. Further, Colonel Rutherford hadn't shown up to answer his subpoena.

The clattering of voices and impatient foot shuffling quieted as General Stevens entered from the side door, accompanied by his uniformed aide and Douglas Anderson, a lawyer from Minnesota, the civilian head of the Freedmen's Bureau. As in the morning session, General Stevens stepped up to the judge's chair, with Mr. Anderson and the aide taking seats flanking him. The general banged the gavel twice to begin.

Durk had seldom felt so pressured, and so powerless. The fate of all these people, brave enough to file complaints, had fallen on his shoulders like an avalanche. And with Antoinette and Josh on the road to Jackson, he had no one to advise him, to calm him when his fears and doubts raged, to place an arm around his shoulders and offer him encouragement. It was up to him and him alone.

"Mr. Hurst," General Stevens said, drawing Durk's attention. "Please present your next plaintiff."

"The next complaint is from Miss Missy Collins, a field hand, against her employer, Mr. J.J. Parker, owner of Parker Manor, a plantation of about two hundred acres," Durk announced. "On August fourth, Miss

Collins walked off Mr. Parker's place to file a complaint with the Freedmen's Bureau about Mr. Parker's physical violence against her. But Mr. Parker overtook her before she could reach my office. He wrapped one end of a rope around her neck and tied the other around the neck of his mule. Then he proceeded to drag her more than two miles back to his plantation. When Mr. Parker was away on business later that week, Miss Collins ran away to meet with me."

Hearing this, those in the back of the courtroom burst into angry shouts. General Stevens slammed down his gavel repeatedly until the room quieted. Mr. Anderson and the general merely glanced at each other, no consultation needed.

General Stevens studied the older, unshaven planter sitting at the defense table. Then he turned to the young woman sitting beside Durk, staring at her lap, her hands fiddling with her apron strings.

"Is that what happened to you, Miss?" General Stevens asked her.

"Yes, sir," she replied slyly. "Mr. Parker drag me till I was dead. Then he woke me and drag me some more. Three times he done it . . ."

"Let us see your neck," the general requested.

"Yes, sir," Miss Collins said and pulled down her collar to show red and purple welts, bruises, and scabs caused by the rope.

"Your injuries are noted for the record, Miss Collins. Now, Mr. Parker," the general said to the defendant, "do you have any response?"

"Nobody can tell me how to treat my nigras," Mr. Parker shot back defiantly. "Especially not no Yankee. I' been running my place for near forty years. What do you know about them people? A man's got to show them kind who's boss. Understand?"

"Mr. Parker, whether you accept it or not, Miss Collins is a freedwoman, whom you assaulted in the most brutal manner. I don't believe this kind of treatment was acceptable even before the war, but it certainly isn't now.

"I think I've heard enough to make a ruling," the general continued, clearly disgusted. "In any employer-employee contract, the law assumes that both parties will adhere to minimum standards of decency. In this case, the employer clearly has not. Miss Collins was pursing her right to file a complaint to the Freedmen's Bureau, and Mr. Parker intervened to prevent her from doing so. Therefore, the bench rules that the plaintiff's contract tying her to the defendant's plantation is no longer valid. Miss Collins, you can be released from your contract if you so desire. Do you still want to work for Mr. Parker?"

"No, sir, I don't want nothing to do with him; I don't never want to see that man again."

"Do you have somewhere to go?" the general asked.

"Yes, sir. I can stay with my sister and her husband out to *FrenchAcres.* They put me up."

"All right, you are now free to move in with your sister. Further, defendant will pay plaintiff back wages that have been withheld from her on a *pro rata* basis for the three months she labored at his plantation, minus what he has already paid her for that period. Mr. Parker, how much have you paid her so far?"

"Paid her? General, we pay once't a year, after harvest. That's standard for them nigra contracts."

"Regardless," the general said, figuring the numbers, "you owe Miss Collins a total of . . . of sixty dollars for the three months she's worked for you. Additionally, due to the mistreatment she's obviously suffered, I am granting her damages of . . . of sixty dollars more added to her wages.

"Mr. Parker, you will pay one hundred twenty dollars to Miss Collins. I also am filing a complaint with the local sheriff here for your assault upon this woman, even though I assume my referral will go nowhere."

"A hundred twenty dollars!" the planter shouted. "She ain't worth more than ten. And what about the money I spent on her living expenses, to house, feed, and clothe her. I deduct that from they wages when I pay them after harvest. It's in the contract."

The general looked over the rags the plaintiff was wearing. "Mr. Parker, I have no doubt you spared no expense shipping in the finest provisions for Miss Collins, and she's likely been sleeping on a feather bed in the big house. Nevertheless, I am invalidating that part of the contract as well. The one-twenty still stands with no deductions."

Stunned and fuming, the planter stared at the general. "You ain't heard the last of this. You ain't heard the last!"

"I'm sure that's true, sir. I thank you for the warning." The general turned to his aide. "Draw up a writ for assault against Mr. Parker and give it to the sheriff. He can burn it along with the others we've given him."

"No, sir," the sheriff said, a sly grin on his face. "I'm gonna do my duty with all these nigra complaints."

"I'm sure that's the case," the general grumbled.

While J.J. Parker was counting out crumpled bills and slamming them one by one onto Durk's table, Durk glanced up to examine the face of James Clifton in the jury box. During the proceedings, Clifton's expression had grown increasingly grim and, following Missy Collins' testimony, now evidenced a dark shame. Durk took this as a good sign.

The general's voice caught Durk's attention. "All right, Mr. Hurst. Next case, please." Just at that moment there was a commotion at the door. Turning to see the cause of the disturbance, a smile crept across Durk's face: Long Lou was inching toward him supported on crutches with the help of Ellen Purely. Everyone watched as Lou struggled forward, one painful step at a time, his hollow face drawn in a grimace. The sight was excruciating, but Durk's spirit lifted: at least he'd have his shot at Rutherford and Stubbs. When Lou reached the front of the courtroom, Durk seated him, while Ellen retreated to find a place to stand in the gallery.

"The next complaint is against Colonel J.B. Rutherford and Sheriff Bake Stubbs," Durk declared, "but I don't see the colonel in the courtroom."

The general's aide stepped forward. "Are Colonel Rutherford and Mr. Stubbs in the courtroom?"

The sheriff worked himself to his feet. "I'm here. The colonel ain't."

The general's eyes narrowed on Bake. "Colonel Rutherford was subpoenaed to be here, Sheriff. Send one of your men to fetch him."

"Well, sir, the colonel is doing poorly," Bake replied.

"Poorly or not, send someone to get him or I will place him under Federal arrest," the general threatened.

Bake threw up his hands. "I will, but he ain't gonna be happy about it." He whispered urgently to his deputy, and the man ran from the courthouse.

Rather than wait for the colonel, the general began calling other cases, both dire and of less consequence. In some, the general referred writs to the sheriff, who by now had a whole collection of them stacked on the table at his side; but no one had illusions about them being enforced. One man testified that his employer had knocked him down. The planter defended himself by claiming "the Negro had been insolent, calling him 'Mister Williams' instead of 'Master.'" Another complained his employer had whipped him for going off the plantation to see his cousin, and threatened to whip him again when he filed the complaint. Another had been sick with fever for two months and was not yet recovered when his employer came to his cabin and beat him severely with a buggy trace for not being at work. The man lifted his shirt to show the court the scars on his back. And so it went.

Finally, Colonel Rutherford appeared at the door, supported by a crutch, being aided by two of his gun club ruffians. In defiance of the proceedings, he wore his full-dress Confederate military uniform, sporting gold epaulettes and a medal pinned to his chest, his officer hat worn at a jaunty angle. The ungainly trio made its way to the defense table and seated the colonel, while a third gun club member placed a stool under his legs. Their lawyer, Wayne Dunham, sat beside him.

Relieved, Durk quickly reviewed his presentation. "The next complaint is from Mr. Lou Jones and others working involuntarily at the Rutherford Plantation versus Colonel J.B. Rutherford and Sheriff Bake Stubbs. It entails both property claims—and crimes of murder."

# CHAPTER TWENTY-ONE

# LONG LOU'S TALE

"Murder?" General Stevens puzzled. "This is not a criminal court, Mr. Hurst." He thought over his options. "But let's see what this is about. And you are Colonel Rutherford?"

"I am. You should recognize this uniform, sir," Rutherford shot back. "It made you boys run more times than I can count."

The general's aide interjected, "Please remove your hat in the courtroom, Colonel."

"I will do no such thing," Rutherford replied, straightening his back. "Mind your own damn business."

"Let's go on," the general said, brushing off the controversy. "Mr. Hurst, please state the complaint."

Durk stood to speak and indicated Lou seated beside him. "This is Mr. Lou Jones, General. He served under me during the war and has been contracted with me since we were discharged. He is a resident of Turkle, originally married with children in Carolina. Because he was sold away, Mr. Jones hasn't seen his family in seven years. Therefore, as a reward for his bravery, diligence, and honesty, I gave Lou permission to travel to Carolina. As his employer, I provided him with a road pass and a copy of his contract.

"While Lou was on the road, on foot, Sheriff Stubbs' deputies arrested him without cause. Lou had a pass and a labor contract, but they simply tore them up. They justified this arrest citing the vagrancy clause in Turkle's Black Codes, which I maintain is merely a cover for what is really taking place."

"I am familiar with the practice," the general acknowledged. "Turkle isn't the only place these types of law are being used to supply field labor. Go on."

"Yes, but what Colonel Rutherford and Sheriff Stubbs are doing is worse, far worse. Colonel Rutherford has contracted with Sheriff Stubbs to supply him with field labor at a set price per head, without any hope of redemption for the freedman. It is a form of perpetual slavery in another guise."

"Is this true, Sheriff Stubbs?" the general asked.

"Y-yes, I-I guess so," the sheriff demurred, glancing at Colonel Rutherford for guidance. "It's a legal agreement. Everything open and above board, sir."

"Is this true, Colonel?" the general asked.

"Yes. It was strictly business, which is my right."

"Go on, Mr. Hurst," the general said.

"Thank you, General," Durk continued. "Colonel Rutherford works the men supplied by Sheriff Stubbs seven days a week from before dawn until after dark, provides them with inadequate rations, and quarters them in crowded conditions worse than animal pens. General, many of these men have been worked literally to death. Besides starvation and exhaustion, many die from untreated disease. They are not given a chance to see a doctor. When they die, the colonel simply has them buried in large pits. Under guarantees in the contract between these two men, the laborers who perish are replaced by the sheriff without charge."

"Is that how it works, Sheriff?" the general asked. "Is your contract written so that you must replace any Negro laborers who die on the job?"

"Yes, sir, I honor the contract," the sheriff said defensively. "I don't charge the colonel another penny."

"Continue, Mr. Hurst," the general said.

Durk cleared his throat. "Under this arrangement, which has been quite lucrative for the sheriff, the colonel has no incentive to treat his laborers humanely. It was under these conditions that Mr. Jones found himself after being kidnapped by the sheriff's men. Please note that he had two good legs when he was taken to the Rutherford Plantation."

The general couldn't speak for a moment. "Mr. Jones, these are serious charges. Let us hear what you have to say. You needn't try to stand." Durk took his seat.

Wayne Dunham, the colonel's lawyer, sprung to his feet. "General, here in Turkle, a Negro cannot testify against a white man. That's the law."

"I will remind you that this hearing is being held under the authority of the United States Congress, Mr. Dunham. The Freedmen's Bureau is represented by Mr. Douglas Anderson, and I represent the U.S. Army. We will, indeed, hear Mr. Jones' testimony."

Rutherford slammed his fist on the table. "Putting a nigra on equal footing as a white man violates God's law and natural law," he shouted. "Those are laws Washington cannot repeal!"

"In that case, Colonel, I suggest your lawyer file a formal appeal with God; I'm sure he'll be sympathetic to your predicament. As for our purposes, we will gather all the pertinent facts. Now, Mr. Jones, I am most interested in your claim of a mass pit for Colonel Rutherford's laborers. How did you come to know about this?"

"The day they take me to the colonel's place, the overseer put me on what they calls 'burial duty'. Another man on the duty, Joe Patton, tole me they always put the new men on burial, kind of as a warnin'. So's they tole us to carry out a Negro field hand who die' and bury his body at the edge of the woods, no coffin or nothing. Turns out, we didn't have to dig much 'cause they was other Negros buried in that hole. And Joe tells me they is more than one of them pits."

"This is hearsay, General," lawyer Dunham objected. "Hearsay!"

"Hearsay from a nigra!" Rutherford shouted. "It's a nigra's word against a white man."

"Hearsay, yes," the General replied. "Let's hear what else this man has to say. Continue, Mr. Jones."

"Yes, sir. So's we start to dig, but the pit weren't too well-covered. Mostly, it was loose dirt. Pretty soon, my shovel hits a body, and as I keep on digging there is other bodies and skulls and bones. 'All dead nigras', Joe say to me, 'kill by hunger and disease'. And that's what I saw, General."

"This man is lying," Dunham objected. "No such thing exists on Rutherford Plantation."

"You can't believe a crazy nigra!" Rutherford shouted. "He's just telling a story that Hurst made up. It's a total fabrication, a fiction."

"We'll see about that," the general said. He turned to his aide. "Have Corporal Birney take a company out to Rutherford's. If these graves do exist, have the freedman there exhume the evidence, and have Birney take the overseers into custody as witnesses. Then bring all of Rutherford's freedmen to our camp for their own safety. Tell Birney to get the report to me tonight."

The aide saluted. "Yes, sir, right away." He turned to go, but was halted by General Stevens.

"Oh, one more thing," the general added. "Tell Birney to bring decent rations to feed those poor souls. I'm sure they've been malnourished for quite some time. And commandeer the colonel's wagons and stock to transport them to our camp. I'm certain they're not in much condition to travel."

"Yes, sir," the aide said.

"You have no right to trespass on my property, nor to take my men into custody. And you dang sure can't run off with my nigras! I've got a business to run," Rutherford bellowed, his face contorted in anger.

"Well, I'm ordering it done, Colonel. You can appeal to Washington if you object to my actions. Get going now," he ordered the aide, who saluted and disappeared out the side door.

"Rule at the end of a bayonet, that's what you Yankees brought us," Rutherford growled. "You'll burn in Hell for this, General."

"Good. I look forward to a warm chat with you then, Colonel." The general turned to Lou. "All right, Mr. Jones. Tell me in your own words about how you came to Rutherford Plantation, what you saw, and what happened to your leg."

"Well, General, two of the sheriff's men stop me in the road. 'What you doin', nigra?' they say. 'I'm going to find my family', I says. 'You ain't going nowhere', they say."

Nervous, Lou took a deep breath and turned to Durk, who gave him a reassuring nod, and Lou continued. "I tell them I work for Mr. Hurst, but they just laugh. 'Show me your paper', they say; so I do. But they just tear it up. Then they grab me.

"I try to pull away, but I ain't so young no more. Finally, one of them smack me on the leg with his rifle. Then he hit me again. My leg starts bleeding. 'You coming to jail, is what you doing', one says. 'But my leg is cut; I can't make it', I say. They tie a rope around my neck, get on their horses, and pull me to walk all the way to town. I'm stumbling and bleeding; I fall, but they just laugh, call me 'clumsy nigra'. Then they throw me in jail."

"Did the sheriff have your injury treated?" Mr. Anderson of the Freedmen's Bureau interjected.

"No, sir. I beg the sheriff, but Bake say, 'The doctor a busy man, nigra. You keep quiet'. I ask him to fetch Mr. Hurst; he speak for me, he got papers. But Bake just laugh. He tell me if I don't shut my mouth something worse than my leg be bleeding. Meantime, my leg is hurting terrible bad, and the blood ain't stopped yet."

The general turned to the sheriff. "So this man was injured, bleeding, and you didn't fetch the doctor for him?"

"I couldn't, General," Bake replied. "I was in the jailhouse by myself; I didn't have nobody to send."

"Noted," the general said.

"So then, you were fined by the court. . . ?" Mr. Anderson asked Lou, continuing the questioning.

Durk interjected: "Note that Turkle has separate courts for whites and Negros, sir. Lou was fined in the court for Negros, which, by strange coincidence, finds all freedmen guilty."

"How's that for justice?" Mr. Anderson remarked to the general. "Continue, Mr. Jones."

"I tell the judge to call Mr. Hurst, he's got my papers, but the judge won't hear it," Lou added. "So next thing, I'm drag' off by Rutherford and his people. I can hardly walk. My leg swelling and yellow stuff oozing from the wound."

"Did you show Colonel Rutherford your leg when you arrived at his plantation? Did you ask for a doctor?" the general asked.

"Yes, sir. I beg him. But he just laugh. He tell his man to get me to work. And the other freedmen tell me they ain't never seen no doctor."

"That's a lie," Colonel Rutherford said. "You can't take a nigra's word against mine. I had the doctor out every week to examine those people."

"That so?" the general said. "How about if we bring the doctor in to testify?"

The colonel's face flushed. "There is nothing in writing that says I have to provide medical services to these people," he sputtered. "They're all vagrants. Vagrants! I don't run a charity, General. I'm giving them useful work, keeping them out of jail."

"I'm sure they appreciate your beneficence, Colonel," the general quipped.

"I have a question for Mr. Hurst, General," Anderson said. "Mr. Hurst. If the sheriff is supplying labor to Colonel Rutherford *gratis*, why would the colonel pay a fine to acquire Mr. Jones for his plantation?"

"I'll tell you why," Lou answered. "Colonel Rutherford been to the jail. He pick' out the men he want; he say I'm too old for his place. So's they took me to auction me off with the ones left. When the colonel see Durk trying to pay my fine, he outbid him. We just got out of the army, so Durk don't have much money. Later the colonel tole his overseers to treat me special 'cause I'm a friend of Mr. Hurst. Then they begin to work me to death. When I fall, they whip me on my bad leg."

"I see, Mr. Jones. And how did you get back with Mr. Hurst?" Anderson asked.

Durk rose to address the bench. "I can explain that. Judge Fairbanks gave me a court order saying I could retrieve Lou after I reimbursed the colonel for Lou's fine. I raised the money, but by that time his leg was too infected. The doctor had to amputate it."

At that moment, Lou trembled and doubled over, falling off his chair. Durk bent to help him as Ellen rushed to their side through the startled crowd. She felt Lou's head. "His fever's getting bad again," she said. "I'll get him back home."

General Stevens glanced at his pocket watch. "Well, it's Friday, and we've had enough this week. Colonel Rutherford, I will receive a report tonight on what my men discover at your plantation relating to Mr. Jones' claims. Further, Mr. Anderson and I plan to take depositions this weekend from your overseers and from your Negro laborers. I am not yet prepared to make a judgment on this case, against you or Sheriff Stubbs. However, I am seriously considering your financial and legal responsibility to transport Mr. Jones to his family as soon as he becomes well enough to travel.

"We are adjourned until Monday, gentlemen, at which time these hearings will resume. Both Colonel Rutherford and Sheriff Stubbs will report here that morning. That is all for today." General Stevens brought down the gavel and rose to leave.

Rutherford turned to Durk. "You'd best draw up a will for yourself, Mr. Lawyer Man. This is the last treachery you'll ever foist upon this country. I promise I'll get you for this!"

"I know you will, Colonel," Durk said calmly.

Colonel Rutherford merely stared at Durk in bewilderment.

The courtroom cleared out faster than a water bucket with a hole at the bottom. As dusk settled, a weary General Stevens left the courthouse through the side door, followed by his entourage. Durk looked toward James Clifton, who signaled that he'd be in his office and exited through the main entrance. As soon as Clifton was gone, Durk hurried out the side door and caught the general under the courthouse eaves, surrounded by a half-dozen troopers.

"To your mounts," the general ordered his men, then turned to speak with Durk. "So, Mr. Hurst, how close are you to the end of your list?"

"At this rate, a day or two at most, sir. A few more freedmen may show up, but most fear retaliation if they confront their employer. And many don't even know the bureau is in town. Perhaps next time we'll be better prepared."

"I encounter the same damned situation everywhere," the general said. "What a road show this has been! I know we've neglected Turkle— my resources are stretched past the limit. However, I assure you this town will not wait so long for my next visit."

"I appreciate that, General."

"Now, Hurst, how goes your plan on the rifles? The last thing I need is for my men to be outgunned by local rebel holdouts; it would be a bloodbath."

"Yes, sir. I intend to set things in motion tonight. The forest out where I suspect the guns are being hidden is treacherous, but I know it well. If you'll trust me to guide your men, we can recover the rifles and trap those who would place them in the wrong hands. How does that sit with you?"

"I'll have a company or two ready for you. Do hurry though, Hurst. This regiment must be back in Jaron's Ferry by the end of the month. That gives us very little time to enact your scheme. Understand?"

"I couldn't be in more of a hurry if my house was on fire, General."

Durk re-entered the courthouse through the side door hoping to avoid any encounter with an aggrieved landowner still lingering about. Once inside, he hurried up the back stairs and through the upstairs hallway to Clifton's office, where he found him sorting papers.

"Thank you for agreeing to see me, sir."

"Listen, Hurst, I only consented to your request because Ellen asked me to as a personal favor. You came to my house, and insulted one of my *invited* guests. Now please make it quick."

"May I sit?" Durk asked.

"No need to get comfortable. State your business."

"Mr. Clifton," Durk said, "I apologize for my unforgivable behavior the other night. I don't know what came over me . . ."

"To the business at hand, Hurst," Clifton interrupted. "It's getting late."

"All right. How do you honestly feel about what you witnessed today?"

"How do I feel?" Clifton reluctantly dredged up his memories of the afternoon. "Disgusted. Disgusted, disappointed, and *ashamed* by the actions of men I've known all my life, some of whom are good friends. That's how I feel, Mr. Hurst. What is your point?"

"My point is: I believe you are a good Christian man who wants Turkle to be a fair and harmonious place in which to live and raise children, to be a lawful community. Am I correct?" Clifton nodded perfunctorily. "But that is not what you observed today, sir, and that realization is gnawing at your guts right now. Mr. Clifton, the blood of our friends and their sons have been spilled, but Turkle has not found peace. Quite the opposite: we are devolving further into chaos every day. If things continue like this, we're going to see worse, much worse. You and I both know there's going to be violence and plenty of it; men like Colonel Rutherford promise just that, and I for one believe him." Durk's eyes bore into Clifton's.

"Yes? So what can I do about it? I'm just one man."

"Mr. Clifton, you are head of the town council. More than anyone, you can stop this."

"How, Mr. Hurst? How?"

Durk slid two documents across the desk. "The constitution says that citizens have a right to petition their government. The top document asks that the council repeal Turkle's Black Codes, which gut the very concept of civil law. Such laws have brought nothing but instability wherever they've been instituted—even up North.

"The second paper asks the council to repeal the legal code drawn up originally for slaves, now being applied to freedmen. That's a travesty, and you know it. The petition also requests the elimination of the separate court for Negros. They should be tried in the same court under the same rules as white men; it's only fair."

"If I brought these petitions before the council, they'd impeach me. I'd be a pariah in this town like you. Surely you can understand that, Mr. Hurst."

"I do understand the dilemma you face, sir. This will require a great act of courage on your part, perhaps even more courage than men like Colonel Rutherford displayed on the battlefield. But you can see that something must be done—and quickly."

Clifton studied the documents. "These are not signed by anyone but you and Mrs. DuVallier-French. Petitions must have more than two signatures."

"There would be many, many more, I assure you, but the freedmen are afraid to sign petitions like these," Durk replied. "You can understand that after what you witnessed today. But I assure you, Mr. Clifton, the entire freedman community wants these unjust laws repealed. You must know that."

Clifton rubbed his eyes, his face flushing red. Finally, he spoke. "You will need to get a substantial number of signatures on these to even be considered. Understand?"

"All right, Mr. Clifton. Assuming I can get them. . . ?"

"About the first petition, you know full well the legislature will be passing Black Codes for the whole state in November. At that time, Turkle will follow state law to the letter, making Turkle's Black Codes moot. I won't waste the council's time on this.

"On the second petition, regardless of what I think, folks don't want Negros in their courtroom. It would be foolish to present such a petition to the council. I won't besmirch my own reputation by allowing it to come to a vote. Is my position clear?" He rose, turned off the oil lamp, and headed for the door.

As he passed, Durk offered his hand. "Thank you for your time, Mr. Clifton."

"This is a futile crusade, Hurst," Clifton said, ignoring the gesture, and hurriedly left the room.

Durk turned to follow him out, heading for the store. He wished he could see Antoinette and Josh to tell them of the day's victories in the courtroom. But they were on their way to Jackson. Besides, he had to effect his trap on Colonel Rutherford and his cohorts. Durk wouldn't be sleeping that night.

The long trail of marchers wound their way down the country road. Spirits were high, but dusk was falling rapidly and people were growing weary. The tall cypress lining the road and spotty patches of clouds overhead created splashes of shade, cooling the hot, humid slog.

A young man who'd been sent ahead returned at a run, having found a good place nearby to camp for the night. Hearing this, the marchers' spirits picked up. One woman broke into song, as she was soon joined by other powerful voices.

Just then, a shot rang out from the wooded area not far ahead. Everyone froze in place, listening. Then a second blast echoed, as the orderly march turned into a disturbed anthill, with the women ducking behind wagons, as the men formed a phalanx of bodies to confront whatever came.

Big Josh strode directly toward the source of the disturbance and shouted, "Who fired them shots? Show yourself!" There was a pause, and Josh shouted again, "Come face us like men, bushwhackers. We ready for you!" Again, there was no response from the shooters. "Come on out or we're coming after you!"

Before everyone's eyes, a pair of boys not more than fifteen, with hunting rifles, emerged from the trees, looking sheepish, frightened, and confused. Seeing the looming threat to the marchers reduced to two half-grown pranksters, marchers started angrily toward the pair, yelling and waving fists. When the boys saw them approaching, one shouted defiantly, "Nigras!" Then the pair turned and ran away.

Seeing the boys in flight, the group of marchers returned to the road laughing.

"All right," Josh said. "It's just a couple children. Let's go on." Soon the march continued with voices raised in song stronger than before. Nothing was going to stop them. Their petition would be presented to the constitutional convention. And hope would live.

# Chapter Twenty-two
# PULLING THE TRIGGER

Heartsick and exhausted, Durk dragged himself through the store and into the parlor, fell onto the sofa, and rubbed his temples. The hearings had been hard, and Lou's testimony especially excruciating. Night was falling, but Durk didn't light the oil lamp or candle, preferring the calm of darkness.

Everything was going as planned—which surprised and scared him. The hearing, only the first move in the gambit he'd envisioned, had turned Colonel Rutherford boiling hot—pointing the diehard secessionist toward Durk's trap. But the next move would be risky, and could even endanger Caleb. And the boy didn't deserve that.

Durk had tried for days to devise a plan that wouldn't involve Caleb, but none held nearly the promise. Too much was at stake; he had no choice.

Caleb entered the parlor. "Ellen said you want to see me, Durk."

"Come sit beside me," Durk said. When Caleb joined him, Durk placed his arm around the boy's shoulders. "Listen, Caleb, I have a plan that I believe could sink Colonel Rutherford's boat—with him in it. But I'll need your help. I hate to ask you because it could be dangerous. *Real* dangerous. If you don't want to do this, I'll understand."

"I ain't no coward, Durk. You know that."

"Yes. But this isn't a game, Caleb. Rutherford's men are killers, and if something goes wrong, he'll have it in for you. Understand?"

"What do you need me to do, Durk? Tell me."

"All right. You know how you've been running messages for the colonel?"

"Dang right."

"I need you to take a message to him tonight. But it's forged. I've signed another man's name to it. You're to tell him that man with the Henry rifle gave it to you to deliver. Are you following me?"

"I guess so. So I'm going to bring the colonel this note and tell him it's from that man who held the rifle on you and Antoinette?"

"That is right, Caleb. The man's name is French. Rutherford will probably give you a reply to take back to him. French is holed up in an old house belonging to his partner, a man named Jenkins, who's a dangerous man. It's a long ride out there on an old road near the Chickasaw swamp. I'll be right beside you on the ride there and back. But the most dangerous parts—passing the notes—you'll have to do by yourself. I can't be with you. Understand?"

"I do, Durk."

"Good. Now when the colonel asks you where you'll be taking his reply, tell him, 'the man said not to tell; he said he don't want no one but me bringing your answer'. If Rutherford pressures you, just tell him Jenkins' place; that's okay. Then bring his reply around to the back of the store, and I'll rewrite it for you to take to Jenkins'.

"But, Caleb, you'll have to ride up to Jenkins' house alone. I'll hide and wait for you. That will be your moment of greatest danger. French will probably recognize you from that night he came by. And he'll wonder why you're delivering a message from Colonel Rutherford. Just tell him you're Rutherford's regular messenger. Got it?"

Caleb nodded.

"Now, tell Jenkins and French and that Rutherford wants you to wait for a reply. Just stay on your horse; never dismount. If they invite you inside, tell them no thanks. If they insist, ride away immediately. Don't be brave.

"If French does send a note back for Rutherford, we'll return to the store and I'll duplicate it so the handwriting matches our original note to Rutherford. Got it?"

"I'm ready."

Durk handed Caleb the forged note to Rutherford sealed with wax. "Don't break the seal, Caleb. The colonel must feel confident that you haven't read it."

"I won't."

Then Durk handed Caleb a worn gold coin with a dent in its center. "Now Caleb, this is my lucky coin. It's yours now. I've had it for many years: it's saved my life more than once. When you take the message to Colonel Rutherford, show this to him, brag that the man who gave you the message paid you with this coin to be their go-between. Understand?"

"I do." Caleb's face lit up as he admired the coin. He felt its weight in his palm and fingered the dent at its center, then slipped it into his pocket.

"Listen, Caleb," Durk spoke quietly, "I know we haven't spent enough time together since we arrived in Turkle. First there was the war, and here in Turkle I've been busy trying to help the freedmen. Plus there's the store. I've wanted to take you camping, to teach you the ways of the Chickasaw, how to track and trap game, how to survive in the wilds. But things are as we found them, unfortunately for both of us. But I love you, Caleb. I want you to know that."

Caleb was quiet a moment. "I love you, too, Durk."

"Okay now, I want you to leave through the kitchen, circle around, and approach Rutherford's house from the east, like you're coming from the other side of town. I'll meet you back here in thirty minutes or so. Get it?"

"I'm ready."

"Good. Now if Rutherford asks where I am, I headed out to *French-Acres*."

Caleb took up the message and scurried out through back. Durk watched him go, chastising himself for placing the boy in jeopardy to attempt the most harebrained scheme he'd ever conceived. If anything happened to the boy, Antoinette would certainly leave him. At one fell swoop, Durk would lose everyone he'd ever loved. And he'd have no one to blame but himself.

Colonel Rutherford was apoplectic. The dang army had taken his overseers into custody, stolen his field hands, and confiscated his wagons, horses, and mules. He hadn't been this furious since that traitor Bobby Lee surrendered, rendering four years of fighting for naught.

He sat in the study of the house he rented in town, trying to compose a letter to the *Turkle Tower*. He crumbled up a draft and threw it onto the floor, where it landed on a pile of other failed attempts. Then he heard a faint knock on the study door.

"Yes?"

His elderly servant, Wheeler, stuck his head in. "Boy, want to see you, Colonel. Say it's urgent."

"A boy?" the colonel exclaimed. Then he realized who it likely was. "Send him in, Wheeler." The colonel tied his robe closed over his nightshirt, as Wheeler ushered Caleb into the room, then departed, closing the door behind him.

Caleb took a deep breath. "A man give me a message for you, Colonel," Caleb said nervously, laying the note onto the desk. "He told me to bring him your answer."

"A man? What man?" the colonel asked, suspicious.

"Just a man," Caleb replied. "He didn't tell me his name or nothing."

Colonel Rutherford studied Caleb's face in the shadows, seeking hints of guile. Finally, he took up the letter opener, sliced open the seal, and brought the lamp closer. Keeping an eye on the boy, he read through the message.

"What did he look like? Was he a big man?"

"No, sir, he was kind of scrawny; didn't even fit into his suit."

"Did he have a beard or a mustache, any facial hair?"

"No, sir, Colonel. His face was pink as a baby. He was just a little guy, see?"

Rutherford thought it over. "Did the man have freckles? Brown-red hair? Voice kind of high?"

"That's him." Caleb pulled the coin from his pocket and fingered it nervously. "Paid me with a gold piece."

"Let me see that, boy," the colonel said. Caleb slid the coin across the desk. Rutherford held it to the light and rubbed the dent at its center. "This dent, it's from a bullet."

"Yes, sir, I seen that. But I weren't asking no questions."

"No, you wouldn't." The colonel slid the coin back to the boy, who pocketed it. "Why would you accept gold from a stranger, but you never accept payment from me?"

"Durk told me not to take money from you. He didn't tell me not to take it from nobody else."

"Where is Mr. Hurst this evening?"

"Ain't seen him, Colonel. Miss Ellen says he rode out to *FrenchAcres* after supper. That's all I know."

Rutherford laughed angrily to himself. "Probably thinks he'll be safe out there among the nigras. Man's a coward. You know that, don't you, boy? I read that on his face first time I saw him."

"I don't know."

Rutherford thought over his situation. "I want you to run a message out to my plantation. Can you do that, Caleb?"

"No, sir. Durk forbid me to go to your place. I'd be in big trouble."

Rutherford considered his options. "How did this stranger know to give this note to you?"

"Everybody knows I'm your messenger."

"All right," Colonel Rutherford said, pointing across the room. "Sit over there." Caleb took the chair against the opposite wall to wait.

Rutherford picked up his quill, dipped it in the inkwell, and wrote out a message. At the bottom, under his signature, he wrote: "If the seal is broken on this correspondence, my offer is invalid. Take whatever actions you feel are appropriate." Then he folded the note, melted red wax over a candle, and sealed the missive tightly.

"How long will it take you to deliver this message to that man and return with a reply."

"It's gonna be hours, Colonel. He lives a far piece."

"Are you sure you can you find him?"

"Sure. He gave me easy directions."

"Where's he staying, Caleb?"

"I don't know whose place it is, Colonel. All I know is it's out the old road to Lethe Creek."

"Can you deliver my note tonight? It'll be very late when you get back."

"Durk ain't home. Guess I can do it. He never told me not to."

"Wait for his reply. Then bring it straight back tonight. Don't worry about waking me. You hear? Now go on, Caleb, time is wasting."

Caleb took the sealed message and was out the door. Rutherford watched him go, then sat back to consider his next set of moves.

His strategy determined, he pulled a stack of new foolscap writing paper from the drawer and squared the pile. Then he dipped the quill. He had quite a few notes for the sheriff's deputies to deliver around town in the morning. Quite a few.

Caleb rushed into the kitchen and landed in Durk's waiting embrace. Beaming, the boy handed over Rutherford's reply.

"He took your note, Durk. Wrote this out for French," Caleb said, still breathing hard.

Durk slit the seal with the kitchen knife and read. Clearly, Rutherford's anger had made the heady bait irresistible. Smiling, Durk sat to write, then sealed the new message.

"Caleb, I know you're tired. I am, too. But we have to ride out to Jenkins'. Ready?"

"The turnoff to Jenkins' is just ahead; you can't miss it. Give me about fifteen minutes to slip around. I want to be in position to watch what happens, in case you have a problem. Remember, if for any reason you think it's too dangerous, you can always turn back; no shame in that. Either way, we'll meet at that bridge we passed; wait where I showed you."

Caleb watched Durk disappear on Contrition into the wooded blackness, where he'd planned to hide his horse. The boy waited for what he guessed was fifteen minutes, then spurred Old Nancy.

Now alone, the road was scary and getting scarier. The overcast night was black with spotty clouds and few patches of stars visible. The forests and abandoned brushlands were encroaching stealthily onto the seldom-used road, which was pitted with gullies and cavities, making it hard for Old Nancy to traverse. The twisted limbs of trees overhead were poised like witches' talons poised to pierce the boy's flesh, closing in on him as the wild vegetation inched in ever closer.

The outline of Jenkins' roof appeared against the half-moon just ahead. Caleb thought about turning back and telling Durk he couldn't go through with it. But he was so close, he had to keep on.

# CHAPTER TWENTY-THREE

# FINAL MANEUVERS

"Come on out!" Caleb shouted from horseback. "I got a message."

Tense and fearful, he waited in the pervading darkness. And waited. A whippoorwill sang in the distance, but supplied no distraction. Caleb called out again. But no window showed a lantern. The rundown old house appeared deserted. "I said, a message," he repeated more loudly.

Without warning, two figures appeared from behind the house, pistols leveled at him, approaching cautiously but steadily. "What kind of message, boy?" the disheveled older man snarled. Caleb stretched out the note, and the man swiped it from his hand, never lowering his pistol.

"It's from Colonel Rutherford," Caleb said, voice shaking. "He tole me to wait for your answer."

Seeing the message was sealed with wax, the grizzled man pulled a knife out of his boot and sliced it open. Then, holding onto Old Nancy's reins, he passed the note to Devereau French. Devereau struck a match and read the memo. "Aren't you Durksen Hurst's boy?" she asked, crumbling the note into her pocket.

"I am," Caleb replied.

"What are you doing delivering messages this time of night for Colonel Rutherford?"

"I'm the colonel's regular boy," Caleb answered, keeping an eye on the pistols aimed his way. "He sends me all over. This is his horse."

"It's Old Nancy, all right," the older man confirmed. "Belongs to the colonel."

The two looked quizzically at each other, then turned back toward their unexpected visitor. "Come into the house," the older man said.

"I got orders," Caleb replied, refusing to take the bait. "I'm waitin' here."

The two men looked at each other again, then conferred in whispers. "Our writing paper's inside," Devereau said invitingly. "Sure you won't come in for a bite of cake, perhaps a sup of water?"

"Colonel says not to."

The two turned and went up the front steps and through the door. Caleb sat the war-scarred brown, listening, watching the shadows for any sign of movement. Soon he heard them shouting at each other. It seemed to Caleb they were taking a long time to resolve their differences. Finally, the pair returned. The older man kept a pistol trained on Caleb, taking hold of Nancy's reins again to prevent his escape. The smaller one displayed a sealed note.

"How do we know this isn't some kind of trick?" Devereau asked.

"Deliver it yourself if you don't trust me," Caleb answered. "The colonel's at his house in town."

The two men glanced at each other. Then Devereau handed the boy the note.

"If you ain't being square," the older man said, "we know where to find you. And it won't be no mercy killing neither." He let go of Old Nancy's reins. "Just remember, boy: I'm a dead shot, *dead.*"

Caleb spit, then spurred the horse away, not looking back—relieved to still be alive. As he trotted down the road, Caleb listened for hoof beats, but none followed. He rode a quarter mile, then drew rein. He remembered Durk's instructions: if he was chased, escape into the brush. After a while he saw a rider approaching from just ahead. He strained his eyes to see who it was and, recognizing Durk, displayed the note with a pleased grin.

Everything seemed to be going according to plan.

Durk and Caleb hid their horses in a thick grove a hundred yards back of the store. Durk could see how exhausted the boy was, but there was no alternative: Caleb had to visit Rutherford one last time before the boy could sleep. Durk, too, was near the point of collapse and still had to ride out to General Stevens' camp. The die was nearly cast.

It was pitch black when they reached the kitchen. Closing the curtains by feel, Durk lit a candle on the table. He told Caleb to rest on the floor, then opened and read Devereau's instructions for the exchange. It was a well-chosen location, with discovery by outsiders nearly impossible. He tried to imagine a strategy that would enable the cavalry to surround the site without being seen, but knew he would have to rely on his instincts when the time came. In all likelihood there would be a shootout, something Durk hoped to avoid. But better the troopers initiate a surprise entrapment against a half-dozen men bearing pistols than being ambushed at some future date by pro-secessionist bushwhackers armed with repeater rifles.

Taking a deep breath, Durk copied Devereau's message, using his own paper, matching the other note he'd sent to Rutherford. Then he sealed it with a thick layer of wax. When he tried to raise Caleb, sleep had already sunk its claws into the wrung-out boy, and it took time to get him on his feet. He handed Caleb the note.

"Just come straight back and go to bed," Durk told him, making sure the drowsy boy understood. "Tie Nancy up out front. You can return her to the stable in the morning."

"Okay, Durk," he yawned, rubbing his eyes.

When Caleb was out the door, Durk sunk into the parlor sofa to rest, but his worrying about the boy wouldn't allow it. Caleb was heading directly into the lions' den—and Durk could not be there to protect him.

When Wheeler opened the door, his hands shook as he fumbled to button up his nightshirt. "Go on home, boy. Shoo," Wheeler whispered.

Caleb brushed past him. "Gotta deliver this note."

Wheeler showed him into the colonel's study, lit only by a single silver desk lamp. Its light flickered across Rutherford's face, contorting his wry expression into a daemonic leer. Standing around the perimeter were six gunmen, none looking too friendly, with Sheriff Stubbs sitting to the colonel's side. Caleb was taken aback by the unexpected sight. He steadied himself and entered, as Wheeler quickly disappeared, closing the door carefully behind him.

Bucking up his courage, Caleb walked right up to the desk and slid the note to the colonel, ignoring the sheriff and the men leaning against the walls. "Here's your reply, Colonel," he said.

Rutherford studied Caleb's face, then examined the message. "Did that man tell you his name this time, Caleb?"

"No, sir. And I didn't ask."

His movements slow, deliberate, Rutherford cut the seal on the note, which he read before turning his attention back to the boy. "You've done well, Caleb," he said smooth as butter. "It took some time to ride there and back. Can you tell me, son, where you delivered my note?"

Caleb stretched and yawned. "Well, I shouldn't tell, Colonel. I just want to go home and sleep."

"Of course, son. But first, I need to know where you were. You can tell me. If it wasn't important, I wouldn't ask." As he spoke, the sheriff turned to face Caleb squarely, and two of the rowdies sidled forward to stand at his shoulders.

Caleb was in a panic, his heart beating rapidly. Then he remembered through the haze of his fatigue that Durk said he should tell the location if pressed. "He's living out east off the old Lethe Creek road," Caleb said. "Next turnoff past that bridge with the rocks. It weren't hard to find; it was just far."

Rutherford grinned to the sheriff, who nodded in return. "Our old friend Jenkins," Rutherford said. "We figured right. All right, Caleb, you go home and get some sleep. I'm going to have another ride for you tomorrow, to the west this time. Think you can do that?"

"Sure I can."

The sheriff reached in his pocket and pulled out a roll of money. He pulled a bill off the top and offered it to Caleb. "I can't take that," Caleb told the sheriff.

"It's not from me," Rutherford interjected. "It's from the sheriff. This has all been town business. Mr. Hurst didn't tell you not to take money for helping the law, did he?"

"I guess not," a yawning Caleb said, pocketing the money. "I may have to give it back, though, if Durk says."

"All right, Caleb, you can go home," Rutherford said. "Come back tomorrow after supper."

Caleb turned and retired, glad to be leaving the study's threatening atmosphere.

When the boy was gone, Colonel Rutherford asked the six gunmen, "Which of you is the fastest rider?" All pointed at one man. "Bill, do you know Jenkins' place?"

"I do," Bill said.

"Good," Rutherford said. "Go wait out in the parlor. Have Wheeler get you something to eat and drink. The rest of you get plenty of sleep. I'm going to need you wide awake tomorrow night. Now git." The hired men funneled out the door, leaving Rutherford alone with the sheriff.

"What do you want with the boy tomorrow?" Stubbs asked.

Rutherford winked slyly. "Nothing special. Just to keep me company—as an insurance policy you could say."

The sheriff swallowed hard. Whatever the colonel was fixing to do about those rifles, he clearly planned to use the boy as a shield. Bake knew which side his bread was buttered on, but, heck, he *was* the town law and order. Letting a child face that kind of danger might be more than he could sanction. He bit his lip, keeping his mouth shut.

Rutherford sat quietly a moment, then exploded: "I want to know who crippled me, Stubbs! If you can't find out, I'll get someone who can. And when I do, we won't need lawyers or paperwork to extract the full price for his perfidy."

Shaken by the raw venom of Rutherford's vow, the sheriff took several seconds to compose himself. Then in a trembling voice, he said, "Look, Colonel, you know you can't buy Henrys nowhere in Miss'ippi. There's only them stolen ones out at Jenkins'. So your shooter must have got the gun either from Jenkins or his partner. When we make the exchange tomorrow, I'll find out who they sold that rifle to. Simple."

"If they won't tell us voluntarily, I'll have my men persuade them. They'll talk," Rutherford said ominously "And if they did have a hand in it, there's plenty of places to dump them in that swamp." He took a moment to consider the situation. "Do you think it was Jenkins that shot me, Bake? He owns the Henrys."

"Why would he shoot you, Colonel?"

"We've had our differences. Jenkins still owes me money after reneging on our last deal. And that wasn't the first time. He's owed me money on and off for years."

The sheriff thought this over. "If Jenkins shot you, why would he turn around and try to sell you those rifles? That would point the guilt straight at him. Besides, Jenkins don't miss. If he'd wanted to kill you from that range—using a Henry, no less—you wouldn't be here."

"Do you think it could have been Devereau French? The boy's description of Jenkins' partner sounds just like him. My sources tell me French has been spotted around Turkle recently."

"I heard that, too, Colonel. But from what I know about him, Devereau French wouldn't even know how to load and fire a fine firearm like the one that clipped you. No, sir, Colonel, French is a bad bet."

Rutherford ruminated on everything he knew. "Then it had to be Hurst," he concluded. "Hurst's man lost his leg at the knee, and I was crippled in the knee. He'd think that evened us up. I promise you this, Stubbs, Hurst is done troubling this town. There won't be any trial either, nor any fine last words, that I assure you."

The sheriff blinked, then blinked again. The colonel wasn't talking about killing no freedman; this was a white man, or nearly one.

"Is Hurst a good shot?" Rutherford asked.

"I ain't never seen him shoot, but folks swear he can shoot around corners with a pistol."

"Even if it wasn't him, he's the one responsible for General Stevens' humiliating me in that courtroom. Listen, friend, Hurst is going to pay, I swear it on my country's flag. You'd better accept that." Stubbs spit. Hurst's death was no great loss to him, not if it meant standing in the colonel's way.

The colonel grew pensive. "After four years of war, I know when something doesn't smell right, and this rifle deal troubles my nostrils. You know the area around Jenkins' place, don't you, Stubbs?"

"Oh, sure. A bunch of us used to go huntin' up that a-way right before planting time. Know it well, Colonel."

Rutherford handed him the forged note from French the boy had brought. "This is where they want to transfer those guns. Know it?"

Stubbs read the missive. "Sure, generally speaking."

"Do you know another spot that would serve just as well?"

Stubbs took a bite of chew and thought this over. "I do, Colonel. Closer to town, too." The sheriff described the proposed site.

Rutherford wrote, then stopped and tore the note into small pieces. "I'm going to change the location for the exchange in case someone's planning to lay a trap for us. But I'm not dumb enough to put it in writing." He called in their hired man. "Bill, I want you to ride out to Jenkins' place. Tell him the deal is as agreed, but there's a change of plan. We're going to meet near that abandoned sawmill instead of where they wanted." He turned to Bake. "This is why the Yankees never did catch me. I'm always somewhere other than where they expect me to be."

Rutherford gave the man his final instructions and sent him off.

"Once we have those guns, this region's gonna be the meanest hornets' nest those Yankees ever imagined. And the first thing I'm gonna do is clean out the vermin infesting *FrenchAcres*."

# CHAPTER TWENTY-FOUR
# THE TORCH PASSED

## JACKSON, MISSISSIPPI

Under the great dome of the capitol building in Jackson, the convention for the new state constitution was a seething, roiling cauldron of contentious argument and quiet deal-making. For a secessionist state to be re-admitted to the Union, the Federal government required that ten percent of its citizens sign a loyalty pledge, and Mississippi had achieved that penurious minimum. Among the convention leaders were a dozen delegates to the secession convention of 1860: its president, who had entered the motion for secession; a few Confederate generals; a Confederate senator; and a Confederate governor.

Suddenly, a wave of silence settled upon the great mass as an assembly of black faces in dark Sunday suits, colorful dresses, and field garb filed through the front door, led by Big Josh and accompanied by Antoinette, the pastor, other leaders, and two white landowners. Making their way down the center aisle, the marchers halted before the convention leaders seated at the dais.

The convention president repeatedly slammed his gavel. "What do you people mean barging in here like this?" A chorus of delegates beside him echoed the remark.

Steeling their nerves, Antoinette and Josh glanced at each other for reassurance. Their desire to construct a rudimentary bridge between Mississippi's former slaves and those who had owned them could now begin in earnest.

Josh took a calming breath and stepped forward, hoping his stutter would remain under control. "We've brought a petition to submit to this honorable body for your consideration," his baritone voice echoed through the chamber. "The right to petition is in the U.S. Constitution.

I would remind you gentlemen that you personally, and Mississippi as a people, have pledged to honor that sacred document in order to reenter the Union."

The men on the dais began to object, but were silenced when the president pounded the gavel. When things quieted, he turned to one of the two planters accompanying the marchers. "Do you have anything to say about this?" he asked.

"No, sir," the man replied. "These people can speak for themselves. I'm just here to listen, as should you."

The president pointed the gavel at the second planter. "You have anything to say?"

"Same with me, sir," the man replied. "Just showing support."

The president grew quiet. The man beside him leaned over and said under his breath, "How are we going to get these people out of here without calling in the militia?"

Frustrated and perplexed, the president pointed his gavel at Antoinette. "You, madam, what is the nature of this invasion of our proceedings?"

"My name is Mrs. Antoinette DuVallier, Mr. President," she stated. "You gentlemen have taken on the great responsibility of rebuilding our civilization after the terrible destruction brought about by your own misguided policies. And I salute you for that. But you can't build, or rebuild, a castle on a swamp. Today, our state is in great turmoil, and these good folks, representing half the state's population, want to help you create a firm foundation for a new Mississippi. I urge you to give them your full attention and scrupulous consideration of the document they present to you."

The president turned to his right to examine the reaction of his noteworthy cohorts, then to the left. Quizzical expressions up and down the line. Then he spoke, directing his comment to Big Josh: "All right then. Let's hear what you have to say. What is your name and occupation?"

Big Josh pulled the remarks his committee had prepared from his breast pocket and unfolded it. They had heard of a similar petition the black citizens of South Carolina had put before city authorities when the war ended. Though that effort had not been fruitful, it had inspired their composition. "My name is Josh Tyler, sir. I am and have been for most of my life a plantation manager, both in Tennessee and here in Mississippi, formerly as a slave. And now I r-represent these people as a free man."

A rumble of whispers spread throughout the gathering. The president brought down his gavel. "Proceed, Mr. Tyler."

"Thank you, Mr. President," he said, straightening himself to his full six-foot-four.

"Sirs," he began to read. "We are well aware that to some members of your honorable body it may seem little short of presumption in us, thus, to knock at the door of your convention with the request that, in your deliberations, we shall be recognized as a component of the state. But you cannot deny that the basic aspirations of the free colored man are no different from those of the free white man. Both are inseparably woven into the welfare of Mississippi. We all share a stake in this state's future prosperity." He took a breath.

"More importantly, the equality of all men before the *law* provides a practical foundation on which both should stand, regardless of antagonisms that might exist between the two classes of men.

"Therefore, we respectfully ask that no clause shall be inserted into the new constitution which will deny any man from exercising the rights and privileges of citizenship because of the color of his skin." He paused as his words rang throughout the assembly.

"We know the deplorable ignorance of the majority of our people; we also are aware of the limitations of those among us who have acquired some degree of education. However, we do ask that if the ignorant white man is allowed to vote, that the ignorant colored man shall be given the privilege to vote also.

"We readily admit we are pleased by the turn of events which struck from our limbs the chains of slavery. But we also willingly express our sorrow that freedom for our race was accomplished by the ruin or death of thousands of those for whom, notwithstanding the bitterness of the past, and of the present, we cherish feelings of respect and affection.

"Let us also assure your honorable body that nothing short of this, our respectful demand for equal treatment, will satisfy our people. If our prayers are not granted, we will bide our time. The day for which we watched and prayed came when we least expected it; the day of our complete enfranchisement will also come. And in that faith, we will work and wait.

"We fully understand what long-held prejudices must be overcome before our prayers can be granted; but we must believe that the people of Mississippi are capable of rising above past habits and persuasion; and buoyed up by this hope we respectfully ask that our prayer may be granted, and we will ever pray.

"Signed: The colored citizens of Mississippi."

The pastor beside him strode to the head table and laid the petition before the president. The chairmen perused it briefly, then brought down the gavel. "Mr. Secretary, you will add this petition to the agenda."

"Yes, Mr. President," a man replied, making notes on a list.

"Thank you," Josh said, turned, and rejoined the marchers. Within minutes, the group had filed out of the chamber—all but Josh who hung back near the door to watch.

The president took some moments to collect himself as the hubbub in the chamber resumed. Finally, he called, "Do I hear a motion on this petition?"

"I move the petition be tabled," one delegate at the head table cried.

"It is moved that the petition from the colored citizens of Mississippi be tabled without being entered into the record," the president announced. "Second?"

"Second!" a chorus shouted.

"All for the motion?" A loud animal roar greeted the invitation to dismiss the petition.

"Opposed?" the president barked. Silence prevailed. The president banged his gavel. "The petition will be tabled. Next order of business . . ."

Josh drifted slowly outside into the sunshine to join the others, determined to keep what he'd just witnessed to himself. What mattered most, he believed, was that they'd made the long march in spite of the danger and hardship, that they'd made history that couldn't be erased. And that meant other marches would take place—and would actually succeed one day.

\* \* \*

Durk drew the curtains in hopes that the parlor would appear unoccupied from the street. After what seemed a long time, he lit a match, straining to read the clock in the blackness. But the hands had moved little since he last checked. He blew out the match and paced the room, unable to rest with Caleb still at Rutherford's. Durk berated himself for allowing Caleb to deliver the message, for involving the boy in the first place. Now, with his nerves screaming from exhaustion and fear, all he could do was wait. And worry. He collapsed onto the sofa.

Finally, he heard the back door squeak and light footsteps pad across the floorboards. Using his balled-up fists, Durk pushed himself to his feet and made for the kitchen. There—relief! He made out Caleb's form in the darkness and ran to him. The boy, spent from his long ordeal, fell into Durk's arms.

"What happened, Caleb?" Durk asked. "Did Rutherford believe the note was from French?"

"It went good, Durk. He told me to come back tomorrow night at six."

"Come back. . . ?" Durk was stunned. He hadn't considered that the colonel would want Caleb at the transfer, undoubtedly as a hostage. His mind reeled at the prospect of the boy being in the line of fire between Rutherford's killers and the army. Far worse, Durk realized that if Caleb were a witness to the rifle exchange, there was little chance Rutherford would let the boy live if things went badly.

Of course, Rutherford would be suspicious if the boy didn't show. That would likely spell the end of Durk's plan. But there was no question of sending the boy into such a dire situation.

Durk faced Caleb squarely. "Caleb, listen, you cannot go there tomorrow. They'll kill you for sure. I'll take you to *FrenchAcres* on my way to meet the army."

"But, Durk, the plan . . ." Caleb said, his eyes starting to tear.

"I don't care about that; you can't go. You hear? It isn't safe. Now go to bed. You're asleep on your feet."

Reluctantly, a depleted Caleb stumbled through the house to his bedroom. Durk listened to his footsteps, then sighed. Caleb wasn't the only one who needed sleep. He'd need sharp wits about him tomorrow and knew he'd have trouble sleeping, but he had to try.

Durk made his way to the bedroom, removed his boots, and draped his britches over the chair. Then he made sure the curtains were open and, settling wearily into bed, lay down facing the window. That way, if he managed to fall asleep, daybreak would wake him. As it was, taking Caleb out to *FrenchAcres* would take precious time away from meeting General Stevens and getting the army in place. For the first time, Durk regretted his naive attempt to set Turkle right.

He must have overslept! Through the haze of waking consciousness, Durk bolted upright, suddenly realizing the sun had already risen. Frantic, he rolled across the mattress to his feet to check the time. His fears were confirmed: he was late!

He hurriedly pulled on his trousers and boots, then rushed into Caleb's room, only to find the blanket and sheets tangled on the unmade bed—but no Caleb. Quickly, Durk searched the house, running from room to room. No Caleb anywhere.

Durk was panic-stricken. He figured Caleb must have it in his head to show up at Rutherford's that night despite his warning. Durk understood the boy saw this as an act of bravery, saw himself as the link critical to the scheme working. Foolhardy, but what was Durk to do?

In the kitchen, Durk filled a canteen and grabbed a hunk of bread to eat in the saddle, then hurried out the back. He called out Caleb's name, but the boy had obviously run off.

Durk hurried to the secluded grove where he'd tied up Contrition and continued his search for Caleb on horseback, but there was no time. He had to carry on with the plan to meet General Stevens. And hope . . .

It was sheer torture for a man of constant motion to sit and watch the grandfather clock tick away his existence. Being practically crippled, his once-good leg useless, Rutherford was unable to pace the room to ease his anxiety, or even to rise from his chair without the help of people in his employ, all of whom he loathed. The weight of inert, empty time had become unbearable. Making matters worse, he'd been made a fool before the whole town.

The colonel had eaten an early supper, knowing he wouldn't have time later. Afterward, he'd had Wheeler dress him in his officer's uniform, strapping on his ceremonial sword and full pistol belt.

Thankfully, the waiting was almost over. Rutherford slid the envelope of cash into his breast pocket. The envelope contained most of what remained of his liquid assets, but by tomorrow nothing would have value in Mississippi except guns and blood, and there'd be plenty of both.

As evening descended, he called out, "Sully! Come in here and bring Frank with you." Two of his hands appeared and hurried to his desk. "Hand me my crutches," he said. One of the men retrieved them. "Help me stand and scoot me over to the couch. Then bring me my Bible," the colonel ordered.

Lifting him by the elbows, the pair of gunmen half-carried, half-dragged him across the room like an awkward six-legged beast with two defective legs, while Rutherford cursed and shouted.

"Now send Stubbs in here, and close the door behind you," he snapped. The men hurried to obey. The sheriff entered and took a moment to let his eyes adjust to the gloom. "Sit close, Stubbs. I don't want anyone else to hear this."

"Yes, sir, Colonel," the sheriff said, pulling up a chair to face Rutherford.

"You'd better get this right, Stubbs, or we're both dead. Now after we get the rifles, we'll meet up with the gun club. Did your deputies deliver my messages to the members?"

Peering into the colonel's red-rimmed eyes, Stubbs hands trembled. He'd seen the colonel angry, even seen him disposed to violent means; but the venom he saw there now terrified him. "Y-yes, sir. They're to meet us at the b-branch. Our old spot under the elm where the road meets the ford."

"Good. Now listen hard, here's what we're going to do. You will ride with me and my men to make the exchange with Jenkins and French.

"Then we'll take that wagon full of guns to the branch to meet the club. We'll distribute rifles to them there; then you and Sully will take what's left to the hiding place. That'll be most of them.

"Once that's done, I'm going to lead the club out to *FrenchAcres*, let the boys break in their new firearms. That infestation has hung on long enough. We're going to burn out and chase away every nigra on the place—men, women, and younguns—and shoot down the ones who won't go. It'll be open season."

Stubbs blinked once, twice, three times. "But . . . but Colonel, there's a court order . . . Nobody ain't supposed to go out there . . ."

"The Confederate States of America does not recognize any order related to French's wife.

"Besides, Stubbs, I think Hurst is hiding out there. There'll be a substantial reward for the man who brings him to me. It's going to be shoot to kill as far as that turncoat is concerned."

The sheriff felt a chill run down his spine. The colonel was planning to defy the judge's order. What should he do? Stubbs put that quandary out of his mind for the moment. Heck, when all the burning and shooting starts, he'd be miles away hiding the rifles. Wouldn't be none of his business.

The short walk through the streets of Turkle seemed to take forever. Caleb was scared, and he had good reason to be. It was getting dark by the time he reached Rutherford's house on the well-kept stretch of Main Street, and what he saw frightened him. Nine saddled horses were tied along the picket fence lining the street. He tried treading quietly, but a spotted mare neighed loudly and stamped a warning, startling the boy. Walking past the horses, Caleb recognized Rebel, the colonel's mount; Old Nancy; the sheriff's graying brown; and six others. Caleb slowed, then stopped at the gate. This was his last chance to change his mind. Once he went up the walk, he couldn't back out.

He forced himself forward, climbed the porch steps, and knocked on the oak door. In seconds the door swung inward, revealing one of the colonel's gunmen, an emaciated ruffian with a patchy beard and grim expression. Inside, the house was dark, thick with the odor of stale tobacco. "Get in," the man growled. "Colonel's waiting."

"Where's Wheeler?" Caleb asked, eyes searching for Rutherford's servant.

"Got the night off," the man replied, slamming the door closed. "Go on back."

Caleb made his way through the hall and into Rutherford's study, the man following closely behind. The study was lit by a single lantern, as it had been the previous night, and Caleb instantly regretted coming. When his eyes adjusted to the darkness, he was startled to see the colonel seated on his couch, dressed in his Confederate uniform, surrounded by the sheriff and Rutherford's hired men, who stared at Caleb like a pack of hungry wolves.

"Well, here's our little rebel," Rutherford replied in a low, flat tone. "Loyal to the cause, are you?"

"I saw Nancy tied up outside. Where do you need to send me, Colonel?"

"Does Mr. Hurst know you're here?" Rutherford asked.

Caleb grew nervous. "No, sir. Ain't seen him since he left for *FrenchAcres* Friday."

"You wouldn't lie to me, would you, boy?"

"Course not, sir," Caleb replied, holding the colonel's gaze.

Rutherford watched Caleb shift uncomfortably amid the roomful of glaring eyes. "Hiding out, is he? Leaving that crippled nigra and the girl to mind the store?"

"I guess. So who do you have a message for? I want to get home."

"No message this evening, boy. We're going to avenge your two brothers who died for the Cause. You're going to strike a real blow tonight." Caleb didn't reply. Rutherford studied Caleb's face, then nodded to the bearded man, who closed in and slapped a hand on Caleb's shoulder, making him wince.

Just then, the grandfather clock chimed from the shadowy recesses of the study. "All right, it's time," the colonel said. "Let him loose, Frank. Evans, Larson, help me to my horse." The two picked up his crutches and went to his side.

The men standing around the room headed for the door, their bootheels hard on the wood, spurs clattering. Caleb walked among them but slowed to drop behind, hoping when they stepped outside, he could run around the house and disappear. No luck. One man shoved him forward with a sharp order to hurry on. Two men led him over to Nancy and waited for him to mount, one holding the reins so he couldn't ride off. All Caleb could do was sit the saddle.

Shortly thereafter, two of Rutherford's hands helped him mount Rebel. "Caleb, you're my aide de camp; you'll ride at my side," the colonel said. "Frank, you'll flank him."

Caleb swallowed hard. There'd be no escape now. He didn't know what scared him more: being killed by these men or facing Durk's wrath from having disobeyed him.

Colonel Rutherford took a moment to think. He'd changed the location of the meeting, so there was no chance Hurst or the army would know where the transaction was taking place—even if the boy had betrayed him in some manner.

Then his angry mind flooded with visions of what was soon to come. He saw Negro cabins ablaze, lighting up the night sky, women crying, grabbing their children, and fleeing through the blackness. He heard shots fired, the screams of terror and agony.

And he envisioned clearly what he would do to Mr. Hurst, saw the man's body writhe in pain, heard his pleas for mercy. It would be pretty. Oh, yes, it was going to be very pretty.

The colonel turned Rebel to the east. "Lead the way, Stubbs. We're going to acquire ordinance to arm the Confederate States of America."

# CHAPTER TWENTY-FIVE

# AN ELUSIVE PREY

The trap was set, but Rutherford hadn't shown. Frustrated, Durk lifted his head above his hiding place to view the forest-enclosed clearing below, but there was nothing to see. No sounds broke the gentle cacophony of chirping crickets, croaking frogs, and the rustle of night creatures scurrying through the underbrush. The soldiers, spread around the area, were positioned perfectly. Jenkins and Devereau would have to bring the wagonload of rifles up the dirt road from the east, teeing into Colonel Rutherford's trail from the west. But where was Jenkins? Or Rutherford and his men? Durk scrambled back through the trees and squatted beside General Stevens.

"They should have been here by now, Mr. Hurst," General Stevens stated.

Durk took a moment to think this over. "Rutherford is a suspicious man, General. He must have changed the location. Let me think . . ."

The general watched Durk ruminate, his brow creased in thought. Durk's *DarkHorse* property had encompassed much of this area, and he knew it well. Finally, his face lit up.

"I think I know another good spot where they might affect the exchange," Durk said. "And the road leading from it to Rutherford's plantation it is wide enough for a wagon. I'll scout east of here to make sure."

General Stevens removed his hat and lit his pipe. Failure could mean statewide insurrection.

"All right; I just hope we're not too late," Stevens said.

Rutherford's group turned off the main road onto what was little more than a rutted trail shrouded in tree trunks and black limbs blocking the moon. Caleb's anxiety grew; he had no escape. As the riders descended into the dense forest, Caleb knew right away they weren't on the road Durk had described. He glanced at Rutherford beside him, but the colonel, body rigid in the saddle, stared straight ahead, eyes ablaze, visualizing a war waged on an imaginary battlefield.

Thirty yards ahead, someone lit a match. Following the light to a clearing, they found Jenkins standing beside a wagon, his horse nearby, while Devereau French hung back some distance on the McCorkle chestnut. Rutherford drew rein and leaned on Rebel's pommel, taking a moment to admire the boxes of Henrys stacked in the wagon bed. Real firepower there.

Rutherford's men and the sheriff dismounted. Noting Caleb still on the horse, Rutherford nodded to the man assigned to watch the boy, indicating Caleb, too, must dismount. The man grabbed Caleb by the sleeve and pulled him off the horse.

Both sides faced one another. "You got my money, Colonel?" Jenkins asked.

"I do." Rutherford turned to his gunmen. "Keep these two in your sights, boys." The hired men drew their pistols, aiming at Jenkins and French.

"You planning to cheat me?" Jenkins asked.

"No, I'm good pay," Rutherford said, "But first I want to know who shot me last week, and I want to know now."

"I have no idear, Colonel," Jenkins replied. "I ain't been into town."

"I was shot with a Henry, and you're the only man in Turkle who has any. The shooter got that rifle from you, didn't he?"

"Why would I shoot you?" Jenkins asked. He spit in the dirt. "And why would I sell one measly gun and put my whole supply at risk? That don't make no sense."

Rutherford studied Jenkins' face, thinking the situation over. "Your partner there, maybe he sold it to someone when your back was turned. What about it, French? Did you sell one of those Henrys?"

Every eye turned toward Devereau. Her eyes fixed with horror at Caleb, who'd seen her with the rifle at Ahronson's. If the boy revealed the encounter, she'd have to explain that she'd lost the gun and had no idea who'd stolen it. They'd never believe her. Surely she'd be tortured to get a name, and failing that, Rutherford would hang her on the spot.

Caleb's heart pounded rapidly, face flushing in panic. The boy knew that if he didn't speak up, he'd be passing a death sentence onto the little man. But if he admitted being the shooter, the colonel would have him killed.

"It's absurd to think that I shot you, Colonel," Devereau declared. "Has anyone ever accused me of being a marksman?"

Without warning, Sheriff Stubbs strode toward French, a suspicious leer across his face. "What a minute," Stubbs said. "That horse you're riding. Chestnut with white muzzle, white stockings on right front and rear? Why, I'd bet anything that's the McCorkle horse." He turned back toward Rutherford. "Colonel, that horse was stolen by whoever murdered a widow a couple counties over. Heck, I think I've got my man." There'd been a reward offered, but the sheriff kept that to himself.

Rutherford considered the situation. "That's of no consequence to me, Stubbs. Mr. Jenkins, who knew the location of these rifles, besides you that is?"

Jenkins spit toward French. "Just my partner here, Colonel."

In an instant, Devereau spurred the chestnut and galloped off. "Stubbs, get after him," Rutherford shouted. "I want to talk to him. Hurry!" The sheriff ran to his horse as fast as his stumpy legs could take him and mounted up.

Hearing this, Caleb couldn't contain himself. "Don't kill him, Colonel!" he shouted. "It couldn't be him."

"Wait a minute," Rutherford ordered, halting the sheriff. He turned his fury on the boy. "How do you know it wasn't French, boy?"

Caleb looked from face to face; every eye on him. "I . . .I . . ." he stuttered. "I weren't far away when they shot you, Colonel. I saw that man at the same time I heard the shot."

"Oh, you did?" Rutherford said with bitter sarcasm. "That's a marvelous coincidence. You didn't mention it when I asked about it before."

"It didn't come to mind, Colonel. It just now . . ."

"Say, Caleb, you bragged to me you were a dead shot, didn't you? Didn't you?"

"Well, sure . . ."

"Why would you protect Mr. French? Tell me that, boy. You've never seen him before tonight? Well, have you?"

Caleb stared at the ground; he had nothing to say.

"Frank, tie that boy's hands. He'll ride up front of you. He's slippery now. If he tries to run, you men shoot him down. Don't think a thing of it."

"Yes, sir, Colonel." The man grabbed Caleb by the arm and dragged him to the horse. Caleb pulled and resisted, but Frank struck him across the face. When Caleb touched his lip, his fingers came away with blood. Then two of Rutherford's men tied his hands in front of him and lifted him onto Frank's horse, and Frank climbed up behind him.

"All right, Stubbs, forget French. Let's finish our business here."

"Take in a dang partner!" Jenkins groused. He strutted to where Rutherford sat Rebel. "All right, Colonel. Give me my money and this hardware is your'n. That includes the wagon and stock pulling it. I wash my hands of it."

"Darrell, you teamster the wagon," Rutherford ordered, handing Jenkins the envelope with the cash. "The rest of you, mount up. We've got some friends waiting for their new firearms."

Jenkins mounted his own horse. "I guess there'll be a reward for French?" he asked the sheriff. Stubbs nodded. "Well, if he thinks he's safe at my place, he's mistaken." He tipped his hat and rode off.

Caleb was terrified but wouldn't let them see him cry. His hands were bound and he was bleeding. Rutherford was only waiting for the right time to have him killed. The colonel's face left no doubt about that.

One by one, the members of the gun club trickled into the nighttime clearing, an assortment of wealthy planters, small-plot dirt farmers, handymen, sharecroppers, townsmen, and a few with little to do but cause trouble. They tied up their horses in a nearby grove, then made their way on foot to a large bonfire lighting up the surrounding trees. Men sat on fallen trunks and squatted on their heels drinking coffee from pots over the fire. Some passed jugs.

Each had received the colonel's summons that day, but none knew why he'd gathered them together. The urgency in Rutherford's notes, however, spoke volumes. Anticipation was in the air.

"When's he going to get here?" one planter asked. "We've been waiting some time now."

"I don't know the colonel's business," a man replied. "Left town about suppertime."

"Well, he'd better hurry. If it starts raining, the ford might be dangerous to cross. We'll have to ride four miles north to that old bridge to make it back home."

"He be coming. Yes, sir, if the colonel say he coming, he be coming."

Caleb twisted restlessly, uncomfortable riding with his hands tied, only to be struck in the back of the head by the man behind him. "Settle down, boy, or I'll hurt you bad."

Rutherford led the group down the trail, followed by five riders and the wagon. When they passed a turnoff to the southwest, one of the riders asked, "Ain't that the way to your plantation, Colonel?"

"We're taking a different route. I've got to make a stop."

In panic, Caleb turned to watch as they passed the trail to Rutherford's. Now they weren't even taking the alternate route!

Desperate to leave some message on the chance Durk searched this area, Caleb leaned over and carefully worked his boot off, dropping it in the road. Durk had recently gifted the pair to him and would recognize it. "Straighten up, boy," the man behind him growled. "No tricks or I'll shoot you right here."

The caravan pressed on, riders and wagon. Caleb glanced back at his boot lying in the road. He prayed Durk would find it and that his life would be saved—a pretty slim chance.

# CHAPTER TWENTY-SIX

# PRECIPICE

Durk tied Contrition to a sapling and slipped rapidly through the tangle of swamp, slinking from tree to tree, creeper and vine tugging at his heels. Soon he came within sight of the road junction where he expected Rutherford would have to turn off, headed for his plantation. He crept toward the forested trail and knelt to examine the ground. No wagon tracks had broken the soil, nor was there any evidence of men passing. He was shocked. Rutherford wasn't taking this route either!

He followed the trail to where it joined the main road. Here, he did, indeed, find wagon tracks and the unmistakable disturbance of passing horses. But they were headed directly west, a route that would take Rutherford at least five miles out of his way. This was puzzling.

Still on foot, Durk followed the tracks another twenty yards. And then he saw it: a boot lying on the road, too small to be a man's. He ran to where it lay and picked it up. It was Caleb's! Clearly, the boy had dropped it as a signal that he was in trouble.

Durk's heart dropped into his stomach. He tried to think through the situation, but he was gripped by the fear of what Rutherford might do to the boy.

Breaking his paralysis, Durk ran to Contrition, grabbed the reins, leaped into the saddle, and galloped back to notify the general. While he rode, Durk would have to figure out where Rutherford was headed and design another trap. He just hoped there was enough time.

Rutherford tried to settle in the saddle, but riding with one bad leg and one useless one allowed him no leverage or balance. He studied Caleb, the cause of his loss of free movement. He wanted to be done with the boy, but the sound of a shot might expose their group, and besides, the sheriff was there. The weapons and the nigras came first.

"Frank. Tie that boy across Nancy's saddle and take him to my place. Take that trail we passed about a mile back." The colonel waved Frank over to whisper in his ear: "When you get there, put him down. And have fun with it; don't feel rushed to put a bullet in his head. Then bury him in the south woods."

"Yes, sir, Colonel. Be my pleasure."

"I believe I know where they're going. The road crosses the Chickasaw branch at a ford about seven miles further west. I haven't been up there, but folks tell me that's where Rutherford's gun club meets. The tracks I found were still pretty fresh. If we hurry, we should be able to get into position ahead of him."

The general paced, uncertain of what to do. He stopped and turned to Durk. "Are you sure it's Rutherford?"

"Yes, sir. Riders and deep wagon ruts; that's the rifles. I saw one spot where a wheel had sunk into backwash up to the axle. Rutherford's men must have had to push it free; their bootmarks were deep."

In contemplation, the general slapped his gloves into his open hand. Finally, he turned to his officers. "All right, men, one last attempt. Satisfy you, Mr. Hurst?"

"Yes, sir! Let's go. We'll circle south through rough ground to circumvent them."

"Mount up, everyone. Follow Hurst here."

For the first time that day, Durk was able to breathe. He climbed up on Contrition to wait for the soldiers to organize themselves. The chase wasn't over—and there was still a chance to save Caleb. He actually didn't know the area they were headed toward, nor the route to get there. But he wasn't going to tell anyone that. He just had to trust to luck.

Contrition splashed through the slough of low-lying swamp, sliding and stumbling up an incline until the horse emerged onto dry land. The circular route to the ford had been more treacherous than Durk had anticipated, slow going through heavily overgrown stretches, forced to retreat to avoid deep water in others. Behind him, the troopers grumbled at every setback. But Durk was determined to get there—and fast.

Durk turned aside and waited as the line of mounted troopers behind him worked their way up the bank. At last, they neared a patch where the forest thinned and were able to spur their tired horses to a cantor. Durk sensed they were getting close to the ford. Drawing rein, he held up his hand as the soldiers behind him halted. Looking up at the summit before them, they could see the sky lit by what appeared to be a large bonfire coming from the other side. The general rode up to join him.

"The ford should be just the other side this hill, sir."

"All right, men," the general said. "Dismount. Draw weapons and fan out." The soldiers drew their rifles from their saddles and formed a crescent-shaped line. Satisfied, the general ordered them to surmount the hill. "Quiet, men, we don't know how many are down there, nor if we have the benefit of surprise. Hurst, you wait back with the horses."

"Don't forget, General," Durk said, "Rutherford has my boy."

"Horses! Other side of the hill," one man shouted, pointing to the southern hillside.

The others around the campfire quieted. "Must be the colonel." Relieved, the gun club members rose and brushed off their pants. They'd waited some time and were anxious to know what mischief Rutherford had in store for them. Men hurriedly shoveled dirt onto the fire, and a few began drifting toward their waiting mounts.

"Soldiers!" someone shouted, as the trees became alive with army troops descending toward them like a blue wave through the forest. A number of men drew their pistols. Others ran to their saddles and drew rifles.

"Hold on," one planter shouted. "Put up your arms, boys! We aren't fighting no army. Don't give them an excuse to shoot." The citizens lowered their weapons as the regiment advanced, surrounding them.

When it was certain there would be no gunfire, General Stevens rode leisurely down the hill to the planter who had assumed spokesman duties. "What are you men doing here? Seems an odd place to gather for a bit of comradeship this far from town."

"None of your damn business, Yankee. We aren't breaking any law."

The general examined the area, fixing his sight on the road to the east. "That's true. Is there a Colonel Rutherford among you? I need to talk to him."

"He ain't here," a man shouted.

"That so?" General Stevens waved an officer to come to his side. He leaned over and whispered, "Rutherford hasn't made it this far yet. Take one company to intercept him. And take Hurst. Hurry."

"Yes, sir." While the officer assembled a company and ascended the hill double-time, the general contemplated what to do with the people around the site. If he released them now, one would surely ride ahead to warn Rutherford he was headed into a trap. But there were no legal grounds to hold them. Finally, he decided on a delaying tactic.

"All right," the general announced. "I won't hold you. But just for the record, you will all register your names with the sergeant. Once that is done, you are all free to go. Line up under that oak."

The spokesman confronted the general. "I am sorry, General. But you cannot require us to put our names on any list. Our identities are none of the army's damn business."

"So you refuse?"

"We do." The men behind him voiced their agreement.

"All right. Corporal, go get your writing materials. You men will all line up and, one at a time, refuse to be identified, after which you are all free to return home." General Stevens leaned over and whispered, "And take your time doing it, Corporal."

That would be delay enough.


Colonel Rutherford slumped in the saddle, his back burning and legs throbbing like hot poker stabs. Nevertheless, he felt victorious, straining to hold his head high. He glanced proudly at his arsenal. Soon it would be distributed to hands throughout the region, hands that will rectify a great injustice. And even tonight, many Henrys will be in hands that will burn out the nest of blacks at *FrenchAcres* once and for all. And won't that be a pleasure to witness.

Snapped from his reverie, Rutherford heard riders thundering toward them. He instinctively wanted to spur Rebel and dissolve into the forest, but his eyes lit on the guns. Abandoning them would mean abandoning his chance for revenge. Besides, with his legs practically useless, attempting to escape, even on horseback, would be futile.

"Draw your pistols, boys. We'll fight it out along this line," he ordered, as if on the battlefield.

But the company of uniformed soldiers, rifles and pistols at the ready, had already galloped to encircle them. Panicked, Rutherford looked around to issue an order, but saw the sheriff and all five of his hirelings with their hands raised. There would be no shootout: he was trapped. "Draw your weapons!" he repeated, but no one moved. "Fire, you cowards! Shoot them!"

The company officer rode up to Rutherford. "Drop that pistol, Colonel. I don't want any bloodshed."

Seeing no way out, Rutherford fell into a black despair. His inclination was to die a warrior's death, to charge at his captors, pistol blazing. But then he realized he hadn't been defeated yet, not completely: he still had the rifles.

"Do you own that wagon and cargo?" the officer asked, pointing.

"Yes, they belong to me," Rutherford replied, sliding his pistol into the holster.

"What do those boxes contain?"

"Farm equipment. It's private property, Lieutenant."

"We'll see about that. Dolan, open one of those crates."

"Don't touch them. I'm not breaking any law."

"Open it, Dolan."

As Rutherford issued a barrage of epithets, the trooper slid off his horse, slammed the rifle stock hard against one of the boxes, and pried it open. Then he reached in and withdrew a Henry rifle, holding it high for all to see.

"Colonel Rutherford, I am arresting you for possession of stolen military weapons. Seize him. And seize the others."

Durk rode up as one trooper took the reins from Rutherford, holding his pistol on him. "Where's Caleb, Rutherford?" Durk demanded.

"I don't know anything about the boy."

"Yes, you do," Durk said, holding up Caleb's boot. "He was with you. Now where is he?"

"The boy who crippled me!" Rutherford said bitterly. "He's free to go where he wants."

"Where you're going, that's more than I can say for you, Colonel. Those cells can get quite cold in the winter, steaming hot in the summer. You won't have Wheeler or trash like these to keep after you."

"If I had my pistol, you'd be dead now, Hurst, you traitor, you coward," Rutherford spewed.

"Yes, but you have neither a pistol nor rifles it seems. Lieutenant, this man kidnapped my boy. Could you lend me a few troopers to recover him—if he's still alive?"

Furious and despairing, Rutherford yanked off his hat and threw it at Durk, but it fell limply to the ground, pin of crossed swords falling into the dirt. No one bothered to retrieve it for him.


Retracing the route Rutherford had taken, Durk tried to think of what the colonel might have done with Caleb. Leading three troopers, Durk saw no break in wagon ruts and hoofprints. Then a mile further east, he noticed a change in the pattern. He dismounted and examined the road. Two horses had left Rutherford's group and turned back riding single file, as if one was leading the other. That meant if Caleb was on one, there was only one man guarding him.

"A man has taken Caleb this way, likely headed directly to Rutherford's plantation. Let's get him, boys!" Durk shouted, mounting and spurring Contrition. And the four were off in a cloud of dust.


Frank rode at a leisurely pace down the wide forested trail, leading Old Nancy by the reins. The boy, hogtied across Nancy's saddle, had squealed at first, but stopped when Frank threatened to quiet him permanently. Frank had already shaken off any reluctance to shoot a child. He'd put men down before, and each was easier than the last. This one wouldn't appreciably trouble his conscience. He relaxed in the saddle, letting his mind wander untroubled.

Then he heard hooves thundering toward him. Could it be a message from the colonel? He drew his pistol, uncertain of what to do.

Durk and one trooper thundered toward him, then halted thirty yards away.

"Hold it there, Hurst. I've got a bead on you."

"I just want the boy," Durk shouted. "Hand him over."

This was a quandary. If Frank lost the boy, the colonel would be angry—and he wouldn't have any bargaining leverage. He aimed his pistol at Caleb's head. "Can't do that."

Without warning, two other troopers appeared behind him, rifles leveled. "We've got you surrounded," Durk said. "Let us have the boy, and we'll let you go. Drop the reins."

Seeing he had no choice, Frank dropped Nancy's reins, turned his mount, and spurred it southwest, heading for the colonel's place. In moments, he was out of sight.

"Let him go!" the army officer shouted to his troops. "We've got the boy."

Spooked from the excitement, Old Nancy, with Caleb trussed and tied across her saddle, bucked and kicked. Durk quickly dismounted, hurrying to secure her bridle and settle her down. Then he lifted Caleb to the ground and untied him. He threw the ropes aside and helped Caleb to his feet, offering him his boot. Ignoring the boot, Caleb threw a big hug around Durk.

"He was gonna kill me, Durk," Caleb said, voice cracking.

"I know he was, son. Let's get you home." Caleb pulled on his boot and mounted Old Nancy. Then he sat admiring Durk, waiting for his rescuer, his friend, his father to begin the journey home.

Beside him, Durk climbed up on Contrition and settled back in the saddle. In an instant, Durk grew lightheaded, as if every drop of energy had drained from his skull. The ride home seemed to stretch to the far side of the earth. He closed his eyes, nearly dozing off, then mentally slapped himself awake. So he'd surmounted the first barrier, a high one, indeed: the colonel and his minions. He knew he'd been lucky.

His mind cleared, and his thinking fixed on the tasks ahead. The odds seemed exceedingly long; but they were far longer just yesterday. It would be up to the courts. But perhaps he could place his thumb on the scales of justice—and do it in a most unexpected manner.

# Chapter Twenty-seven
# RESTING PLACE

Antoinette stepped onto the sidewalk boards outside Ahronson's, weary and covered with a film of road dust. It had been a long time since she'd slept in her own bed, spending her nights on roadsides or in squatter cabins en route to Jackson and back. Turning, she exchanged her good-byes with Big Josh. "You're welcome to stay tonight."

"I got business in *FrenchAcres*," Josh replied with a final wave.

Antoinette watched him trudge on, then entered the store. She nodded to a townswoman leaving, the last customer of the day. Then Antoinette examined the shelves: not as empty as when she'd left. Ellen must have done enough business to build up their depleted inventory. A good sign.

She approached Ellen sitting at Durk's desk, immersed in her Bible. "Ellen, I'm back from Jackson!"

Ellen looked up. "Thank the Lord."

"How is Lou doing?"

"The poison's mostly out of him. He gets up on his crutches once't in a while. He's sleeping now, poor thing."

"That's good news. Where are Durk and Caleb?"

"I'm scared. They didn't come home last night. They been running in and out at all hours, all very secret-like. I don't know what they been up to."

Antoinette felt a tinge of fear run down her spine. "Well, thank you for taking over. You've done a wonderful job. Would you like some time off? You've earned it."

"I would. Ain't hardly been to church since the day you left."

"Why don't you go now? Would you like to do that?"

"Yes, mam. Thank you kindly."

Ellen closed her Bible and, marking her place with a strip of cloth, departed. Exhausted and anxious about Durk and Caleb, Antoinette collapsed into Durk's chair. She opened the store ledger, but was unable to focus on the columns of numbers. Feeling weary, she closed the book and buried her head in her arms to rest just a moment.

Through the haze of sleep, she heard the back door slam and light footsteps cross the kitchen, coming her way. She sat up with a start. Perhaps it was them.

Suddenly, Devereau French appeared from the hallway, pointing a pistol at her. "Well, Mrs. DuVallier . . . or is it Mrs. *French*," Devereau said through gritted teeth. "Or is it, in fact, Mrs. Hurst? Which surname do you belong to these days, Antoinette?"

"Does it really matter, Devereau? Is it Miss French now . . . or still *Mr.* French? Which do *you* belong to? What is it you want?"

"Well, sister—or should I say *wife*? Little matter. We're going to take a ride together, just you and me."

"I can't leave. I'm caring for a sick man."

"The health of your nigra isn't my concern. Get out of that chair. Now!" Devereau's pistol waved Antoinette toward the hall. "My horse is out back. Come on or I'll put a bullet through your lovely head right here."

Seeing the zealousness in Devereau's eyes, Antoinette rose and headed for the kitchen, followed by Devereau pressing the pistol into her back. Outside, Devereau ordered Antoinette up on a dusty thoroughbred and climbed up behind her. Once mounted, they circled behind the stores lining Main Street, then took the first side street they came to. This muddy lane ran through the poorest part of town, a row of dilapidated shacks sitting on debris-filled lots. The dirt-caked children running about ceased their games to stare at the odd pair. Finally, the riders reached the road to *FrenchAcres*.

"You're taking us home?" Antoinette teased.

"*My* home, not yours. *Mine*."

"Nothing is left there for you, Devereau. You know very well the place burned down. People say you were the cause."

"*You* were the cause, sister. Of that—and of Mother's demise. I was merely the instrument of those calamities. You're the guilty party, not me."

"How could I. . . ? You're mad."

"No, dear, I've grown quite sane over the last few years. Quite sane." Antoinette thought it best not to argue.

—*I know what you're planning, fool. Don't you do it!*

—I'll do what I want. And I'm nobody's fool, not any more. Especially not yours.

—*You are deranged, my darling.*

—Not at all. I've never seen things so clearly. I see everything like in stark bright sunlight, every detail.

Devereau began mumbling incoherently, her voice trailing off to a whisper, as if in conversation with a ghost. This puzzled Antoinette, but she said nothing. Where was this madwoman taking her, and why?

It was growing late as they approached the grounds of *FrenchAcres*. Reaching the former mansion's weed-covered front lawn, they rode through the fallen gateway and up the dirt drive, passing the ashes of the once-proud French edifice.

—*I've kept your room waiting for you, daughter. Make yourself at home.*

—Ha! There'll be no more prisons for me, Mother, especially not that one.

—*You may be right, child. You know, they hang you for murdering old ladies.*

—That's my business. You just keep to yourself.

They passed the burnt remains of the stable. Further along, Antoinette noticed a construction site, probably to replace it.

Finally, they reached the French family graveyard, drawing Antoinette's attention immediately to Louis Edward's grave. Devereau drew rein and slid off the horse. "Climb down, sister."

Antoinette obeyed. "What are we doing here?"

"I think you deserve a last visit to his grave. Go ahead, I'm right behind you."

"What do you mean 'a last visit'?" a suddenly terrified Antoinette asked, her heart racing.

"Never you mind. Go on. Say goodbye to Louis Edward." Devereau stuck the pistol into Antoinette's ribs, prodding her through the entrance. Antoinette pulled aside the loosely hanging gate, and it fell onto the ground. Devereau kicked it aside. "Go on."

ED PROTZEL

Antoinette lifted her skirt and made her way through the fallen stones and weeds, stopping before the boy's grave. "What has gotten into your head, Devereau?" Antoinette asked. "Haven't we both suffered enough?"

"What do you know about suffering? You had your social seasons in New Orleans, your gowns, jewels, and carriages. You had your handsome, rich husband. And you had Louis Edward for most of his three years of life. Me?" she spit angrily. "I had no one but my jailer, that lunatic. No husband, no friends. You talk about suffering? I suffered."

—*Still an ingrate! Without me you'd have been an indigent orphan. You'd probably have starved. I gave you everything, and you threw it all away! Why? Because of that man. You're pathetic . . .*

—I had nothing, Mother. Nothing but sorrow and heartbreak. You hated me. Don't deny it.

Shocked at seeing Devereau's face contorted by a disjointed diatribe, Antoinette understood enough to know that Devereau was chastising her dead mother. If she was to survive this episode, she would have to find some accommodation, some common ground, with her half-sister.

"Devereau, you forget," Antoinette said gently. "When I was very small, still a little girl, our mother *sold* me—yes, sold me—to an old man as his concubine, to be, in effect, his slave. Why? So she could be free to marry your rich father without the evidence of her sordid past. Can you comprehend that?"

"You don't know the half of it!" Devereau chided. "She was making me into a recluse, just like her. Now do you see it? Do you see what a completely, utterly hopeless existence Mother forced upon me? Loneliness, sister. That is suffering . . ." Devereau broke into tears, her body trembling.

"I'm so sorry, Devereau," Antoinette said sympathetically. "Truly. To impose such misery on one's own daughter is unimaginable." She tried to put an arm around Devereau, but Devereau forced her back with the pistol barrel.

Wiping her eyes and nose with her sleeve, Devereau commanded, "Kneel before his grave. Kneel! Say your final goodbye to our child."

"I won't," Antoinette said.

"You're ruining everything!" Devereau shouted. "This is not the way I pictured it. You must kneel at Louis Edward's grave."

"I won't do it."

*—She won't kneel for you, fool. Let her go. Do you want to kill our only remaining blood?"*

"I . . .I . . ." Devereau didn't know what to do.

Seeing Devereau's obvious confusion, Antoinette's voice softened. "Listen, Devereau, you don't want to kill me. I'm your sister, the only one who understands you. Haven't you had enough killing?"

A morose Devereau sat on a fallen monument, sobbing. "All I ever wanted was my own family: a man of my own, children, a home—a *real* home. Can you imagine, I was jealous of my own slaves!"

"Devereau," Antoinette ventured, sympathizing, "you are a pretty woman. Yes. You can start over, begin your life as the real woman you want to be."

"It's too late for me," Devereau said, rising to her feet. "Too late. I'm wanted for murder . . ."

"For shooting Mother? No one will bother about that. Durk will get those old charges thrown out."

"No, not just Mother. Where do you think I got that horse I'm riding? A few counties over, I killed a widow and stole it. They have me dead to rights. It's hopeless . . ."

*—When they hang you for killing the old widow, they'll discover your charade. "Why, Devereau French has been a woman all along." they'll say. They'll laugh at you, daughter, as I told you they would. Oh, how they'll laugh.*

Devereau's head swam, the trees and monuments swirling about. Then, sobbing uncontrollably, she threw herself face-first onto the boy's grave. Like a drunk, she clawed at the earth above him, rubbing her cheek into the dirt as if into a pillow, trying in vain to hug the body lying six feet below.

Horrified by this sight, Antoinette stumbled away, but tripped on a grave marker and fell backwards, losing her breath. When she managed to sit up, she saw Devereau on her knees, clinging to Louis Edward's stone. She wanted to reach for her, to console her, but was unable to move.

"Enough of this torment," Devereau cried into the darkness. "Enough of your deceit, your greed, your cold, unfeeling heart—enough of that hateful voice. I am going to free myself from you, Mother, forever. For once in my life, I'm going to act like a man." She put the pistol into her mouth.

"Don't, Devereau! Stop!" Antoinette shouted. "Devereau . . ."

There was a single loud explosion, and Devereau French collapsed in a spray of crimson. Her trials were, indeed, at an end.

Antoinette pushed herself to her feet and made her way to her sister's lifeless body. "Poor Devereau, finally liberated from your bondage."

Shaken, Antoinette brushed off her dress and ran her fingers through her hair. Then she made her way in the darkness toward the McCorkle thoroughbred, careful not to stumble. What was she to do now? She tried to gather her thoughts. When Turkle learns Devereau was a woman, then Antoinette's sham marriage to her would be exposed. She would not inherit *FrenchAcres*; consequently, she could not grant rights to the freedmen occupying the land.

Still shaking, she mounted the horse and headed back to find Josh. She needed his advice and his help. Her thoughts kept returning to Devereau. Yes, they would bury her immediately—beside Louis Edward; it was the only kind thing to do.

Hopefully, that would ensure Devereau's true gender stayed concealed, if the authorities did not exhume the body. And then there's the matter of the death certificate. If Durk could make it all work somehow, perhaps she might be able to complete her plan. There was some justice in that. After all, hadn't these folks earned it after generations of toil?

If only Durk could pull it off.

# Chapter Twenty-eight

# DURK'S GRAND STRATEGY

It was well after midnight by the time Caleb was rescued and Rutherford was taken into custody. A pretty good result, even if the ordeal had shattered Durk's nerves. Figuring Antoinette was due back any time now, he wanted to return to town immediately, but the boy was far too exhausted to make the long trip back, and Durk was dog-tired himself. Searching for a place to rest, Durk found a shack near a ferry crossing by the Chickasaw branch. There the two slept on horse blankets spread out on the dirt floor, exposed to the elements through the hovel's missing boards.

The next morning, the sunlight broke through the absent slats in the roof and walls to wake them from a deep sleep. After trapping and cooking a squirrel for breakfast, they mounted up.

It was mid-afternoon when Durk and Caleb reached Ahronson's. "Hello, we're back," Durk called. Seeing Ellen, he asked, "Has Antoinette returned from Jackson?"

"She was here when I left for church last evening, but not when I got back. Left Lou here all by hisself. I been scared for her, Durk."

"Did you ask Lou about her?"

"He don't know nothing neither."

"I'll go look for her, Durk," Caleb offered.

If Antoinette was in trouble, as Durk feared, he wasn't going to let Caleb fall into it. "No, Caleb, you're not leaving this store. You disobeyed me once and almost got yourself killed. Now go to your room and get some rest. We'll talk later." Caleb slunk off to his room, slamming the door in frustration.

Durk had to search for Antoinette. But where? She wouldn't have left Lou alone if she had a choice, so that implied she'd been coerced.

The only place he could imagine her going was to *FrenchAcres*. Why or with whom, he had no idea, but he had to find out.

It was evening by the time he rode through the fallen French gateway and past the mansion ruins. Approaching the graveyard, he spotted a group of people congregated there and an unfamiliar thoroughbred tied at the fence. He dismounted, concealing Contrition behind a cluster of trees, then soundlessly stalked the gathering from the wooded side. Hiding behind a large oak, he could make out Antoinette talking quietly with Big Josh and a few other freedmen who were leaning on shovels. Durk breathed a sigh of relief.

He emerged from the darkness. "Antoinette," he called. Seeing him, Antoinette ran into his arms. "What's going on? What are you doing here?"

She led Durk to the freshly covered grave beside Louis Edward's, relating Devereau's confession of the McCorkle murder, her confounding suicide and hurried burial.

"Why'd you stick her in the ground so fast?" Durk asked.

"We had to conceal her body," Antoinette replied. "If folks knew she was a woman, my claim as French's widow would become a fraud. I'd likely face prison."

"Well," Durk remarked, staring at the grave, "at least she's with Louis Edward. He's the only thing that gave her any comfort." He then embraced Big Josh, relieved that he'd returned safely from Jackson. While the freedmen, who had come to help bury their former owner, said their goodbyes and returned to their homes, the three made their way to the drive and led the McCorkle horse away.

"Where were you and Caleb?" Antoinette asked. "Ellen said you were acting secretive before you disappeared yesterday. What were you up to, Durk?"

Durk described what had happened just the night before—although it seemed much longer ago. When he told them that Rutherford and his henchmen, as well as the sheriff, had been arrested for possession of stolen military rifles, Josh and Antoinette cheered, their greatest fears erased, their fondest hope suddenly revived.

"But what we going to do 'bout Devereau?" Josh asked Durk. "That horse been stolen after a murder. You the lawyer."

Durk took a moment to consider the situation. "First, we have to let folks know she's dead—somehow. If they think she's still alive, Antoinette's claim would be highly problematic."

"But the doctor won't sign no death certificate if he can't see the body," Josh interjected.

"You're right about that," Durk admitted. He paused to study the McCorkle horse. "Too bad Bake's been arrested. I could have convinced him to sign the certificate."

"My so-called marriage tactic still seems flimsy," Antoinette cautioned. "I fear the planters and the lawyers will storm right through our argument."

Durk scratched his head. "I've been thinking. You know Mrs. French wasn't one to leave loose ends. And she surely wouldn't hang the future of her empire on such a slender thread as Devereau's sham marriage to Antoinette. There's another avenue I want to explore before I go to court." This raised spirits a bit.

"What about *DarkHorse*?" Josh asked. "Any chance of getting it back?"

"Didn't you say the back taxes on that land are substantial?" Antoinette asked.

"Yes," Durk granted. "The taxes I owe are far out of our reach. Even if I win the rights in court, the authorities can still confiscate it. There'd be nothing I could do, unless . . ."

"You got some kind of trick up your sleeve?" Josh asked.

"Maybe," Durk replied, pacing back and forth. "It's a bit farfetched, and won't be easy to pull off. If I succeed, though, there'll be some justice served. But Turkle will be mad. Yes, sir, folks will certainly be mad."

Durk glanced through the window at the evening shadows encroaching upon the verbena outside the judge's home. Evening was coming. He pushed his rook to the eighth rank and declared, "Check."

Judge Fairbanks took a sip from his whiskey and studied the chessboard. Seeing his position was hopeless, he turned over his king.

"Mate," the judge responded. He rose and crossed his study to refill his glass. "Another drink?"

"Neither a drink nor another game, your honor. You've worn me out. I have to be home."

The judge returned to his seat. Forehead lined in thought, the elderly man studied his opponent with profound intensity, as if making a momentous ruling. He took one sip, then another.

"Your hearings Friday, Mr. Hurst. You have quite a task ahead, what with every lawyer and moneyed interest in the county lined up against you. Have you planned your strategy as deeply as you did on these sixty-four squares?"

Durk downed his whiskey. "I've prepared as best I can, Judge. Both cases will be difficult, to say the least. Have you thought about the two items I mentioned when I arrived? They could make an enormous difference." Durk waited nervously for the judge's reply.

"You say Mrs. DuVallier-French intends to deed *FrenchAcres* to the freedmen who are currently living there. Do you think these people can possibly succeed?"

"I'm more than certain of it, Judge. They will succeed and prosper."

"But they seem so primitive, so lacking in management skills. You realize, they face a very competitive world out there."

"They've been treated as chattel for generations, Judge Fairbanks, deprived of an education. But they will learn, I assure you; many have already. Moreover, it is our moral duty to give them a chance. If they fail, of course, the local planters will wind up with the land anyway."

Judge Fairbanks thought long and hard. "I've something for you," he said. He rose and went to his desk, where he withdrew a document from the top drawer and returned.

"The late-Mrs. French used to entrust certain papers to me which she didn't want made public. They would come to me in sealed envelopes, identified only by date, number, and title marked on the cover. Sometimes she had me witness and notarize signature pages without making the relevant document available to me, then she'd send me the full document in a sealed envelope later. I never opened them unless she requested that I do so. Being private matters, I kept a whole stack of these in a locked box in my home, not here in my office. Many were never opened; I assume these were for contingencies that didn't bear fruit. I never asked questions.

"Well, the ownership of *FrenchAcres* will be contested in my courtroom this week. So last night, I unlocked that box. Mrs. French has been dead four years now, you understand, so I took the liberty of unsealing each one. Most were meaningless to me or moot. However, there was this one dated five years ago, in 1860."

He handed Durk the document. "This may prove pivotal in one of your cases, but don't tell anyone I gave it to you. Understand? And only use it if you're sure it can make a difference. If you see you're going to lose the case anyway, please return it to me. We won't speak of it again."

Durk studied the document as a smile lit his face. "I won't betray your trust, Judge Fairbanks." He folded the papers into his jacket pocket and withdrew a single sheet. "One last favor, Judge. Will you sign Devereau French's death certificate for me?"

"No, Durk, I'm sorry. I can't do that. You'll have to ask the doctor."

"But the body is buried . . ."

"I'm sorry; it wouldn't be proper."

Both men stood to shake hands. "Good luck," the judge said. "To prevail in my courtroom, you will need more good fortune than you probably deserve."

"Those depending on me deserve more good fortune than I can ever provide. I only hope I can prove worthy of their trust."


As Durk passed the stable, a breathless Walker ran to catch him. "Mr. Durk," he shouted. "Mr. Durk!"

Durk turned back. "What's the emergency, Walker?"

"He back," Walker coughed, catching his breath. "He lef' his horse wit' me 'bout a hour ago."

Durk couldn't help but laugh. "Well, my friend, let's get to saddling a horse."


Sheriff Stubbs trundled down the sidewalk from the boarding house where he stayed, fed and prepared to enter his office for the first time in days. He'd been arrested along with Rutherford and his henchmen, but now he was back, having been released on General Stevens' orders. He took a moment to pull down his vest, which had ridden up above his considerable belly, then took a plug of tobacco from his back pocket and bit off a chew.

"Sheriff," someone shouted. "Sheriff Stubbs!"

The sheriff turned to examine the town square. Headed toward him from the stable, Durksen Hurst led a beautiful thoroughbred horse with two white stockings, its coat brushed, its saddle of expensive, finely worked leather polished. When Stubbs saw the stallion, he coughed, nearly swallowing his chew.

"Good to see you back, Sheriff. I see the army let you go. I imagine you signed a statement, or you'd still be their prisoner."

"Never you mind what I signed, Hurst. I'm a public servant, not one of the colonel's hired thugs. I told the army the truth, the whole truth, and nothin' but the truth. Chips fall where they may; I had my honor to consider."

Durk laughed. "Looks like the chips are falling on Colonel Rutherford. He's got some hard years in prison ahead of him, especially given his condition. I'd love to see his face when they sentence him. Fortunately, Sheriff, your honor is still unblemished!" He handed Stubbs the horse's reins. "Thought you'd want this."

"How . . . how'd you come by this animal, Hurst? This is the McCorkle horse. People been looking for it . . ."

". . . since Devereau French showed in town, I bet."

"That's right. It seems French killed McCorkle's widow and stole this animal. It was me who identified French as the killer, you know."

Durk reached inside his coat pocket and handed Stubbs two copies of an official document. "Well, Sheriff, looks like justice has prevailed in the McCorkle murder: Mr. French is dead and buried. Sign these death certificates and you can claim the reward. Are you going to return the horse—or is the horse worth more than the reward?" he added, an amused glint in his eye.

"Oh, I'll get the reward. And there ain't no family left to claim that horse neither. McCorkle was killed in the war, you see, and they had no surviving children. This horse is being held in the custody of the Turkle public trust," he said, patting the horse's neck. "I've done impounded it for civic purposes, at least temporarily."

"Might be a pretty good mount for law enforcement duties," Durk laughed.

"It'll be a sweet ride, that's for sure."

"Taxpayers will have to pay the upkeep, though," Durk teased, "being owned by the public trust and all. Just sign the death certificates, two copies."

Stubbs studied the documents. "This says French committed suicide, shot himself in the head."

"You just need to sign off, and everything's square."

"But I ain't seen the body. How can I sign a paper when I ain't seen the *corpus*?"

"You were out of commission, Sheriff, off doing army business— keeping your honor and all. Listen, we had to get French in the ground; he was a bloody mess." Durk stuck his finger deep into his mouth and made a shooting sound.

"Now if you want him dug up, your department will have to pay the labor. We paid for the burial." Seeing a suspicious look enter the sheriff's eye, Durk yanked the reins from his hand. "I'll hold the horse till you sign. It's an open-and-shut matter of 'lawful discovery and legitimate confiscation', right there in the law book." Durk chuckled at his imaginary reference to a book which he knew the sheriff had never read—and maybe couldn't.

"Besides, I know where French is buried. Can't claim that reward without the *corpus*, right? And possession of this exceptional stud is ninety percent of the law, ain't it?"

Stubbs studied the McCorkle horse, a fine animal for sure. Hoping to mask his glee, he pretended to grow serious. "Well, I guess there's no sense in spending public money on a deceased killer. Least he's in the ground. After all, like you said, it is a' open-and-shut case of that law you done cited. Yep, you done this right for a change, Hurst. You done right. Come into my office, and I'll sign these here papers. You can file one at the courthouse for me. Will you do that? I'll send a copy to the folks over in McCorkle's hometown."

"Of course I will, Bake," Durk replied, handing him back the reins. "I'm just here to be a good citizen."

"Well, don't you forget that, Hurst. I got my eye on you."

"I know you do, Sheriff. You're way ahead of me."

"By the way, where is Mr. French buried?"

"Where? Why the French family graveyard, of course. What did you expect?"

*Death certificate: check. Judge Fairbanks' document: check. A day's ride to visit Wounded Wolf tomorrow: checkmate! Unless Wounded Wolf takes it into his head to kill me, always a possibility.*

It was mid-afternoon by the time Durk emerged from thick forest to reach the Chickasaw village. Everyone turned to watch as he led Contrition on foot through the common areas.

Asking after Wounded Wolf, Durk was directed to where the Indian was throwing knives into a tree trunk with a friend. The Indian yanked his knife from the tree and confronted Durk.

"What do you want here, Dark Horse?" Wounded Wolf threatened, brandishing the knife.

"I want nothing. I have something *for* you."

"The horse is yours; we are even. I don't want it."

"That's not it, Wounded Wolf. I mean I have something for the Chickasaw, for the tribe."

"We have seen the white man's gifts, Golden Tongue. The Indian ends up holding nothing, the white man everything. You stole the land you call *DarkHorse* from our people. Haven't you taken enough? Go away."

"Just let me say what I came for."

"Say it, then go, or I will plant this knife in you. We have nothing left for you to steal."

"All right, my old friend. Listen to my words . . ."

# Chapter Twenty-nine
# THE TRIAL

There hadn't been such an exciting spectacle in Turkle since last spring when that famous preacher came to town to save souls in a Chautauqua tent! The sweltering courtroom was jammed, with the wealthier claimants from throughout the county—the planters, merchants, cotton traders, and their lawyers—taking the prime seats in front to wait their turn. Spectators filled the remaining seats and stood crammed together in the back, spilling out the doorway into the hall. Every window had been thrown open in hopes a non-existent breeze would alleviate the suffocating heat, to no avail, as the curious jostled for position on the lawn to view the proceedings.

Durk watched anxiously from one of the tables set out for the claimants. Beside him sat Antoinette wearing modest calico, hoping to gain the court's sympathy. Their case would be called next, the last on the morning docket. Then it would be up to the judge.

Nearby, Turkle's leading citizen, James Clifton, sat at what normally would be the prosecutor's table, nervously fiddling with his hat brim. Standing beside him, his lawyer, Wayne Dunham, his face a mask of confidence, was finishing up his presentation.

"Lastly, I present to the court this registered bond, the legal obligation of Mrs. Marie Brussard French, the deceased owner of *FrenchAcres* plantation and majority stockholder of Turkle Bank." He handed the paper to the bailiff, who carried it to the judge. Judge Fairbanks took a moment to peruse it.

"This legal obligation is recognized by the court," Judge Fairbanks announced. "Please continue, Mr. Dunham."

"As this bond proves, your honor, my client, Mr. Clifton, was owed two thousand dollars by the French family at the time of Mrs. French's untimely death. Therefore, in the absence of any *legitimate* heir to Mrs. French's estate, I move that Mr. Clifton be made executor of said estate, with first option to purchase or complete discretion to sell any assets of said estate without restriction; to recover his losses and be made whole; and to revive the fortunes of the poorly run bank. That concludes my case, your honor." Dunham closed his briefcase.

As he took his chair, Clifton shared a congratulatory handshake with him. Smiling and exchanging pleasantries, the pair, emanating assurance of their victory, awaited the judge's ruling.

"Call the final claimant," the judge told the bailiff.

"Mrs. Antoinette DuVallier-French, present your case," the bailiff called out.

"I represent Mrs. DuVallier-French," Durk said, striding to the bench, brushing past Clifton and Dunham. "Well done, gentleman. That's the best rationale—so far." Raising his chin in a snub, Clifton turned away, with neither of the two acknowledging the remark.

"May I please have a look at that bond, your honor?" Durk asked.

"You may," Judge Fairbanks replied. The judge handed him the bond, and Durk studied it a moment. Then he returned to the table and untied his stack of documents.

"Let it be recorded," Durk said, "that the bond in question is an *unsecured* note signed by the late-*Devereau* French, not by his mother, the late-Mrs. Marie Brussard French. Therefore, Devereau French was *personally* liable for this debt, not the Marie Brussard French estate."

Dunham angrily snapped to his feet. "Devereau was signing for his momma, Judge. Everybody knows the old lady was a recluse. And her gnarly hands: she could barely use them. No, sir, the note represents a *family* obligation *in toto*. The bond still belongs to the late-Mrs. French."

There was a loud murmur throughout the courtroom, which took several moments to die. The judge slammed his gavel once: "I will withhold judgment on that for the moment. Continue, Mr. Hurst. What else do you have for the court?"

Durk cleared his throat. "Misters Clifton and Dunham have made a very compelling argument, your honor. However, I will produce evidence that will supersede the merits of their case. The fact is, Mrs.

French's entire estate, including *FrenchAcres* and her bank shares, rightfully belong to my client, Mrs. Antoinette DuVallier-French." There was a loud hubbub in the room, and Judge Fairbanks had to bang his gavel twice to restore order. Durk glanced at Antoinette, who forced a nervous smile.

"You're going to have to prove such a outrageous claim!" Dunham shouted.

"I will do just that, gentlemen. First, if it pleases the court, I would like to present a certificate of marriage between the recently deceased Devereau French and his lawfully wedded wife, Antoinette. Also, I would like to enter this death certificate for Devereau French, signed by Sheriff Bake Stubbs." The bailiff carried the two certificates to the judge, who glanced at them. "Clearly, Devereau French, being Mrs. French's only remaining blood relation, would automatically inherit her estate. All rulings on the plantation and the bank since Mrs. French's death would be invalid."

"Your honor," Dunham called out, snapping to his feet, "we concede the marriage of Mr. French. A man as scrawny and useless as Devereau French could not have resisted a handsome piece of womanflesh like her." The crowd guffawed as he pointed at Antoinette, who maintained her silent composure.

"However, Judge, both are moot points," Dunham continued. "The marriage doesn't matter. It is written into law that a man cannot benefit financially by committing a crime. Everyone in Turkle knows that Devereau French murdered his mother; therefore, Devereau cannot inherit her estate. And since Devereau cannot inherit her estate, upon Devereau's demise, his wife cannot inherit it from him. That is the law, your honor."

A pleased expression crossed Dunham's face. "If you want to adjudicate the late-Mr. French murdering his mother back in '61, there were witnesses in the house that night. Even if we can't locate those witnesses—after all, four years of war have passed—the sheriff's office has on file signed testimonials from them contemporaneous to the time of the murder, stating that Devereau shot her. I need not mention, your honor, that at the time of his suicide, Devereau French was also wanted for murdering the widow McCorkle. That being so, Mrs. French died *intestate*—without a will, for Mr. Hurst's elucidation." He glared triumphantly at Durk and returned to his seat. His client, James Clifton, patted him on the back.

Durk glanced at Antoinette, who'd been wringing her hands under the table. Her face, however, remained stoic.

"I will not dispute that, your honor," Durk said. "However, the claim that Mrs. French died *intestate* is false." Durk handed the bailiff a sheath of papers, which was handed to the judge. The judge needed only glance at the documents—since they were the ones he'd given Durk after their chess match. "This document, dated August seventeen, eighteen-sixty, is, indeed, Mrs. French's will, notarized, witnessed, and signed by all parties, including yourself, Judge." Durk gave Judge Fairbanks a glance, as if saying, Sorry, I had to do it."

Durk continued. "This will states that Devereau French is Mrs. French's heir, certainly. But it also contains language that stipulates, and I quote: 'if Devereau cannot take possession because he has either predeceased his mother *or for any other reason*, then Antoinette DuVallier-French will inherit her entire estate'. Antoinette DuVallier is blameless in the death of Mrs. French. Therefore, your honor, *FrenchAcres* and the bank stock clearly belong to my client, Mrs. DuVallier-French." With that, the room broke into an uproar, and the judge had to bang the gavel repeatedly.

"I object, your honor!" Dunham shouted. "Let me see this *supposed* will!"

"Both parties will approach the bench," the judge ordered. Durk and Antoinette made their way to the bench, joined by Clifton and Dunham. "This is a complicated case, which could take quite some time to resolve," the judge said quietly so only the four principals could hear. "Perhaps you can come to some agreement, and we can avoid lengthy adjudication that could stretch far into the future."

As the crowd watched, unable to hear what was transpiring at the bench, the five continued their heated discussion. Clifton spoke angrily, as did his lawyer; Durk spoke forcefully, and his opponents retorted furiously. Arguments ensued until Durk laid out a compromise proposal calmly, logically. Debate continued until the four finally nodded agreement.

Durk offered his hand to Clifton, but Clifton refused to shake, and he and his lawyer returned to their seats in a huff. Durk and Antoinette did likewise. The courtroom grew quiet.

"I'm pleased that the two parties have reached an agreement to settle the French estate," the judge announced. "James Clifton, you will be the trustee for Mrs. French's majority holdings in Turkle Bank. I am granting you complete fiduciary powers over Mrs. French's shares in the bank, not to be limited by any other authority. All prior rulings in favor of Colonel Rutherford are overturned and dismissed. Colonel Rutherford has one week to appeal this ruling. Mr. Hurst, do you agree?"

"I do, your honor," Durk responded, knowing Rutherford would be tied up in the Federal judicial system and unable to appear for years, much less within the week.

Judge Fairbanks struck the gavel once. "So ruled." Loud cheering split the room, silenced again by the gavel.

"I further rule, Mrs. Antoinette DuVallier-French to be the sole owner of *FrenchAcres*. All prior debt obligations of her husband, Devereau French, or her mother-in-law, Mrs. Marie Brussard French, are hereby relinquished by Mr. James Clifton. Mr. Clifton, do you agree?"

Clifton waved his hand, bitterly accepting the statement.

"We will take a one-hour dinner break at this time," the judge said. "When we return, we will take up the matter of the property encompassing the *DarkHorse* plantation." He slammed the gavel. "Court is adjourned for sixty minutes." The judge stood and exited the courtroom for his chambers. He needed a drink.

Durk and Antoinette rose and calmly made their way out of the courtroom. Around them folks grew quiet, moving aside to let them pass. The fact that this woman, proud of bearing and striking to behold, was now the sole owner of what had been the largest plantation in Lethe Creek County began to settle into the public mind. That the old rumors about that weasel Devereau French being married to this lovely creature had been true only added to their sense of awe.

Outside, Durk and Antoinette continued silently across Turkle's main square, heads erect, eyes straight ahead, trailed by a gathering crowd of the curious. When they entered Ahronson's, Durk closed the door behind them and turned the sign in the window to CLOSED. Disappointed, the crowd groaned and began to disperse.

"Ellen, we won *FrenchAcres*!" Antoinette exclaimed, hugging her tightly. "The folks working there are safe!"

The three broke into jubilation. Durk and Antoinette embraced, and she gave him a kiss. "You did it, Durk. You saved them."

"Let's all thank Mrs. French and her tricks," Durk exclaimed. "She was always a move ahead of everyone. Well, almost."

Soon, however, Durk grew grim, taking a seat to calm himself, as Ellen scurried to fix them a quick dinner. Only half the job was done. The future of *DarkHorse* was still in limbo.

# Chapter Thirty

# RESURRECTION

An hour later, the bailiff called the court to order. If anything, after the morning's startling decision, the room was more crowded than before. Everyone rose as the elderly jurist in black robe climbed the steps to the bench, his years weighing heavily upon his soft frame. Once seated, he caught his breath and brought the gavel down. "Call Mr. Hurst, please, bailiff."

"Mr. Durksen Hurst will appear before the court." But Durk's table was empty. A buzz arose. There was a commotion at the courtroom door, and all heads turned to see what new surprises were in store.

To everyone's astonishment, Durk entered and made his way up the aisle accompanied by a strongly built Chickasaw donning a gray Confederate tunic over his bare chest, and buckskin breechcloth and boots. Crowning the Indian's strong, impassive face was a roach style headdress adorned with the tall hawk feathers of a chief or high dignitary. Durk took his seat and gestured for the Indian to sit beside him.

"Well, Mr. Hurst," James Clifton chided, "I see you've brought a reliable witness in your *DarkHorse* matter."

"I haven't said he's a witness, sir. Perhaps he's a plaintiff."

"So, Mr. Hurst," the judge intoned, ignoring Durk's remark, "I understand you have received no transfer document from the Indian Bureau to present to the court. That would have helped your case immensely."

"That's true, your honor. I requested a copy, but I suspect Colonel Rutherford's man at the post office intercepted it." Durk smiled to himself, knowing that with Rutherford out of the picture, the only proof left of Durk's ownership was the scrap of paper Wounded Wolf signed. And that's precisely what he wanted.

"Well, sir, this court cannot assume such a transfer agreement exists merely upon your word. The only documentation you've presented is this note from six years ago with an Indian's mark on it. Am I stating the situation correctly?" Judge Fairbanks held up a heavily weathered sheet of paper, frayed and torn along its folds.

"That is correct, your honor. But that will be enough to prove my point."

"We'll see about that. Proceed, Mr. Hurst," the judge said. "But I warn you: this is very flimsy evidence. Very flimsy."

Wayne Dunham, Clifton's lawyer, snapped to his feet. "Your honor," he said, "we concede that the Chickasaw signed that property over to Mr. Hurst. The issue is: taxes on that land accumulated throughout the war. Can Mr. Hurst reimburse the town for what he owes? If not, the land must be put up for auction to recover this debt."

"I concur. The back taxes *are* the issue, Mr. Hurst, the only issue," the judge said. "I hereby validate the document transferring *DarkHorse* to you based on Mr. Dunham's concession."

Durk repressed a smile. "Now with your permission, I call Wounded Wolf to the stand."

The large Chickasaw rose and strode to the witness chair. The bailiff offered up the Bible to swear him in. But when asked if he would tell the truth, the Chickasaw glared at the bailiff so threateningly, the crowd gasped. "I do not lie like the white man," he stated, and took his seat.

"Mr. Wounded Wolf," the judge asked, "are you qualified to represent your tribe?"

The Indian pointed at his headdress. "Do you see this? The president of the United States does not wear hawk feathers."

"Acknowledged. Continue," the judge said.

Durk handed Wounded Wolf the agreement. "Wounded Wolf, is that your mark on this piece of paper, dated 1859?"

"It is my mark."

"At the time you signed this paper, were you officially chief of the tribe? Had they conducted the traditional ceremony installing you as chief yet?"

"No. The ceremony was not performed for another moon."

"So, in effect, you were not legally in a position to sign away that land. Is that right?"

"That is true, Dark Horse. I was not chief yet. I could not give the land to you."

"Your honor, we are operating on a flawed assumption," Durk said. "The fact is, this agreement signed by Wounded Wolf is invalid. I could not—and did not—legally own that land. Therefore, *DarkHorse* still belongs to the Chickasaw."

Hearing this, the courtroom erupted. The judge had to bang the gavel repeatedly before order was restored. "This is another of your tricks," Clifton shouted.

"I object! This is without precedent," Dunham bellowed.

"Nevertheless, what I say is true," Durk continued. "Furthermore, your honor, Turkle has no legal taxing authority over the Chickasaw nation. Thus, the land known as *DarkHorse* must revert to the tribe, unencumbered by debt, free and clear."

The crowd rose in an uproar.

"Your honor," Durk said when order was restored. "There also is the matter of the few remaining small farms on *DarkHorse* that survived the war. Mr. Wounded Wolf, as chief, do you pledge these plots to be held in *fee simple* ownership to the people living upon them now?"

"I do grant them," Wounded Wolf said.

"And that two square miles of land that runs along the Chickasaw branch bordered by *FrenchAcres*, do you also pledge that land in perpetuity to be a school for Negros?"

"I do so pledge that land."

"Then my case is completed." As Durk sat down, the room exploded in acrimony. Insults were hurled; objections were shouted by lawyers and planters alike; a boot flew by Durk's ear, barely missing him. The judge slammed the gavel repeatedly as Sheriff Stubbs and his deputies struggled to establish order. Finally, the crowd simmered down.

Judge Fairbanks cleared his throat. "As Mr. Dunham has pointed out, this case is, indeed, unprecedented. I know of no situation where a transfer of land registered with the Indian Bureau was returned to the Indians. However, this court has seen no registration documents from the Bureau, whether they were stolen by Colonel Rutherford, as Mr. Hurst asserts, or not. Absent official Federal registration, therefore, the court is forced to rule on this case as if the document does not exist." The courthouse came to a hush.

The judge took a deep breath. "The duly appointed court of Turkle, Mississippi, hereby rules that the witness known as Wounded Wolf was not legally authorized to sell, trade, barter, or relinquish in any way the land known as *DarkHorse*. Therefore, documentation filed with the Indian Bureau by Mr. Hurst, if any, is moot and invalid. With the exceptions noted of the small farm plots and the two square miles of land bordering *FrenchAcres*, the land hereby reverts to the Chickasaw nation as of 1859.

"Furthermore, since Turkle has no taxing authority over the Chickasaw, the tax lien on said land is likewise invalid. Court is adjourned." Judge Fairbanks slammed down his gavel.

Durk took a deep breath and exhaled. The money interests eyeing that raw land would appeal the ruling, but he had an ironclad case. Justice had been done for the Chickasaw. At long last, his conscience was clear.

Their bellies were full and the evening pleasant, lit by a full moon suspended upon a diamond-studded black canvas. The sweet, aromatic smoke from the cookfires of the *FrenchAcres* common drifted on the breeze, dissipating like the effusion of gratitude given to Durk and Antoinette for having lifted the sword of Damocles from above their homes and families. Moreover, a week had passed since news of the courtroom pyrotechnics flashed through Lethe Creek County, then faded to whispers. Ahronson's hadn't been looted or burned; no one had been shot. Turkle and environs seemed to be in repair.

Leaving the festivities behind, Big Josh strolled toward the entrance of the former plantation, leading Durk and Antoinette, arm in arm. He carried a large object wrapped in a blanket under his arm, but refused to reveal what the object was, saying it was a surprise. Long Lou hobbled alongside them on crutches, smiling from the sheer joy of being outdoors after his long convalescence. Even Caleb had shaken off his recent huff, playing imaginary games in circles around them.

The friends had good reason to feel at peace. The *FrenchAcres* plots had been deeded over to the freedman, who as owners no longer feared expulsion. The new community building they'd erected had a roof and walls, needing only a coat of paint to be respectable, and already sheltered Sunday church, children's classes, and political and social gatherings. Further afield, Big Josh was already negotiating with lumber companies to clear the heavily forested Chickasaw land grant by the river. This enterprise would fund a college to train black teachers, who would spread learning to freedmen throughout the South. Things had never seemed so hopeful.

They reached the entrance gate, and Josh stopped to look it over. The current residents had reassembled the gateway's brick towers, connecting them at the top by a stout hickory wood arch. Durk and the others also halted, wondering why the community had spent precious time and labor on this meaningless monolith.

"So what is it you have there, Josh?" Durk asked, indicating the mysterious blanket under his friend's arm.

"Yes, Josh, what is it?" Antoinette prompted.

"The folks took a vote," Josh said, a sly smile on his lips.

"Yes? And that was. . . ?"

"Folks don't want to live on *FrenchAcres* no more. They was slaves here; it hurts to remember that."

"But . . . But they own the place now. . . ?" Durk sputtered.

"That's right," Josh answered, barely containing his glee. "Everybody vote to rename the place, to honor our partnership. We voted to call it *DarkHorse*."

Stunned, the friends looked at each other, then broke into laughter at the irony of the French plantation, once an apotheosis of the Old South, the dead South of slavery and cruelty, being replaced by their long-sought dream of each man his own master, reaping the rewards of his own labors.

Then with a flourish, Josh unwrapped the large bundle to reveal a wooden carving of a galloping horse, head to tail about a yard long, painted solid black. The workmanship was detailed, with a finely etched mane and face, muscular body and legs.

"What's this?" Antoinette asked.

"Old Joe Williams, does woodwork at night, carved this special."

Durk and Antoinette grasped each other's hand and locked eyes. "Joe Williams has quite a talent," Antoinette remarked.

"Josh . . ." Durk teared up, his voice catching. "Is this what I think it is?"

Josh pointed to the wooden arch with hooks on its underside stretching from tower to tower. "Gonna hang it. Let folks know they entering our *DarkHorse*."

"How are we going to get it up there?" Durk asked, peering up. The arch wouldn't hold Big Josh, and Durk certainly wasn't a climber. He thought it over. "Caleb, come over here. You think you could climb up there?"

"Sure, Durk," Caleb replied. "Easy."

"Good. You do the honors. Climb on up, will you? We want to hang this horse up there."

"There are hooks up under that hickory," Josh said.

Caleb removed his boots and began to climb, his hands and feet finding holes and protrusions in the rough brick tower. As he ascended, Durk and Josh stood below in case he fell, watching him, their hearts in their throats.

Nestled in the warm bosom of the first peace he'd felt in years, Durk's mind drifted back until he found himself standing at the former *DarkHorse*, feeling the same exultation and harmony he'd known during that heady time. Transfixed, he watched as Isaac shinnied up the rugged pillar to hang their carved black horse, encircled by the gleaming eyes and happy faces of his twelve partners, nearly all of them gone now. He knew how moved they'd be at this moment of triumph.

Snapping to the present, Durk wistfully studied his friends. Lou would soon resume his long and difficult travels east, and Durk would likely never see him again.

He took a long look at Josh, realizing that they were at the end of their partnership. Both led separate lives now, and he knew Josh would succeed, that his schools would one day dot Mississippi top to bottom. Durk would spend his life trying to emulate him. Having this friend had made Durk a man, a true man.

And then there was Antoinette. Without her, there'd simply be no reason to continue. He thought it paradoxical that fate can gift a man perfection, yet he must spend his days learning how to receive it properly. He vowed to marry her legally one day.

Once Caleb reached the top of the tower, he climbed out along the arch until he was seated unsteadily upon it high in the air. As he did, Durk removed his boots and climbed cautiously halfway up the tower. When both were in place, Josh handed the wooden horse up to Durk, who, steadying his grip, managed to hold it with one hand without falling. Then Durk handed the horse up to Caleb, who attached it to the hooks before both descended the way they'd come.

In the moonlight, the long-time friends and the once-orphaned boy stood admiring the sign against the evening sky. Durk slipped his arm around Antoinette's waist, and Josh stretched his big arm around their shoulders. Lou leaned on his crutches, wiping his eyes with his sleeve. Suddenly, the weight of what they'd gone through pressed upon Durk: the horror of slavery, the naked brutality of war, the chaos of the fighting's aftermath. And from what he'd seen, the road ahead wouldn't be easier, nor short-lived. It was as if they'd climbed a mountain, only to find a greater one looming above them. He knew gun clubs would block the roads to the polls in November to keep freedmen from attempting to vote; he'd already heard rumblings of that circulating around the courthouse. And the new legislature would institute Black Codes for the whole state, a foregone conclusion. They'd just have to face those trials as they came, in court or, failing there, through means not yet discovered.

"Folks gonna be proud to say they own a piece of *DarkHorse*," Josh commented. "*DarkHorse* still lives, brother!" Josh's deep baritone broke into a rich belly laugh.

Josh's statement brought tears again to Durk's eyes. *Brother*, he'd said. Durk sighed deeply. Well, he thought, on to the new challenges facing us. Someday folks will wonder what was so difficult about what we did here. But these friends here, they know. And so will their children and their children's children.

"Yes, indeed, brother, *DarkHorse* does live," Durk replied. "*DarkHorse* certainly lives on."

# Acknowledgments

Researching the *DarkHorse Trilogy*'s tumultuous period—from slavery, to Civil War, to Reconstruction—often proved a double-edged sword. I am, of course, grateful to the dedicated historians who inspired these volumes, including those cited below, for preserving an insightful store of knowledge for posterity. But while delving into the immediate aftermath of the Civil War for *Something in Madness*, there were times I had to close the books because public sentiments commonly written and expressed about African-Americans were so troubling to read.

It is for that reason I felt a duty to accurately reflect those times as best I could and let the characters speak for themselves, often using words taken directly from history.

Of course, my *DarkHorse Trilogy* would not have been possible without the invaluable support of my publisher, Sheri Williams at TouchPoint Press, and my agent, Jeanie Loiacono of the Loiacono Literary Agency. And finally, my everlasting thanks to my wife, Janet, for her encouragement and patience as I struggled to tell a story so emotionally charged and heartbreaking at its core, yet sure of man's ability to endure and to triumph in the face of overwhelming adversity.

BELZ, Herman, *Emancipation and Equal Rights: Politics and Constitutionalism in the Civil War Era* (W. W. Norton & Company).

BUDIANSKY, Stephen, *The Bloody Shirt: Terror After Appomattox* (Viking).

EGERTON, Douglas R., *The Wars of Reconstruction: The Brief, Violent History of America's Most Progressive Era* (Bloomsbury Press).

FONER, Eric, *Reconstruction: America's Unfinished Revolution, 1863–1877* (Harper Perennial).

FONER, Eric and Joshua Brown, *Forever Free: The Story of Emancipation and Reconstruction* (Alfred A. Knopf).

# ACKNOWLEDGMENTS

KLINGAMAN, William K., *Abraham Lincoln and the Road to Emancipation: 1861–1865* (Viking, a member of Penguin Putnam Inc.).

PHILLIPS, Jason, *Reconstruction in Mississippi, 1865–1876* (Mississippi History Now, May 2006).

SPAN, Christopher M., *From Cotton Field to Schoolhouse: African American Education in Mississippi, 1862–1875* (The University of North Carolina Press-Chapel Hill).

# About the Author

Ed Protzel grew up in St. Louis, the son of a Jewish father and a part-Cherokee mother. For a time he lived in an orphanage when his parents divorced, and left home after high school to live in St. Louis's bohemian Gaslight Square entertainment district. These experiences gave Protzel a unique perspective, which is reflected in the traits of many of his fictional characters: outsiders and gamesters—male or female—on lonely quests, seeking justice, love, and fulfillment against society's blindness.

Protzel began writing both novels and screenplays while in college, working on them in his spare time while employed in securities management. He kept writing as he moved around the United States. He did some freelance work for 20th Century Studios and completed several original screenplays, one of which optioned by a producer. But Protzel couldn't abide what he calls Hollywood's "hyper-Darwinism," so he enrolled in grad school at the University of Missouri-St. Louis, where he earned his master's in English and creative writing.

# THE DARKHORSE TRILOGY

## FROM OPEN ROAD MEDIA

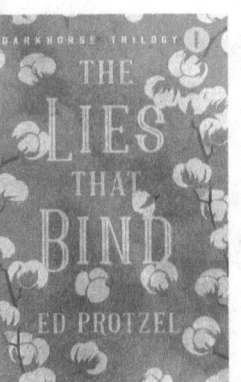

OPEN ROAD

INTEGRATED MEDIA

Find a full list of our authors and titles at www.openroadmedia.com

FOLLOW US
@OpenRoadMedia